1989

# POPULAR MUSIC
# AND
# COMMUNICATION

# SOME OTHER VOLUMES IN THE
# SAGE FOCUS EDITIONS

# POPULAR MUSIC
# AND
# COMMUNICATION

### Edited by
## James Lull

**SAGE** PUBLICATIONS
The Publishers of Professional Social Science
Newbury Park   Beverly Hills   London   New Delhi

*For information address:*

SAGE Publications, Inc.
2111 West Hillcrest Drive
Newbury Park, California 91320

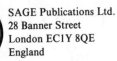

SAGE Publications Inc.
275 South Beverly Drive
Beverly Hills
California 90212

SAGE Publications Ltd.
28 Banner Street
London EC1Y 8QE
England

SAGE PUBLICATIONS India Pvt. Ltd.
M-32 Market
Greater Kailash I
New Delhi 110 048 India

Printed in the United States of America

Library of Congress Cataloging-in-Publication Data

Main entry under title:

Popular music and communication.

(Sage focus editions ; 89)
1. Popular music—Social aspects.  2. Communication.
I. Lull, James.
ML3470.P67   1987      780'.42      87-16548
ISBN 0-8039-2825-4
ISBN 0-8039-2826-2 (pbk.)


SECOND PRINTING, 1988

# Contents

# *Preface*

Rock and roll came along just in time for me. I'd hate to think of what my life might have been like without that beat, that feeling. Elvis, Bill Haley, Little Richard, Fats Domino, Gene Vincent, Jerry Lee Lewis, The Dell Vikings, The Diamonds, and Buddy Holly were the most important of that first generation of American rockers for me. Now, many years later, it is very satisfying to have assembled a collection of essays that helps illuminate the importance, indeed the necessity, of popular music in the lives of young people. It's really a kind of personal victory too since the academy has never embraced the serious study of things that matter in the way that popular music does, and I've had more than one bout with those who prefer to define our field narrowly, let's say shortsightedly. Nearly everybody (including college students) knows about the power and pertinence of music as a form of communication. The task that we faced in this book was to articulate this understanding in a serious and compelling way that could be appreciated by rock and pop music listeners, communication scholars, and students alike.

The contributors to this volume have certainly done just that. I owe much to them for their participation in this project, and I have learned a tremendous amount from each by reading and editing their superb essays. Collaborating with a group of *scholars* who love and appreciate *popular music* was indeed a rare and valued experience. We were united in this effort by our love for music and for youth culture, and by the idea that this book could help elevate the study of popular music closer to its deserved place in the academy. Our objective was to provide an analysis of popular music that was scholarly, but contemporary and culturally informed as well.

Several people have made special contributions to this book. For several years now, Larry Grossberg has inspired me to continue my work in popular music, and his support, suggestions, and encouragement are reflected in this volume. Lisa Freeman-Miller signed the book with Sage Publications and supported the concept from the very beginning. Mitch Allen and Ann West, editors for Sage Publications, were very positive and helpful. Others who have influenced this work are Larry Johnson, Jill Stein, Phil Wander, Joe Verbalis, my students in Santa Barbara and San Jose, and my colleagues in the Radio-Television-Film program at San Jose State University.

The book also reflects the many thousands of hours I have spent listening, dancing, stretching, and contemplating to popular music. The book is dedicated to everyone who deeply believes in the power of popular music as a form of communication, and especially to a select group of popular musicians whose spirit I respect and admire greatly. Among them are Kate Bush, David Sylvian, David Byrne, Bryan Ferry, Jim Kerr, the Cocteau Twins, and especially, the late Tim Buckley, for whom I cared greatly.

—James Lull
San Francisco

# PART I

# Music Sources:
## Artists and Industries

# 1

# *Popular Music and Communication:*

## *An Introduction*

### JAMES LULL

Music is a passionate sequencing of thoughts and feelings that expresses meaning in a manner that has no parallel in human life. It is a universally recognized synthesis of the substance and style of our existence—a blending of personal, social, and cultural signification that is confused with no other variety of communication. Music promotes experiences of the extreme for its makers and listeners, turning the perilous emotional edges, vulnerabilities, triumphs, celebrations, and antagonisms of life into hypnotic, reflective tempos that can be experienced privately or shared with others.

This book is about the role of music in human communication, especially as it pertains to the sociocultural behavior that is characteristic of youth. For that reason there is far more emphasis given here to various forms of contemporary popular music (for instance, rock, soul, punk, dance, heavy metal) than to classical, traditional, or period music. Popular music is a unique and extremely influential communications form that deserves serious analysis—not just on the street and in the popular press, but in the scholarly literature and in the classroom as well. The articles that comprise this volume, therefore, variously consider the communicative roles of musicians, the music, the means by which music is transferred to its audiences, and the ways in which music is received, interpreted, and used by listeners in a wide variety of important contexts. A diversity of theoretical and methodological approaches is represented.

Exploration of music-as-communication invites analysis in many areas. There are, of course, many varieties of popular music and new genres constantly evolve. But, whatever its sound and meaning, music originates and resides in the social and cultural worlds of people. The composition and performance (live or recorded) of music is communicative activity that is highly valued in all societies. For music fans in the more developed parts of the world, nothing may be more exciting than that moment of anticipation when band members step onto the darkened stage, pick up their instruments, and enact one last momentary tuning of guitars and crashing of cymbals are before the lights come up and the music begins. Popular musicians are loved, even worshipped, not only for their abilities to write songs and perform them publicly, but for their ability to "speak" to their audiences. Even an artist whose only contact with the audience is through the sale of millions of records and tapes in a way communicates "personally" with each listener.

For musicians or bands to become popular today and occupy positions of significant influence, however, the audio textures they create must undergo considerable industrialization. Artists and bands who want to become popular must get recording contracts from the record/tape/disc industry and receive exposure for their work from radio stations and the music video channels. The music and electronic media industries, therefore, are intimately involved in the flow of music from artists to audiences. Various considerations that bear upon the creation and distribution of popular music are treated in depth by contributors to Part I of this book. Authors from several academic fields and from industry comment on the fundamental processes of musical encoding—its creation, recording, marketing, and worldwide distribution.

In Part II ("Music Audiences: Culture and Subculture"), the experience of receiving music—listening to it, interpreting it, using it—is the focus of analyses provided by authors from several countries. Music pervades the social and cultural realms of its listeners ranging in type from the stylistic dandyism of English subcultures to the street life of inner city black youth and the routine affairs of midwestern American farm kids. My own primary interests in the study of popular music and communication fall into the area of audience analysis as well, and I will reserve the bulk of my descriptions, commentaries, and theoretical reasoning for the chapter that appears later on. In the next several pages, however, I will discuss some of the current issues that bear on music artists and industries.

Before doing so, I want to assert two fundamental theoretical assumptions that generally guide the analysis provided by the collection of articles contained in this volume. First, *participants in human communication that involves popular music, and in all forms of symbolic interaction for that matter, act willingly and imaginatively in nearly every instance of its occurrence.* The encoding and decoding of music are intentional human activities that serve a wide range of purposes, many of which are discussed in the various chapters of this book.

Second, *the potential for exercising these communicative capacities is indeed influenced by the structural circumstances that surround their existence.* Music, like other forms of communication, is constrained and given direction by the relations that people have with each other. These relationships may take the form of patterns reflecting hierarchical displays of interpersonal power among small groups of audience members or demonstrate differential evidences of economic and political power among representatives of the most far-reaching social structuring apparatuses, including decision makers from the music business, related industries, and the consuming public. Technology plays a roll in all of this, at once providing a resource for the creative construction, consumption, and use of music by its makers and audiences, and at the same time providing a mechanism through which corporate profits are realized and social relations affected.

## Music and Industry

Record companies and radio stations are commanding elements of the popular culture industry that have as fundamental tasks the production and marketing of various forms of music as a commodity for consumption. The development and management of these commodities are processes that understandably promote the preferred ideological orientations of the controlling economic interests. But, because artists sometimes make music that does not fall within the favored ideological parameters of the culture industry, and because that music frequently has significant appeal to young consumers of records, tapes, compact discs, and radio and television signals, the ideological mantelpiece of the music business in its several manifestations does not solely represent prevailing modes of thought.

In the following paragraphs some of the major issues inherent in this contradictory arrangement are raised. Essentially, there is a tension between forces of conventionality and forces of resistance in the production of popular culture. We shall refer to the first of these influences as "patterns of control," wherein dominant ideologies (referring here to conservative, safe, or "status quo" ways of thinking about political, economic, social, and cultural issues in the general sense, and to the "ways of doing business" that characterize activities of the record and radio industries) are asserted in the manufacture and promotion of popular music. In conflict with this are the less financially viable "patterns of resistance," wherein musical artists use industry to assert subcultural or alternative orientations, sometimes with profound implications. The following discussion, then, will identify and trace some of the more important themes in this enduring dialectical process. The music and broadcast industries are regarded here to be complementary forces in patterns of both control and resistance.

**Patterns of Control**

There are numerous indicators of conservatism and conventionality in all phases of the production of popular music. Inheriting a tradition of imitation from the Tin Pan Alley era, popular recording artists of all types typically write songs that follow a predictable structure of sound. Most pop music writers, for instance, believe that a song should display the chorus as soon as possible, that dissonant instrumentation should be avoided, and that instrumental solos should be kept short if they are used at all. Artists who create successful songs often try later to imitate their earlier work. Many bands try to win record contracts by imitating other artists or groups that are successful, placing their sound within the range of textures that the record companies believe are marketable.

Record companies avoid signing artists or groups whose music does not appear to fit into one of the established radio station formats. Individual songs typically must start on the road to popularity by achieving success within a particular format (for instance, urban, album rock, adult contemporary) before they expand to airplay on the lucrative contemporary hits (a.k.a. "top forty") or the new "crossover" format stations. There are, therefore categories of music with varying amounts of acceptability, attributable to the sorting system of the commercial radio industry.

For the most part, lyrical content is conventional too. Even rock music, seemingly deviant because of its rough textures, loud volume, and sometimes suggestive or rebellious lyrics, fundamentally belongs to the family of ideas that constitute normative culture. Rock music's primary audience, youth, is expected to quarrel with institutional forces such as parents, teachers, and bosses. Songs that describe philosophical conflict from the point of view of youth are common in rock music. With some important historical exceptions, however, conflict in contemporary music is limited primarily to the problems of adolescents.

Perhaps to a greater extent than any other art form, popular music has the ability to penetrate the consciousness of its audience through sheer repetition of its themes. Songs become popular when certain melodic components (riffs or choruses) catch the attention of the public. These recognizable elements of popular songs are also called "hooks," referring to their ability to capture and hold the interest of listeners. The hook is usually repeated several times within a song. Dance club deejays often superimpose the hook of one song over instrumental fills of other songs, thereby further increasing its impact.

And, unlike any other media form, the top "hits" in music are played with great repetition on radio stations, further transmitting the fundamental information contained in the songs to a large audience. Popular music sends particular musical and lyrical fragments deep into the society for the duration of its first-run popularity through repetition, then reappears with systematic frequency as "oldies."

As Simon Frith points out in his chapter in this volume and in previous writing (Frith, 1981), the record and tape market is still controlled by a small number of "major" companies. This influence can be seen in the signing of artists and groups, the production of albums, the pressing of records, tapes, and discs, and the distribution of music throughout the world. Record companies are also involved in the sale of musical instruments, record, tape, and compact disc players, and electronic equipment used in the production of music. The major record companies are intimately involved in the arrangement of live performances made by artists under contract with them. They also supervise plans for radio interviews and orchestrate retail appearances of their acts.

Thousands of radio stations operate in the United States with formats that represent a variety of genres of popular music. Radio has become a "companion" medium since the arrival of television and the various formats are each tailored to the anticipated interests of demographic or "taste" subgroups. The high number of stations has led to a high degree of marketplace competition, thereby encouraging managers to rely on proven programming material. Consequently, radio stations within each format typically try to copy the sound achieved by financially successful stations in large markets.

Some of the effects of this competition can be observed in the decision-making processes that take place in radio stations as they select songs to be played regularly on the air. First, the technical quality of recorded music that is played on the radio generally must meet a high standard that only well-financed major labels can produce, a problem that is akin to the inability of local cable television producers to create shows that can compete with the technical excellence of network television. Given this restricted range of recorded music to choose from, most programmers rely on external indicators of potential and realized popularity to determine what songs will be played. Data from industry trade journals that report what other stations are playing is the first evidentiary criterion that most program/music directors use to choose songs for their stations. Actual record sales is another measure. The "track record" of artists and groups influences decisions, providing greater consideration for those who have had a "hit" record before. In the 1980s, many radio stations throughout the country employ a national consultant who tells stations what songs they must play. All of these techniques contribute to a homogenization of music on radio and a market-by-market replication of sound that is more sensitive to the national industry than to local musical and cultural circumstances (Rothenbuhler, 1985). There is a tremendous amount of cooperation taking place between the record industry and the radio industry, an alliance that further standardizes the sound.

The radio term "top 40" persists even today (though now the format to which this originally referred is more often called "contemporary hits") and represents a manner of thinking that characterizes programmers' attitudes toward their listeners. The common belief is that people only want to hear their very favorite songs (the ones with the best hooks) over and over again until they "burn out" on them. When this happens with a particular song it is replaced with another safe potential favorite in the radio station's music rotation. The rotation system is used by most radio programmers and is not specific to any particular format. Rock, country-western, pop, urban, nostalgia and all other formats typically operate with rotation systems and "tight playlists." In their attempts to create a consistent and predictable air sound, radio programmers have simultaneously indicated to their audiences that there is a limited, self-contained universe of popular music over which they exercise considerable control. How decisions are made at radio stations about what music is played is taken up in depth by Eric

Rothenbuhler in Chapter 4. The same basic processes also characterize the programming philosophy of the music video channels.

## Patterns of Resistance

Perhaps more than any other cultural form, music is capable of providing a widespread, unified voice of protest. As David Dunaway points out in Chapter 2, the United States has a rich history of music as an agent of organized resistance to many forms of oppression. Music has played such a role in resistance to slavery, racial and gender discrimination, labor abuses, war, and poverty, among other issues. The history of music as a form of protest in the United States began in colonial times and continues now, sometimes suffused with video and television, as was the case of the Live Aid, Farm Aid, and Sun City events among others in the mid-1980s.

Protest music in America began long prior to the declaration of national independence. There were anti-British anthems during the colonial period and political songs ("topical broadsides") that repre- sented the sentiments of Americans who resented and fought the economic power wielded by the aristocracy. Major issues in American history have invariably stimulated the writing, singing, and recording of protest music. Therefore, songs have addressed slavery and racial discrimination held toward blacks, Irish, Italians, and others; war in general and each particular war; labor abuses suffered by mining, manufacturing, and agricultural workers; conformity, automation, and dehumanization; commercialism and other forces of control that confront particular social groups (Rosen, 1972; Denisoff, 1983).

Labor struggles have produced strong protest songs in the United States. The famous ballad "John Henry was a Steel Drivin' Man" at the turn of the century was actually a commentary on the labor position of man versus the new steam drill (Hamm, 1983). The "hillbilly" music that was created largely by nonliterate immigrants from the British Isles who settled along the Eastern seaboard, particularly in the Appalachian mountains, was a genre of music that represented protest in the labor disputes that took place between mainly white workers and bosses. The famous Harlan County, Kentucky coal mining battles between union organizers and mine owners produced much protest music among the workers. The message was clear:

Don't scab for the bosses,
Don't listen to their lies.

Us poor folks haven't got a chance
Unless we organize [Denisoff, 1972: 21].

Two songwriters/singers (Welling and McGhee) documented the infamous Marion Massacre of textile workers in North Carolina in 1930. More than 600 workers of the Marion Manufacturing Company had gone on strike the year before. After a settlement was reached that was extremely favorable to the textile company, local police killed or wounded 30 workers who refused to return to work. The song ("The Marion Massacre") documented the underlying root of the class struggle that led to the murders:

It started over money,
The world's most vain desire,
Yet we realize the laborer
Is worthy of his hire.

These men were only asking
Their rights and nothing more
That their families would not suffer
With a wolf at every door.

Historically, much subcultural music has come from oppressed groups that are often defined along lines of socioeconomic class. Consequently, the conditions experienced by American workers has been expressed frequently in subcultural protest music, particularly in the early part of the century.

The experience of black America has been reflected in rural and urban protest music including especially blues, jazz, country, soul, funk, gospel, and rap. Conditions of oppression have influenced much black music in the United States, obvious not only in the lyrics and arrangements of various musics, but also in the vocal treatment and inflection (Hamm, 1983).

Folk singers such as Woody Guthrie and Pete Seeger are well known for their songs and performances in the early and middle parts of this century. They have stood on the side of the poor and downtrodden, the workers, and the oppressed by writing, performing, and recording music that reflects the class interests of the poor. These men were often banned from mainstream media exposure in the United States, perhaps the most famous instance being the censorship of Pete Seeger from the Smothers Brothers Comedy Hour on the CBS television network in the 1960s.

Perhaps the most compelling illustration of the power of music as an agent of resistance in the United States during this century, however, is the period from the middle 1960s to the early 1970s. Americans were torn by the hostile involvement in Vietnam, the civil rights movement, the "credibility gap" and the "generation gap," a stirring of feminist concerns, a dramatic increase in drug use among middle-class and upper-class youth, the assassination of some of the nation's most charismatic leaders, a new awareness of environmental issues, and a general retrenchment of the ideological orientation among those youth who were fortunate enough not to have day-to-day matters of survival interfere with their ability to reflect on the many major issues of the day.

The atmosphere of social change directly involved music. Different styles of rock music developed, emphasizing alternative lyrics and melodies and the increased length of individual songs. Virtuoso "guitar heroes" such as Jimi Hendrix, Eric Clapton, and Alvin Lee emerged. "Folk rock" developed as a separate genre, one that typically spoke of protest sentiments. Barry McGuire forcefully sang out that the world was on the "Eve of Destruction" and Country Joe McDonald and the Fish sang the "Fixin' to Die Rag," a not-so-lighthearted spoof of the fate of young men who were sent to Vietnam. Bob Dylan, who had already written songs and sung about racial discrimination and other sensitive issues wrote the classic antiwar song, "Blowin' in the Wind."

The music legitimized, even glamorized, civil protest. San Francisco was the place to go "with flowers in your hair." If you grew your hair long, used illegal drugs (especially pot or acid), listened to Bay Area bands such as the Jefferson Airplane, Grateful Dead, Quicksilver Messenger Service, or Big Brother and the Holding Company, you were categorized outside mainstream culture.

Protest messages were widely accessible to the public on record and on the new underground, progressive rock FM radio stations. The music reinforced those who were ideologically committed to the "revolutionary" politics. Music created by these artists also became a medium with which to extend the influence of the subcultural movement by reaching listeners who were beginning to shape their opinions on the various controversies.

The ideological imperatives of the antiwar movement in the 1960s and early 1970s in the United States and elsewhere were part of a seeming cultural revolution going on in the West. The so-called hippy subculture, with its ideological and stylistic departures from "establishment" values and lifestyles, was evidence of the power of subculture to ascend to prominence in the right context. The mass media, which generally represent and support institutional power, were vital in providing communication within the subcultural community, thereby increasing its numbers and amplifying its impact on the rest of society. Not only did some popular artists become subcultural spokespersons, but an entire assortment of new media became important personal communication resources for young people. Frequency-modulated (FM) radio especially, but also underground newspapers and magazines, foreign films, even alternative comic books were among a new assortment of deviant media.

Just as people are known to have interpersonal "reference groups" and "significant others," subcultural media of the 1960s, especially the FM radio stations, became "reference media" programmed by mediated significant others attractive to young people who had assumed, temporarily at least, a new set of values and attendant lifestyle activities. Of course, agents of mainstream culture including its media at the same time continued to function the same way for those committed to more status quo values. But the ability of deviant or alternative media to encourage identification with the tenets of subcultural ideologies can be seen as an historical catalyst for social change.

In the very important case of progressive rock radio, many stations adopted alternative programming because previous formats were not financially successful. Owners were willing to play "radical" music and hire long-haired announcers because it seemed to promise them at least short-term profits given the growth of the subculture within the enormously expanding youth market directly attributable to the entry of the baby-boom generation into consumer activity. Many station owners and managers were personally offended when the programmers, announcers, and newspersons that took over the programming of these stations began to recommend alternative action: Stop the war, integrate the races, get off the commercial treadmill, radicalize your appearance, break away from your parents, question authority, take drugs.

Progressive rock radio stations and other alternative media of the Vietnam war era were forums wherein the politics and art of a new consciousness were experienced. The presence of alternative information and entertainment in these media reinforced the social movement, confirming its ideological foundation. The mass media were effective means of information sharing and political organizing. They were the tools of subcultural protest.

Even the presentational styles of the various media had ideological implications. The then new progressive rock radio stations, for example, typically presented music "sets" of 15, 30, or 60 minutes without commercial interruptions. This differed sharply from the Top 40 presentational style characteristic of most mainstream radio where commercial breaks generally took place after every record was played.

During the progressive rock movement of the 1960s, many of the assumptions of record industry executives and radio station managers seemed no longer valid. Albums sold without benefit of a "hit single." The length of songs on albums increased way beyond the two- or three-minute limit expected during the heyday of Top 40 radio. There were underground radio stations, underground recording artists and companies, and underground newspapers that reported on the albums, concerts, and lifestyles that accompanied the new music.

## Back to the Mainstream

After the conclusion of the Vietnam war, however, deviant elements of the music and radio industries gradually returned to the operating principles that were in place before the disruption of the decade of war. Political themes in music of all types were rare, and the emerging forms—heavy metal, album rock, and disco—were useful primarily as hedonistic escape routes from personal troubles or as avenues for pure entertainment. The progressive rock radio stations had become "album rock" stations and bore little resemblance to their predecessors.

It is true that when the Sex Pistols, the Clash, and other punk bands crashed onto the music scene in London in the mid-1970s, the music industry was again destabilized. The period was reminiscent of the 1950s when the original American rock music upset the normative Tin Pan Alley ballad sound and of the 1960s when progressive rock disturbed the comfortable position of its forerunners in music and radio. But the fallout of punk, "new wave," has also developed a largely uncritical, predictable sound. The heavily synthesized dance beat of this music became a staple of nightclubs, discos, and radio stations that were looking to modernize their airsound, and, of course, of the music video channels.

The first radio station in a major market in the United States to air exclusively new wave music in its early days was KROQ-FM in Los Angeles. While other radio stations were programming traditional rock or pop music for their young adult and teen audience, KROQ was playing nonstop new wave music mixed with pop "oldies" from bands such as the Beatles, Rolling Stones, Yardbirds, Dave Clark Five, and the Who. The station fought a license revocation, low transmitter power, a high turnover of employees, and other misfortunes in order to present the unfamiliar new sounds to Southern California.

The program director of this station, Rick Carroll, became a popular national consultant to radio stations throughout the United States when the new wave (or "modern") sound started to become popular. His syndicated format was termed "Rock of the Eighties." *Success of the format, however, depended not only on the distinctive beat and atmosphere of the new music, but also on the strict, tight rotations that these radio stations adopted.*

Many radio stations that had programmed progressive rock or album rock music for years became contemporary FM versions of the old AM Top 40 stations. This systematic return to frequently repeated, now familiar music signalled the reemergence of the basic popular radio format in the United States. Album rock stations debated whether or not to include bands like the Talking Heads, B 52's, and the Police on their playlists. Contemporary hits stations played the new sounds regularly, blending the basically white modern music with dance-beat grooves and ballads of black artists. Many of these stations were able to build coalitions of listeners especially among teens, young women, and ethnic minorities that challenged the hard rock stations for ratings points. Decisions about what format to adopt are not unimportant to the owners of radio stations. In 1986, about a decade after its humble beginning, modern music king KROQ was sold for $45 million.

Shortly after the emergence of the "Rock of the Eighties" and other modern music radio stations, the first national video outlet, MTV Music Television, began to have an impact on the television and cable industries. Both modern rock stations and MTV relied on a "heavy rotation" of the biggest new wave hits, playing the same songs several times per day. Record companies contributed to the mainstreaming of new music too. They hired bands that sounded like the ones that were getting airplay on the modern rock stations and on MTV.

By the middle 1980s the music business and popular radio had returned again to fairly stable, homogeneous patterns of record/tape sales and airplay. Music that had been on the very edges of the culture was now substantially modified, marketed, and made profitable to the owners and managers of the popular culture industries. The radio and record industries historically cooperate to create a pervasive sameness of sound that benefits them both. This phenomenon is episodic in the United States since the insipid cultural product that this convergence creates is persistently challenged by subcultural artists who offer something different. When alternative music first develops it is resisted by industry primarily on financial grounds, then is reluctantly accommodated by them when profit potential is more clear, and is finally brought under their financial and artistic control, a process that almost always demands substantial modification in the music itself. Recording artists and industry decision makers who initiate or tolerate these changes in order to make a profit are sometimes accused of "selling out."

The mainstream music and broadcast industry of the late 1980s assumed some exciting yet confusing contours. The status of industry technology, radio and video formats, and the music itself was in flux.

Compact disc and digital audio tape (DAT) made repeated listening to recorded music an unsurpassed aesthetic experience. Record companies began to record their talent with digital equipment. Not only music fans, but managers of radio stations traded in their turntables for disc players as digital technology began to replace analog/mechanical recording and reproduction systems en masse for consumers of music too. The record companies began to supply radio stations with "CD singles" rather than LPs, 12-inch singles, or (forget about them, they're history), 45 rpm records. Record companies began to market the "cassingle," a one- or two-song audio cassette that was designed to replace 45 rpm records in stores.

Corporate alliances with rock and pop stars developed to an unprecedented degree. Genesis became the house band of the Anheuser-Busch Corporation (brewers of Michelob), recording an MTV-style commercial for the beer and a hit single ("Tonight, Tonight, Tonight") that sound exactly alike. Beyond that, the band went on tour in 1986 and 1987 under the corporate flag and financing of the brewery. Michael Jackson suffered through flaming hair and the delayed release of his 1987 album on behalf of the advertising strategy designed in the corporate boardroom at Pepsi-Cola. Tina Turner went on tour under the logo of the same company.

The music underwent unthinkable changes. The stars of hip television shows (Don Johnson, Bruce Willis) became pop music stars. Herb Alpert went from perhaps the least cool recording artist in history, to one of the coolest through his association with Janet Jackson. Rappers Run DMC recorded an old Aerosmith song ("Walk This Way") with members of the dinosaur group. The governor of Minnesota took out a full page ad in *Billboard* to praise the cultural contribution of Prince, Morris Day, Hüsker Dü, the Jets, and other Twin City recording stars.

Such juxtapositions influenced radio and video. "Dance" and "cross-over" formats began to emerge in the urban centers. Some stations (the "power" stations) used white deejays to play mainly black artists. Some "modern rock" stations toned down their uptempo, top 40 style with a more laid-back announcer style in order to broaden their demographic composition at the top end. The "new age" format evolved, wherein a comfortable texture comprized mainly of new age (i.e. Windham Hill style) artists, jazz, and light pop was designed primarily to capture part of the yuppie market.

Several album rock stations cut back on the variety of their playlists and focused on hard rock. There was an overall reduction of recurrent or "oldies" tracks on most formats, except, of course, on the nostalgia stations. MTV went "back to the basics" for a white rock image while other video outlets, notably Night Tracks, moved to expand their playlist with more black artists. Videos began to appear more frequently in retail record stores, often formatted by section of the store (i.e. the appropriate videos were being played in the corresponding part of the store to encourage buying). The profit motive has never been healthier in the music business than it is today and corporate marshalling of economic power remain a fundamental characteristic of the industry.

Nonetheless, various substreams of culture continue to express alternative messages through music. Small, independent companies in the United States, England, and elsewhere record and distribute music that falls outside conventional textural and lyrical constructions. These recordings often have irregular, unmelodic tunes and harsher instrumentation. The production quality may not meet the standard set by the majors. Typically the music is marketed without the advantage of large budgets for promotion to record stores and radio stations.

And, of course, the musicians themselves exercise considerable control over the potential social impact of their work. Famous musicians in the 1980s organized and produced records and live concerts that raised considerable amounts of money for various causes. The USA for Africa group of American singers raised more that $50 million for relief of the starvation in Ethiopia with their song, "We are the World." The "Live Aid" concerts staged simultaneously in the United States and England raised more than $80 million for famine relief. Country singers staged "Farm Aid" in the United States in an event organized by superstar Willie Nelson that raised millions for financially pressed American farmers. Little Steven produced an album and video ("Sun City") that spoke out against the racist apartheid system of South Africa. Peter, Paul, and Mary joined with South Africa's Bishop Tutu in a Washington, DC protest over the same issue. Paul Simon also took up the cause with his Grammy winning album, *Graceland*. Grupo Mancotal, a folk group from Nicaragua, toured the United States singing songs and raising money in protest of the U.S. presence in Central America. Simple Minds' Jim Kerr donated proceeds from some concerts and arranged a letter-writing campaign for Amnesty International, an organization that works for the release of political prisoners worldwide, that was hardly known to young pop music fans before the music activity. Bryan Adams, Peter Gabriel, U2, Sting, Lou Reed, Jackson Browne, and Joan Baez later went on a U.S. tour, part of which was shown on MTV, to benefit the same organization. Huey Lewis donated nearly $250,000 to benefit AIDS Research in San Francisco. Steve Jones, Sheena Easton, Michael Des Barres, Gregory Abbott, and Gene Simmons, among others, endorsed a government and industry backed anti-drug campaign. James Taylor, Bonnie Raitt, Santana, and the Doobie Brothers were among the American musicians who put on (with the considerable help of Bill Graham) a Fourth of July rock concert/peace demonstration together with Soviet musicians in Moscow in 1987.

Social activism on the part of popular musicians is not limited to the West. In the wake of the Chernobyl nuclear power plant accident, pop and rock musicians in the Soviet Union representing several genres (including heavy metal and new wave) performed before more than 30,000 young people in Moscow. The concert (titled "Account 904" in reference to the bank account established in support of those who suffered from the accident) and subsequent release of an album raised the equivalent of more than $200,000.

Musicians are behind contemporary protest movements in Latin America and Africa. In Asia political resistance movements in Korea and Japan have support among young musicians. There is an acute critical awareness among some young Chinese in Taiwan, Singapore, and Hong Kong that traditional culture has been greatly influenced by styles from the West. One young Hong Kong rock band, The Cicada, has written a satirical description of the cultural transformation:

I wear Japanese fashion and Italian shoes;
I wear a Swiss watch and a French necklace;
I gotta tell you,
I will not be a "descendant of the Dragon."

I appreciate the moon in Europe,
And I love the sunshine in California;
Statue of Liberty, Eiffel Tower
I will not stay on the Yangtze River!

The contrast of the social impact of mainstream culture and subculture, of mainstream media and alternative media, should not be drawn too sharply. Most audience members have been influenced by each. Still, the hegemony of popular ideologies is challenged by the presence of alternative media and content that advocate deviant perspectives on sociocultural and political-economic issues. This influence is dramatically affected by the sociopolitical context as was illustrated in the relevance of protest music to the national mood surrounding the civil rights movement in the early and mid-1960s and the Vietnam war in the mid-1960s to the early 1970s. Should the United States' involvement in Central America, the Middle East, or elsewhere become more intense, musicians and their protest music would again contribute to the inevitable resistance movement.

### The Music Video Phenomenon

Cable television has grown rapidly in the 1980s, finally fulfilling the promise that was projected for it long ago. Among the more attractive "services" that cable companies can offer audiences is MTV Music Television and its spinoffs. Music video has become a fact of life in the realm of popular culture, raising grave concerns by some about its effects on young viewers; stimulating great interest in the music industry that has looked upon this programming as an unparalleled marketing tool; and causing musicians to think about their creations visually as well as aurally. The music channels were not overnight financial successes, but few would believe now that they will disappear in the near future.

Just what is music video? It reverses the normative aesthetic and semiotic relationship between picture and sound in television and film, in that the visuals are there to enhance the sound rather than the other way around (that is, there is a "visual track" to accompany the sound rather than a "sound track" to accompany the visuals). Motives normally associated with exposure to television and to music simply do not describe their reasons for contact with MTV (Sun & Lull, 1986). Music video is a separate kind of medium, one that uses the convention of popular radio (rotation of favorite songs played repeatedly throughout the day; the presence of "veejays"; concert and music information, and so on) but is transmitted via cable television technology and sends pictures as well as sounds. The fact that popular videos are repeated so often gives them a forum for exposure that is more similar to television *commercials* than to entertainment programming.

It is not yet possible to assess fully the impact of music video on the audience. Could it be that the basic experience of decoding music will be permanently changed with the addition of the visual track? In what ways has the music industry's approach to signing and promoting artists and groups changed since the arrival of music video? Does the emergence of music video programming signal the triumph of shallow musical and cultural style?

There are concerns that music videos destroy the imaginations of young viewers since they provide ready-made, repeated interpretations of popular songs. Does this common experience mean that viewers are somehow "robbed" of their own abilities to visualize or otherwise interpret popular songs? The presentation of violence, sexual innuendo, and sexism on many videos has elicited some extreme reactions.

Music critics have been hard on music videos too. For instance, the *San Francisco Chronicle* chastised the popular British band the Thompson Twins for their MTV-oriented music:

> The Twins make music that is not deep, only opaque enough to keep the light from shining through. That has always been the key to success on television, a medium that apparently thrives on platitudes and doesn't comfortably support deep emotional expression or strong, pointed intellectual material.

Bands like the Thompson Twins, Wham!, and especially Duran, Duran are generally thought to be "creatures" of MTV, owing their enormous popular success to the effectiveness of their videos. Every kid in the suburbs knows the MTV bands.

There are some bands that for ideological or financial reasons will not make videos. Punk bands, as might be expected, are especially negative about music videos, though it is interesting to speculate about what their videos might look like. The popular punk band, The Dead Kennedys, has a song in their repertoire titled, "MTV—Get Off the Air!" And there has been much controversy during the early history of music video about the lack of black and other minority musicians in the rotation systems of the new video channels, though separate black music video programs have now arrived. Asians, Latinos and other minority groups in the United States also make videos but have almost no access to the music video channels on cable television. The Vietnamese-American population in California, for example, has an extremely lively pop music scene that unfortunately is almost entirely contained within the ethnic culture. Vietnamese pop music videos are sold in Vietnamese stores and played back by fans on their VCRs at home.

Despite the problems and fears, the presence of music video is by no means entirely negative. It is an artistic phenomenon that has been appreciated by many musicians and music fans. Music videos incorporate a compelling synthesis of many art forms into one. Videos involve not only a visual conceptualization of the song and its performance, but also dance, choreography, storytelling, fashion, costuming, lighting, acting, visual techniques (including digital effects and animation), and editing, and call upon managerial skills in directing and producing. The result is action-packed visuals combined with the sound of pulsating rock and pop music, a dynamic and attractive package for young viewers who are known to watch and enjoy it a lot (Brown et al., 1986; Sun & Lull, 1986), and often share the experience of viewing music videos with their friends (Miller & Baran, 1984).

Many of the issues raised above are discussed in considerable length by Dean Abt in his piece in this volume. Another issue taken up by him is the impact of music video on the purchase of albums and tapes. The relationship between music videos on television and the music industry is a sensitive one. Wolfe (1983) has summarized the history of this relationship and concludes that MTV and other video outlets believe that the industry needs them. The record industry, on the other hand, has asserted itself more strongly since 1985 when major manufacturers of music videos began to charge stations to play them. The ultimate goal of the music industry, of course, is to move as many "units of product" as possible to a consuming public. But the willingness of music buyers to act accordingly depends in part on the person's "involvement with music and with music video" (Abt, this volume) and with the way in which the "meaning" of music is communicated via video vis-à-vis audio (Rubin et al., 1986).

MTV Music Television has diversified its programming to include not only music videos, commercials, concert news, music information, and friendly "raps" by the veejays, but also comedy and drama. Programmers will keep an eye on the dynamic music scene since MTV benefited so much in its early days by its enthusiasm for "new wave" or "modern" music. However, ratings problems in the middle 1980s motivated MTV programmers to narrow their playlist to more conventional hard rock artists in an effort to find a sellable audience demographic composition. Whatever the current musical trends, what programmers of the video channels seek is not just what sounds good, but what looks good too.

## Cultural Sovereignty and the World Beat

World cultures differ in virtually every aspect of their existence, but the creation and use of music is as common to them as finding the means for survival. Of course, the kinds of music that are made and the contexts in which music appears differ greatly from one culture to another. Lomax, in his impressive and controversial analysis of world cultures, placed music at the heart of culture and argued that song style reflects social structure so clearly that the globe can be mapped into regions by music type (Lomax, 1968). He related music to the division of labor, gender relations, sexual mores, social cohesiveness, and the rate of production and political activity, among other considerations.

Blacking's (1973) long-term study of South Africa's Venda tribe similarly considered music in relation to social functions and the division of labor in society. He postulated that music is "not a language that describes the way society *seems* to be, but a metaphorical expression of feelings associated with the way society *really* is" (Blacking, 1973: 104; italics mine). An anthropologist, Blacking saw music in the Venda tribe as a "reflection and response" to the circumstances of life, especially of work roles among tribe members and activities that confirm their cultural identities. These studies and others provide convincing evidence that music has cultural importance that greatly transcends its obvious ability to provide entertainment. Music is a cultural resource of great value.

But the world's cultures are not insular. With the development of communications technologies and the fundamentally unregulated practices of international business, cultures all over the world have been influenced from the "outside." Consequently, there has been justifiable concern expressed especially in recent years about the impact of the "flow of information" from the more developed to the less developed parts of the world. Critical theorists and other observers worry about the impact of media technologies and their content on nations that have had to import these materials in order to "modernize." The focus of concern usually has been on television, since program materials for the visual medium are so costly to produce, often causing receiver nations to depend on nations that supply them with telecommunications hardware and to also provide abundant, low-cost software. With the arrival of these materials is value-laden program content that sometimes conflicts with at least some of the cultural traditions and orientations of the receiver countries.

Music technology and the songs themselves arrive in all parts of the world with far less technical or bureaucratic difficulty than television does. Especially with the development of audio cassette units, "dubbed" or "pirated" tapes make it easy to disseminate music throughout the world. People from all classes of nearly all cultures seem to have found ways to obtain cassette playback or record/playback systems and tapes to use with them. The immediate problem that this distribution of music raises is the question of modern "cultural imperialism," the disruption, alteration, or replacement of local culture stimulated by the worldwide diffusion of software originating in more developed societies. If this homogenization is occurring, an "international youth culture" may emerge and lead to the gradual erosion of local music, the values it embodies, and its characteristic music-making styles and sounds (Robinson, 1986).

The Soviet bloc governments have certainly feared this influence and its ideological implications. A distinctly American genre, jazz music, has been popular in the Soviet Union for many years with unsteady government approval (Starr, 1983). Soviet youth were aware of Western rock music before the early 1960s, but when the Beatles and other English bands achieved such great international attention, the news also filtered into the USSR, where young people wanted to listen to and make this kind of music. There have been serious obstacles standing between the will of youth in Eastern Europe to hear and play contemporary Western rock music and the willingness of local authorities to grant this permission. In these countries, for instance, bands must be licensed by the state. Rock concerts are approved by the government. Electric instruments are difficult to find. Records of some of the most popular bands outside Soviet-controlled nations are not available. In late summer 1984, for instance, when Michael Jackson's international fame was starting to fade from overexposure, youth in Czechoslovakia could not yet buy his records. Punk bands are allowed to play in East Germany, but they must be approved by the Communist Party there (Wicke, 1984).

The control exercised over music in the Soviet Union and its allied nations serves two fundamental purposes for the state—economic and ideological. The economic policy of the Eastern bloc clearly prescribes international trade among Russia, Poland, East Germany, Czechoslovakia, Hungary, Yugoslavia, and Rumania in as many areas as possible, including music. So, musical instruments and equipment not manufactured in one Eastern European country may be imported from another. Similarly, consumers in any one of these countries may freely purchase rock (and other kinds of music) records made by bands from the other bloc countries. Albums that are imported from outside countries, including the United States, are actually pressed in Eastern European countries from master tapes that are sold to them.

Restrictions on availability of records and tapes, recording equipment, instruments, and the licensing requirements imposed on musicians keep the culture-producing practices and its messages under government supervision. Of course, absolute control is impossible. In Prague, Czechoslovakia, for instance, American and British dance music pours out of a disco where young people dress in modern fashions and dance in contemporary Western styles to a low-quality sound system with a deejay who interjects comments in English over the music. There is little apparent censoring of the music that is played, or of the actions of the club's occupants. In the Soviet Union, young people create "purposeful deviance" and partake in some of the lifestyle activities that accompany playing and listening to rock music, including marijuana smoking, wearing cosmetics, and dressing and dancing in Western styles (Starr, 1983). The black market is a common resource for access to these controlled materials (Rauth, 1982).

A measured tolerance for rock music is permitted by Soviet and Eastern European governments so as not to lose the confidence of the younger generation (Szemere, 1985). By the late 1980s, the underground rock scene there was growing to significant proportions. Still, as Bill Graham told the New Music Seminar in New York after his return from Moscow, several Soviet rock musicians who he invited to participate in the 1987 Fourth of July concert in Moscow did not appear for fear of official recrimination.

The kind of control in evidence in the Soviet-influenced countries does not typify the international situation regarding music. In general, popular music travels quite freely from one nation to the next. Often the artists and organizations responsible for creation of the music do not receive financial compensation for the sale of sound in foreign places, since copyright laws generally cannot prohibit duplication of tapes when it occurs across national borders. Despite this problem, international record companies have distributed popular music throughout the world. With few exceptions, the *lingua franca* for this dissemination of culture is English. Even the famous Swedish band, Abba, that has outsold every recording group in the history of worldwide marketing of music, sings primarily in English.

Roger Wallis and Krister Malm present the various sides to the controversies that characterize international communication through music in their article in this volume. Perhaps the most important point that can be made here is that even those nations that do not protect themselves from outside influence do *not* become irretrievably damaged by foreign music. There is ample evidence to demonstrate that indigenous cultures use music coming from the outside for their own purposes. They often turn these foreign materials into sources to fit their own musical and cultural needs (Mark, 1983; Rutten, 1984).

There is a typical historical pattern. At first, a band may try to imitate exactly the music that comes from abroad. But in a short period of time the tendency is to incorporate the new material into their own cultural experience rather than try to create something culturally unfamiliar. Rock bands in Sweden or Norway, for instance, now may continue to use electric guitar, electric bass, and a synthesizer, but they may also employ an electric accordion or other instrument more generally associated with their own musical heritage. Many musicians in these countries have returned to singing all or most of their material in their own language, reflecting a reborn nationalism and pride—a means of asserting their own culture in the face of the international culture, one that speaks English.

This movement established certain expectations that musicians perform in a manner true to their native culture. I'll never forget attending a concert given in Copenhagen by the popular Danish band SW-80 in support of political activism calling for the removal of American missiles from Europe. A fully modern rock band with sophisticated electronic instrumentation, SW-80 sang in Danish until the very last song. When the band began to sing in English, the large crowd booed loudly and threw objects onto the stage, demonstrating not only strong anti-American sentiment but also a desire to have creators of local culture do so in the native language.

At times the crossing of international and national musical experiences is mixed or juxtaposed. In countries such as India, for instance, affluent young people may listen to a Prince record while dressed in Western clothes visiting a friend's home, then change clothes and join a wedding ceremony where traditional Indian music is played and everyone takes part in the traditional dances (Reddi, 1985). In Mexico, young adults attend discos and dance for hours to Western music, but during the last hour deejays typically play slow Mexican ballads to which the young women scream in delight as each new song begins. There is a spark to this part of the evening's entertainment—an apparent variety of cultural resonance—that greatly transcends the earlier moments.

International influence through music is not just a recent phenomenon. Jamaican reggae music has borrowed considerably from the influence of American soul music that was beamed to the island from Miami AM radio stations in the 1960s (White, 1983). More recently reggae music produced there has begun to sound more like disco music, presumably to help break the genre into foreign markets (Cuthbert, 1985). Dutch musicians have taken the disco beat, given it a profoundly national interpretation, and turned out a distinctive style of northern European dance music (Rutten, 1984).

This international blending of sounds and styles is what Wallis and Malm refer to as "transculturation" (see their article in this volume). Their research in 12 small countries around the world demonstrates that indigenous music is not simply replaced by imported sounds. Rather, various "hybrid" forms develop "of either local music with a transnational flavor, or transnational music with a local flavor." This process takes place in the United States and England too, where instruments such as the sitar from India and the African finger piano have been incorporated into mainstream popular Western music.

The integration of culturally varying musical styles is not new. But today, the term "world beat" music refers to a developing intention to turn the synthesis into a contemporary genre. In various parts of the United States, at least, world beat sounds, depending largely on African rhythms but also featuring European, Latin, and Asian influences, resound in dance halls and clubs. World beat music has taken on political connotations as well, signifying the "one world, one people" orientation that some young listeners embrace. The recent popular music of Sting (with the Police and as a solo artist) and Talking Heads are striking examples of the "world beat" influence on established artists.

Still, the United States, England, Holland, West Germany, and now Japan with its superb sound reproduction techniques have a major influence on the international music scene. And, despite the fact that cultures around the world have demonstrated the ability to absorb and use foreign music within their own contexts, concern still exists about the potential influence of external music. For that reason countries as diverse as the Soviet Union, Canada, and Nigeria have all imposed restrictions on the amount of foreign music that can be played on the radio.

### Summary

The foremost objective of this book is to analyze some of the important roles of music in human communication. This goal requires that the processes of communication in which music has influence be examined from the point of view of all contributors to this special variety of symbolic activity. The issues raised in the preceding paragraphs have been devoted primarily to the roles played by persons who send musical messages to their audiences—the musicians, the music industry, the radio industry, and the television/cable industry. The chapters that follow in Part I take up specific issues related to questions of the *making* and *distribution* of music.

Analyses of industrial relations to art, in this case to music, should, it seems to me, be set in a theoretical framework that invokes consideration of the pertinent political, economic, social, and cultural influences. Strangely, these factors are seldom raised in the analysis of much human communication, particularly that which is measured and interpreted "scientifically." We can see in the history of music making around the world important implications of the intimate relationships that exist among artists, the cultural products they create, and the contexts where they do their work. Struggles among forces of control and resistance are still apparent in the industrial and cultural realms. The economic, political, social, and cultural issues become more complicated as new technologies develop in musical instrumentation, recording techniques, and delivery systems. The impact of electronic recording and playback gadgetry, the explosion of radio formats that feature virtually all genres of popular music, the music video phenomenon, and the recent surge in world popularity for cassette tapes are evident among other innovations in the industrialization of music.

Of course, communication involves much more than the simple encoding of particular meanings in musical, verbal, filmic, or any other form. There is the robust and inspiring activity of the listener-users of music to consider. We need to ask, *what do people do with music?* Part II of this book is devoted to the study of music's audiences. The collection of articles presented in the second section demonstrates the notable importance of music ranging from the routine behaviors of people immersed comfortably in the mainstream of popular culture to the "radical" behavior of music-based subcultures such as punks and rastas. The ways in which popular music is interpreted and used by its listener-users is an area in social science, cultural studies, and communication theory and research that is just now beginning to assume its fair share of importance, given the vast amount of time that people, especially youth, spend with music. The activities of music's audiences will be taken up in depth in the several chapters that compose Part II. But, first, let's continue our examination of music artists and industries.

## REFERENCES

Blacking, J. (1973) *How Musical Is Man?* Seattle: University of Washington Press.

Brown, J. D., Campbell, K. P., & Fischer, L. (1986) American adolescents and music videos: Why do they watch? *Gazette, 37,* 19-32.

Cuthbert, M. (1985) Cultural autonomy and popular music: A survey of Jamaican youth. *Communication Research, 12,* 381-393.

Denisoff, R. S. (1971) *Great day coming: Folk music and the American left.* Baltimore: Penguin.

Denisoff, R. S. (1983) *Sing a song of social significance.* Bowling Green, OH: Bowling Green University Popular Press.

Denisoff, R. S., & Peterson, R. A. (1972) *Sounds of social change.* Chicago: Rand McNally.

Frith, S. (1981) *Sound effects: Youth, leisure, and the politics of rock and roll.* New York: Pantheon Books.

Hamm, C. (1983) *Music in the new world.* New York: Norton.

Lomax, A. (1968) *Folk song style and culture.* Washington, DC: American Association for the Advancement of Science.

Mark, D. (1983) Pop and folk as a going concern for sociological research. *International Review of the Aesthetics and Sociology of Music, 14,* 93-98.

Miller, D., & Baran, S. (1984) *Music television: An assessment of aesthetic and functional attributes.* Paper presented at the meeting of the International Communication Association, San Francisco.

Rauth, R. (1982) Back in the U.S.S.R.: Rock and roll in the Soviet Union. *Popular Music and Society, 8,* 3-11.

Reddi, U. (1985) An Indian perspective on youth culture. *Communication Research, 12,* 373-380.

Robinson, D. (1986) Youth and popular music: A theoretical rationale for an international study. *Gazette, 37,* 33-50.

Rosen, D. (1972) *Protest songs in America.* Westlake Village, CA: Aware Press.

Rothenbuhler, E. W. (1985) Programming decision making in popular music radio. *Communication Research, 12,* 209-232.

Rubin, R., Rubin, A. M., Perse, E. M., Armstrong, C., McHugh, M., & Faix, N. (1986) Media use and meaning: A music video exploration. *Journalism Quarterly, 63,* 353-359.

Rutten, P. (1984) *Youth and music in the Netherlands.* Paper presented to the International Association for Mass Communication Research, Prague, Czechoslovakia.

Starr, S. F. (1983) The rock inundation. *Wilson Quarterly, 51,* 58-67.

Sun, S.-W., & Lull, J. (1986) The adolescent audience for music television and why they watch. *Journal of Communication, 36,* 108-115.

Szemere, A. (1985) Pop music in Hungary. *Communication Research,* 12, 401-411.

White, T. (1983) *Catch a fire.* New York: Holt, Rinehart & Winston.

Wicke, P. (1984) *Young people and popular music in the GDR: Social realities and some theoretical views.* Paper presented to the International Association for Mass Communication Research, Prague, Czechoslovakia.

Wolfe, A. S. (1983) Rock on cable: On MTV Music Television, the first video music channel. *Popular Music and Society, 9,* 41-50.

# 2

# *Music as Political Communication in the United States*

## DAVID KING DUNAWAY

The instinct to communicate political sentiments through music is by no means new or uniquely American. As far back as the Hsia Dynasty—2000 B.C.—Chinese emperors advised officers of the court to listen to the songs of their workers as a rudimentary opinion poll (Wang, 1935). In Europe's middle ages, anticlerical feelings found expression in the songs of wandering goliards. In seventeenth century England, the egalitarian Diggers composed anthems of class consciousness, and the song "Lillabullero" helped topple James II from his throne. In 1703, Scottish patriot Andrew Fletcher wrote, "If a man were permitted to make all the ballads, he need not care who should make the laws of a nation."

Through the oral tradition, songs of political dissent have entered and changed American culture, much as "Little Jack Horner" became a children's nursery rhyme long after its barbed reference to Henry VIII's expropriation of church property was forgotten (Brand, 1962). As folklorist Richard Dorson has pointed out, songs and oral tradition articulate popular history: "The historian accustomed to relying on published sources" can find little without oral sources (Dorson, 1971). In his study *Oral Tradition,* Jan Vansina suggests that oral testimony, even when it challenges the status quo, serves a critical social function. A tradition of rebellion, such as the political song, "provides members the concrete proof that they are no longer dependent upon another community."

The history of political communication in American music predates the founding of the union of the English colonies. From West Africa, the British Isles, and Europe, colonists brought a rich musical tradition; and with each music came a social context. It is said that on their ships crossing to the new land, the Puritans—and the slaves—each sang of their troubles and hopes (Hamm, 1983). While their songs reflected different societies, power relations, and musical scales, the function of song was for both groups similar: "the ultimate social glue," as ethnomusicologist Bess Lomax Hawes commented.

### Defining Political Music

While political music often has roots in traditional song and balladry, it is not often popular music—rarely are these creations current among the masses. It is not necessarily folk music—though folklorists and ethnomusicologists have debated this point. Nor is it art music, in the sense of a work consistently performed from its original written version for entertainment. Yet music of all of these types has served for utterances of a political or dissident nature (Dunaway, 1977).

The field of political music includes everything from an electoral song of the 1730s to a punk-rock protest of the 1980s. Among the most common types are: political campaign songs and the music of political protest, including labor, abolitionist and slavery, and suffragist and populist songs.

*Music may be said to be political when its lyrics or melody evoke or reflect a political judgment by the listener.* The politics of a piece of music are communicated by its time, performer, and audience. Thus the most comprehensive definition of political music would take into account its specific context: the communicative function of a particular work in a particular setting at a particular place in time.

Across *history* the politics of a piece of music may undergo radical transformation. A song too politically sensitive to be published in one era—such as "If I Had a Hammer" (originally composed on the occasion of the 1949 trial of leaders of the Communist Party)—can become the Muzak of another generation (Dunaway, 1981). When the historical context of a song changes, so does its meaning.

A second factor in context is *performance.* Under different circumstances, music communicates different meanings to different groups. "Un Canadien Errant," a song of a Canadian driven from his home after a war, has far less political impact sung in a coffeehouse in California than performed before French Canadian separatists in Montreal. Even the same performer singing the same song before the same audience can produce dramatically different results, as someone invited to sing the country and western hit, "Take This Job And Shove It" might discover when presenting it at both the union picnic and the annual company dinner.

Besides the historical reference and the performance context, the individual performer's *style and tradition* communicates the politics of music. Should a singer introduce a song with "I learned this one from a friend, who used to sing it as a child," he will evoke a less political reception than if he begins: "This next song was written 40 years ago, during a bitter mining strike in Harlan County . . ."

By focusing on the effect, rather than the intent of the music, this definition avoids judgments on the overt politics of a specific piece of music. The question remains, however, whether a piece of political music can itself—as opposed to the larger political movement it serves—ever achieve a political end.

### Song as Communication

The song, that most populist of art forms, has traditionally been a medium for expression by those who do not leave a printed record. This is particularly true for protest songs, which have given voice to sentiments that had no other outlet, from slave songs sung under the whip of plantation foremen to the songs of political allegory of the People's Songs movement of the 1950s. As one communications theorist pointed out, this oppositionist function of music today legitimizes "cultural alternatives to the values and lifestyles of the dominant culture so thoroughly represented in the popular media and the home, neighborhood, work, and school environments" (Lull, 1985). Song texts and their accompanying music enfranchise groups in important ways.

First, the lyrics of songs inevitably express the worldview of their authors and singers. This is particularly true for anonymous works, which often reflect a folk or popular consciousness. Songs are part of the unofficial culture of their time, though they are generally ignored by scholars more comfortable with the printed word. The thoughtful student explores not merely the lyrics but the song's underlying sentiment and ideals as well.

Second, music itself acts as a historical indicator. Musical forms have their own identifiable history, which tells us the origins and worldview of those who choose them as means of exhortation. A country singer such as Kentucky's Jim Garland and a citybilly like New Englander Pete Seeger both create protest songs out of traditional Appalachian tunes, but the songs they select and what they do with them musically (as well as textually) differ enormously. In addition, the communicative mode of the music adapted—dancing, entertainment, education—may determine its success as political communication. A civil rights protest song based on gospel and one based on a Broadway show tune are likely to be received very differently among black Americans—both were tried in the civil rights movement of the 1960s, but the gospel-based compositions were far more widely sung.

In an ethnological context, the communicative effect of music "is to give the listener a feeling of security for it symbolizes the place where he was born, his religious experience, his pleasure in community doings, his courtship, and his work—any or all of these personality-shaping experiences" (Lomax, 1959). Lomax was referring to traditional song in a traditional community, but similar elements apply for most groups— union supporters in a loft in Greenwich Village, for example. Across time, songs provide a key to community dynamics and history, a cultural inventory of a group.

### Types and Functions of American Political Music

Having briefly defined political music, we can now offer general patterns in its types and functions. While these typologies are based on research in Anglo-American and Afro-American music, they may prove applicable internationally.

In terms of *topic,* the lyrics of political music fall into a number of basic types:

(1) Protest and complaint, direct or indirect, against exploitation and oppression.
(2) Aspiration toward a better life, a more just society.
(3) Topical satire of governments, politicians, landlords, capitalists.
(4) Political philosophical themes; political and ethical ideals.

(5) Campaign songs of particular parties and movements.
(6) Commemoration of popular struggles past and present.
(7) Tributes to heroes and martyrs in the popular cause.
(8) Expressions of international working-class solidarity.
(9) Comment on industrial conditions and working life and the role of trade unions.
(10) Protest against racial and sexual stereotyping.
(11) Appeals for renewable energy sources and environmental betterment [Ashraf, 1975].

These categories are descriptive, however, and reveal little of the mechanisms by which songs penetrate a culture and express sentiments that often cannot be uttered in words or print. Political music as a genre might benefit from a sociological-anthropological typology of the *functions* of the idiom. From this perspective, music attempts to:

(1) Solicit or arouse support for a movement.
(2) Reinforce the value structure of individuals who support this movement.
(3) Create cohesion, solidarity, and morale for members of this movement.
(4) Recruit individuals into a specific movement.
(5) Evoke solutions to a social problem via action.
(6) Describe a social problem, in emotional terms.
(7) Divide supporters from the world around them (an esoteric-exoteric function).
(8) Counteract despair in social reformers, when hoped-for change does not materialize (Denisoff, 1983).

These categories are also descriptive and by no means mutually exclusive; a singer could describe a social problem in one breath and recruit supporters in the next. These communicative functions vary in importance from one group or time to the next.

**Political Campaigns**

In campaigns, music unifies a nation by evoking national and local electoral rituals; this has been true since the first colonial broadsides were sold on the streets of Boston. In New York in the early 1700s, during a period when non-property-owning classes were disenfranchised, election day brought out class-conscious songs and verses:

Now the pleasant time approaches;
Gentlemen do ride in coaches.

But poor men they don't regard
That to maintain them labour hard.

In 1734, maverick writer and printer John Peter Zenger used political songs so successfully in an electoral campaign that the then governor of New York proclaimed a reward for the authors of the "Scandalous Songs or Ballads" and conducted a public burning of the broadsides he collected. Songs circulated in political campaigns against the Stamp and Game Acts and the British presence in North America (Foner, 1975). These are only a few of the hundreds of incidents where Americans have turned to song to make a point:

> From the earliest periods of American history the oppressed people forming the broad base of the social and economic pyramid have been singing of their discontent. What they have said has not always been pleasant, but it has always been worth listening to, if only as the expression of a people whose pride and expectation of a better life have traditionally been considered attributes of the American nation [Greenway, 1953].

As America became a nation in the 1780s, songs such as "God Save Washington" (to the tune of "God Save the King") helped elect the first president; others aided the campaign to ratify the Constitution. American campaign songs had perhaps their most sweeping effect in the election of 1840, where supporters of W. H. Harrison assembled songbooks such as the *Tippicanoe Songbook* (Silber, 1971). The result was not only victory but the emergence, for the next 75 years, of a stream of presidential odes, songs, waltzes, marches, and polkas for presidential candidates.

The music of the political campaign circulated in political journals; no one knows how widely the songs were sung. By the mid-nineteenth century, the campaign songster (a collection of lyrics without printed music) had become standard equipment in electoral campaigns, aided by sheet music publishers who hoped to find a bonanza in a song about a popular candidate. Most of the melodies of these parodies were popular tunes or patriotic airs.

Campaign music began to decline in importance after World War I. While "Keep Cool and Keep With Coolidge" inspired adherents, the candidates to use song most effectively were probably Franklin Roosevelt (whose "Happy Days Are Here Again" and "We've Got

Franklin D. Roosevelt Back Again" came to symbolize his era) and the ill-fated 1948 left-wing presidential campaign of Henry Wallace. After 1948, media exposure and advertising gradually took precedence over campaign songs, a symbol of the decreased role of face-to-face campaigning. Songs such as "Happy Landin' with Landon," "We're Madly for Adlai," and "Go With Goldwater" passed quickly into the realm of historical artifact.

### Labor and Union-Building

From its birth, the labor movement was rich in music, and with the first unions came the first union songs. As in later years, the early guild and union movements used music to express resistance to economic and social injustice. A scholar of this movement has summarized the themes of nineteenth century labor song as "the organizations and struggles of working people, their hatred for the oppressors, their affirmation of the dignity and worth of labor, their determination to endure hardships together and to fight together for a better life" (Foner, 1975). These early songs occasionally found their way into the songsters or hymnals such as the *Pocket Hymn Book* but more commonly circulated as broadsides and at processions and parades. The tunes for many of these parodies were popular songs or hymns, reflecting the exhortative tradition of American religious music.

In the first labor newspapers, such as the *Philadelphia Mechanics' Free Press,* songs of class protest made a regular appearance. Though editors did not often publish melodies, they frequently had columns of songs and doggerel contributed by readers and union members. When hard times hit industrial and self-employed craftsmen, songs became a convenient means of voicing discontent; and the labor press became a principal forum for sentiments which before had circulated only orally. Yet much musical-political expression was excluded—particularly that of Afro-Americans in slavery, Native Americans, recent immigrants, and those in occupations without unions or guilds.

With the widespread industrialization of New England in the early 1800s came child labor and some of the most famous American factory protest ballads: "The Factory Girl" was the title given to a half-dozen songs. Each wave of industrial and social change was reflected in the songs of the time: the depression of 1837, the utopian movements of the 1840s and 1850s. Music was a part of political meetings and rallies, much in the way religious revivalists encouraged singing at camp meetings.

To return to our earlier typology, in the eighteenth and nineteenth centuries early labor songs aired grievances, satirized corrupt officials and practices, commented on industrial conditions and unions, and served as campaign songs; by and large they functioned to arouse support, describe social problems, counteract despair, and evoke positive solutions.

Toward the end of the nineteenth century, the most bitter and prominent strikes and labor battles produced memorable political songs, such as the "Coal Creek Rebellion" (1892), where mine owners in Tennessee used convicts as forced labor in the mines. The first national strike of the United Mineworkers in 1897 gave rise to "Miner's Lifeguard." The Haymarket affair of 1886, where Chicago workers met to campaign for a shorter workday and against police brutality, popularized songs promoting the eight-hour work day. The Homestead steel strike of 1892 and the Pullman strike of 1894, two watershed events in the development of American unionism, each produced a wealth of political music, some written to popular tunes such as "After the Ball."

Miners also contributed important political music. The isolation of working underground and the feudal conditions under which many miners labored produced the most extensive collection of labor-protest songs of any American industry. Since miners traditionally lived in encampments near their workplace—which lacked outside diversions— they fashioned music and entertainment from their isolated sur- roundings. The alienation and poverty of mineworkers found expression in the only art form most understood and unself-consciously practiced: singing.

In 1905, the IWW was formed out of the remains of the Socialist Labor Party, the Western Federation of Miners, and other socialist groups. Its practice of combining singing and rabble-rousing speeches is said to have originated in Spokane in the 1900s, when an organizer decided to compete with the Salvation Army's street bands by parodying their hymns with lyrics pleading the IWW cause (Greenway, 1953). Unlike the more conservative American Federation of Labor, the IWW opened its meetings with songs, and their songbook included the first printing of "Solidarity Forever," "The Preacher and the Slave (Pie in the Sky)," "Hallelujah I'm a Bum," and "The Red Flag." Their tunes were largely taken from popular song hits of the 1909-1915 period, or from familiar gospel revival tunes.

The IWW called itself the "Singingest Union of them all." The IWW's use of music as a direct organizing arm inspired later song agitators by offering songs as a front-line device for building morale, recruiting new members, and garnering publicity. Their music also functioned as a continuing oral history: many of their major strikes, campaigns, and martyrs were recorded in song.

During America's Great Depression, grass-roots efforts at labor organizing and education produced topical songs in the nineteenth century labor song tradition. Commonwealth College, Brookwood Labor College, and the Highlander Folk School collected and popularized the rural southern labor song, through songbooks. The early drives of the new Congress of Industrial Organizations stimulated union songs where the initials C.I.O. were zipped into choruses. Only rarely did these songs leave their local communities in the 1930s, the exception being those which emerged from the bitter mining strikes in Gastonia and Marion, North Carolina.

The Almanac Singers (1941-1944) were a dozen or so young musicians who lived and performed together in the early 1940s to provide musical support to the American Communist Party and to the Congress of Industrial Organizations. The Almanacs adapted Appalachian folk songs to topical issues and sang them as widely as they could, though their most common audience was among Eastern European immigrants in unions in New York City (Reuss, 1986).

People's Songs (1945-1949)—conceived during World War II, before the postwar anticommunist campaigns were foreseen—set out to spread labor and political protest songs through a national organization of radical songwriters and performers. The association, the bulletin of which numbered at its highest 2000 subscribers, employed a variety of forms (cabaret, jazz, ethnic, and folk music) to communicate political sentiments.

Both the Almanacs and People's Songs featured Pete Seeger and Woody Guthrie, who (with Joe Hill of the IWW) are the most celebrated of American labor songsters. Guthrie's songs of the dust-bowl migrants in the 1930s and Seeger's union songs of the 1940s and 1950s helped establish a revival of interest in American folk song at the same time as they spurred radical union organizing.

The ultimate failure of twentieth century labor song groups such as People's Songs may have resulted from their reluctance to heed the changing functions of political music. Where, before World War II, labor songs recruited members and bolstered morale, after the war the situation of unions had changed. The postwar era's emphasis on management-labor collaboration nearly ended singing in the unions; during the anticommunist blacklist period, union organizers turned away from music, due to its earlier association with left-wing groups.

### Slavery and Abolitionism

Living in isolation on the plantation, deliberately kept from literacy by their masters, blacks preserved many elements of their distinctive oral culture, at least through the nineteenth century. For Afro-Americans, more than for most other groups, political sentiments surfaced in folklore and folk songs, particularly in the music of black protest: the field holler (as a means of communication beyond the hearing of the field boss); the spiritual (with its veiled references to that "Great Getting-Up Morning"); work songs (which allowed a degree of control over the pace of labor); and folk songs encoded with directions to the Underground Railroad (such as "Follow the Drinking Gourd"—the Big Dipper, north). Likewise, slaves made up ballads of outlaws, tricksters, and "bad" slaves, such as High John the Conqueror. This music fed political protests and more overt activities of defiance, such as sabotage, escape, and revolt by Afro-Americans. For slaves, musical protest had to be coded in religious terms. There were overt descriptions of brutal working conditions and aspirations toward a better life; the trickster tales and native protest songs often served as tributes to heroes and martyrs. These songs functioned by recruiting members of anti-slavery campaigns and escapes and by dividing the slave community into "ins" and "outs" according to those who understood the codes of the singers. Thus a song about the elusive "Grey Goose" ("The hounds couldn't catch him. . . . The knife couldn't cut him . . .") effectively divided listeners into those who understood this as a tale of a goose, and those who heard this as a symbol of resistance.

Initially, musicologists failed to probe beneath the surface of Afro-American culture and the racial supremacist attitudes of the eighteenth and nineteenth centuries. As late as 1914, a scholar wrote: "Nowhere in these songs can we trace any suggestion of hatred or revenge, two qualities usually developed under slavery" (Howe, 1922). Contemporary researchers, such as historian Lawrence Levine in *Black Culture and Black Consciousness,* disputed these conclusions:

> Those who have argued that Negroes did not oppose slavery in any meaningful way are writing from a modern political context. What they really mean is that the slaves found no political means to oppose slavery. But slaves . . . had other means of escape and opposition. [They] were able to perpetuate much of the centrality and functional importance that music had for their African ancestors.

To the disenfranchised and the nonliterate in a slave society, music expressed those sentiments which could otherwise not be uttered.

Throughout the nineteenth century, Afro-American spirituals echoed themes of release from bondage on earth. The symbolic content of this music ranged from the fairly explicit "We Shall Be Free" to elaborate justifications of biblical narratives, such as "Didn't My Lord Deliver Daniel (and Why Not You or I)." Times of crisis brought secular political songs about specific events, such as the songs of the slave revolt of Nat Turner in 1831.

Songs proposing the abolition of slavery reflected the dissatisfaction that had characterized slave songs for the previous two centuries. As abolitionism grew in support in the North, it produced a large body of songs regularly sung at public meetings. The Hutchinsons, a singing family of entertainers, performed traditional songs and these new "topical songs" for the abolitionist cause, parodying traditional tunes such "Old Dan Tucker." Performing before the Civil War, the Hutchinsons may have been the first professional song agitators in the United States (Jordan, 1946).

### Suffrage and Populism

Besides the music of labor and slaves, two other political movements used political music for communication in the nineteenth century: the suffragists, demanding the franchise for women, and the populist, farmer-labor alliances.

Widespread agitation for women's suffrage began soon after the Civil War, with a referendum in Kansas. Characteristic of songs of that era was "Female Suffrage," composed in 1867:

You may wear your silks and satins
Go when and where you please
Make embroidery and tattin'
And live quite at your ease

You may go to ball and concert
In gaudy hat and coat.
In fact, my charming creatures
Do everything but vote [Silber, 1971].


Contemporaneous to the suffragist activity after the Civil War was the movement (and music) of populism. As the army had cleared the frontier of native American settlements in the 1800s, farming had spread through the midwestern and western states. Unfortunately for the farmers, throughout the nineteenth century their working conditions were determined by large landholders, banks, and railroads, themselves combined in enormous trusts.

After the Civil War, with costs for rail transportation rising and mortgages foreclosing, farm tenancy increased dramatically. With these developments came the Farmer's Alliance, founded in 1877. This populist political movement parodied many popular tunes, such as "Johnny Comes Marching Home" and "John Brown's Body." In the 1890s, the Alliance movement merged with the Knights of Labor and published the popular political songsters the *Alliance and Labor Songster* and the *Labor Reform Songster*. The simple, familiar tunes and direct, exhortative lyrics were sung in many farmhouses and grange meetings.

In 1892, the Alliance-Knights of Labor coalition formed the briefly successful Populist (or People's) Party, who used traditional tunes like "Rosin the Bow" for campaign songs such as "The Hayseed:"

I once was a tool of oppression
As green as I could be;
And monopolies banded together
To beat a poor hayseed like me. . . .
But now I've roused up a little
Their greed and corruption I see
And the ticket we vote next November
Will be made up of Hayseeds like me.

### Contemporary American Political Music

In the twentieth century, political groups communicating through music have, with a few exceptions, been of a radical cast. A variety of musical forms have been used, including everything from musical comedy to hillbilly-country and western to folksongs of social protest to avant-garde jazz and atonal compositions. Emergent technology has brought new media for musical communication. Anthems for political change are today created by mass political movements, a development aided by the instantaneous electronic journalism of radio and television.

Besides the labor and union groups mentioned above, Afro-Americans have relied on music in contemporary political movements. From 1954 to 1965, civil rights campaigns in the South made a most effective use of music, beginning with the spirituals which had served slaves in their protests, songs such as "We Are Soldiers in the Army." In a second phase, this movement adapted traditional songs—and their melodies—in the same way union organizers had in the radical labor schools of the 1930s. Perhaps the most famous example was "I'll Overcome," a traditional hymn which had its lyrics, tempo, and meter revised for mass singing over a period of 15 years, ultimately becoming "We Shall Overcome" (Carawan and Carawan, 1963). The musical-religious roots of songs such as this one were so deeply embedded in the culture of the black southern masses that they succeeded in a way previous political song campaigns did not. By 1965, however, songs started to disappear from civil rights marches, as their novelty—and that of the nonviolent tactics this music dramatized—began to fade.

When black musicians forsook the folk-gospel styles of the civil rights period, many sought new musical forms for the issues of the day: soul music, for black nationalism and cultural pride (James Brown, "Say It Loud, I'm Black and I'm Proud"); funk, for economic redistribution and rejection of the culture of poverty (War, "The World Is a Ghetto"); and typical blues (John Lee Hooker, "Vietnam Blues"). Black jazz musicians such as Archie Shepp and Charles Mingus experimented with new tonalities, which evoked a dissident sociopolitical message without need of lyrics (Backus, 1976). The overtly revolutionary lyrics of Jamaicans Bob Marley and Peter Tosh popularized Afro-Caribean-American political music, or reggae.

Songs of the nuclear disarmament movement, sung by a few in the late 1950s, found new life in the 1960s amid dissatisfaction with American involvement in Vietnam. Though rarely broadcast, underground antiwar songs such as "Feel Like I'm Fixing To Die" by Country Joe McDonald received wide popularity.

In the 1960s, insurgent groups increasingly relied on music for political, even revolutionary, sentiments. Feminist, environmentalist, even fantasist political groups generated their own music. Singers such as Holly Near crossed political movements, uniting new and old leftists.

In the 1970s, advocates of renewable energy sources turned a grass-roots campaign against the spread of nuclear-generated power and nuclear weapons into the most musically fruitful one of the decade, including most contemporary musical styles: folk, rock, disco, country and western, new wave, and punk rock. In the 1980s, a fusion of international pop music styles and a series of benefit recordings raised interest in African culture and demonstrated once again how music can promote international understanding.

Scattered right-wing protest songs emerged in the 1950s and 1960s: barbershop quartets advocating the Ku Klux Klan's doctrines of racial supremacy, songs reflecting a backlash to civil rights and labor-organizing campaigns, and satires of social protesters in a country and western vein (Triuzzi, 1969). Right-wing activists tried occasionally to imitate left-wing success with folk-protest song. A leader of the Christian Anti-Communist Crusade hired a singer to perform compositions such as "Be Careful of Communist Lies," to the tune of "Jimmie Cracked Corn." These efforts found few audiences.

## A Theoretical Perspective

Music's political signification (or code and sign system in terms of semiotics) is evolutionary. How does a traditional or popular tune take on and retain political meaning in a community? Three paths are discernible. First, an old song takes on new meanings as historical circumstances change—such as the above-mentioned "Little Jack Horner" from the times of Henry VIII, or "We Are Soldiers in the Army," a hymn adopted "as is" by bus boycotters in Montgomery, Alabama in the mid-1950s. Once a clear historic referent ceases to be shared by audience and performer, such music often re-enters tradition as folk music.

The second, and by far the most common, method is when a tune remains in its traditional or popular version, but lyrics are added on. Musicologists refer to this as a parody, with no reference or implication of satire; American populist songs of the nineteenth century were largely parodies of Appalachian or music hall tunes.

A third possibility—when the words of a song remain the same but the tune changes—rarely occurs. Perhaps this is because outside of outright satire, music itself rarely carries an explicit political message. One example of this variety is the live recording of rock guitarist Jimi Hendrix at the Monterey Pop Festival in 1967, where he bends the tune of "Star-Spangled Banner" into an electric-psychedelic frenzy.

These last categories suggest directions for future study, particularly through analysis of tune-text relationships. At issue in studying parodies, where the text changes but not the tune, are: (1) the parallels with earlier texts, (2) the transmission and currency of the next text (who sings and listens to it?); and (3) the performance context of the new version (that is, where and how is it sung?). At issue in the study of a traditional or popular tune modified to fit a topical reference is: (1) the degree and type of variation with the traditional version; (2) why and where the change came about—whether from musicians, propagandists, a folk group, and so on; and (3) whether the change is significant and enduring (such as in the case of "We Shall Overcome," where the original version "I'll Overcome" had been eclipsed by a variant).

Music cannot be studied as political communication without examining the music itself. Songs are not poems; they live and travel in relation to their tunes. As musical styles change, so will the nature of the meanings which songs communicate. The choice of tune (and its musical ancestry and context) may determine the transmission, reception, and endurance of the text's message.

A final issue is performance context. Obviously, each performer brings a musical style, tradition, and repertoire which projects an intrinsic message to an audience. If a performer sings a protest song after telling jokes and singing love songs, the audience will receive it as entertainment; but if the performer does nothing but political music, interspersing singing with autobiography and social commentary, a different result will be produced. What effect does audience expectation have on performers of political music? What happens when groups in an audience have mixed reactions to a political message—with some desiring entertainment and escape, others in agreement with the musician's political intent, and a third group in entire disagreement?

Serious analyses of music as a vehicle for communication should examine the performance as a communicative event, in terms of the cultural rules of communication which surround it—what is communicated (content), to whom (audience), and at what places and times (context). Thus the communicative event, rather than the text communicated, is the actual focus of analysis.

## Conclusion

In the 3½ centuries since settlers landed in America, music has always served as a barometer of political sentiments, whether or not those listening reflected on what it told of their era. Politically oriented musicians have tried to collapse the distance separating singing and organizing, but music has often seemed ephemeral when compared with bullets or votes. Music's effect on the political process is subtle and virtually impossible to measure, even in retrospect. The impact of a political song is often separate in time and space from the original performance.

Music's limited effectiveness in political organizing may be inherent. As the poet Stephen Spender pointed out, those writing revolutionary songs or poetry may be thwarted by the antimaterialist nature of their craft: "Music is the most powerful of idealist drugs except religion."

Political music most successfully evokes not the bitterness of repression but the glory of a world remade. Ever since the blasts of Joshua's trumpets, political movements have turned to music to express their causes.

## REFERENCES

Ashraf, M. (1975) *Political verse and song*. Berlin: Seven Seas.

Backus, R. (1976) *Fire music: A Political history of jazz*. New York: Vanguard Books.

Brand, O. (1962) *The ballad mongers*. New York: Funk and Wagnalls.

Carawan, G., & Carawan, C. (1963) *We shall overcome*. New York: Oak Publications.

Denisoff, R. S. (1970) Religious roots of the song of persuasion. *Western Folklore, 29,* 175-184.

Denisoff, R. S. (1983) *Sing a song of social significance*. Bowling Green, OH: Bowling Green University Popular Press.

Dorson, R. (1971) *American folklore and the historian*. Chicago: University of Chicago Press.

Dunaway, D. K. (1977) Protest-song in the U.S.: A select bibliography. *Folklore Forum, 10,* 8-25.

Dunaway, D. K. (1981) *How can I keep from singing: Pete Seeger*. New York: McGraw-Hill.

Foner, P. (1975) *American labor songs of the 19th century*. Urbana: University of Illinois Press.

Greenway, J. (1953) *American folksongs of protest*. Philadelphia: University of Pennsylvania Press.

Hamm, C. (1983) *Music in the New World*. New York: Norton.

Howe, W. R. (1922). The negro and his songs. *Southern Workman, 51,* 382.

Jordan, P. (1946) *Singing Yankees*. Minneapolis: University of Minnesota Press.

Levine, L. (1977) *Black culture and black consciousness*. New York: Oxford University Press.

Lomax, A. (1959) Folksong style. *American Anthropologist, 61*, 11-13.

Lull, J. (1985) On the communicative properties of music. *Communication Research, 12*, 363-372.

Reuss, R. (1986) *American folklore and left-wing politics*. Urbana: University of Illinois Press.

Silber, I. (1971) *Songs America voted by*. Harrisburg, PN: Stackpole Books.

Triuzzi, M. (1969) The 100 American songbag: Conservative folksongs. *Western Folklore, 28*, 27-40.

Vansina, J. (1984) Oral tradition and historical methodology. In W. K. Baum & D. K. Dunaway (Eds.) *Oral History: An Interdisciplinary Anthology*. Nashville: American Association for State and Local History.

Wang, B. (1935) Folksongs as regulators of politics. In A. Dundes (Ed.) *The Study of Folklore*. Englewood Cliffs, NJ: Prentice-Hall.

# 3

# *The Industrialization of Popular Music*

## SIMON FRITH

When I was a child I lived in dread of having to sing in public. This was a common forfeit in party games, but I'd do anything else humiliating in preference. Singing was too personal, too exposed an activity.

Singing still seems to me the rawest form of personal expression (which is why I love soul music) and music making, more generally, still seems the most spontaneously human activity. Without thinking much about it, people sing in the bath and on the playground, beat out rhythms on the dance floor, and whistle while they work. It is because of our experience of the *immediacy* of music making that its industrial production has always been somehow suspect. In fact, of course, people today work with piped-in music and skip to the beat of a ghetto blaster; they're more likely to listen to the radio than to sing in the bath. Most of the music we hear now, in public or private, has been mechanically produced and reproduced. It reaches us via an elaborate industrial process and is tied into a complex system of money making. And we take these "artificial" sounds for granted. A couple of years ago I went to see Al Green in concert in the Royal Albert Hall in London. At one point he left the stage (and his microphone) and walked through the audience, still singing. As he passed me I realized that this was the first time, in 30 years as a pop fan, that I'd ever heard a star's "natural" voice!

The contrast between music as expression and music as commodity defines twentieth century pop experience and means that however much we may use and enjoy its products, we retain a sense that the music industry is a bad thing—bad for music, bad for us. Read any pop history and you'll find in outline the same sorry tale. However the story starts, and whatever the authors' politics, the industrialization of music means a shift from active musical production to passive pop consumption, the decline of folk or community or subcultural traditions, and a general musical deskilling—the only instruments people like me can play today are their record players and tape decks. The rise of multinational leisure corporation means, inevitably, the efficient manipulation of a new, global pop taste that reaches into every first, second, and Third World household like Coca Cola (and with the same irrelevance to real needs).

What such arguments assume (and they're part of the common sense of every rock fan) is that there is some essential human activity, music making, which has been colonized by commerce. Pop is a classic case of what Marx called alienation: Something human is taken from us and returned in the form of a commodity. Songs and singers are fetishized, made magical, and we can only reclaim them through possession, via a cash transaction in the marketplace. In the language of rock criticism, what's at issue here is the *truth* of music—truth to the people who created it, truth to our experience. What's bad about the music industry is the layer of deceit and hype and exploitation it places between us and our creation.

The flaw in this argument is the suggestion that music is the starting point of the industrial process—the raw material over which everyone fights—when it is, in fact, the final product. The "industrialization of music" can't be understood as something that happens *to* music but describes a process in which music itself is made—a process, that is, which fuses (and confuses) capital, technical, and musical arguments. Twentieth century popular music means the twentieth century popular record; not the record of something (a song? a singer? a performance?) which exists independently of the music industry, but a form of communication which determines what songs, singers, and performances are and can be.

We're coming to the end of the record era now (and so, perhaps, to the end of pop music as we know it) and I'll return to the future later. What I want to stress here is that from a historical perspective rock and roll was not a revolutionary form or moment, but an evolutionary one, the climax of (or possibly footnote to) a story that begins with Edison's phonograph. To explain the music industry we have, then, is to adopt a much wider time perspective than rock scholars usually allow. The pop business itself—the nature of its sales activities—is in a constant state of "crisis." Business analysts should, by contrast, keep cool. To be examining always the entrails of the "latest thing" is to mistake the trees for the wood, and, as I hope to show, there is more to be learned from the continuities in pop history than from the constantly publicized changes. "New things" are rarely as novel as suggested. In 1892, for example, "song slides" became a promotional craze for sheet music publishers: Pictures telling the story were, for years, a necessary sales aid for a new song sheet—they survived the coming of radio and talkies and had a measurable effect on the types of songs marketed and sold (Witmark and Goldberg, 1939). Video promotion, in short, doesn't just go back to 1930s jazz shorts!

To analyze the music industry through its history means focusing on three issues.

### The Effects of Technological Change.

The origins of recording and the recording industry lie in the nineteenth century, but the emergence of the gramophone record as the predominant musical commodity took place after the 1914-1918 war. The history of the record industry is an aspect of the general history of the electrical goods industry, and has to be related to the development of radio, the cinema, and television. The new media had a profound effect on the social and economic organization of entertainment so that, for example, the rise of record companies meant the decline of the music publishing and piano-making empires, shifting roles for concert hall owners and live-music promoters.

### The Economics of Pop

The early history of the record industry is marked by cycles of boom (1920s), slump (1930s), and boom (1940s). Record company practices reflected first the competition for new technologies and then the even more intense competition for a shrinking market. By the 1950s the record business was clearly divided into the "major" companies and the "independents." Rock analysts have always taken the oligopolistic control of the industry for granted, without paying much attention to how the majors reached their position. What were the business practices that enabled them to survive the slump? What is their role in boom times?

**A New Musical Culture**

The development of a large-scale record industry marked a profound transformation in musical experience, a decline in amateur music making, the rise of a new sort of musical consumption and use. Records and radio made possible both new national (and international, American-based) musical tastes and new social divisions between "classical" and "pop" audiences. The 1920s and 1930s marked the appearance of new music professionals—pop singers, session musicians, record company A & R people, record producers, disc jockeys, studio engineers, record critics, and so on. These were the personnel who both resisted and absorbed the "threat" of rock and roll in the 1950s and rock in the 1960s.

## The Making of a Record Industry

The origins of the record industry are worth describing in some detail because of the light they cast on recent developments. The story really begins with the North American Phonograph Company which, in 1888, got licenses to market both Edison's phonograph and the "graphophone," a version of the phonograph developed by employees of the Bell Telephone Company. When Edison had predicted, 10 years earlier, how his invention would "benefit mankind," he had cited the reproduction of music as one of its capacities, but this was not the sales pitch of the North American Phonograph Company. They sought to rent machines (as telephones were rented) via regional franchises to offices—the phonograph was offered as a dictating device.

The resulting marketing campaign was a flop. The only regional company to have any success was the Columbia Phonograph Co. (Washington had more offices than anywhere else!) but even it soon found that the phonograph was more successful as a coin-operated "entertainment" machine, a novelty attraction (like the early cinema) at fairs and medicine shows and on the vaudeville circuit. And for this purpose, "entertaining" cylinders were needed. Columbia took the lead in providing a choice of "Sentimental," "Topical," "Comic," "Irish," and "Negro" songs.

Meanwhile, Emile Berlinger, who in 1887-1888 was developing the gramophone, a means of reproducing sounds using discs, not cylinders, was equally concerned in making recordings—he needed to demonstrate the superiority of his machine over Edison's. The United States Gramophone Company was formed in 1893, and the following year

Fred Gaisberg, who'd started there as a piano accompanist and thus taken charge of recording, was poached from Columbia to be Berlinger's recording director and talent scout. Berlinger, unlike Edison, regarded the gramophone as primarily a machine for home entertainment and the mass production of music discs such that "prominent singers, speakers or performers may derive an income from royalties on the sale of their phonautograms" (Gelatt, 1977, p. 13), and in 1897 Gaisberg opened the first commercial recording studio. For the next five years there was an intense legal struggle between disc and cylinder.

It is useful at this point to make the usual industry distinction between hardware and software: hardware is the equipment, the furniture, the "permanent" capital of home entertainment; software is what the equipment plays—particular records, tapes, or discs. The invention, manufacture, and selling of hardware must, obviously, precede the manufacture and selling of software. What normally happens, then, is that hardware companies get involved in software production simply in order to have something on which to demonstrate their equipment—we can thus compare the early history of the record industry with the recent history of video: Video manufacturers too have been confused about what video owners would, in practice, use them for. Software is, in fact, first regarded as a means of advertising hardware (where the initial profits lie)—think of the original marketing of stereo equipment, with records of train noises that could be heard to move from one speaker to the other!

At a certain moment in the development of a new electronic medium, though, the logic changes. If people begin buying records, any will do (train noises, the first compact disc releases, whatever one's tastes), just to have *something* to play. Then, as ownership of the new equipment becomes widespread, records are bought for their own sake, and people begin to buy new, improved players in order to listen to specific sounds. Records cease to be a novelty. In the record industry this switch began in the 1920s, the real boom time for companies making both phonographs and phonograph records. In the words of Edward Lewis, a stockbroker who helped Decca become a public company in 1928, "A company manufacturing gramophones but not records was rather like making razors but not the consumable blades" (Lewis, 1956). In the video industry the switch means a changing source of the best profits—from the hardware makers (in Britain, for example, the home video market is pretty well exhausted; after its remarkable growth figures the manufacturers can now expect a steady decline in sales) to software (that is, film) rights, hence the interest of mass media moguls such as Rupert Murdoch in film companies: Their back catalogs are the basic resource for both home video users and cable television stations.

By the 1920s there were, in both Britain and the United States, numerous phonograph manufacturers, competing for sales by references to technical advances, design qualities, a variety of gimmicks and, of necessity, all issuing their own records. At this stage record companies were part of the electrical goods industry, and quite separate in terms of financial control and ownership from previous musical entrepreneurs. They were owned and run by engineers, inventors, and stock market speculators that had little to do with song publishers, theater owners, agents and promoters, performers, and managers. They don't even seem to have been much interested in music. Gaisberg comments in his memoirs that "for many years Berlinger was the only one of the many people I knew connected with the gramophone who was genuinely musical" (Gaisberg, 1946, p. 25).

It follows that these companies' musical decisions, their policies on who and what to record, were entirely dependent on the judgments and tastes of the "live" music entrepreneur (just as the "new" form, pop video, has been dependent so far on the skills and tastes of existing short film—that is, advertisement—makers). Companies competed to issue material by the same successful stage and concert hall performers, to offer versions of the latest stage show hit or dance floor craze, a practice that continued into the 1950s and rock and roll with the "cover version". Few companies were interested in promoting new members or new stars, and there was a widely held assumption in the industry that while pop records were a useful novelty in the initial publicizing of phonographs, in the long run the industry's returns would depend on people wanting to build up permanent libraries of "serious" music. Fred Gaisberg, for example, the first A & R man, whose work soon took him from America to Britain and then across Europe and Asia, was, essentially, a classical music impresario.

There is an irony here that has a continuing resonance: While each new technological change in mass music making is seen to be a further threat to "authentic" popular music, classical music is seen to benefit from such changes, which from hi-fidelity recordings to compact discs have, indeed, been pioneered by record companies' classical divisions. The record industry has always sold itself by what it could do for "serious" music. As Cyril Ehrlich points out, the gramophone began as not quite respectable (because of its public novelty use) and so an emphasis on its use for playing classical music was seen as necessary to sell it to middle-class families (Ehrlich, 1976). The early cinema went respectable with similar tactics—using classical music for its accompaniment to silent films. The important point here is that in the history of electronic media, the initial "mass market" (this was true for radio, television, and video as well) is the relatively affluent middle-class household. The organization of the record industry around the pop record (and the pop audience) was a later development, a consequence, indeed, of the economic slump.

For anyone writing the history of the record industry in 1932, there would have been as little doubt that the phonograph was a novelty machine that had come and gone as there was about the passing of the piano roll. Sales of records had dropped from 104 million in 1927 to 6 million; the number of phonograph machines manufactured had fallen from 987,000 to 40,000.

The 1930s slump was marked not just by an overall decline in leisure spending but also by a major reorganization of people's leisure habits. The spread of radio and arrival of talking pictures meant that a declining share of a declining income went toward records (just as in the late 1970s and early 1980s, when there was, after the rise in gas prices, less money overall to spend on leisure and new products like video recorders and computer games). I won't go into the details of the slump here, but simply note its consequences. First, it caused the collapse of all small recording companies and reestablished the record business as an oligoply, a form of production dominated by a small number of "major" companies. This wasn't just a matter of rationalization in the recording business itself—failing companies going bankrupt or being taken over— but also involved the surviving companies covering the crisis in record sales by putting together more wide-ranging music interests.

The development of American radio had parallels with the history of the record industry. Various companies were working out how best to exploit a new medium (by carving up the patents) and were discovering that to persuade people to rent transmitters (and make money from advertisement sales) they'd also need to provide entertaining programs. By 1926, RCA was networking shows via its National Broadcasting Company. There was also an early broadcasting emphasis on "potted palm music" (to attract relatively affluent and respectable listeners), which meant that while radio did "kill" record sales it also left pockets of tastes unsatisfied. Early radio stations were not interested in black audiences and so the market for jazz and blues records became much more significant.

As radios replaced record players in people's homes, the primary source of music profit shifted from record sales to performing rights and royalties, and the basic technological achievement of this period, the development of electrical recording by Western Electric, marked a fusion of interests among the radio, cinema, and record industries. Western Electric could claim a royalty on all electrical recordings and was the principal manufacturer of theater talkie installation. Film studios such as Warners had to start thinking about the costs (and profits) of publishers' performing rights, and began the Hollywood entry into the music business by taking over the Tin Pan Alley publishers Witmark in 1928.

The following year RCA (with money advanced by GE and Westinghouse) took over the Victor Talking Machine Company and, with General Motors, formed GM Radio Corporation, to exploit the possibilities of car radio. The subsequent making (and unmaking) of the United States's electrical-entertainment corporations is too complicated to go into here, but in the resulting oligopoly, competition for sales got more intense and, quickly, changed its terms. The initial response to falling sales was a price war—records were sold for less and less and the assumption was that people would go for the cheapest record on the market, but this eventually came up against the "irrationality" of tastes—people's musical choices aren't just a matter of price. New sales tactics had to be developed and, for the first time, record companies, led by Decca, ran aggressive advertising campaigns in newspapers and on billboards:

> Here they are—your favourites of radio, screen and stage—in their greatest performances of instrument and voice! Not obsolete records, cut in price to meet a market, but the latest, newest smash hits—exclusively DECCA. Hear them when you want—as often as you want—right in your own home [Gelatt, 1977, 268].

Decca was the first company to realize that an investment in advertisement and promotion was more than justified by the consequent increase in sales. The peculiarity of record making is that once the break-even point is past, the accumulation of profit is stunningly quick. The costs of reproduction are a small proportion of the costs of producing the original master disc or tape. It follows that huge sales of one title are much more profitable than even cost-covering sales of lots of titles and that the costs of ensuring huge sales are necessary costs. Decca thus developed the marketing logic that was to become familiar to rock fans in the late 1960s: Promotion costs were established at whatever figure seemed necessary to guarantee huge sales. Only major companies can afford such risks (and have the necessary capital available) and the strategy is dependent also on a star system, on performers whose general popularity is guaranteed in advance.

In the 1930s the recording star system was dependent on a tie-up with film and radio (hence the arrival of Bing Crosby—again, Decca was the first company to realize how valuable he was). But in the 1980s, again in a time of recession, we've seen very similar strategies being followed—an emphasis on a few superstars at the expense of the mass of groups just getting by, those stars in turn being marketed via films and film soundtracks and, more especially, with video promotion on MTV. Industry statistics suggest that the average of 4,000-5,000 new albums per year in the 1970s had become less than 2,000 per year in the 1980s.[1]

Aggressive selling and a star system in the 1930s meant a new recording strategy. Companies became less concerned to exploit existing big names, more interested in building stars from scratch, as recording stars; they became less concerned to service an existing public taste than to create new tastes, to manipulate demand. Electrical recording helped here. New crooning stars like Crosby could suggest an intimate, personal relationship with fans that worked best for domestic listeners: His live performances had to reproduce a recorded experience rather than vice versa, and jukebox programmers offered a direct way to control national taste. But radio mattered most of all, and by the end of the 1930s it was the most important musical medium. It gave record companies a means of promoting their stars and record companies provided radio stations with their cheapest form of programming. Media that had seemed totally incompatible—radio killed the record star—ended up inseparable.

The 1930s marked, in short, a shift in cultural and material musical power—from Tin Pan Alley to broadcasting networks and Hollywood studios, from the publisher/showman/song system to a record/radio/ film star system—and the judgment of what was a good song or performance shifted accordingly—from suitability for a live audience to suitability for a radio show or a jukebox. It was in the 1930s that the "popularity" of music came to be measured (and thus defined) by record sales figures and radio plays. Popular music came to describe a fixed performance, a recording with the right qualities of intimacy or personality, emotional intensity or ease. "Broad" styles of singing taken from vaudeville or music hall began to sound crude and quaint; pop expression now had to be limited to the two or three minutes of a 78rpm disc, and while musicians still had much the same concerns—to write a good tune, to develop a hook, to sum up a feeling in a lyric, to give people something to whistle or to dance to—the gatekeepers of this new music industry, the people who now determined what music was recorded, broadcast, and heard, were quite different from their pre-decessors in the music business. They were no longer directly connected to a public, trying to please it on the spot; their concern was a market, popularity as revealed by the sales that consumers delivered to advertisers. For the record industry (as for the film industry) the audience was essentially anonymous; popularity meant, by definition, something that crossed class and regional boundaries; the secret of success was to offend nobody. The record industry became a mass medium in the 1930s on the back of two assumptions: first, that the pop audience was essentially malleable; second, that pop music (and musicians) were, in cultural terms, vacuous. These were assumptions challenged after World War II by the rise of rock and roll.

### The Making of the Rock Industry

By 1945 the basic structure of the modern music industry was in place. Pop music meant pop records, commodities, a technological and commercial process under the control of a small number of larger companies. Such control depended on the ownership of the means of record production and distribution and was organized around the marketing of stars and star performances (just as the music publishing business had been organized around the manufacture and distribution of songs). Live music making was still important but its organization and profits were increasingly dependent on the exigencies of record making. The most important way of publicizing pop now—the way most people heard most music—was on the radio, and records were made with radio formats and radio audiences in mind.

The resulting shifts in the distribution of musical power and wealth didn't occur without a struggle. The declining significance of New York publishing houses and big city session musicians, the growing importance of radio programmers and record company A & R people, were marked by strikes, recording bans, disputes over broadcasting rights and studio fees, and, outside the United States, such disputes were inflected with the issue of "Americanization" (and anti-Americanism). The United States's influence on international popular music, beginning with the worldwide showing of Hollywood talkies, was accelerated by the U.S. entry into World War II—members of the service became the record industry's most effective exporters. By the end of the war the pop music people heard on radio and records across Europe—and even in parts of Southeast Asia—was either directly or indirectly (cover versions, copied styles) American. Hollywood's 1930s success in defining internationally what "popular cinema" meant was reinforced in the 1940s and 1950s by the American record industry's success in defining the worldwide sound of "popular music."

Outside the United States the ending of the war and wartime austerity and restraint meant a new boom for the record industry (in Britain, for example, Decca's turnover increased eight-fold between 1946 and 1956). In the United States, postwar euphoria was short lived. By the end of the 1940s, television seemed to carry the same threat to the pop industry as radio had 20 years earlier. The industry's resistance to this threat and its subsequent unprecedented profits were due to technological and social changes which, eventually, turned the record industry into the rock business.

The technological developments that began with CBS's experiments with microgroove recording in the late 1940s and culminated with digital recording and the compact disc in the 1980s, had two objects: to improve recorded sound quality and to make record storage and preservation easier. For the electrical engineers who worked to give their companies a competitive edge in the playback market, the musical aspects of their experiments were straightforward. What they were trying to do was to make recorded sound a more accurate reproduction of "real" sound—from the start the new processes were marketed in the name of "high *fidelity*." But this sales talk of records reaching nearer and nearer to the "complete" experience of "live" music is just that—sales talk. Each new advance—stereo discs in the 1960s, compact discs' elimination of surface noise and wear in the 1980s—*changes* our experience of music (and some changes, such as quadraphonic, have been rejected by consumers despite their supposed superior truth-to-concert-experience). Hi-fi opened our ears to a new appreciation of dynamic range and subtlety. By the end of the 1960s, records, not concerts, defined the "best" sound. Nowadays both classical and popular musicians have to make sure that their live performances meet the sound standards of their records. The acoustic design of concert halls has changed accordingly, and rock groups take sound checks, sound mixers, and elaborate amplification systems for granted. The increasing "purity" of recorded sound—no extraneous or accidental noises—is the mark of its artificiality. Prewar records were always heard as a more or less crackly mediation between listeners and actual musical events; their musical qualities often depended on listeners' own imaginations. To modern listeners these old discs (and particularly classical 78s) are "unlistenable"—we're used to treating records as musical events in themselves.

A second point follows from this. All hi-fi inventions (and this includes the compact disc) have been marketed, at first, on the assumption that the consumers most concerned about sound quality and a permanent record library are "serious" consumers, consuming "serious" music. The late 1940s "battle of the speeds" between CBS's 33 1/3 LPs and RCA's 45 rpm records was resolved with a simple market division—LPs were for classical music collectors, 45s for pop, which continued to be organized in three-minute segments, as music of convenience and of the moment (a definition reinforced by the continuing significance of jukeboxes for pop sales).

Record companies' assumptions about "true" reproduction and pop triviality were, in the event, undermined by the invention that made hi-fi records feasible—magnetic tape. In the long term the importance of tape recording was to be its availability to domestic consumers:

> In 1969 the industry produced small, self-contained tape cassettes that could run backward or forward, record or replay, skip to specific selections, and hold as much as an LP. These mass-produced cassettes made all the advantages of tape—high quality sound, long wear and ease of storage—available, affordable, easy to use, and very popular. By 1970 cassettes accounted for nearly a third of recorded music sales, and in 1971 the value of tape players sold exceeded that of phonographs [Toll, 1982, p. 74].

Hence arose the problem of home taping which, in the 1950s, was certainly not foreseen. Tape recording, initially developed by German scientists for broadcasting purposes in the war, was initially picked up not by the music biz but by radio stations (as a relatively cheap way of prerecording talk and jingles) and film studios (as an aid to making soundtracks), but record companies quickly realized tape's flexibility and cheapness too, and by 1950 tape recording had replaced disc recording entirely. This was the technological change which allowed new, independent producers into the market—the cost of recording fell dramatically even if the problems of large-scale manufacture and distribution remained. Mid-1950s United States indie labels such as Sun were as dependent on falling studio costs as late-1970s punk labels in Britain, the latter benefiting from scientific breakthroughs and falling prices in electronic recording.

But tape's importance wasn't just in terms of costs. Tape was an intermediary in the recording process. The performance was recorded on tape, the tape was used to make the master disc. And it was what could be done during this intermediary stage, to the tape itself, that transformed pop music making. Producers no longer had to take performances in their entirety. They could cut and splice, edit the best bits of performances together, cut out the mistakes, make records of ideal, not real, events. And on tape sounds could be added artifically. Instruments could be recorded separately; a singer could be taped, sing over the tape, and be taped again. Such techniques gave producers a new flexibility that enabled them to make records of performances, like a double tracked vocal, that were impossible live (though musicians and equipment manufacturers were soon looking for ways to get the same effects on stage). By the mid-1960s the development of multitrack recording enabled sounds to be stored separately on the same tape and altered in relationship to each other at the final mixing stage, rather than through the continuous process of sound addition. Producers could now work on the tape itself to "record" a performance that was actually put together from numerous, quite separate events, happening at different times and, increasingly, in different studios. The musical judgments, choices, and skills of producers and engineers became as significant as those of the musicians and, indeed, the distinction between engineers and musicians has become meaningless. Studio-made music need no longer bear any relationship to anything that can be performed live; records use sounds, the effects of tape tricks and electronic equipment, that no one has ever heard before as music (Frith, 1983).

It is a pleasing irony of pop history that while *classical* divisions of record companies have led the way in studio technology, their pursuit of authenticity has limited their studio imagination. It was *pop* producers, unashamedly using technology to "cheat" audiences (double tracking weak voices, filling out a fragile beat, faking strings) who, in the 1950s and 1960s, developed recording as an art form, thus enabling rock to develop as a "serious" music in its own right. The emergence of rock as art was symbolized by the Beatles' self-conscious studio artifact, *Sgt. Pepper's Lonely Hearts Club.*

The rise of rock depended too on a broader social change—the appearance of youth as the pop music market. This was partly the result of general demographic and economic trends—the increasing number of teenagers in the 1950s (a period of full employment) gave their consumer choices a new market weight—and partly reflected changes within the leisure industry itself. As television became the basic medium of family entertainment, previous leisure businesses such as the cinema, radio, dance halls, and theater went into decline. Teenagers were the one age group that still wanted to be out of the house and they began to take over public leisure spaces, to display a distinct teen culture, their own codes of dress and noise. These new leisure consumers were not, at first, catered for by the major leisure companies, and American teenagers had to find their style where they could—in black music, in certain Hollywood images. The resulting demands for records and clothes were first met by small, independent companies, looking for opportunities not already covered by the majors. Their success (and need for further advertisement outlets and promotion) opened the new market to media like radio and cinema desperately in need of it. The Elvis Presley story is typical. His commercial potential was first realized by his local independent label, Sun, but once his potential was realized (and his television appearances proved to the doubters that he could, indeed, be a national youth star) then he was quickly used as a way of selling records, cinema seats, magazines, merchandise, and advertising time on radio (which was adapting easily to Top 40 and rock and roll formats). From the industry perspective rock and roll was a means to an end. As music it was taken to be silly, gimmicky, and with a short shelf life; but as a way to control teenage spending, it couldn't be beaten. As deejay Dick Clark remembers,

> It was during this time that I decided to go into the record business. I got into talent management, music publishing, record pressing, label making, distribution, domestic and foreign rights, motion pictures, show promotion and teenage merchandise [Frith, 1981, p. 96].

The record industry's post-Presley focus on youth had spectacular results. In 1955 U.S. record sales increased 30% (from their postwar low point) to $277 million; in 1956 they reached $377 million; in 1957 $460 million; and in 1959 a peak of $603 million.

For the moment it seemed as if a sales plateau had been reached. The discovery of teenagers had given the industry a new lease on life but the exploitation of this market by a new network of teenage records/ stars/films/tv shows/magazines/concerts/dance steps/radio shows had the effect of confining teenage culture and teenage music to a combination of vacuous fun and romantic self-pity. After the trashy, erotic excitement of the original rock and rollers, teen music had become, under the tutelage of the record biz, an aspect of white middle-class conformity, and it took the arrival of the Beatles to suggest how limited this market was, even in commercial terms. The Beatles revealed a "youth" market that crossed age and class lines, a "pop" market that confounded the distinctions between "serious" and "trivial" records. Beatles fans were the first generation to grow up with hi-fi sounds as the norm. They bought pop records to play on sophisticated equipment, collected LPs, assumed that their stars would be available in stereo.

In the United States this market was first tapped not by local independent producers (though significant independent servicing companies were involved—FM radio stations, *Rolling Stone,* new promoters like Bill Graham) but by British acts, and the immediate result of this was the direct entry of the U.S. majors, CBS, RCA, and Warners, into the British pop scene. They set up offices in London in pursuit of British musicians, not fans. The Beatles and Rolling Stones, Dave Clark, Herman's Hermits, and the rest of the British invasion groups were almost all signed to EMI or Decca, which made them vast profits, but by the end of the 1960s British rock groups such as Led Zeppelin, who made even vaster profits, were on American labels. By the end of the 1970s Decca itself had been taken over by the German-Dutch company Polygram, and EMI had been reabsorbed by Thorn, the electrical goods manufacturer it had sold off 50 years earlier.

Rock, even more dramatically than rock and roll, reached sales levels previously thought impossible. In 1967 the American record industry passed the billion dollar annual sales mark for the first time. By 1973 annual sales had reached $2 billion, record companies were taking two million sales of single rock LPs for granted, and classical music's market share, 25% in the 1950s, had dropped to 5%. By 1978 the industry had reached sales of more than $4 billion. This was the industry I described in my book, *Sound Effects*: "music had become the most popular form of entertainment—the sales of records and tapes easily outgrossed the returns on movies or sport" (Frith, 1981, pp. 4-5).

The 1970s rock industry was focused almost exclusively on record sales. The major music corporations' profits derived from their manufacture and distribution of vast numbers of discs and, as in the 1930s, the fixed costs of record making were such that the profit rate accelerated rapidly as sales rose. By the mid-1970s the potential sales figures of rock's superstars seemed limitless. All other aspects of the music business were subordinated to this record sales campaign. Live performance, radio and television appearances, music press interviews, photo sessions, and the like were all developed as promotional tools. Every rise in costs seemed to be justified by the resulting rise in sales:

> By the end of the 1970s the average rock and roll album cost between $70,000 and $100,000 in studio time, and any "sweetening" (adding strings, for example) could add another $50,000 to the bill; promotion budgets began at around $150,000 and rose rapidly. At the beginning of the decade there was still some sense of "normal" production costs, "normal" sales and "normal" profits. Now the decision was made the other way round: the object became platinum sales—a million copies as a starting point. Company bosses began to turn their noses up at gold records—500,000 sales; studios and promotion costs were established at whatever would ensure platinum [Frith, 1981, p. 147].

Throughout the 1970s, on the other hand, 90% of records released failed to cover their costs and so there developed a sharp distinction between "hit" groups, for whom the first sign of success meant a sudden surge of record company investment designed to realize the sales potential to the full, and "miss" groups, the majority, whose records were released without fanfare, vanished without a trace. The record industry can't control pop purchasers—partly because people's musical tastes are "irrational," partly because some of the crucial gatekeepers in the business such as disc jockeys and journalists have their own interests to pursue. Record companies' usual strategy is, therefore, to release far too much product while trying to maximize the returns of success and to minimize the costs of failure. It's worth noting two points about this. First, stars are the best guarantors of success record companies can get, which is why established stars such as Stevie Wonder can negotiate such good deals when their contracts lapse: The record company ideal is to have a record go platinum before it's even released. Second, all record companies seek to exploit fully their fixed capital—the pressing plants, A & R departments, sales teams, and studios, which cost money whether they're being used or not. Record flops are made, then, with little additional costs for the companies, and just often enough a hit is released which covers all these costs anyway.

One of the most peculiar aspects of this business in the 1970s was that it was a hugely profitable corporate structure resting on two anticorporate myths. Myth 1 pitched artists and their audiences against an industry which, supposedly, denied people access to their music with a series of greedy, profit-obsessed gatekeepers. Myth 2 celebrated independent labels as rock's real creative entrepreneurs—the majors were accused of simply taking over and homogenizing the original sounds and styles the indies developed. Neither of these myths made much sense about how the rock business actually worked—as a highly efficient organization of market servicing.

This involved, first of all, the steady professionalization of every facet of music making. Hucksters, amateurs, and gamblers were replaced by responsible team players—musicians, managers, promoters, pluggers, agents, and so on, who were paid not to take risks but to provide a fixed skill. The industry began to be dominated by lawyers and accountants and by the mid-1970s there was very little tension between musicians and the business. Rock performers were more likely to complain about companies not exploiting them properly than to object to being "commercialized."

Second, "independent" producers and label owners were part of this system. They became, in effect, talent scouts and market researchers for the major companies, while being driven, for survival, into dependent manufacturing and distribution deals. They were the main victims of the ever-increasing financial demands made by each professional in the system, made by the artists and producers and engineers and promotion crews. The costs of success were inflationary and it made sense to let the majors bear them.

The rock industry was, in short, not only profitable on an unprecedented scale, it also seemed all-enveloping. It was no longer possible to talk sensibly about the moguls' exploitation of the musicians (rock musicians were making enough money to be moguls), or the unfair competition between the majors and the independents ("independence" no longer described how small companies worked), or consumers' unmet demands—rock audiences wallowed in the music they got. There was no grit in the system, and when it did appear, as punk, it was in the form of a challenge not to the entertainment business as such but to the very idea of entertainment itself.

The punk argument was that rock no longer excited or challenged or threatened anyone. Something new was needed and, according to cyclical theorists, this was an inevitable turn of rock's wheel—independent labels develop new forms of music, the majors tame them, independent labels thus develop new forms of music, the majors tame them. But punk didn't feed into the industry this way. Its do-it-yourself ideology was both too radical for the record industry and too feeble. The punk musicians who wanted to be stars signed up to major labels anyway; the musicians who didn't want to be stars were no commercial threat.

The rock business faced a crisis at the end of the 1970s not because of punk or the cycle of business competition but because of "outside" technological and social changes parallel to those that gave birth to rock and roll in the first place. On the one hand, the demographic structure of Western countries was shifting (the number of teenagers fell, the number of people over 25 increased) while mass youth unemployment meant young people had less money to spend on leisure goods anyway. On the other hand, the spread of home taping, computer games, and video recording gave recorded music new sorts of competition for people's time and interest. In Britain, for instance, 1984 market research suggested that 97% of teenagers had access to tape recorders and that 85% used them to record music. By the same year 35% of households had videocassette recorders and 20% home computers, equipment that no one had in 1976. As the British Phonographic Industry comment on computer software (85% of which is "game-oriented"):

> The consumer profile is similar, especially in age group, to music buyers, and the pricing level of a game is only marginally more than a top price LP. There is strong evidence that recorded music purchasers are diverting some of their leisure spending to computer software [BPI, 1985, p. 35].

This is the context for the end of the rock boom. Between 1973-1978 world record sales expanded from $4.75 to $7 billion, but in 1978-1979 there was a 20% drop in record sales in Britain, an 11% fall off in the United States. The growth rate of the rock business (which had reached 25% per year in 1976) was down to 5%-6%, and record companies had to stop assuming ever-increasing sales, an expanding number of platinum discs. The industry in the United States did recover in the mid-1980s but as *Billboard* noted:

> The industry's total haul of gold and platinum albums declined for the third straight year. This supports the contention that the trade's recovery in '83 was due more to the runaway success of a handful of smash hits than to an across-the-board pickup in album sales [Billboard, 1984].

### The Politics of Technology

Most explanations of change in the music industry are derived from general theories of corporate strategy and market control. As I summarized this in *Sound Effects*:

> Historians of American popular music argue that musical innovation has always come from outside the major record companies. "Independent" companies have been the outlet for the expression of new ideas and interests, and only when such ideas have been shown to be popular have the major companies used their financial advantages to take them over, to turn them into new, "safe" products. Innovation in such an oligopolistic industry, is only possible because technological changes open gaps in existing market control, and if, in the long run, competition means creativity (the more sources of capital, the more chance of musical progress), in the short run, the music business is intensely conservative, more concerned with avoiding loss than risking profit, confirming tastes than disrupting them. Records are made according to what the public is known to want already [Frith, 1981, p. 89].

What this analysis describes is a particular pattern of market competition—at one moment intense (new producers, new sounds, new media outlets, newly discovered audiences), at another moment stagnant (a small number of large companies producing a homogeneous product for a known consumer group). Technological change has a role in this cycle of competition and consolidation (it affects market conditions), but the underlying dynamo of pop history is human nature: People's musical "needs" are increasingly ill-met by conservative corporations until they burst out in a ferment of exciting new styles and stars (and new companies to market them).

I'm dubious about this model. It both feeds into and derives from the 1960s rock delusion that it was possible, at moments, to have a mass produced music (rock and roll, British beat) that wasn't really "commercial," and there is little evidence today, as we've seen, that major and independent record companies are really competing with each other. As Heikki Hellman puts it:

> The pattern is rather that the smaller companies offer a test market for the competition between the larger companies, through which these companies can outline their music production. The smaller companies have gained a permanent and important although subordinate position in the

music industry. The cycles have changed into symbiosis [Hellman, 1983, p. 355].

This is not to say that there are no longer contradictions and struggles in the music business, but that they can't be reduced to a simple line up of goodies and baddies (independent companies, bold musicians, and adventurous fans versus the multinationals, designer groups, and easy listeners). If there's one thing to be learned from twentieth century pop history it is that technological inventions have unexpected consequences. The "industrialization of music" has changed what we do when we play or listen to music, and it has changed our sense of what "music" is, both in itself and as an aspect of our lives and leisure, but these changes aren't just the result of producer decisions and control. They also reflect musicians' and consumers' responses.

Music "machines" have not, in short, been as dehumanizing as mass media critics from both left and right perspectives have suggested. For a start, it was technological developments that made our present understanding of musical "authenticity" possible. Recording devices enabled previously unreproducible aspects of performance—improvisation, spontaneity—to be reproduced exactly, and so enabled Afro-American music to replace European art and folk musics at the heart of Western popular culture (and the global reach of black American sounds is even more remarkable than the global reach of white American capital). This affected not just what sort of music people listened to but also how they listened to it, how they registered the emotional meanings to sounds and the musical shape of their own emotions. Recording gave a public means of communication to otherwise socially inarticulate people, and its continuing technical refinement, particularly since the development of the electrical microphone, has extended the possibilities of expression in all pop genres. Out of such developments came the star system—the marketing of individual performers as spuriously "knowable" friends and idols—but out of these same developments also came new means of self-definition, musical identities that could (as in "minority" cultures and subcultures) challenge the common sense of bourgeois ideology (Frith, 1986).

Technological change has also been the basic source of resistance to the corporate control of popular music. Examine the history of inventions in the recording industry and you find that those which catch on are the ones that lead, at least in the short term, to the decentralization of music making and listening—video tapes caught on, for example, video discs did not. The music industry uses new instruments and devices to do old things more efficiently or cheaply; it is musicians and consumers who discover their real possibilities. The mechanization of popular music has not, then, been a simple story of capitalist takeover. Think, for example, of how Jamaican dub culture and New York hip-hop took over the technology of recording to undermine the status of the record as a finished product; scratching and mixing "found" sounds together, challenging the whole idea of copyright.

But the most significant example of new technological habits challenging old record company ways is home taping. Cassette recorders have given fans a new means of control over their sounds; they can compile LPs and radio shows for themselves, use a Walkman to carry their soundscapes around with them. And, for the industry, this is the source of all its troubles. Behind the recurring (and increasingly successful) campaigns for levies to be imposed on blank tapes is the suggestion that people are using them to acquire music illicitly, without paying for it, without even giving the musicians involved their just reward. Every blank tape sold is a record not sold. This is another example of the multinationals' inability to control the use of their own inventions (the effects of home taping were not anticipated) and their failure to grasp the point that to throw another electronic toy into the leisure market is to disrupt all consumer habits. The suggestion that blank tapes are simply replacing records is, therefore, misleading. What home taping signifies, rather, is the changing place of music in leisure generally. Records are being replaced not by tapes as such but by other leisure activities; music is being used differently and in different, more flexible forms.

If record companies often misread the future they also regularly mistake passing fads for lasting habits (hence Warners' fateful over-investment in Atari computer games) and this raises a third point: how leisure pattern change can vary remarkably among countries even when they have similar entertainment setups. In 1975, for example, sales of Stereo 8 cartridges reached 25% of all recorded music sales in the United States but were statistically insignificant in Britain. By contrast, the "penetration" of videocassette recorders was an estimated 40% of households in Britain in 1985 and only 14% in the United States (no one in Britain had expected this VCR boom—Thorn-EMI even decided not to invest in its initial development). Britain, meanwhile, lags far behind both the United States and the rest of Northern Europe in cable TV connections and it is still not clear that this situation will change. This has had the interesting consequence that Britain's basic cable pop channel, Music Box, has actually developed, instead, as a record promotion tool in Holland and Belgium.

This is the context in which two terms of nineteenth century ideology—nationalism and romanticism—have become crucial to the politics of twentieth century technology. Countries are increasingly defending their music industries against the spread of cable and satellite broadcasting, against the marketing decisions of multinational communications groups, in the name of their "national heritage." The Dutch government demanded that Music Box give time to Dutch pop groups; the Swedish government uses blank tape levies to subsidize the production of Swedish music; the Canadians have a quota system for Canadian records on Canadian radio; Third World countries establish state-funded recording studios. And the irony is that the resulting "national" music is, more often than not, just a local variant of a global style; the real idea is that small countries will generate international hits of their own.

Multinational profits are, meanwhile, being defended against new technology in the language of individual creativity. Home taping, scratch mixing, and the various forms of piracy have disrupted the equation of artists' "ownership" of their creative work and companies' ownership of the resulting commodities—the latter is being defended by reference to the former. Copyright has become the legal and ideological weapon with which to attack "illegal" copying, and the battle is being fought in the name of justice for the artist.

## Conclusion

> Rock is the sound of a commercial, the sound of people chasing each other on Miami Vice, the music to a World Series or a Broadway show. The 60s discovered that voice and that voice has now become the voice of corporate America [Bill Graham in Guardian, May 30, 1986].

Record executives no longer wake up in the night sweating that they were the ones who turned the next Michael Jackson down. They've got a worse nightmare now: They sign up the next MJ and then make no money out of him! For every record they sell, 1,000 are copied on to tape by fans at home and 100,000 are produced illicitly in Singapore and Taiwan! His video clips are stolen from satellite services and the world is awash with unauthorized posters and tee-shirts!

Even by 1982 the piracy figures were daunting—66% of the Asian record and tape market, 30% in Africa and the Middle East, 21% in South America, 11% in Canada and the United States. European figures were lower (3% in Britain) but only by dint of expensive and time-consuming legal and detective work (and even in Eastern Europe "piracy," the ability of small producers and private consumers to use their own taping facilities to bypass state recording policy, is now a major problem—in countries such as East Germany there is more sophisticated recording equipment in private than in public hands). And if there's one thing we can predict with certainty it is that by the end of the century copying and reproducing equipment (developed relentlessly by Japanese electronic hardware firms) will be cheaper, better, and more widely owned. Not even the rise of the compact disc will solve this problem: domestic digital recording equipment, blank CDs, the compact Walkman, and the rest of the necessary items for "home discing" are already being developed.

What we're now seeing is, effectively, the "death of black vinyl." As John Qualen points out, the "crisis" in the music industry in the last decade has been marked by three important shifts in the organization of profit making. First, recording and publishing companies are now integrated, and an increasing proportion of record company profits come from the exploitation of publishing copyrights. Second, the majors now derive a regular source of income from licensing material from their back catalogs to independent TV and specialist music packagers. Third, record companies have begun to treat radio and TV use of records and videos not as advertisements for which they provide new material cheaply, but as entertainment services which should pay competitive prices for the recordings they use:

> In many ways the record industry is facing similar problems to the film industry. Its base market is being eroded and fragmented (pre-recorded music sales are down, as are cinema admissions), costs are spiralling and the traditional distribution system is threatened by new technologies.

> Though there will always be box-office biggies like *ET* (or *Thriller*), for the most part the earnings of the producers of films (pre-recorded music) will come not from their physical sale but from the exploitation by the producers of the rights they hold in their productions to broadcast and cable TV. The double advantage of this strategy for the record industry (which is far more vertically integrated than the film industry) is that, for

the majors, it could eliminate the high cost of manufacturing and distribution [Qualen, 1985, p. 16].

The move from record sales to rights exploitation as the basic source of music income has two implications. First, as Bill Graham suggests, it roots rock in corporate America. Already the biggest stars, like Michael Jackson and Bruce Springsteen, are being offered their biggest pay checks by companies keen to use their names in advertisements, and get their biggest concert returns not from ticket sales but from the tie-in merchandise. Companies are lining up to sponsor rock tours and TV shows. The British "group of the future," Sigue Sigue Sputnik, has even offered, only half-jokingly, to sell advertising space in the grooves between their LP tracks. Such multimedia tie-ups—record/film/advertisement/book/cable/clothes—change the purpose of pop, the reason why companies sign and develop their stars in the first place. Like films, the best-selling records of the 1990s will be made only when they've been presold as a sound/video/image packet—presold, that is, not to consumers direct, but to television shows and advertisers. The basic source of the multinational leisure corporations' income will be the licensing fees they charge for the use of their productions by other companies and across all the mass media.

Second, as the majors' interest in individual record buyers falls and the promotional drive shifts from radio to TV and video, new opportunities will arise for the independents. As Qualen says:

> The one trend that is positive is the likelihood of the continued growth and expansion of the independent sector into the manufacture and distribution of black vinyl as the majors continue their process of withdrawal, as well as into production by capitalizing on the possibilities for producing music with the aid of the new technologies and keeping in touch with the sound of the streets [Qualen, 1985, p. 33].

And this reference to "the sound of the streets" brings me back to my starting point—music as a human activity. The industrialization of music hasn't stopped people using it to express private joys or public griefs; it has given us new means to do so, new ways of having an impact, new ideas of what music can be. Street music is certainly an industrial noise now, but it's a human noise, too—the struggle for fun continues!

*NOTE*

1. Thanks to Reebee Garofalo for these figures.

# REFERENCES

BPI (1985) *British phonographic industry yearbook*. London: BPI.

Ehrlich, C. (1976) *The piano*. London: Dent.

Frith, S. (1981) *Sound effects*. New York: Pantheon.

Frith, S. (1983) Popular music 1950-1980. In G. Martin (Ed.), *Making music*. London: Muller.

Frith, S. (1986) Art vs. technology. *Media, Culture and Society, 8*.

Gaisberg, F. W. (1946) *Music on record*. London: Robert Hale.

Gelatt, R. (1977) *The fabulous phonograph 1877-1977*. London: Cassell.

Hellman, H. (1983) The new state of competition in the record industry. *Sociologia, 20*.

Lewis, E. (1956) *No. C.I.C.* London: Decca.

Qualen, J. (1985) *The music industry*. London: Comedia.

Toll, R. C. (1982) *The entertainment machine*. Oxford: Oxford University Press.

Wittmark, I., & Goldberg, I. (1939) *From ragtime to swingtime: The story of the house of Witmark*. New York: Lee Furman.

# 4

# Commercial Radio and Popular Music:

## Processes of Selection
## and Factors of Influence

ERIC W. ROTHENBUHLER

The commercial radio industry in the United States is among the most powerful influences on contemporary popular music. While it is clear that popular music evolves within a tradition, answers to subcultural and generational experiences, registers the creativity of individuals and movements, it is also clear that "stylistic trends in popular sound recordings cannot be separated from the social organizations that produce them" (Anderson, Hesbacher, Etzkorn, & Denisoff, 1980, p. 42). I do not claim that by knowing the actions of the radio industry we can explain popular music, only that the actions of radio are a force in the system by which some music comes to be popular and other music does not.

### Radio as the Popularizer of Music

The first issue to dispense with is the old story that it is popular songs that get played on the radio—that radio plays the songs the public wants to hear. First, it is obvious to any social observer that radio airplay precedes, rather than follows, massive public popularity. It is then impossible for radio to use "popularity" as a criterion for play, for it is not popular until after radio plays it. As Simon Frith puts it: "The BBC is contemptuously certain that Radio 1 satisfies its listeners, but it can only be so certain because its argument is circular. . . . The BBC moulds as well as responds to public taste" (Frith, 1978, p. 91). This, of course, is clear in any of the studies of the operation of the popular music industry system (for example, MacDougald, 1941; Hirsch, 1969; Frith, 1978; Ryan & Peterson, 1982). McPhee (1963, 1977) models this as a system in which a cultural item, once chosen by and given exposure by media, gains popularity that motivates further exposure, which eventually exhausts popularity. Exposure multiplies exposure while increasing popularity until growth in popularity accelerates to the limit.

If radio broadcasters are simply responding to popularity, then their decisions need only be based on some indicator of popularity. The objectification of popularity is a "hit" list such as *Billboard*'s "Hot-100." But the hit list is made up of some combination of measures of radio play and sales (Hesbacher, Downing, & Berger, 1975), so that even "popularity" is not entirely dependent on the public's vote. To the extent that these or similar charts are sources of information for programming decisions (and they are), radio airplay in part determines radio airplay. This is the multiplicative process McPhee (1977) discusses as leading to "abortions" and "runaways."

The commercial radio music system has a measurable effect on the audience's attitudes and behaviors. Erdelyi (1940), Jakobovits (1966), and Wiebe (1940) have examined the relation between radio exposure of songs and music sales, and popularity and liking, respectively. The relationship is an inverse-U with radio airplay as the leading variable in the time order. That is, increasing exposure, up to a point, leads to increasing popularity or affect, at which point further increasing exposure leads to decreasing popularity or affect.

Fathi and Heath (1974) find that their "mass culture listeners" (as opposed to "high culture listeners") most frequently report the radio as the source of their original interest in music. Lull and Miller (1982) in their pre-MTV study of exposure to new wave music, report that 59% of their respondents cite the radio as their "principal source," with 35% for records and tapes, 3% clubs, 2% concerts, and 2% television.

The 1981 Warner study of record buyers found that 61% of album purchases are planned, that 56% of record buyers most often go to record stores only to make a particular purchase, and that 63% of record buyers are usually searching for a particular record while in a store. For most record buyers, then, the record store does not serve as a source of information about music. Consumers must be learning about the records they plan to purchase elsewhere and, given the evidence of other studies, radio would seem the most likely source.

Despite what some broadcasters say, then, radio does serve as a principal popularizer of popular music. As Duncan MacDougald put it long ago:

> The making of the majority of "hits" is largely predetermined by and within the industry. It is in direct contrast to the general opinion of Tin Pan Alley which clings to the ideology that the success of songs represents the spontaneous, free-will acceptance of the public because of the inherent merit of the number [MacDougald, 1941, pp. 65-66].

Radio, then, is the main machine of popularization.

### The System

If we locate radio within the context of the popular music industry *system*, its function as a popularizer of music is clarified. The first use of the concept *system* to characterize the popular music industry was probably made by MacDougald (1941). In recent times the roles in the system include the recording musicians, the record producers, the record company policymakers, the record promoters, radio programmers, and both the record buying public and the radio listening public (Hirsch, 1969, p. 18; Ryan & Peterson, 1982).

Hirsch (1969) has characterized the industry components of the system as a *preselection system*—a system for anticipating or preselecting the public's selections. This is a sequential, staged filtering of an overabundant product in anticipation of an uncertain demand. Recorded musical products move through the system in a linear manner, being filtered at each stage—either rejected or passed on to the next stage. The filter criteria at any given stage are based upon the past successes of similar items at later stages. That is, decision makers try to anticipate what will be successful at later points in the system by using feedback about what has been successful in the recent past (for use of feedback information, see Hirsch, 1969, 1972; Peterson & Berger, 1971, 1975; Davis & Willwerth, 1974). As products move through the system each role acts as a surrogate consumer for the previous role (Hirsch, 1972). The activators of roles early in the system work to offer goods that will be successful with activators of the next role in the system rather than the ultimate consumer. Record companies are at least as interested in offering records that are of interest to radio programmers as what they think will be of interest to the public. The system works in both a value-added and power-added manner so that later role activators—such as radio programmers—have much more influence on what will be popular than do earlier roles—such as record producers.[1]

## Making Money

Radio stations are in the business of making money, not the business of playing music. It is clear that people that are attracted to radio as a place to work are often people who love music, but few if any people own a radio station because they love music. People own radio stations to make money. If there is any doubt about this aspect of the radio business, it can be laid to rest quickly and easily.

There are three principal types of things that are broadcast on American commercial music radio stations: songs, advertisements, and talk. If for one reason or another a song that should have been played was not, let us say the disc jockey made an error or an emergency weather report interrupted the music, there would be no mention of it, no apology, no adjustment of the playlist to see that the song got all of its alloted airtime. If an announcer didn't say everything that he or she meant to say during a particular break, that also would receive no notice. But if an advertisement is not played, or is interrupted, or placed next to a competitor's ad, repair work must be done. In most stations the disc jockey on the air at the time must make a note on the station log and fill out a form. Later what is called a "make-good" must be run. This is a free repetition of the advertisement during equally valuable airtime. This indicates with perfect empirical clarity that advertisements are the most important portion of the broadcast program.

## Managing the Means for Making Money

If radio statons are owned for the making of money, where does the music enter? Clearly, music is a part of the means for making money. Commercial music radio will be invested in financially to the extent that it is more attractive than other ways to make money. (Exactly what constitutes an attractive way to make money is surely highly variable; it may have to do with personal taste or personal history as well as efficiency in the light of tax structures.) As long as a radio station is owned because it is a more efficient way to make money than some other equally available options, then the efficiency of broadcasting music as a means for making money is important. Many of the ways in which the structure of the commercial radio industry in the United States affects the range of available popular music has to do with increasing the efficiency of the radio station operation.

Broadcasters earn their money, as Meehan (1984) points out, not by producing messages, or even audiences, but by selling ratings points to advertisers. Advertisers buy time slots that represent a certain number of ratings points for certain types of audience; presumably an audience similar to the one described by the ratings will be attending the advertisements placed in the purchased time slots. The music that is played on commercial radio stations is designed to attract audiences that contribute to ratings that are attractive to advertisers that are in turn attractive to radio station management. It must be noted that some demographic categories, such as young males, cooperate less with the ratings companies and so produce apparently lower ratings for the same size audience. Also, some advertisers are more interested in some demographic categories than in others. And, station management may be more interested in some advertisers than in others—this would have to do with market strategies as well as matters of taste.

Just as any other activity, these processes can be efficiently performed to the extent that they can be standardized. It is to the economic advantage of commercial radio stations, then, to make predictable choices in what music to play. This not only increases the efficiency of station operation, but of audience flow—the audience attracted by one song will stay tuned for the next. To the extent that the audience is predictable, the ratings will show patterns. To the extent that these patterns are attractive to advertisers, the station will be in a good position to make money by playing music.

**The Format**

The way that this standardization or predictability has come to be institutionalized is in the format. A format is a style or genre or system. Formats define the boundaries of the types of music that a station will play and the general guidelines for presentation of that music.

The format, however, is not a choice dictated by musical concerns, but by business concerns. Formats were invented as mechanisms to manage audiences:

Formats are not sought by radio stations to provide diversity for its own sake. . . . Nor are they provided in order to satisfy listeners' demands. The purpose of these formats is to enable radio stations to deliver to advertisers a measured and defined group of consumers, known as a segment [Fornatale and Mills, 1980, p. 61].

Formats can be used as ways to avoid competition; consultants often recommend that radio station management choose a format that is not duplicated by other stations in the market (see Routt, McGrath, & Weiss, 1978). In this way the total radio audience is divided up among the radio stations within a market in order to minimize competition among stations.

But as Glasser (1984) points out, format choices are based on expected ability to maximize profits, which is not necessarily the same thing as avoiding competition. This means "a station will duplicate an existing format [within a market] rather than produce a unique format if its share of the audience for a duplicated format yields higher profits than the profits generated by the entire audience for a unique format" (Glasser, 1984, p. 129). Maximum profits are not even tied to maximum audience size, but to maximum attractiveness of the ratings to those advertisers that do the most radio business.

For the concerns of this chapter, however, the point remains the same. Whether used to avoid competition, to maximize audience size, or to maximize profits, the format is a mechanism for managing the audience and selling airtime to advertisers; it is not a musical concern.

Once a format choice is made, however, the songs that will be played within that format still have to be selected. The effect that commercial radio has on popular music depends first on formatting and second on choices within formats. Since songs need radio exposure to become popular, record company decision makers will try to anticipate what radio station decision makers want to play when they are producing and releasing records. Since radio stations work within formats, this serves as a form of pressure for record companies to work within formats as well. Records that fall between formats, or that overlap formats, may be perceived as belonging to no format and so receive no radio play. With no radio play the chance of a financial success on the scale of a popular music hit is almost none. The "crossover" hit is that rare, apparent exception—the song that becomes a hit in more than one format.[2]

## The Nature of the Decision Makers

To specify the nature of radio's influence on popular music further we should examine those persons who have decision-making power within radio stations—the gatekeepers. The more systemic concerns already raised should be kept in mind, however, for there is always an extent to which "the organization is the gatekeeper" (Bailey & Lichty, 1972, p. 229; see also Whitney's 1982 review).

The disc jockeys on the air do not usually have significant decision-making power regarding the music that they play. Both radio station format and song selection within formats are decisions made by owners of radio stations, managers of radio stations, and radio consultants. These people may have entered the radio business because they loved music, but they have risen into decision-making positions by, among other things, never letting their love of music interfere with the money-making functions of a radio station.

As Elliott (1979) points out, one approach to the study of media organizations is to focus on occupational roles. This would include studies of recruitment, socialization, and career paths. Such information would be useful to know in the cases of the consultants, tradesheet editors, program directors, music directors, and record promoters that influence and control popular music radio. In the absence of such information we can turn to a *Program Director's Handbook* (Paiva, 1983). Here we note that in 160 pages of text only one 12-page chapter is given to music. Even that little consideration is cast in management and business terms, not in musical terms. The point, here as above, is that music is a management tool in commercial radio stations. Employees who accept and understand that may be given decision-making power, others will not.

### The Taken-for-Granted

Just as any other form of work, radio programming poses certain problems, some of which occur regularly. When solutions are found to recurring problems, the solutions often become part of routine work procedures and are taken for granted. They become a part of the way things are done *unreflectively* so that they are performed as if they were the only way of getting things done. This form of taken-for-granted knowledge is very resistant to change (see Schutz, 1970).

Among these routines is a peculiar pattern I have observed—that radio personnel tend to treat records as if they were *already* sorted into four categories. First, records are either current or not current (this has to do not only with how recently they were released but with their continued popularity). Second, records are either played on the air now, or not played on the air now.

As the radio station personnel categorize the albums they isolate those that are problematic. A decision must be made about those that are current but not played now. Are they something that won't be played or something that is not played yet? If the latter is the case, when will they be considered for airplay and how seriously?

But this system does not just isolate the problematic albums, it defines some albums as unproblematic, and this means they will not be thought about as requiring a decision. Whatever they were first considered is what they will remain. This sort of unreflective acting can completely block some records from being given airplay without any careful decision having been made about them.

The same style of the taken-for-granted routine operates in other aspects of the decision making. Certain performers will never be considered for airplay because they are categorized in a taken-for-granted manner as being outside the format, or too new, or too different. This is most likely based on their past, not on the sound of their current music.

Perceptions of the audience and perceptions of the competition work the same way. In 1982, MTV Music Television was new. The Music Director and Program Director at the radio station I was studying at the time told me that they didn't compete with MTV, it was television after all, and that the performers that were becoming popular there—predominantly new-wavers in those early months—were too weird for their midwest rock and roll audience. These inferences were logically based on their previous experiences and could naturally be taken for granted—and be taken confidently for they were *the* rock and roll station in the market; they controlled the scene.

But six months later one of the new bands regularly featured on MTV, the Stray Cats, sold out a show in town without ever receiving any radio airplay! This violated the programmer's taken-for-granted knowledge. This sort of violation is what is required to call old routines into question, to reproblematize the taken-for-granted. A few weeks later they were paying close attention to MTV when making their programming decisions.

## Song Selection in Rock and Roll Radio: The Division of Labor

The decision-making process in radio programming is a two-stage system. This is the same as has been found in other gatekeeping systems, and has been posited as a general attribute of such systems by Dimmick (1974).

In the case of music programming on radio, there is a universe of potentially useful albums from which the decision makers choose those that have the greatest potential for being useful. This choosing is the first stage of the decision making and is what Dimmick (1974) calls the *sensing* process. Those albums that are chosen by this process are then given serious consideration for airplay. Their worth is considered relative to (a) the "space" available to use them (that is, how many available spots of what size there are on the playlist), and (b) the other albums available, which have the greatest potential for becoming a hit, which fit into the format. This consideration of airplay worthiness is the same as the *valuation* process in Dimmick's conception of gatekeeping.

Someone at a radio station—usually a music director—is primarily in charge of the sensing stage of the decision making and is responsible for gathering the necessary information for the valuation process. At the station I studied a few years ago, this meant the music director built a list as the week wore on of the accumulating records that should be considered for airplay and made notes of evidence as to their usefulness to the station. He also kept track of all the songs they were currently playing: who else was playing them and how much, what were their sales figures, if they were getting requests, how long they had been on the playlist, whether or not the disc jockeys were tired of them, and so on.

In the sensing and information-gathering processes the agenda is set. The reduction in the size of the population of albums made at this step of the decision making is remarkable. Of the 467 albums that were available during 10 weeks of my earlier study (Rothenbuhler, 1982), only 81 received serious consideration for adding to the playlist (about 17%). Of the 81 albums considered, 35 received airplay (about 43%). In other words, the sensing process, which was primarily the music director's job at this station, reduced the size of the potential universe by a factor of almost 6, where the valuation process reduced the population by a factor of just over 2. Overall, only about 7% of the albums available to the station in those 10 weeks got any airplay at all.

**The Routine**

The programming task is cast into a weekly work routine (see Rothenbuhler, 1982, 1985). The actual playlist decisions were made on Tuesday afternoons at the station I studied; as far as I could tell at the time this was also true of all or most other Album-Oriented Rock (AOR) stations in the country. Directors of a Contemporary Hits station in the same market tended to wait until Wednesday to make up their playlist—perhaps to see what the other stations in town were doing. The few stations I have observed since then also make their decisions on Tuesdays or Wednesdays; this appears to be a general pattern around the industry. This pattern is useful for information sharing, among other things.

This decision-making schedule fits neatly with the publication schedule of the trade sheets—one of the major purveyors of information in the business. The trade sheets come out late in the week arriving in the mail at radio stations sometime between Friday and Monday. The trade sheets provide general record and radio industry news, lists of record airplay and sales aggregated nationally, sometimes broken down by market, sometimes by station. Some sheets list versions of station playlists, and lists of what stations added what songs to their playlists the week before. Most trade sheets also publish schedules of upcoming record releases, artist tours, and promotional events. The sheets also print tips from the editors and quotations from radio programmers and record promoters evaluating new records, artists, industry trends, or answering a question of the week. These types of information are vitally important to programming decision makers and the sheets are carefully studied beginning the moment they arrive.

Most stations also gather local market information. Usually this means that on Monday afternoon someone compiles all of the telephone requests that have been logged in the last week and by one means or another gathers data concerning local record sales.

Most of the record promoters that visit radio stations in a given week do so on Monday or Tuesday. They come bearing copies of records, promotional items to be given away to the audience, more sales and airplay data, information on what other radio stations have been deciding that very afternoon, and a sales pitch.

Late in the day on Tuesday or early on Wednesday the playlist decisions are made while, or shortly after, conferring with any consultant the station may be using—and consultants are no longer unusual. Someone makes sure there are sufficient copies of the record in the studio and contacts the promoters for more copies if needed. The rotation cards, or whatever system is used, are changed in the studio so the disc jockeys know what to play. A version of the playlist in terms of "heavy, medium, and light rotation" (referring to the amount of scheduled airplay) is typed up for public release, and a version in full operational detail is documented for internal use. The music director or program director reports to the trade sheets providing their portion of the information that will be published later in the week. At some point the promoters call back to see how their product fared in that week's round of decision making.

### Sources of Information

The radio programming task is an information-devouring one in an information-starved environment. To predict the future has always been difficult. To predict the future of the capricious and seemingly random behavior of mass media audiences can be frightening (see Goodhart, Erenberg, & Collins, 1975; Headon, Klompmaker, & Rust, 1979). Though programmers claim to be able to hear a hit when it comes along, the fact is that their job requires information that doesn't exist. Given this fact, they become information sponges. They clutch for information. They grab at information. I have seen a song boosted into higher rotation because the program director heard his little sister turn up the radio when the song came on (Rothenbuhler, 1982). Another time at the same station, a second song from an album was added to the playlist because the music director had seen the girl that cleans up at the barber shop singing along with the first song, and she knew every word. These examples are typical of the atmosphere of a popular music radio station.

The sharing of information holds the industry together. The consultant's role also can be conceptualized as a link in an information network. The trade sheets serve as organizers and distributors of information. Programmers and promoters compete to be quoted in the sheets. Long distance phone calls are more common than office memos.

Trade sheets, the gathering of local market information, and meetings with colleagues and consultants have already been mentioned as sources of information. The promoters also work as a source of information. Promoters are salespeople. What they say about an album will be viewed with skepticism, sometimes contempt. But what they say can also be taken as advice. A variety of promotion situations offer information to radio programmers.

Most promoters work with more than one album at a time. In their presentation of albums to stations there is an implicit rank ordering. Albums are presented one at a time in a given order, each is given a different amount of time, some are accompanied by promotional items and advertising buys. Promoters also sometimes offer an explicit rank ordering. They may say something like, "this one is our priority . . . if this other one catches on, OK, we'll be behind it, but we think this one has a better chance out of the box."

Promoters offer advice. This advice can be positive or negative. First, they tell the programmers which "tracks" or "cuts" (particular songs) to listen to and therefore establish the impetus for a "consensus cut." Second, they can tell programmers not to worry about a particular album, saying such things as "nobody else knows what to do with it" or "there probably won't be a tour." This sounds like odd behavior for a salesperson, but it does happen. This sort of negative advice is rare; it probably serves to maintain the promoter's credibility.

To what extent do programmers get information from or about their audience or the people that make up the local market? At one point in my field notes for the 1982 study I listed 35 different types of contact the programmers had with the social environment outside the station. Of those 35 only 8 could be considered as sources of information from or about their audience. At another point in the same study I listed 42 factors that I had observed as potentially influential in programming. Of these 42 only 4 could be considered as having something to do with the audience. Except as a mental image held by the programmers, the audience enters little into programming decision making.

It could be argued that the broadcasters do not have good sources of information about their audiences. That is probably true. But the sources they do have are the ones they have institutionalized; and even these are not used. Even when information about the audience is available, it is dismissed, rationalized, misattributed, or interpreted strictly in terms useful to the routine contingencies of the radio world.

For example, my informants tell me that you can't tell much from requests, the people who call in are not representative of the audience. But when phones are for something that's new that the radio community is hot about, they are reported enthusiastically in the trade sheets and used as evidence for additional airplay.

My informants also say that you have to be careful with sales data. People might buy records for different reasons than they listen to the radio and not everyone in the audience buys records. But every station collects sales data, all the trade sheets report sales data, individual stations cite sales data in their trade sheet reports, and most important, when there is a disagreement about the worth of an album, sales data are marshalled in support of one or the other side.

When faced with evidence of the popularity of music that is not played by a station, its programmers will ignore it. An Album-Oriented Rock station music director once told me about new wave fans "[they're] not our audience . . . just look at the way they dress. We're a rock and roll station."

### The Consensus Cut

One outcome of the characteristic uncertainty and information sharing of the industry is the consensus cut phenomenon. No one knows what song on a new album or which of the new albums the public will want to hear most, if any. So they look around to see what everyone else is doing—this is one of the main functions of the editor's tips and the quotations of industry players in the trade sheets.

If an album receives none of this sort of attention it is almost precluded from consideration for airplay. Even if an album receives a lot of attention, but that attention is divided over different songs, unless the album is by a superstar its chances of becoming a hit are decreased. This is because cautious stations or stations in markets without direct competition will put the album in a lighter rotation or not play it at all until they see some consensus on which cut to play. In markets with competing stations, many different cuts could well be played and the audience's attention divided. The national aggregate airplay will be considerably less for any one song than what it takes to make a hit.

If, however, all of the attention given to an album is devoted to one particular cut, a hit is almost guaranteed. Given this industry consensus, everyone feels confident predicting a hit. They slide the record right into heavy rotation. It becomes a hit and is seen as yet more evidence of programmers' ability to predict public taste. The result is that only what *everybody* plays will *anybody* play.

### Effective Criteria

The question here is what makes a difference when it comes down to the point that some songs get played on the radio and some do not? Baskerville's handbook lists five "factors that will influence a station's programming": (1) habit; (2) competition; (3) trade charts; (4) record promoters; and (5) change of management (Baskerville, 1981, pp. 365-

366). Where is the audience? It is presumed; conditions of audience taste are not as important as conditions of industry. For example:

> The first decision was which cut to use from the albums that were being added. This decision was made between MD and PD [the music director and the program director] when there was a perceived choice, and primarily based on the sound of the cuts and what cuts others stations were playing. Consensus on cut is very important. A visitor one day asked: "do you always play what they [record companies] recommend?" PD: "usually . . . if you don't and everyone else does you end up looking stupid." Asked about trade sheets and recommended cuts, MD said: "Yeah, if you don't know what to go with . . . this gives you a consensus cut . . . if you need a reason to play this and not something else, you can say this is a consensus cut." "[We follow] programmers with supposedly good ears . . . or a station where you know the people and you know what they're doin' and they do well in their market, then you look to see what they're playing" [Rothenbuhler, 1982, pp. 66-67].

Subsumed here are a number of reasons to play a song, but only one has the remotest connection to the audience. This quotation makes clear the extent to which programmers work for each other. They worry about "looking stupid" in front of their peers. The audience members do not read the trades so how could they know what the other stations are playing? How could they make a programmer feel stupid? The one reference to the audience in this quotation is cast strictly in radio terms: "They do well in their market." They are not looking to the members of their audience for advice; they are looking to their coprofessionals in the radio and record business.

Elsewhere I have estimated a variety of statistical models to predict airplay based on the various forms of information available to the programmers (Rothenbuhler, 1985). Based on those analyses and qualitative observations it is clear that the most effective criteria in programming decisions are industry factors. Information about the local market, whether in the form of record sales, requests, or what other stations were playing, was shown to be of little utility to the decision makers. Rather, such industry factors as national airplay as reported in trade sheets, artists' track records, the consultant's recommendation, and the fit of the song being considered with currently available space on the playlist (how many other songs of nearly the same style are currently being played, and so on), and whether or not the program director thought it sounded like a hit, were the predominating factors in the decision.

The end result of all of the above, and especially the fact that national industry system criteria so outweigh local criteria in the final playlist decision-making process, is that a very small proportion of the music recorded is selected for massive amounts of broadcast exposure, in every market across the United States, at about the same time, to about the same extent. It is inevitable that most of the selected songs become hits while few if any of those not selected do. As entire industries are oriented to capitalizing on hit songs, it is inevitable that what becomes a hit today will affect what is offered as recorded music tomorrow. As the degree of concentration and control in the recording end of the system continues to increase (see Peterson & Berger, 1975; Rothenbuhler & Dimmick, 1982), these effects will be exacerbated.

### Conclusion

The conclusion is straightforward: Given contemporary commercial radio's place in the popular music industry system, the huge audience for broadcast programming, the repeated playing of songs that has become typical, and the influence of such factors as formats, trade sheets, promoters, and consultants on the decision making that tend to reproduce the same choices at station after station—given all this, commercial radio cannot but have a profound effect on popular music. Second, given such system attributes and decision-making criteria as imitating success, following track records, waiting for consensus, formatting, promoters' influence, taken-for-granted work routines, and the business orientation—given this and the above, contemporary commercial radio's influence on popular music *must* be limiting and conservative.

### NOTES

1. The remainder of this chapter focuses on radio and its workings in this system. The discussion is based on my readings of the extant literature, a study of radio programming decision making I conducted in 1981-1982, and my less formal observations and experiences in and around rock and roll radio since that time. Passages of this chapter reproduce in a slightly revised form passages of my *Radio and the Popular Music Industry: A Case Study of Programming Decision Making*, unpublished Master's Thesis, Department of Communication, Ohio State University, and various convention papers based on that work.

The earlier study (Rothenbuhler, 1982) included eight months of observation in a commercial Album-Oriented Rock (AOR) station in a large midwestern American city. The first five months of that period were devoted exclusively to in-depth participant observation of the radio station, its personnel, their visitors, and their work. The center of this observation was the programming task itself; the study focused on how what songs were picked to play how much. The last three months of the study were devoted to a set of quantitative measures of factors that had been identified by the qualitative study as influential in the programming decision making. The full report of that study is Rothenbuhler (1982); portions of the study are reported in Rothenbuhler (1985).

2. Anderson and Hesbacher (1979); Hesbacher, Clasby, Clasby, and Berger (1977); Hesbacher, Simon, Anderson, and Berger (1978), provide information on the attributes and market performance of substream musical styles and cross-over hits. Baskerville (1981); Hesbacher, Clasby, Anderson, and Berger, (1976); Hesbacher, Rosenow, Anderson, and Berger (1975); Lull, Johnson, and Edmond (1981); Routt, McGrath, and Weiss (1978) give background information in varying detail on contemporary formats and radio programming strategies. Fornatale and Mills (1980) provide a short, standard, and useful history of the radio formats. Baskerville (1981); and Warner (1981) give information on record buyers.

## REFERENCES

Anderson, B., & Hesbacher, P. (1979). Country and soul hits: Manufacturer strategies and crossover characteristics. *Popular Music and Society, 6*, 284-292.

Anderson, B., Hesbacher, P., Etzkorn, K. P., & Denisoff, R. S. (1980). Hit record trends, 1940-1977. *Journal of Communication, 30*, 31-43.

Bailey, G. A. & Lichty, L. W. (1972). Rough justice on a Saigon street: A gatekeeper study of NBC's Tet execution film. *Journalism Quarterly, 49*, 221-229, 238.

Baskerville, D. (1981). *Music business handbook and career guide* (3rd ed.). Los Angeles: The Sherwood Company.

Davis, C. & Willwerth, J. (1974). *Clive: Inside the record business.* New York: Morrow.

Dimmick, J. (1974). The gate-keeper: An uncertainty theory. *Journalism Monographs, 37*.

Elliott, P. (1979). Media organizations and occupations: An overview. In J. Curran, M. Gurevitch, & J. Woollacott (Eds.), *Mass communication and society.* Beverly Hills, CA: Sage.

Erdelyi, M. (1940). The relation between "radio plugs" and sheet sales of popular music. *Journal of Applied Psychology, 24*, 696-702.

Fathi, A. & Heath, C. L. (1974). Group influence, mass media and musical taste among Canadian students. *Journalism Quarterly, 51*, 705-709.

Fornatale, P. & Mills, J. E. (1980). *Radio in the television age.* Woodstock, NY: Overlook.

Frith, S. (1978). *The sociology of rock.* London: Constable.

Glasser, T. L. (1984). Competition and diversity among radio formats: Legal and structural issues. *Journal of Broadcasting, 28*, 122-142.

Goodhart, G. J., Erenberg, A.S.C., & Collins, M. A. (1975). *The television audience: Patterns of viewing.* Lexington, MA: D. C. Heath.

Headon, R. S., Klompmaker, J. E., & Rust, R. T. (1979). The duplication of viewing law and television media schedule evaluation. *Journal of Marketing Research, 16,* 333-340.

Hesbacher, P., Clasby, N., Anderson, R., & Berger, D. G. (1976). Radio format strategies *Journal of Communication, 26,* 110-119.

Hesbacher, P., Clasby, N., Clasby, H. G., & Berger, D. G. (1977). Solo female vocalists: Some shifts in stature and alterations in song. *Popular Music and Society, 5,* 1-16.

Hesbacher, P., Downing, R., & Berger, D. G. (1975). Sound recording popularity charts: A useful tool for music research. I. Why and how they are compiled. *Popular Music and Society, 4,* 3-18.

Hesbacher, P., Rosenow, R., Anderson, B., & Berger, D. G. (1975). Radio programming: Relating ratings to revenues in a major market. *Popular Music and Society, 4,* 208-225.

Hesbacher, P., Simon, E., Anderson, B., & Berger, D. G. (1978). "Substream" recordings: Some shifts in stature and alterations in song. *Popular Music and Society, 6,* 11-26.

Hirsch, P. (1969). *The structure of the popular music industry.* Ann Arbor, MI: Institute for Social Research.

Hirsch, P. (1972). Processing fads and fashions: An organization-set analysis of cultural industry systems. *American Journal of Sociology, 77,* 639-659.

Jakobovits, L. A. (1966). Studies of fads: I. The hit parade. *Psychological Reports, 18,* 443-450.

Lull, J., Johnson, L. M., & Edmond, D. (1981). Radio listeners' electronic media habits. *Journal of Broadcasting, 25,* 25-36.

Lull, J. & Miller, D. (1982). *Media and interpersonal socialization to new wave music.* Paper presented to the annual convention of the International Communication Association. Boston, MA.

MacDougald, D., Jr., (1941). The popular music industry. In P. F. Lazarsfeld & F. N. Stanton (Eds.), *Radio Research 1941.* New York: Duell, Sloan, and Pearce.

McPhee, W. N. (1963). *Formal theories of mass behavior.* New York: Free Press.

McPhee, W. N. (1977). When culture becomes a business. In P. M. Hirsch, P. V. Miller, & F. G. Kline (Eds.)., *Strategies for communication research.* Beverly Hills, CA: Sage.

Meehan, E. (1984). Ratings and the institutional approach: A third answer to the commodity question. *Critical Studies in Mass Communication, 1,* 216-225.

Paiva, B. (1983). *The program director's handbook.* Blue Ridge Summit, PA: Tab.

Peterson, R. A. & Berger, D. G. (1971). Entrepreneurship in organizations: Evidence from the popular music industry. *Administrative Science Quarterly 16,* 97-107.

Peterson, R. A. & Berger, D. G. (1975). Cycles in symbol production: The case of popular music. *American Sociological Review, 40,* 158-173.

Rothenbuhler, E. W. (1982). *Radio and the popular music industry: A case study of programming decision making.* Unpublished master's thesis, Department of Communication, Ohio State University.

Rothenbuhler, E. W. (1985). Programming decision making in popular music radio. *Communication Research, 12,* 209-232.

Rothenbuhler, E. W. & Dimmick, J. (1982). Popular music: Concentration and diversity in the industry, 1974-1980. *Journal of Communication, 32,* 143-149.

Routt, E., McGrath, J.B., & Weiss, F. A. (1978). *The radio format conundrum.* New York: Hastings House.

Ryan, J. & Peterson, R. A. (1982). The product image: The fate of creativity in country music songwriting. In J. S. Ettema & D. C. Whitney (Eds.), *Individuals in mass media organizations: Creativity and constraint.* Beverly Hills, CA: Sage.

Schutz, A. (1970). *Reflections on the problem of relevance* (R. M. Zaner, Ed.). New Haven, CT: Yale University Press.

Warner Communications, Inc. (1981). *The prerecorded music market: A consumer survey: 1980.* New York: Author.

Whitney, D. C. (1982). Mass communicator studies: Similarity, difference, and level of analysis. In J. S. Ettema & D. C. Whitney (Eds.), *Individuals in mass media organizations: Creativity and constraint.* Beverly Hills, CA: Sage.

Wiebe, G. (1940) The effect of radio plugging on students' opinions of songs. *Journal of Applied Psychology, 24,* 721-727.

# 5

# *Music Video:*

## *Impact of the Visual Dimension*

### DEAN ABT

Music video came on quickly, overcoming predictions that the visual representation of musical sound would not work well aesthetically or commercially. It is creative, exciting, controversial, and now stands as an accepted form of popular culture throughout the world. This still-growing phenomenon has become one of the most significant developments in the history of popular music.

The impact of music video on the recording industry and consumers of music will take considerable time to assess conclusively. Still, it is certain even now that this new blend of sight and sound is not a whimsical fad that will be replaced by the next innovation. We are, therefore, required to ask some important questions about music video: What are the social and cultural implications of this new cultural form? What are the effects, realized and potential, of music video on the music, television, and radio industries? The purpose of this chapter is to examine and evaluate some of the emerging issues that reveal the significance of music video. The following discussion includes both a review of major critical themes and findings from an empirical analysis of music video's effects on record buyers. This combination of assessments is presented in the hope of better describing music video's

AUTHOR'S NOTE: I wish to thank James Lull for his close association and valuable help with this project, including both the data collection and writing of the manuscript. I also thank Serena Stanford for her advice and assistance in the empirical part of this report.

effects on record buyers. This combination of assessments is presented in the hope of better describing music video's place in the complex, dynamic, and often contradictory relationship between popular music and its audiences.

## Critical Issues in Music Video

Much like the reaction to radio and television in their early days, the swift growth in popularity of Music Television (or "MTV," the dominant and profitable 24-hour cable service) and other music video programming has elicited a wide range of reactions from young viewers, their parents, the popular press, the music, television, and radio industries, musical artists, and the academic community. From this close scrutiny a number of critical themes have emerged during the first few years of the widespread existence of music video. Among these themes are the following: (1) music video's visual styles and characteristics; (2) its potential inhibition of the imaginative use of music; (3) the violent, sexual, and sexist imagery that is said to characterize its content; and (4) the role of this new cultural form as advertising. Of course, these themes do not exhaust the concerns stimulated by the emergence of music video. They are, however, among the major issues considered to be most notable in first analyses of this unique form of entertainment, and they will each be viewed below.

### Visual Styles and Characteristics of Music Video

Most videos are three- to four-minute visual statements that are designed to join artistically with a song in order to accomplish several communicative objectives. They must gain and hold the viewer's attention amidst other videos; help establish, vitalize, or maintain the artist's image; sell that image and the products associated with it; and, perhaps, carry one or several direct or indirect messages (for instance, "war is wrong," "social/sexual life is competitive," and so on). Each video is an interpretation of a song. Exactly whose visual interpretation is presented varies from video to video, depending on the amount of creative influence exerted by the artist(s), the video director, and the record company.

Visual techniques commonly employed in music videos exaggerate the extremes of television's "form complexity" (Watt & Krull, 1977). Interest and excitement is stimulated by rapid cutting, intercutting, dissolves, superimpositions, and other special effects that, taken together with different scenes and characters, make music videos visually and thematically dynamic. Of course, music videos do not confront viewers with completely unfamiliar visual experiences, since the presentational techniques and much of the imagery shown in videos are already common in television and other visual media. Recently, however, many artists have avoided the predictable technical treatment and visual cliches that characterized early music videos. And, of course, critical generalizations that can be made about the appearance of thousands of videos already produced should not minimize their often extreme creativeness.

Currently, most music videos generally fall into one of four basic presentational formats: those sustained primarily by *literal visual imagery*; those carried by a *narrative centered on the lyrics*; those that incorporate substantial *features of both* of the above; and those that are dominated by an array of *abstract and incongruous* images, sometimes likened to dreams or nonlinear experimental films. These various styles are sometimes referred to as "conceptual videos."

Story lines that are developed in videos can usually be understood by the audience. However, experimental videos may be a seemingly illogical jumble of cuts and images that the audience might construe as having little or nothing to do with the song. Techniques in the most abstract videos have been traced to the stylistic traditions of Dada and Surrealism (Lynch, 1984). Recently, some video artists have turned increasingly to other modern production techniques. "Scratch" videos incorporate segments of films or television that are set to the beat of a song. Also, illustrated and animated imagery is being used more frequently as a supplement and sometimes as a main vehicle in music videos.

A contrasting style, the "performance video," may feature the artist(s) playing the entire song or be intercut with a subordinate narrative or brief visual fragments. Distinctions between performance videos and those with a narrative are less clear when the artist is both performing and playing a significant role in the story line. For example, short flashes of a musician playing or singing sometimes accompany his or her role as a savior, catalyst, or power figure in a short conflict-resolution tale.

What, if anything, does music video imagery and style reflect? Keeping in mind the diversity of videos, Kinder (1984) argues that the unique aspects of narrative and dreamlike videos contribute to our personal visions and to a larger "cultural dreampool." Citing the

Hobson-McCarley Activation Synthesis Model (1977), which posits that dreaming entails image selection from memory and cultural imprinting, Kinder notes similarities between music videos and dreams, mainly their structural reliance on memory. After pointing out that one of the most powerful aspects of music video is its ability to stimulate viewers to retrieve specific visual images from memory every time they hear a particular song, Kinder suggests that the "process of retrieving the prefabricated video images from memory may help train viewers to retrieve them more readily during REM (rapid eye movement) sleep" (Kinder, 1984, p. 14). Other similarities between the content of videos and dreams include structural discontinuity and decentering, abrupt scene shifts, and an unpredictable flow of images. Wood (1982) has also addressed the notion of "television as dream" in a world that is fascinated by the "delights of visual communication." If music video reflects recent currents in popular culture and if we acknowledge the possibility that mass media are significant contributors to our cultural dream or image pool, the similarities between dreams and videos may surely be culturally significant.

Does the growth of music video reflect visual trends? According to Turner (1986, p. 381), pop musicians and their fans have entered the 1980s conditioned by a "lifetime of packaged visuality . . . where pictorial entertainment [comes] in briefer, recycled segments," the result being a "new perceptual agenda." Here, an even faster and more complex visual environment requires assimilation of the "teeming image bank." Turner notes that music videos, especially those that allude to and incorporate old iconic imagery such as film clips (for instance, scratch videos), "are showing us how to acknowledge the burdens and reconstitute the pieces of the information explosion" (p. 390).

Thus living in a speeded-up world of rapid fire commercials and messages makes us "media literate" and better able to decode the techniques and messages of music videos. By reflecting familiar visions, videos contribute to and tap those thematic and stylistic conventions of television that are recognized as most attractive, able to hold attention, to affect memory, and to stimulate action.

## Music Video's Potential Inhibition of the Imagination

The effects of television on the imagination have been reviewed in a number of studies represented in the National Institute of Mental

Health update of The Surgeon General's Report On Television (NIMH, 1982). These analyses generally suggest that television impedes creativity, replaces activities such as reading that are known to stimulate imagination, and inhibits creative thinking, especially among children.

Music videos on television may also inhibit creative processes normally inspired by listening to music. The ability of music to facilitate mental imagery is demonstrated by the empirical data presented later in this chapter and by other studies (Osborne, 1981; Quittner & Glueckauf, 1983). Some observers fear that prefabricated visualizations of music destroy the imaginative potential of young people who, presumably, perceive songs largely in terms of the images they are given in music videos. Rock artist Joe Jackson has voiced his concern that the visual dimension actually reduces the ability of a song to bring forth special feelings, memories, or associations for the individual listener (Connelly, 1984). Similarly, Temple argues that:

> A good popular song can mean different things at different times to different people. This kind of social resonance is heavily narrowed down by the imposition of one interpretation through video which accompanies the release of a single. People tend to think of the video when they hear the song, and the constant process of change, which listening or dancing to music entails, is stopped in its tracks [Temple, 1984, p. 71].

The association between a song and its video may be strengthened in the spectator's mind when the experience of the video is repeated within a short period of time (Kinder, 1984). Of course, music video programs often repeat videos of current popular songs, just as current hits are played with varying degrees of frequency on radio stations. On MTV Music Television, videos in "active," "heavy," and "power" playlist rotation positions can be seen four to five times a day. In addition, research indicates that greater familiarity with music video leads to greater appreciation and a desire for future exposure (Miller & Baran, 1984). The likelihood of seeing certain videos repeatedly increases as time spent viewing increases, thus making it more probable that hearing a song will evoke the imagery of the video.

Audiences, however, are "active" in their consumption of mass mediated materials and it would probably be incorrect to assume that videos uniformly destroy or diminish the imagination of all viewers. Experimental research, for instance, has shown that subjects who are high in "imaginal ability" produce more vivid images and spend more time "imaging" while listening to music than do subjects with low levels of imaginal ability (Quittner & Glueckauf, 1983). Also, for "information rich" music consumers (those who buy many records and tapes, read about and talk about music with their friends, and attend many live performances), music videos may merely supplement their vast awareness and use of music.

It can also be argued that for those who are low in imaginal ability or are less knowledgeable about music, music video may be a tool that can help them appreciate and use music imaginatively. For all types of music video viewers, however, it seems likely that some of the packaged imagery comes to mind when the song is heard in nontelevision contexts and even at times when music isn't playing. Keeping in mind that a vast number of songs recorded do not have videos (usually only one to three singles off an album of 10-12 songs are accompanied by a video), the relationship between this particular visual mode and the human imagination is an intriguing and important area for future study.

### Violent, Sexual, and Sexist Trends in Music Videos

Another critical concern regarding music video is one already very familiar to television researchers—the presence on the medium of antisocial themes. Content analyses of music video have revealed some notable trends. Sherman and Dominick's (1986) study of 166 concept videos found them to be largely male dominated. Violence was portrayed in 60% of the videos and 80% of those containing violence also contained sexual suggestions (kissing, fondling, flirtation). Nonwhites were strongly identified with violence and young people were often persecuted by their establishment elders or nonwhite peers. This frequent occurrence of violence, the mixture of sex with violence, and the depiction of youth versus authority are video tendencies identified in other studies (Baxter, de Riemer, Landini, Leslie, & Singletary, 1985; National Coalition on Television Violence, 1984).

Unlike the destructive scenes framed in a prime-time television representation of day-to-day drama, the violent content of music videos is often intertwined with a series of fantasy images not always related to the song. Yet, while depictions of violence in videos are framed differently from those appearing on popular television, the mere presence of aggressive scenes in music videos is cause for concern. As the cultural indicators project and violence profile have shown (Gerbner,

Gross, Morgan, & Signorelli, 1980), violent portrayals common on television may stimulate imitation or contribute to the habituation of violence. The violent content of some music videos may surely have similar "cultivation" effects.

Also prominent in many music vidoes are scenes that display stereotypical visions of women. Females are shown to be predominantly attractive in videos. Sherman and Dominick (1986) report that they are provocatively dressed half of the time they appear. Goldson (1983) cites four female stereotypes in videos: "man-eaters, victims, love objects, and cold bitches." Women Against Pornography predictably has voiced its concern over the violence directed toward women in videos (Jaeger, 1984).

These trends are particularly noteworthy in light of recent research examining the effects of exposure to filmed violence against women (Linz, Donnerstein, & Penrod, 1984). After viewing a series of movies depicting violence against women, a sample of men developed fewer negative emotional reactions to the films, perceived the films to be significantly less violent, and considered them to be significantly less dangerous to women. In effect, prolonged exposure to filmed violence appeared to desensitize the subjects and to lower their emotional reaction to the material. Other studies (Rabinovitch, Markham, & Talbot, 1972; Thomas, Horton, Lippencott, & Brabman, 1977) reveal similar effects of sustained exposure to filmed violence on television. All of these studies are of special concern when one considers that music videos are targeted toward a young, impressionable audience that sees the violence and sexual imagery repeatedly.

Any analysis of the content and its effects is extremely complicated, however, since the lyrics, visual story line(s), style and type of music, the artist's fame and reputation, and the context inhabited by the audience members at home all are variables that need to be considered.

### Music Video as Advertising

First and foremost, music videos function as advertisements for the songs and artists being showcased. Music videos are promotional tools that emphasize the visual packaging of popular music. The advertising nature of music video makes the distinction between entertainment and the sales pitch indeterminate (Levy, 1983). This fusion of television, radio, and music industries as marketing tools and simultaneous resources for leisure time diversion seems ironic when one considers that rock and roll, the focus of most music videos, has been used by both artists and audiences as an important form of resistance to the commercial world (Frith, 1981). One of the many uses of rock and roll music has been that of a vehicle and means of identification for musical subcultures, described as "pockets of resistance" to the dominant culture-producing structure (Lull, 1985). The visualization and commercialization of even "resistant" music perhaps best illustrates the advertising nature of music video. Miller argues that:

> While the MTV format performs a "bardic" function of converging before its audience an array of possible (competing) youth subcultures and lifestyle options, at the same time it negotiates these subcultures and channels any reflective or participatory energy on the part of the audience into the act of consumerism. In this sense MTV functions as a negotiator in the hegemonic process by amplifying and absorbing elements of oppositional culture, while ultimately legitimizing and naturalizing their relationship to the dominant institutions of a consumer society [Miller, 1984, p. 2].

Although some videos display oppositional or subcultural messages and imagery, each video primarily is an effort on the part of the artist and the record company to create and present a popular image before a special music-consuming audience, a target demographic of individuals 12-34 years old. The directors of videos strive to make their products as exciting as the music. In the struggle to establish and maintain a following, artists utilize any number of techniques in order to appear exotic, powerful, tough, sexy, cool, unique.

As music video has become an important part of the popular music marketing process, some critics have complained about the emphasis on visuals instead of on music. Some artists actually may be signed to recording contracts for their video potential rather than for their musical talent. As one video critic laments, "Packaging has always been a key element in the selling of entertainment, but never has this wrapping been so indispensable" (Hoyt, 1985, p. 30). Because the production of videos has increased the price, and thus the risk, of releasing a single, the artist's ability to facilitate the success of a song visually is truly important to the record company.

Popular recording artists offer diverse views regarding music videos as promotional tools. After releasing a number of clips of previous works, rock musician Joe Jackson (Connely, 1984) refused to provide a video in connection with his 1984 "Body and Soul" album. He complained about unreasonable pressure by record companies to force the creation of a visual concept of one's music, a shift in the amount of money from tour expenses to videos, and the devaluation of musicians that takes place as some recording artists suffer by appearing to be bad actors rather than good musicians. On the other hand, British recording artist Thomas Dolby has noted that, "To me, involvement with video is only natural. When I write music I always have images in my head, so the songs are really soundtracks to my internal movies. Now I have the opportunity to externalize these movies" (Shore, 1984, p. 237).

### An Exploration of Record Buyers' Involvement in Music and Music Video and an Assessment of Music Video's Impact

I have recently conducted a study in the San Francisco Bay Area to gain preliminary descriptive information about the relationship between music video and music buying. A nonprobability sample of 385 record buyers completed questionnaires at 15 large, chain record stores. Stores that were selected for sampling stocked contemporary popular records and tapes and were located in areas where MTV was available on cable. Interviewers stood near the entrance of the store and customers who had just purchased a record, tape, or compact disc were asked to respond to a brief survey about music video. Approximately two-thirds of the customers approached agreed to complete the questionnaire. All respondents said they were familiar with music video either through MTV or other music video television programs.

While respondents ranged in age from 10 to 51 years, the sample was predominantly young (39% between 10-18; 30% between 19-24; and 31% 25-51), with a mean age of about 22 years. In all, 39% of the sample was in junior high or high school; 9% had finished high school; 33% were in or had attended college; 17% had finished college; and 8% were in or had finished graduate school. Exactly two-thirds of the subjects were male.

The 21-item questionnaire consisted of fixed choice questions, four- and five-point Likert-type scales, and open-ended questions. Respondents' involvement with music and music video was evaluated. Questions addressed the influence of MTV and music video on interest in music and record buying; the extent to which music videos give audiences visual impressions of music; subjects' interpersonal communi-

cation about music video; music and media preferences; consumption of
MTV; and likes and dislikes about MTV and music video.

### Involvement in Music

Purchasing music was a common activity for most respondents.
More than two-thirds of the subjects said they had previously bought a
record or tape by the same band or artist they were currently buying. All
but 5% of the sample reported a distinct preference for rock and roll or a
closely related style of music. When asked to evaluate eight popular
music types in terms of their appeal, respondents rated "various rock
and roll" highest, followed by "new music or new wave," "rhythm &
blues," "jazz," "soul," "heavy metal," "reggae & ska," and "hardcore
punk," respectively.

To assess involvement in music specifically, respondents were asked
how important music was to them, how often music brought forth
mental images or pictures, and how often they found themselves
appearing in these images. Because videos exist primarily as advertising
for popular music as a commercial product, these measures were based
on the generally accepted notion among consumer researchers that
involvement in a product class reflects a significant degree of personal
relevance or importance (Greenwald & Leavitt, 1984; Park & Young,
1986). Herbert Krugman, who advanced the "involvement" perspective
years ago (1965), more recently commented (1984) that an audience
member may be involved in music to the extent that listening conjures
up mental imagery, and that involvement increases even more if the
person *places himself or herself in these images.* The involvement
measures used for this study therefore differ from other research
approaches that attempt to explain commitment to music by evaluating
criteria such as time spent listening or frequency of purchase (Dixon,
1980; Lewis, 1980).

Overall, members of the sample were highly involved with music. In
all, 70% said music was "very important" and 27% said it was
"somewhat important." Most subjects (95%) said they conjured up
imagery when listening to or thinking about music (35% always; 45%
frequently; 15% occasionally; and 5% rarely or never). A great majority
(82%) found themselves appearing in the imagery brought forth by
music at least occasionally.

Demographics play a role in music involvement too. Women
assigned higher personal importance to music, reported greater amounts

of music-inspired imagery, and had more frequent personal participation in music imagery than males. These findings coincide with other empirical accounts cited in this volume and with music critic Julie Burchill's (1984) argument that females constitute a more "active" popular music audience than do males. In addition, teens (10-18 years old) and young adults (19-24) reported greater frequency of participation in imagery conjured up by music than did older adults.

Thus the young record buyers found music personally important; preferred a rock and roll style of music; experienced mental imagery facilitated by the music they liked; and more often than not, pictured themselves in this music imagery. Female and young respondents were more involved in music overall.

### Involvement in Music Video

As mentioned above, all of the record buyers had seen music video on MTV or on one of the other television or cable channels. Those who said that they watched MTV specifically (74% of the sample) averaged approximately six hours viewing per week, which, at the time of the survey, was consistent with other current research on MTV consumption (Broadcasting, September 1983). Teens averaged four more hours viewing MTV per week than older consumers of popular music.

To provide an indication of the degree and type of audience involvement in music video, respondents were asked if they could recall seeing a video featuring the band or artist purchased; whether they watched MTV as foreground, background, or both; and how often music videos reminded them of people or things that happen in their own life (that is, the "personal connections" with videos). Krugman (1965) defines involvement with advertising as the number of conscious "bridging experiences," connections, or personal references per minute that the viewer makes between his or her own life and the media stimulus.

More than two-thirds of the sample were able to recall seeing a video by the band or artist whose music they had just purchased. Teens were significantly more likely than the older viewers to be able to recall doing so. Most of the subjects who watched MTV said they attended to the channel as both foreground and background (65%), while 21% said they watch it only as foreground, and 13% watched only as background. Those who reported watching MTV as both indicated that viewing time was evenly divided between foreground (51%) and background (49%).

Fifty-three percent of the viewers reported "personal connections" with videos at least occasionally (7% always; 19% frequently; 27% occasionally; 32% rarely; and 15% never). Videos were also significantly more likely to remind females and teens than the rest of the sample of people or things that happen in their own lives.

### Music Video's Impact on Pop Music Fans

Another series of questions asked respondents to indicate if they believed MTV and music video has an effect on their uses of music. Most of the sample cited MTV and music video as a topic for conversation among peers and as an important source of information when they decide what music to buy. A majority (74%) of the subjects reported talking about MTV or music video with their friends at least occasionally. When asked "which is most important to you when deciding what records to buy?" MTV was cited after radio and friends but ahead of concerts, magazines, and other music video programs on television.

Sixty-two percent of the sample indicated that MTV or music video influenced their record purchasing decisions at least occasionally (8% always; 22% frequently; 32% occasionally; 22% rarely; and 16% never). A majority also noted that MTV or music video had increased their interest in music (24% strongly increased; 39% mildly increased; 36% no increase); 34% said they had bought more music since watching MTV specifically.

Videos also left most of the subjects with visual impressions of music. A decisive majority (84%) indicated that they reflect on images contained in the video of a song when hearing that song on radio or record (20% always; 39% frequently; 25% occasionally; 12% rarely; and 4% never).

Significant differences were observed among various demographic groups' responses to most of the questions regarding music videos' impact on the uses of music. Females were significantly more likely than males to have their purchases influenced by music video; to have their interest in music increased because of video; and to think about the video when listening to a song. Teens were significantly more likely than young adults and adults to buy more music since they began watching MTV; to have their purchasing habits influenced by music video and MTV; to have increased interest in music since watching MTV and music video; to think about the video when listening to a song; and to talk to friends about music and music video. The high levels of music video salience and peer interaction among younger viewers are consistent with Clarke's (1973) findings that adolescents frequently use music as a source of information about others and as a coin of exchange in peer interactions.

Interestingly enough, post hoc tests revealed no interaction between gender and age group. Females and young people were found to be distinct subgroups who are most involved in music and music video overall. Nonetheless, the entire sample of record buyers was very familiar with music video. Most respondents said that MTV increased their interest in music, influenced their music purchases, and left them with visual impressions of particular songs. These results are also noteworthy in light of recent research that examined viewer's perceptions of music video. Here, an experimental group of subjects evaluated music videos favorably, and saw them as more active and potent than songs without videos (Rubin, Rubin, Perse, Armstrong, McHugh, & Faix, 1986).

## *Discussion*

While the findings reported here are subject to the usual cautions concerning self-report data and are limited in their generalizability by the nature of the sample, they illuminate some broad trends that are noteworthy in light of the critical themes reviewed earlier. If we acknowledge that visual imagery is one of the cognitive vehicles through which an audience member reaches the highest level of music involvement (or "product" involvement) and video involvement (or "advertising" involvement), the data indicate that music video is successful in achieving the goals of its creators. Music videos give record buyers something special to think about and talk about, to visualize, recall, and to make "personal connections" with. The potential effects of music video depend upon a number of factors, including the degree of involvement in music and in video and the presence of certain demographic characteristics. Moreover, higher levels of music and video exposure among teens and females suggest strongly the importance of considering the sociocultural context of the music video experience. And, while the research shows that record buyers who watch music videos are left with distinct visual impressions of songs, the data presented here do not indicate to what degree videos replace the substance of viewers' own imaginations.

There are numerous indications now of the cultural pervasiveness of music videos. Promotions for major motion pictures, for instance, often include a music video featuring "name" recording artists performing a song written for the film, interspersed with brief segments of the movie. Video projectors and screens featuring the latest videos are common in dance clubs in many parts of the world. And, the visual and auditory style of one of the most popular action-adventure television series of the 1980s, *Miami Vice*, is directly influenced by music video. In fact, Brandon Tartikoff, National Broadcasting Corporation's chief of programming, has stated, "I decided they [MTV] were doing something special, and for a week I overdosed on MTV. After I'd done that I called [producers] Anthony Yerkovitch and Michael Mann and told them to put cops in it [the new series that was to become Miami Vice]. The working title was 'MTV Cops' " (Dalton, 1985, p. 385). The fallout of the *Miami Vice* phenomenon, including spinoffs and influence on television programming and popular culture in general, continues into the late 1980s.

The purpose of this chapter was to review some of the major still-emerging themes that illustrate the social and cultural significance of music video and to present some empirical evidence concerning audience involvement with music and with music video. An abundance of critical analyses and empirical studies pertaining to music video are now filtering into communication journals and books, further signalling its appeal and importance.

## REFERENCES

Baxter, B., de Riemer, C., Landini, A., Leslie, L., & Singletary, M. (1985) A content analysis of music videos. *Journal of Broadcasting and Electronic Media, 29,* 333-340.

Broadcasting (1983) Examining the MTV phenomenon and its effects on radio. (September 5), 60.

Burchill, J. (1984) Idols on parade. *The Face* (March), 57-59.

Clarke, P. (1983) Teenager's coorientation and information seeking about pop music. *American Behavioral Scientist, 16,* 551-556.

Connelly, C. (1984) Why Joe Jackson said no to rock video. *Rolling Stone* (August 30), 32.

Dalton, J. (1985) The televisionary. *Esquire* (December), 380-387.

Dixon, R. D. (1980) Suggested scales for the measurement of musical involvement and genre tastes. *Popular Music and Society, 7,* 223-244.

Frith, S. (1981) *Sound effects: Youth, leisure, and the politics of rock and roll.* New York: Pantheon.

Gerbner, G., Gross, L., Morgan, M., & Signorelli, N. (1980) The mainstreaming of America: Violence profile no. 11. *Journal of Communication, 30,* 10-29.

Goldson, A. (1983) Three minute heroes. *Heresies, 16,* 6-10.

Greenwald, A. G. & Leavitt, C. (1984) Audience involvement in advertising: Four levels. *Journal of Consumer Research, 11,* 581-592.

Hobson, J. A. & McCarley, R. W. (1977) The brain as a dream state generator: An activation-synthesis hypothesis of the dream process. *American Journal of Psychiatry, 134,* 1335-1348.

Hoyt, D. (1985) Four arguments for the elimination of MTV. *Send: Video Communication & Art* (Spring) 30-34.

Jaeger, B. (1984) Violence, sex flare in rock world. *San Francisco Examiner & Chronicle* (April 15), 35, 37.

Kinder, M. (1984) Music video and the spectator: Television, ideology, and dream. *Film Quarterly, 38,* 2-15.

Krugman, H. E. (1965) The impact of television advertising: Learning without involvement. *Public Opinion Quarterly, 29,* 349-356.

Krugman, H. (1984) Personal communication, March 16.

Levy, S. (1983) Ad nauseum: How MTV sells out rock & roll. *Rolling Stone* (December 8), 30, 33, 34, 37, 74, 76, 78, 79.

Lewis, G. H. (1980) Commitment and involvement in popular music: An argument for a mass behavioral approach. *International Review of Aesthetics and Sociology of Music, 8,* 229-237.

Linz, D., Donnerstein, E., & Penrod, S. (1984). The effects of multiple exposures to filmed violence against women. *Journal of Communication, 34,* 130-147.

Lull, J. (1985) On the communicative properties of music. *Communication Research, 12,* 363-372.

Lynch, J. D. (1984) Music videos: From data to surrealism. *Journal of Popular Culture, 18,* 53-57.

Miller, D. S. (1983) *Music television: Negotiated youth culture in the 1980s.* Unpublished manuscript. University of Texas, Department of Radio-Television-Film, Austin.

Miller, D. S., & Baran, S. J. (1984) *Music television: An assessment of functional attributes.* Paper presented at The International Communication Association annual conference, San Francisco, California.

National Coalition on Television Violence (1984) Violence rate in rock videos. *San Francisco Chronicle,* December 19, 60.

National Institute of Mental Health (1982) *Television and behavior: Ten years of scientific progress and implications for the eighties, Vol. 2* (D. Pearl, L. Buthilet, & J. Lazar, Eds.). Washington, DC: Government Printing Office.

Osborne, J. W. (1981) The mapping of thoughts, emotions, sensations, and images as responses to music. *Journal of Mental Imagery, 5,* 133-136.

Park, C. & Young, S. (1986) Consumer response to television commercials: The impact of involvement and background music on brand attitude formation. *Journal of Marketing Research, 23,* 11-24.

Quittner, A. & Glueckauf, R. (1983) The facilitative effects of music on visual imagery. *Journal of Mental Imagery, 7,* 105-120.

Rabinovitch, M. S., Markham, J. W., & Talbot, A. D. (1972) Children's violence perception as a function of television violence. In G. Comstock, E. Rubinstein, & J. M. Murray (Eds.), *Television and social behavior* (Vol. 5). Washington, DC: Government Printing Office.

Rubin, R., Rubin, A., Perse, E., Armstrong, C., McHugh, M., & Faix, N. (1986) Media use and meaning of music video. *Journalism Quarterly, 63,* 353-359.

Sherman, B. L. & Dominick, J. D. (1986) Violence and sex in music videos: TV and rock 'n' roll. *Journal of Communication, 36,* 76-90.

Shore, M. (1984) *The Rolling Stone book of rock video.* New York: Rolling Stone Press/ Quill.

Temple, J. (1984) Videopop. *The Face* (January), 70-73.

Thomas, M. H., Horton, E. C., Lippencott, C. C., & Brabman, R. S. (1977) Desensitization to portrayals of real-life aggression as a function of exposure to television violence. *Journal of Personality and Social Psychology, 35,* 450-458.

Turner, C. (1986) Music videos and the iconic data base. In G. Gumpert & R. Cathcart (Eds.), *Intermedia.* New York: Oxford University Press.

Watt, J. H. & Krull, R. (1977) An information theory measure for television programming. *Communication Research , 3,* 99-112.

Wood, D. H. (1982) Television as dream. In H. Newcomb (Ed.), *Television: The Critical View.* New York: Oxford University Press.

# 6

# The International Music Industry
# and Transcultural Communication

ROGER WALLIS
KRISTER MALM

In the following pages we shall summarize many of the important aspects of our four-year research project on the international music industry, particularly its relationship to local music and culture. The project is termed the Music Industry in Small Countries (MISC). It is a comparative study of the effects of the technological, economic, and organizational changes in the music industry on the lives of people in 12 countries on four continents.

## A Historical Perspective

### The Scenario in a Small Country—Sweden

Throughout the 1950s and 1960s, the international music and entertainment industry brought the sounds of rock and roll to Sweden. Swedish youth, in common with young people in many Western countries, found a group identity by choosing Elvis Presley or Tommy Steele as their idols. This was particularly true of children in middle- or working-class families. A different imported musical culture was often favored by those from more affluent homes, namely Dixieland jazz. The rock and roll fad did not at first lead to much active music making. The sounds of New Orleans, however, did stimulate the formation of some imitative local bands such as the Cave Stompers, Jazz Doctors, and the Storyville Creepers. Some of these bands still exist.

When the full impact of British rock music (for instance, the Beatles, Rolling Stones, Dave Clark Five) hit Sweden in the middle 1960s, however, the stimulus to group activity was remarkable. By this time, Sweden, with its population of only eight million people, could actually boast of several thousand pop groups.[1] All of them played and sang Beatles/Rolling Stones/Animals-inspired songs with words in English. Though many of these Swedish pop singers barely understood the words they sung, all of them seemed to have secret or open ambitions to become local, national, or international heroes through their music. Few of them ever got a chance to make any money as part of the international music industry, with one or two exceptions that arose a decade later. Bjorn and Benny, the male half of the Swedish pop group ABBA, got their basic musical training during the Swedish pop boom of the 1960s. Ten years later, ABBA was the biggest act in the international record industry. ABBA had found a formula for music that could be sold virtually anywhere in the world.

By the year 1968, many of Bjorn and Benny's musical colleagues had disposed of their guitars and amplifiers. Some even went bankrupt trying to pay the bills for their equipment. Others retreated and continued to play in cellars and garages up and down this long, thin country. Two years later, at the turn of the decade, several of these virtually unknown rock groups began to emerge, performing mainly at free festivals organized by the musicians and their fans. They had been inspired by phenomena such as the Woodstock Festival in the United States, which received wide publicity as the hippie movement and student revolts hit Sweden.

The music these groups performed was different from the pop songs of the 1960s in a number of significant ways. Elements of the Swedish folk tradition were often incorporated and adapted for the electric instruments that had been introduced in plenty during the pop boom. Amateurism, the "everyone can join in and play" ideology, prevailed. The orientation at this time was more toward quantity of music rather than quality, an inhibiting obstacle that had limited participation in the music-making process of the 1960s. Group names invariably were outrageous and were in Swedish (for instance, "Flasket Brinner" or "The Bacon's Burning," and "Piska Mig Hart," which we will refrain from translating). Most significantly, song lyrics were now sung in the local language, Swedish. This fact radically affected the communicative role of music in the society. Swedish rock musicians found themselves making a noisy entrance into the political debate of the nation. Songs were sung about everything from the Vietnam war and other international issues to the prevalent "back to nature" ideology that was encouraging many Swedes to leave the cities and set up communes in rural areas. Many songs teased the establishment mercilessly.

Traditional sectors of the music industry were confused by this development. Broadcasters at the national radio monopoly had to decide whether "light music" (in contrast with "serious music") with lyrics that were often political should be incorporated into the normal entertainment output of the Swedish Broadcasting Corporation. While this was happening, the process of integration within the international music industry, which later resulted in the dominance by the "big five" corporations (CBS, Polygram, Warners, EMI, RCA), was beginning to increase their share of the lucrative Swedish market by buying up local producers, distributors, and retailers. The big international record companies, through their local subsidiaries, assumed that the Swedish-language pop groups of the early 1970s were merely a temporary phenomenon. The fact that they sang in a "small" language, and would presumably not sell outside Sweden, made their music even less attractive for locally based representatives of the transnational music industry.

The lack of interest from the music industry establishment stimulated local musicians in Sweden to move to yet another area in which their predecessors in the 1960s would never have been involved. They started their own music businesses with the development of recording studios and record companies for distribution and promotion. Important prerequisites were know-how, funds, and technology. Sweden had sufficient independently owned recording studios (often built by enthusiastic amateurs) and manufacturing facilities to make this development possible. By the mid-1970s, Sweden could boast of an alternative network to that of the transnationals, consisting of 20 or so record companies, studios, joint-distribution organizations, and even a record-manufacturing plant. Most of these ventures were organized as cooperatives, as were most of the clubs where musicians performed up and down the country.

Despite this explosive growth in the early 1970s, the output of these small Swedish companies never managed to exceed more than 5% of the total market for recorded music in Sweden. The five big record companies continued to increase their influence. Warners (United

States) bought up an active, locally owned record company (Metronome) and soon changed the direction of its operations from the recording of local music to the distribution of Warner-controlled records and films. When a Swedish government committee was convened in 1977 to advise on the future for the local Swedish record industry, it was confronted with a confusing picture full of apparent paradoxes.

Sales of music on records had increased fivefold during the 1970s. Teenagers were devoting an average of more than one hour per day listening to their own records and another hour exposed to recorded music on the radio. At the same time, the range of recorded music available had decreased as a result of structural changes in the record industry, favoring a concentration of hit songs. Though the Swedes led the world in purchases of records per capita, local producers using records and cassettes to document and distribute Swedish music were finding it difficult to survive. The large international companies controlled nearly 70% of the Swedish market but were recording less and less Swedish music.

Sweden had provided the world music market with a number of saleable products during the 1970s. Organist Bo Hansson's musical interpretation of Tolkien's Lord of the Rings was recorded by a small alternative record company in Sweden after being refused by the local subsidiaries of the international companies. This recording found its way, via an independent company in London, to the United States, where one of the Warner family record labels, Elektra, sold several hundred thousand copies. And ABBA too, through their own record company (POLAR), were realizing sales exceeding those of the Beatles. ABBA's manager announced proudly that the only places where one could not buy ABBA records were North Korea and the People's Republic of China. ABBA was soon responsible for some 80% of the total copyright income from the use of *all* Swedish music abroad. Even so, almost 70% of the copyright money collected in Sweden left the country. A very real question looming over the horizon was: Would there be a local record industry to help Swedish musicians communicate to their own people in the future?

It was very much with this scenario in mind that the MISC project was conceived. Clearly, Sweden's problems were partly caused by the fact that the country represents a small market in a small language area. How could one ensure that such a small market could use the technology and knowledge of the music industry to enhance its own cultural

Figure 6.1  Music Technology Is Everywhere: An audio recording is made at a key-harp players' gathering in rural Sweden (photo by Roger Wallis).

identity? Would Sweden ultimately become merely a marginal market for the international products of a few gigantic transnational corporations—products marketed globally via superstars, satellites, and expensive video productions?

## The Music Industry in Small Countries (MISC) Research Project

Despite the fact that the phonograph has celebrated its 100th birthday, remarkably few research results have been published regarding the structure, workings, and communicative role of the music and record industry. Mass communication researchers have seldom considered records and tapes to be important means of communication. Some work has been done recently by sociologists interested in patterns of change among youth in relation to music (Frith, 1981; Roe, 1984; Nylov, 1984; Blaukopf, 1977). Others who have endeavored to describe the business side of the music industry have discovered organizations that are unusually adept at concealing their workings.

A great deal of writing, however, has been devoted to the output of the music industry—the artists and the music they record. Still, only a handful of studies attempt to describe how the industry actually functions. Hirsch (1969) concentrated on the financial and organizational structure. Denisoff (1975) has reported on business and contractual relationships and Blaukopf (1977) covers historical aspects. An oft-quoted study of the transitional record companies and their global markets was produced by two Finnish researchers (Soromaki & Haarman, 1978), who have attempted to describe the structure of the industry, providing market statistics gleaned from company reports and trade publications.

Gillet (1972) covers the record company activities concerning the development of blues and rock music. Hennion and Vignolle (1978) analyzed the economic structure of the record industry in France. Hennion has also published a sociological study of different roles played by those involved in the production of records and tapes, looking at who decides what is recorded, by whom, and why. The most valuable British contribution is undoubtedly Frith's book, *Sound Effects* (1981). More recent sources of information regarding the workings of the music industry include Cambridge University Press' *Popular Music Yearbook*, a publication that will soon become a journal. Also, DOPMUS

(Documentation of Popular Music Studies) is a new computerized register of articles and books just established in Sweden.

### Why the Smaller Nations?

The MISC project concentrated on the rapid changes that occurred within the music industry during the 1970s and their effects on the music life in a sample of smaller nations (Chile, Denmark, Finland, Jamaica, Kenya, Norway, Sri Lanka, Sweden, Tanzania, Trinidad, Tunisia, and Wales). The 1970s were chosen since it is an interesting decade, encompassing not only the breakthrough of stereo high fidelity, but also the introduction of the sound cassette and video to virtually every corner of the globe. Concentrating on countries rather than individual cultures was necessary since it is only on a governmental or intergovernmental basis that decisions can be made with sufficient power to contest decisions made by the growing transnational music corporations.

Another assumption was that small countries play a dual role in relation to the music industry. They are marginal markets for international products and they are sources of new, raw material. The role of the small market in the distribution of international music becomes clear as soon as one observes a variety of figures from major music-producing nations such as the United States and the United Kingdom. A major United States copyright organization that collects royalties for composers and publishers claims that "for every one foreign song that is earning money in America, 10 American songs are earning money abroad" (BMI, 1984). Similarly, a study of the British record and tape industry shows that the British have only 6% of the world market, but British exports account for no less than 26% of world sales (Hardy, 1983). As production costs and investment in marketing tools such as television advertising and video clips increase, it becomes more and more important financially for the international companies to sell as much of the same products *in as many countries as possible.*

The fact that the world still has a rich heritage of music expression that can be appreciated and used in different countries explains the smaller nations' role as sources of raw material. Examples are legion. Jamaica has given us reggae music; Trinidad, the calypso. The people of the Carribean have provided much of the repertoire of many artists and composers in the industrialized world. Africa, as one record company executive put it, "is just waiting to be opened up." The industry has an army of talent scouts looking for new sources to tap. Small countries can supply the occasional golden egg, and consume the final product as well, suitably packaged by the industry.

Overall, our aim was to identify major technological, economic, and organizational changes taking place within the music industry and to analyze the resulting patterns of change in the countries we visited. The types of questions we hoped to answer ultimately were:

- How can small countries use the technology of the music industry to document and develop their own musical activity?
- How can small countries avoid having their unique music cultures swamped by a limited number of international cultural products in a world now full of satellites, superstars, and global oligopolies?
- How has the spread of music industry technology affected the traditional communicative role of music?
- How have decision makers in various countries reacted, if at all, to developments within the music industry?
- What is the need for state or other regulatory involvement and cultural policy on a national and international level?

Hopes of answering some of these questions through quantitative statistical analysis were dismissed at an early stage. A look at available statistics produced by UNESCO and other bodies, or released by the record industry, showed a remarkable absence of "hard facts" about the operations of the music industries in general (Gronow, 1980). Statistics in the various countries, when they existed, were often compiled according to widely divergent standards or used methods of measurement that were not appropriate for our purposes. Record albums, it seems, can be measured in kilos! They can also be measured in terms of retail or wholesale value, but seldom in plain units. Compilations using different sets of statistics can lead to completely different conclusions in comparative studies, something we naturally wanted to avoid.

### Sources of Information

Much of the research data for this project was gleaned from interviews with a broad selection of people active in the music scene in our sample countries. This information was supplemented by any available material we could find in the form of usable statistics or reports and with interview material and data on the international music industry collected in London and New York.

In the small countries we interviewed politicians, civil servants, educators, representatives of music organizations, managers and employees of mass media, journalists, people from the music business (from bosses and employees to doormen at night clubs), and, of course, musicians. In short, the sample of informants in each country was made as wide as was practical.

The interviews were geared at getting the informants to identify "significant incidents" in the field of music during the period 1970 through the early 1980s. Interviews were not conducted according to a fixed questionnaire but were adapted to the specific competence of the various informants. Thus it was possible to identify particular incidents that are considered significant by people in different positions and to throw light on these incidents from various angles.

In order to stimulate the memories of respondents, they were each given a list of what we believed were relevant areas of activity. As Figure 6.2 indicates, these areas concerned the organizational development of music (institutions and organizations), the formal development (legislation), the business development (companies involved in music), mass media development with relevance to music, and other activities such as festivals and tourism.

### Analyzing the Data—the MISC Interaction Model

Interviews of the kind described above with more than 200 respondents produced a wealth of data. But as a means of answering the questions we originally posed, the data must be related to a common model of music life in the countries, a model that relates different sectors of the music industry at different levels of enlargement. The model we designed identifies three main levels of action:

- The International Level includes international organizations, the transnational music industry, and related media and electronics industries.
- The National Level includes the domestic music industry, related industries, mass media, and music institutions and organizations.
- The Music Activity level in any country includes the actual music played by different musicians and listened to by members of musical subcultures. This is the level of the public at large.

The MISC Interaction Model (Figure 6.3) demonstrates how all the bodies in this complicated system are related, directly or indirectly. The principle of this approach is that by mapping out the processes that have

1. **The formation of new music institutions or significant changes affecting existing music institutions.**

   *Examples of music institutions*: educational establishments, national concert organisations or orchestras, cultural or research institutes.

2. **The formation of new music organisations or changes in existing music organisations.**

   *Examples of music organisations*: musicians' unions, composers' organisations, concertgoers' associations, other groupings of active musicians or people actively supporting music.

3. **Changes in legislation. The introduction of new national or international agreements.**

   *Examples*: legislation intended to stimulate or control music activity, legislation or agreements affecting copyright, introduction of duties or taxes affecting music productions, legislation or regulations controlling the role of music in the educational system.

4. **Changes regarding business activities in the music sector.**

   *Examples*: changes in the structure of the music industry – record companies, publishers, music periodicals, concert promoters and associated operations. Significant campaigns promoting national or other music. The investment climate for domestic as opposed to imported music.

5. **Changes in the music policies and activities of radio, TV, press organisations.**

   *Examples*: changes in the emphasis on coverage of national as opposed to global music phenomena. The relative roles of live and recorded music. The extent of mass media's commitment to informing about and reviewing music activities such as concerts, workshops, festivals etc.

6. **Other changes or significant events not covered in the above categories.**

   *Examples*: major festivals, cultural debates, acts of individuals, changes in the economic climate, introduction of new music cultures by immigrants/tourists or other processes.

Figure 6.2    Areas of Study in "Significant Incident" Investigation

occurred during the past decade, the current situation can be better understood and questions about the future can be made less ambiguous.

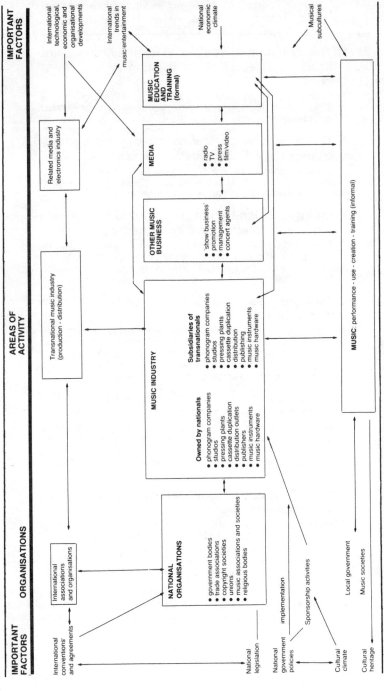

**Figure 6.3 Music Industry in Small Countries (MISC) Interaction Model**

122

## Results of the MISC Research Project

### Advantages and Disadvantages of Low-Cost Technologies

The different countries show remarkable similarities regarding the development of local trends in recorded popular music. These changes often involve the use of electric or electronic instruments and the incorporation of lyrics with local relevance to the modern sound. The Swedes, as was discussed previously, began to produce local-language pop songs in the early 1970s. The first pop records by the Sinhalese people of Sri Lanka, a country very different from Sweden, appeared at about the same time. Welsh-language beat groups also started making their own records in the early 1970s.

A partial explanation for this temporal similarity is the availability of low-cost music technology and its ability to penetrate the various cultures. The most striking example is the sound cassette. It is a simple medium for listening to other peoples' music. Thus the cassette, pioneered by the music industry via Philips of Holland, provided the necessary technology for an enormous pirate industry mainly emanating from Asia. This industry has augmented the flow of international hit music, making cheap copies available in even the poorest countries. This turn of events has made it difficult for local music production that must bear full costs in order to compete in the same marketplace with the "dubbed" foreign music.

The cassette also offers small-scale *advantages* in the form of prerequisites for local industries. Small groups of artists can make their own recordings and distribute them on cassettes, thus avoiding the larger investments required for records. Consequently, records have almost disappeared in countries such as Tunisia and Sri Lanka. In Sri Lanka we found an entire local industry based on cassettes with the so-called Baila-style songs[2] sung in the minority local language, Sinhalese. Many of the lyrics have a strong, local relevance. Some were known as "incident songs," which questioned or reported different events and phenomena in society, much in the same way Calypso does in the Caribbean. The Sri Lanka expressions of popular culture were very rarely featured on local radio channels according to officials for reasons of "quality" and "subject matter." Their creators, the Baila singer-songwriters, were nonetheless extremely popular. Even the inhabitants of the poorest fishing village in Sri Lanka know many of these songs by heart, learned via a cassette player. A survey conducted in a Sri Lankan

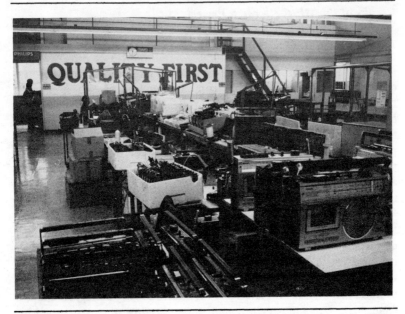

Figure 6.4  Churning out Cassettes in the Third World: In a wing of the Philips
factory in Nairobi, Kenya (photo by Roger Wallis).

village with 1,360 families found that the inhabitants owned no fewer
than 480 cassette players in 1984, according to the Sri Lankan
Broadcasting Corporation.

The local cassette industry in Sri Lanka survives despite the fact that
the cassettes it produces are twice as expensive as the pirate cassettes
that are readily available with stolen material from ABBA, Boney M,
the Beatles, and hundreds of other artists and groups. The introduction
of cheap music industry technologies has provided a new means of
communicating through and entertainment in a popular idiom.

### The Threat to Traditional Music Culture

Not everyone uses the cassette to document and spread the local
culture. Nor has any country, so far as we have seen, been able to block
the flow of music industry technology. Even in cultures where local
music has traditionally played a vital role in communication and the
learning process, the cassette player has made a sudden entrance as a

premiere status symbol. With it have come cheap cassettes transcribed with Anglo-American hit songs.

What are the likely effects of this sudden superimposition of music designed to relax tired workers of the West on top of cultures where music is significant in personal socialization and the development of cultural identity? To discuss the full ramifications of these issues is beyond the scope of this writing. Certain positive observations can be made, however, from the marriage of modern technology and the developing world.

### Warding Off the Threat
### Through Media Policy

Tanzania in East Africa lacks record industry facilities. The national, state-controlled radio service, however, has built its own infrastructure for recording local music and feeding its transmitters with music, not from records, but from its own recorded tapes. This total dedication to national music has had a remarkably stimulating effect on both popular and traditional music in Tanzania. The power of recorded music is even used for teaching purposes. We witnessed a local electric band ("jazz band") that, together with officials from the Ministry of Housing, composed and performed a song about a new way to build huts. To a Westerner, this notion may sound naive, even pathetic. In Tanzania, this use of music is a very efficient way of communicating.

Tanzania's policy regarding local music on the radio may not apply to all other small countries, but its essence should be noted. The principle has been applied in Canada, a small country in relation to its neighbor to the south, where a content of 30% Canadian music is demanded on AM radio stations. No such rule exists in Sweden, however, where the fall off in local record production has led to a decrease of the Swedish music content on the radio in the mid-1980s.

### Positive Cassette Piracy:
### The Case of Chile

Comparing different countries with varying social and economic systems allowed us to observe the exact opposite of the Tanzanian situation. In Chile, prior to the coup that brought General Pinochet to power, local folk music was the heart and soul of the nation. It could be purchased cheaply on records (prices were pegged under inflation) and was played most of the time on radio stations. The major record companies admit that they made their highest profits ever in Chile during the regime of Salvador Allende, head of the elected Marxist government that existed there previously. But the military leaders in Santiago shunned the folk music that had been the hallmark of their predecessors. It was banned from the media. Many performers and composers went into exile. New types of radio stations appeared, playing mainly North American disco music. This suited the intentions of the new government—most of the lyrics were in English, not Spanish, and were guaranteed not to offend. The government's adherence to the free-import policies of the Chicago School of Economics also led to a steady influx of music industry hardware. When restrictions on local concerts were relaxed somewhat in the late 1970s, folk musicians dared to play the songs of Victor Jara again in public. Their audiences were full of enthusiasts clutching cassette recorders, making recordings of the songs they had been denied for so long. The same technology permitted the spread of foreign artists who were firmly disliked by the regime (for example, Sylvio Rodriguez from Cuba). What could strictly be defined as cassette piracy allowed sectors of the Chilean population to enjoy and communicate through their own music culture.

**Small Countries as Laboratories:**
**Tunisian Piracy**

By studying small countries that are very vulnerable to the effects of new technology coming in from the outside, it is possible to understand and even predict developments in larger frames of reference. Piracy and the cassette business in Tunisia is one example.

In 1977, hardly a cassette was available in this Arab country. By 1982, three local factories were churning out between three and five million cassettes for the local market each year. Records have virtually disappeared as a medium for distributing popular music. According to the manufacturers of blank and prerecorded tapes (of their own artists), nearly 90% of the blank tapes manufactured in Tunisia were used for pirated copies. The artists, composers, and companies responsible for producing the original recordings of the pirated items received no royalties. This circumstance gives rise to two interesting questions: First, what effect does this have on the artists and, second, which entrepreneurs can survive in such a business climate?

Artists who were interviewed no longer considered recordings to be

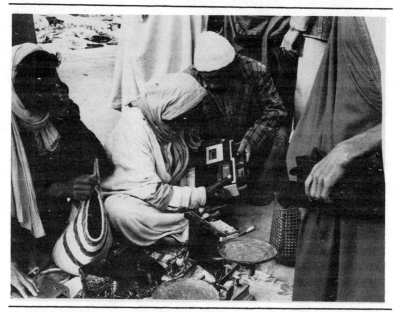

Figure 6.5  Copying Audio Cassettes: Men make copies of popular music cassettes at the Local Market in Douez on the edge of the Sahara Desert in Tunisia (photo by Roger Wallis).

an important source of income. It was regarded as merely a source of publicity—the more the pirate salesmen played a cassette of an artist on loudspeakers in their little shops, the greater the chance of the artist being commissioned to perform in local festivities such as wedding or circumcision ceremonies.

The only entrepreneurs who continued to record the original cassettes (from which the pirates made their recordings) were those with other sources of music industry income. They were mainly the manufacturers of the blank tapes that were the pirates' raw materials. The same principle has applied to the international music industry. Most of the giant corporations whose record divisions claim that they are losing money from home taping and piracy have a financial interest in the manufacture of blank tape. Polygram is 90%-owned by Philips. CBS cooperates closely with SONY in Japan. EMI makes tapes.

### Effects of the Music Industry Spotlight
### on Local Music Culture

Music is never the same once it has been processed by music-industry technology. When exposed to the packaging processes of the international music corporations, the results can be absolutely irreversible. Some examples can be used to illustrate this point:

(1) Popular Tunisian artists are often accompanied by an ensemble with drums, tambourines, and bagpipes. When the first commercial studio was opened in Tunisia, it had acquired a piece of music industry technology—a synthesizer. Musicians then discovered that a new sound could be produced by blending the live bagpipes with the synthesizer. As this sound became popular, other bagpipe players acquired synthesizers to produce the same sound at live concerts. New equipment such as this places new demands (for instance, financing, access to electricity) on musicians in an area traditionally based merely on the ability to play an acoustic instrument.

(2) Steelbands in Trinidad make their music by beating tuned oil drums or "pans." The bands consist of as many as 100 members. Steelbands are difficult to record because of the space they cover. Normally a recording session would involve two microphones near the band in a natural setting, somebody's backyard. The introduction of another new technology, multichannel recording, changed all this. The most technically proficient musicians in a band now record all the various parts on different channels on the tape recorder at different times. The final mix (overdubbing the channels) might be technically perfect, but it no longer represents the collective communication of 100 musicians and their audiences.

(3) Perhaps the most interesting example of the music industry's effect on the music it makes popular is illustrated by the case of Jamaica, renowned for its contribution of reggae to the world music scene. Despite a steady flow of music from the island to the international industry, no transnational music corporation has managed to establish a subsidiary on Jamaica. According to one EMI executive, "It's not a very organized place." Not even CBS, which has an avowed policy of having "a record company in every place it's possible to have one," has managed to open up offices in Kingston, Jamaica. Reggae on Jamaica has a very down-to-earth relationship to everyday life. Local records mainly are songs with a mixture of comments on local current affairs (for example, why the 8:15 bus is always half an hour late) with a fair share of "slack talk" (harmless obscenities). Artists with a Rastafarian religious leaning sing declamatory

Figure 6.6  The Trinidad Steelband: Collective communication, so long as it's live, not recorded (photo by Roger Wallis).

songs expressing hope that Jah (God) will intervene to help the oppressed poor. Bob Marley, of course, was a prophet of this movement.

The international industry has itself become a source of raw materials by spreading music of various cultures. This has resulted in the same process of "mediaization" (adaptation to the media) as the technological changes illustrated in examples above. For example, while the music coming from Jamaica's internationally known artists is becoming more and more oriented toward the outside influence of disco or "easy listening" melodies, the reggae beat that originated on the island has similarly found its way into Western pop music (for instance, James Last from West Germany records "middle of the road" albums that sometimes use a watered-down reggae beat to introduce some color).

The application of the Euro-American legal structure (implied in the operations of the international music industry) can also cause havoc when a local music culture such as reggae is made transnational. The unique beat is the basic element of Jamaican reggae music—lyrics and

Figure 6.7  Downtown Kingston, Jamaica: Where artists sell reggae discs in colorful
outlets (photo by Roger Wallis).

melodies vary more widely than does the fundamental beat. The
European concept of being able to define each combination of rhythm,
harmony, and melody as an individual composition (which can each
earn royalties for the various composers) does not work. The same
reggae "backing track," for instance, might appear on any number of
records. If one of the records becomes an international hit, how are the
spoils to be divided? Suddenly a culture that is used to a collective
ownership of music ends up in turmoil with different individuals
squabbling over the right to differential financial compensation. A good
example is the worldwide hit single, "Pass the Dutchie." This song was
recorded by a group of young black British musicians ("Musical
Youth") but was based on a fusion of at least two different Jamaican
records that used the same backing track (drums, guitars, keyboards).
The question of who should get what in Jamaica and England is still an
ongoing fight. The industry already got its share of money. Those
responsible for the source material will be the last to receive any cash.[3]

## *Transculturation*

To explain the fundamental process described above, it is not enough merely to refer to an established concept such as "cultural imperialism." We are witnessing a two-way process that both dilutes and streamlines culture, but also provides new opportunities for cultural enrichment. For example, a Swedish artist inspired by the songs of Bob Marley might record songs in Swedish over a reggae beat. By doing so the artist is not necessarily the victim of cultural imperialism.

Instead, we have chosen to introduce the concept of "transculturation." The international music industry produces a nationless music with various elements blended together from different cultures. The exposure of new talent continually introduces new elements to the mixture. Some of the new elements subsequently inspire other cultures to create their own new forms of expression, often a synthesis of local music with imported influences. But with the international industry constantly on the outlook for material that makes its product range slightly different, the flow can then go in the opposite direction. This is a process that inevitably leaves its mark on indigenous music cultures, invariably involving the removal of some local communicative aspects.

As low-cost music industry technology becomes more widespread, the transculturation process becomes more marked. Its effect on world music could be devastating if the element of cultural exchange is associated with assumptions about the relative merits of culture in the industrialized and developing worlds. With the development of high-quality, lightweight recording equipment, it has become common for European and American record producers to travel to Africa in order to make indigenous recordings. These are later remixed and supplemented with synthesized sounds or simple melodies in the studios of London or New York. The resulting music can provide a palatable pop-mosaic with what the industry calls "hit potential." If such musical products do become hits, then they will almost certainly find their way back to the Third World countries where they were originally recorded. It would not be surprising, under such circumstances, if local musicians in those nations assumed that this was the way their predecessors played music. Indeed, the music is never the same once it has passed through industry pipelines.

### The Future

The penetration of relatively low-cost music industry technology has had two major consequences. First, the same technical norms have been infused throughout the world. The electronic industry's norm for sound quality produced by the average transistor radio provides global minimum standards for recorded music. This marks the first time in the history of mankind that an entire worldwide generation of people under 30 years old have had access to virtually the same music, wherever they live. And second, the accessibility of music industry technology provides widespread opportunities for local music activists to document their own work and make records and tapes.

While all of this has been happening, the electronics and music industries have poised themselves on the brink of a new technological world. The industry has already developed digital and laser techniques. The large record companies are joining forces with the electronics industries, investing millions of dollars in video disc technology. These same transnationals have also acquired controlling interests in satellite television channels that beam music videos around the world. What will be the consequences of this development for music activity in smaller nations, language groups, or cultures?

Figure 6.8 illustrates the current process. The large companies have succeeded in becoming efficient distributors of transnational music products, occasionally somewhat unwillingly with the support of an informal pirate sector. The electronic industry has provided technology that can be used by both the big transnationals and the small local operator. The record industry and the electronics industry have formed various alliances to capture the market (via standards) for the next generation of technological advances (digital, video discs, laser record players, and the like).

On the local level, musicians are influenced not only by their own cultural traditions but also by the transnational standards of the record industry regarding music content and "sound." The result is the production of various hybrid forms, either of local music with a transnational flavor, or transnational music with a local flavor. Thus we find ABBA being recorded in different forms all over the world—in Sri Lanka with a slightly Asian touch; in Wales sung in Celtic. As one Welsh-language enthusiast put it: "Buying a record in Welsh is an important political decision." Elvis Presley or ABBA material sung in a local language is seen by some as an aid to supporting minority cultures.

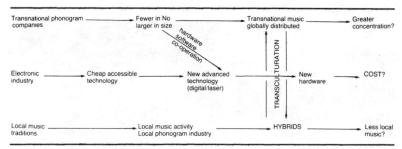

**Figure 6.8  Future Developments**

Much of the recorded music from the political "Swedish music movement" of the 1970s, or the Danish, Norwegian, and Finnish rock scenes, is based on styles of music that have been spread by transnational companies, but with Swedish or other Scandinavian lyrics imposed on top. The interesting question is: How far will the process of imitation and transculturation go? What relationship does this development have to the attempts of nations, groups, or individuals to develop or maintain their own cultural identity? Two possible extreme cases come to mind: a total degree of conformation to transnational norms or a total degree of pluralism among different groups in each society. Either way this will not lead to any identifiable cultural identity for any nation, assuming that this is something worth striving for. The billion dollar question that governments and international bodies concerned with world cultural heritage have to answer is: Can technology be used sensibly to document and enrich, or is the power of the music industry activity that we have outlined so great that we will all ultimately end up with just one song?

It seems clear that if we are to use the opportunities provided by the technology without falling into the pitfalls, then far more research is needed coupled with action on a governmental and international level. Our study provides some basic data, but it really only scratches the surface.

A number of suggestions can be made for further study. First, the relationship between media policy and musical activity must be explored. Since radio, television, video, cable, and satellites rely so greatly on recorded music, then their program policies regarding music assume considerable significance with regard to the retention, development, or even extinction of endangered species of world music. Where commercial organizations cannot satisfy this responsibility, then governments or other regulatory bodies must move in.

Figure 6.9   Two Different Worlds: But both part of the music industry. Above the control room of the tiny Gipsy Studio in Colombo, Sri Lanka, with one of the owners, Neville Perera. At right, where the big decisions are made. Dick Asher, former head of CBS records, in his natural habitat (photos by Roger Wallis).

Second, we must consider the strategies of the international music industry and their significance for local music industries. While the major music corporations are getting bigger in size and fewer in number, a steady stream of small entrepreneurs continually appear on the scene, often working with local modes of expression, providing an important cultural service. We have labelled them "the enthusiasts." How can their survival be guaranteed, irrespective of technological developments?

The effects of concentration and amalgamation within the transnational culture industries as well as the prerequisites for the survival and growth of small independent operations compose an important area for continued study. Such a study should also cover a more detailed look at the relative economic influence of hardware and software.

## Final Thoughts

We have examined the relationship between music and culture in a number of small nations. The results of our work hopefully will be relevant for an analysis of processes of symbolic communication in other contexts. The "sounds" originating in the small countries may not hold worldwide popularity, but they are an important part of the worlds's cultural heritage. Music industry technology can be used to flood them out of recognizable existence. Under other conditions, the technology can be used to retain, develop, and expand the "big sounds from small peoples." We know of no one who has put the case more succinctly than John Blacking (1973, p. 116):

> In a world in which authoritarian power is maintained by superior technology, and the superior technology is supposed to indicate a monopoly of intellect, it is necessary to show that the real sources of technology, of all culture, are to be found in the human body and in co-operative interaction between human bodies. . . . It is necessary to understand why a madrigal of Gesualdo or a Bach Passion, a sitar melody from India or a song from Africa . . . may be profoundly necessary for human survival, quite apart from any merit they may have as examples of human creativity and technical progress.

## NOTES

1. There are no reliable statistics regarding the number of electric pop groups in Sweden during the mid-1960s. Records from the Swedish Broadcasting Corporation's annual "Pop Band Competition" show that more than 1,000 groups entered at the height of its popularity. For every group that considered itself good enough for the competition, there must have been several more in different stages of development.

2. The term "baila" (Portuguese for "dance") reflects the Portuguese colonial influence of the seventeenth century that left its mark in the form of a popular style of music.

3. The ongoing saga of the incomes from this song has been covered extensively in the British trade paper, *Music Week*.

## REFERENCES

Blacking, J. (1973) *How musical is man?* Seattle: University of Washington Press.
Blaukopf, K. (1977) *Massenmedium Schallplatte.* Vienna.
Broadcast Music, Inc. (1984) *Collecting society research report.* New York.
Denisoff, R. S. (1975) *Solid gold: The record industry, its friends and enemies.* New York: Transaction.
Frith, S. (1981) *Sound effects: Youth, leisure, and the politics of rock and roll.* New York: Pantheon.

Gillet, C. (1972) *Sound of the city: The rise of rock and roll*. New York: Dell.

Gronow, P. (1980) *Statistics in the field of sound recordings*. Paris: UNESCO, division of statistics on culture and communication (Report C-21).

Hardy, P. (1983) *The record industry: The case for public intervention*. Report commissioned by the greater London City Council, London.

Hennion, A. & Vignolle, J. P. (1978) *Economie du disque*. Paris.

Hirsch, P. (1969) *The structure of the popular music industry*. Ann Arbor: University of Michigan, Institute for Social Research.

Nylov, G. (1984) *Assorted mimeos*. Stockholm: Rikskonserter.

Roe, K. (1984) *Youth and music in Sweden*. Paper presented to the International Association for Mass Communication Research, Prague.

Rutten, P. (1984) *Youth and music in the Netherlands*. Paper presented to the International Association for Mass Communication Research, Prague.

Soramaki, I & Haarman, J. (1978) *The international record industry*. Helsinki: Finnish Broadcasting Corporation.

# PART II

# Music Audiences:
## Culture and Subculture

# 7

# Listeners' Communicative Uses of Popular Music

## JAMES LULL

Communication research and theory building undertaken in recent years has accorded the audience member a powerful role in the disposition of symbolic imagery, clearly demonstrating that people are not simply the victims of powerful mass media. Social scientists refer to the "uses and gratifications" that people make of their routine contact with media, noting the influence of audiences in the use of media hardware and of content. Cultural theorists suggest that audience members interpret media texts, thereby negotiating meaning in a volitional manner that, similar to the social science perspective, assigns considerable influence to the thoughts and actions of human receivers of media content.

Of course it must always be kept in mind that the owners and managers of media institutions exercise great influence in processes of mass communication too, since they have the collective ability to manipulate the symbolic agenda. Still, no reasonable argument can be made to dismiss the audience as merely an aggregate of passive individuals bound together in some pathetic scenario of submission to the form and content of mass media and the economic edifice that supports it. This most basic theoretical assertion can perhaps be made most clear when audience members' uses and interpretations of *popular music* are examined. The purpose of this chapter and the articles that follow, therefore, is to discuss the lively character of the many different audiences for popular music, paying particular attention to the social and cultural surroundings that bear upon the contexts that constitute everyday life.

In particular, I will describe in this chapter some of the ways that popular music is absorbed, understood, and employed by people with special emphasis given to its most active devotees—youth. Music's role as an agent of socialization is discussed both in terms of shaping the definitions of self that youth acquire and its impact on their introduction to cultural themes. Particular audiences for types of music are explored as "taste cultures" and are examined from a communication rules perspective. Special attention is given to the concept of subculture and how music is so intimately involved in forms of resistance to mainstream culture.

The functions of music in any culture are integrated into the fundamental social operations of its people and these circumstances vary from culture to culture. Nonetheless, listeners create imaginative personal and social uses of music in all cultural contexts. In part, this is because music is available in so many varieties and can be experienced so easily in a large number of situations. Audiences participate in popular music in ways that are *physical* (singing along, tapping, clapping, dancing, sexual arousal, and so on); *emotional* ("feeling" the music, reminiscing, romanticizing, achieving a spiritual "high," and the like); and *cognitive* (processing information, learning, stimulating thought, contributing to memory, framing perceptions, and so forth).

A listener may relate to music directly by experiencing it in a very *personal* way. For instance, one might turn to music for soothing relaxation or to escape and enjoy the sound privately. This variety of communication takes place between the musician and the audience member, an event that is usually technologically mediated rather than "live." But the *social* dimensions of music listening are even more abundant. Music has countless applications in interpersonal communication, many of which will be taken up in this chapter and in the chapters that follow.

Music is a unique form of symbolic expression that can exist alone as a cultural event or product (concert, street performance, private singing and playing, records, tapes, compact discs, digital audio tape, and so on); serve as the content focus for another medium (radio, music video, some movies); or contribute to the overall aesthetics and meaning of another content display (background music for television and film, accompaniment for rituals such as church services, weddings, funeral ceremonies, sporting events, and so on). It is the soundtrack for shopping, driving, studying, and partying, among other activities. Music is sometimes accompanied by extreme physical movement (for instance, dance, aerobics) and is also often experienced in pensive, inactive moments.

In a discussion made more than 35 years ago about human uses of music, Riesman (1950, p. 360) suggested that "the same or virtually the same popular culture materials are used by audiences in radically different ways and for radically different purposes." Similarly, Rosengren and Windahl (1972) noted quite accurately that varying media content can often easily be interchanged to serve the same "function." It's clear that popular music is used by audience members for many of the same purposes that other media are used. One might "relax" with music or with a book. Music is a good "companion" just as television is. Intriguing questions an be asked about the utilitarian role of music given the apparent functional interchangeability of media. Foremost among the questions are: What conditions and contexts encourage utilization of music rather than another medium for the common array of audiences' uses and their presumed gratifications? And, what are the special capabilities of music for uses that are not made of other media? While these questions may never receive definitive answers, they shall help guide the descriptions and analyses that follow.

### Factors in the Use of Music

People who listen to music and incorporate it into their daily lives are typically engaged in purposeful, willing behavior. The assertion by Katz, Blumler, and Gurevitch (1974, p. 12) that "members of the audience put messages to use, and that such usages act as intervening variables in the process of effect" certainly is true of much music listening. It is also difficult to quarrel with their belief that media compete with each other, and with nonmedia sources, as utilitarian agents at the disposal of audience members. And, their claim that it is a "combined product of psychological dispositions, sociological factors, and environmental conditions that determines specific uses of the media" (p. 24) is true also of music since it seems to cover everything, so long as the political/economic facts of life are included under the heading "sociological factors" or "environmental conditions."

## Exposure, Consumption, Use

At the outset, distinctions are made here among three aspects of audience members' involvement with music. In order of complexity, the first consideration is *exposure*, referring only to the amount of contact a person has with music. This facet of the human experience with music refers only to time spent with various kinds of music. The second concept is *consumption*, referring to what is learned or remembered from exposure. This concept implies that music has some kind of impact, since listeners pick up information, feelings, even values from their contact with music. These considerations are difficult to measure because they are amenable to all the problems inherent in assessing mental orientations, notably the difficulties of trying to get people to describe emotional states rather than facts. The third and most complicated factor is *use*, a reference to the personal and social opportunities, applications, satisfactions, and gratifications that are related to exposure and consumption. Exposure, consumption, and use of music may occur in public or private settings, may be part of foreground or background activity, may be important or relatively unimportant, and may be successful or unsuccessful.

Music's many roles in the construction of social and cultural life are by no means limited to moments when audience members are exposed to this special variety of organized sound. Consequences of music listening extend into virtually all time periods and contexts. Delayed uses of music can take the form of conversations, for instance, where someone talks knowledgeably about music recently heard on record, in concert, or on radio. This use of music to qualify oneself as an expert on music was noted long ago by Riesman (1950) and the phenomenon is perhaps even more alive today since music is available in so many forms.

There are many cultural accessories associated with music that are used in postexposure applications. Having the right t-shirt or wall poster in the bedroom, for instance, can be a statement about the values or style of a young music listener. Audience members sometimes identify very strongly with a particular group or type of music (for instance, country & western, jazz, heavy metal, and so on) so that clothing, posters, bumper stickers, and other artifacts that express a musical preference also assert a proud statement from the listener that this artist or genre actually represents his or her personality in some way. These are but a few of the many postexposure applications made of music that will be discussed more fully in the following paragraphs.

## Categories and Contexts of Music Use

In this section, the ways that young people use popular music are analyzed by outlining some of music's attributes and various types of situations that are available as resources for the communicative purposes of music listeners.

### Use of Genres and Lyrics

Some listeners identify strongly with specific types of music and demonstrate their loyalties according to preferences held for particular genres. At times these distinctions are clear. A country & western music fan, for instance, would probably not be mistaken for a punk rocker. But a punk rocker might be confused with a "new waver" or with a heavy metal fan to those who are unfamiliar with the cultural distinctions that obtain between and among fans of these related genres. Some recent research by Christenson and Peterson (1986) found that at least 25 meaningful categories of popular music are distinguished by young listeners, and that this audience (what the authors term "rock's second generation") has strong and variable preferences for the types of music available to them.

Codes are used to signify particular genres, the sociocultural implications they carry, and their corresponding activities. "Rock" music really means "white" music now—hard edged, guitar-based, trebly, aggressive. As Larry Grossberg points out in the next chapter, this label has positive connotations for many fans. But, a club in San Francisco advertizes "absolutely no rock music," which means that patrons will not have to tolerate a Bruce Springsteen, U2, or Billy Idol dance mix. Instead, there is "dance" music, referring to black dance music, with few exceptions (that is non-black artists who have a black beat). The term "high energy" (fast-paced dance music drawing from black, white, and Latino artists) has strong connotations depending on the context. It signals "gay" in some situations, "Latino" or "Asian" in others. And, "new wave," a label that has outlived its original reference to post-punk dance-oriented music, is the generic label now for the Euro-disco dance music craze of California's young and musically active Vietnamese immigrants.

These cultural distinctions are important to pop music fans. The music of Elvis Costello might sound the same as that of Bruce Springsteen to an outsider, but young people know that the difference between these two artists is something more than musical. They represent different lifestyle orientations. Costello is a major exponent of "modern" music while Springsteen is the respected spokesman for blue-collar, East Coast rock and roll. Allegiance to one or the other says something important about the listener. Some modern music fans think Bruce Springsteen is boring old news. Some blue-collar rockers regard Costello as a lightweight, new wave wimp. These are not casual distinctions, and some members of these two camps would rather die than be associated with the other, even though their parents and other naive observers may not be able to tell the difference in their styles of music.

College students in California during the early days of new wave were easily able to describe characteristics that separated the then modern bands (for instance, B-52s, Devo, Costello, and so forth) from more mainstream rock and roll artists of the time (such as Springsteen, Rolling Stones, Fleetwood Mac, and so on). The students preferred traditional rock to new wave and offered a variety of reasons for their resistance to the then new style of pop music (Lull, 1982a). Schisms between genres of rock still exist in some quarters, as we recently found when analyzing reasons that adolescents have for watching or not watching MTV (Sun and Lull, 1986). Fans of hard rock and heavy metal were not enthusiastic about the frequent appearance of new wave bands on MTV in the middle 1980s, and some of them refused to watch for that reason.

There is historical evidence that social and cultural divisions exist among audience members for popular music based on differences in music preference. Teenage girls from the Chicago area were studied in one of the first social scientific analyses of popular music. "Happy" songs were preferred by girls from a wealthy suburb and "blues" songs were more popular in a less affluent area. The type of music that audiences prefer, in some cases, is related to socioeconomic conditions. Historically, of course, blues and country music are the domain of the working and lower classes. Classical music likewise has a cultural association with the socioeconomic elite. Some genres are associated with particular races: Soul, funk, jazz, and rap music have particular appeal to blacks. Country & western and most rock music appeals mainly to white listeners.

Lyrics of popular songs can be used as communicative resources too. Although most listeners claim that the "beat" or "sound" of the music is generally more important to them than the lyrics (for instance, Frith,

1981; Lull, 1982a), the impact of words must not be overlooked. Popular music projected a language that was useful to adolescents in their personal and social lives at least 30 years ago (Horton, 1957). Analyses of lyrics throughout the history of popular music have consistently demonstrated the pertinence of music at various periods (Carey, 1969; Cole, 1971; Harmon, 1972; Denisoff & Peterson, 1972; Pichaske, 1979; Chesebro, Nachman, Yannelli, & Foulger, 1985).

When a personally relevant or amusing lyric is transmitted in music it often becomes a focal point for listeners, sometimes overriding the physical and emotional attractiveness of the beat. The beat can be seen as a medium for delivering the lyric in a rhythmic way, sending it deep into the mind of the listener. Concentrating on the lyrics, the listener may use music in special ways. In situations where two listeners are paying attention to the lyrics, for instance, one of them can use the message to make a point to the other person. Singing along with the words "you're no good, you're no good, you're no good," for example, could be an effective message to someone within hearing distance. People remember key lyrics—those that have special meaning to the self or to someone else who shares the code.

Sometimes lyrics of songs are used in ways that are less benign. In the United States during the middle 1980s the lyrics of songs became big news. One serial murderer (the "Night Stalker," a song title) said that the "satanic" lyrics of the heavy metal band, AC/DC, inspired his crimes. The so-called devil worship of much heavy metal music was criticized by moral majority religious organizations, television evangelists, and others. In another case, a boy said that the lyrics to the song "Suicide Solution" by Ozzy Osborne gave him the idea to take his life, which he did. His father unsuccessfully sued the artist and record company for causing the death. These are extreme examples, of course, but they demonstrate vividly the point that lyrics have communicative potential in interpersonal settings. We will again raise the issue of the importance of lyrics in the next major section of this chapter, when youth socialization to content themes of popular music is discussed.

Perhaps the least productive argument that can take place in the discussion of the impact of popular music is that which attempts to assess the relative power of the lyrics versus the beat or other attributes of music. It is clear that both the lyrics and beat have a profound impact, and that they are not separate factors in the first place. The next step in this attempt to dissect and compare elements of pop music imagery will probably take place in the realm of video, where another unsolvable debate will arise regarding the relative impact of the sight vis-à-vis the sound of the music.

## Use of Aesthetic Properties and Technical Attributes

Music has the ability to stimulate extraordinary emotional feelings. For this reason, audience members often identify in ways with their favorite musicians that differ from their "parasocial interactions" with other media figures. Music can elicit feelings of mental and physical "ecstasy" that can lead to "peak experiences," a kind of sensual stimulation that may be matched only by sex (Panzarella, 1980). Of course, music is often used to accompany sexual activity and sometimes a third element, drugs, is involved. This combination was formalized in the pop music classic, Ian Dury's "Sex, and Drugs, and Rock and Roll."

Unlike television, film, newspapers, magazines, and books, music does not require visual attention. Not only does the audience member have the freedom to experience music in this nonvisually focused way, he or she need not sit down to consume music, a position that generally characterizes reception of other entertainment media. In fact, music stimulates movement of several varieties.

The pleasures of popular music are conveniently available in most countries of the world. Several factors enhance the utility of music. First, music is relatively inexpensive. Although records, tapes, and compact discs purchased in retail outlets are not cheap, there is a lot of trading and loaning of records, buying of used albums, taping of albums, and tape duplication. Music can be recorded off the radio, a practice that is of course regretted by the music industry, which constantly encourages radio stations not to play albums on the air uninterrupted. Further, the technology required for high-quality audio reproduction is portable, permitting the use of music in nearly every imaginable environment. And, except for music programmed on the radio, music is under the control of the user. Desired songs can be played at times and locations chosen by the listener. The user, therefore, is himself or herself an active programmer of music, especially now in the age of the compact disc, thereby asserting great control over the contexts in which music plays a communicative role.

Variable volume is another dimension of music's usefulness. The liner notes on some hard rock albums instruct consumers to PLAY THIS MUSIC LOUD in order to get the full impact of the recorded performance. But high volume is also useful to the person who wants to utilize music for getting attention. A cassette tape system or radio blaring out of a car that cruises the local boulevard is sure to turn heads. Urban inhabitants, especially those of major East Coast cities in the United States, often step out with their "boxes" or "ghetto blasters" pouring out high-volume popular music, a practice that recently has been discouraged through legal ordinances passed in some communities. The "break dance" and "electro-beat" phenomena of the 1980s are among a variety of contemporary street dances/entertainment that involve the use of popular recorded music played back in the public space.

High volume can be used to attract attention for punitive reasons too. Turning up the sound on the stereo is one way to irritate friends, neighbors, parents, or other targets of anger. Even when volume is not being used to punish someone, it is often a part of the total experience of listening to popular music. The potential for incredible volume levels of high-quality sound is a unique aspect of music compared to other forms of entertainment. Nearly every young person in the United States at some point hears a pop music concert live, and comes into thrilling contact with sound so loud and compelling that it seemingly "takes over" the body. Parents and audiologists have warned teenagers for years that high-volume concerts will cause permanent hearing loss. The warnings have had little impact on listening behavior.

## Contexts for the Use of Music

Personal and social applications of music are influenced by users' intentions and the opportunities and limitations that characterize settings where music is heard. The most basic situations are those where the listener employs music alone. Uses of music under these conditions extend from the accompaniment of mundane, practical tasks to powerful moments of personal introspection. Music is used to lessen the drudgery of work in contexts that range from household chores and homework to the aesthetic improvement and humanization of industrial work places. Music emanating from car radios and stereos helps pass the time for travelers, cabbies, and truck drivers. People dance and do exercises at home while listening to music. They escape from personal burdens by turning on the stereo, helping to stimulate fantasies and relax. Music permits reminiscing about times and people in the past. It is a convenient cover-up for unwanted sounds in urban settings. Children and adolescents escape from their families to listen to music, often in their bedrooms (Larson & Kubey, 1983). All of these moments may simply help the person past time, provide companionship, or both.

The social uses of music are just as common and, in some ways, are more complicated since they require interpersonal coordination. Many of the personal uses of music discussed above (for instance, relaxation, dancing, reminiscing, and so on) can also be made in interpersonal or group settings. But there are a variety of formal and informal social situations where music is central to the lively interaction of people.

Cultural collectives are sometimes defined in terms of their associations with music. The definitive moment of punk subculture, for instance, is the live performance where young people meet each other, share the ideology and aesthetic of punk, and engage in the physically involving "thrashing" and "stage diving" (Lull, 1987). The shows bring together members of this oppositional subculture in a ritualistic communal celebration. In a similar way, men and women who appreciate a particular type of music may also share special feelings during concerts. In San Francisco, more than 20,000 classical music fans gather annually for a free outdoor concert put on by the local symphony. This event stirs friendly feelings for those who attend, bringing together some people who may otherwise not have much in common. Music, and contexts of its live creation, become useful to listeners for many purposes. These large outdoor gatherings provoke certain sentiments that may not be achieved any other way.

Music plays utilitarian roles in smaller, more idiosyncratic social contexts too. It helps lessen the inhibitions of people in social situations, facilitates getting attention and approval, provides security in foreign environments, provides topics for conversations, contributes to peer group acceptance and reinforcement, is an appropriate audio backdrop for romantic and sexual exchanges, provides a forum for family communication (for instance, group singing), and generates a constant resource for general entertainment among other uses. Young people use music as a basis for forming impressions of each other and for constructing their friendship networks and daily activities (Clarke, 1973). Adolescents sometimes develop friendship groups on the basis of shared musical taste and certain members of these peer groups become valued opinion leaders in the world of music (Frith, 1981). Music as the primary content of contemporary radio stations also functions well for youth in settings where this medium is useful (Mendelsohn, 1964).

The interpersonal uses of music, then, range from one-to-one situations as diverse as romantic encounters and arguments to informal peer group activities, slightly more formal parties and dances, shows and concerts, and definitive subcultural behavior. Music is also used socially in highly institutionalized setting such as schools, churches, and entire communities. Nations use music for patriotic purposes that in extreme cases can develop into anthems of social control, as happened in Nazi Germany (Warren, 1943). National anthems are routinely played before sporting events in the United States and elsewhere, stimulating thousands of people to stand and face the flag without questioning the curious relationship between sports and patriotism. Recently, live music (usually an organ or synthesizer) is played to accompany the tempo of the action of baseball and basketball games in order to create some excitement, particularly if the home team is losing. Pep bands at football games are a tradition in schools in the United States, and some basketball teams use recorded music as a part of their "warm-up" rituals. The noncompetitive Harlem Globetrotters basketball team has a popular theme song, "Sweet Georgia Brown," that has become famous as part of its basketball show.

### The Importance of Moods

Research on the social and cultural functions of music invariably reflects the mood states of listeners. Music may be used to establish, reinforce, or change moods. The term "mood music" refers to this unique ability of the medium to create or sustain these special feelings. Music can put a person "in the right mood" for romanticizing, for partying, for punk thrashing, for creating the right atmosphere for weddings, funerals, presidential inaugurations, athletic events, meditation, and many other activities. Music helps create an aesthetic ambiance so that events may be maximally enjoyed. This fact can be taken to an unfortunate extreme. One of the country's most beautiful national parks, the Natural Bridge of Virginia, is, as its name implies, a spectacular natural stone edifice that attracts hundreds of thousands of visitors each year. When you walk down along the river and turn the bend to get your first view of this enormous rock arch, you cannot help but notice immediately the sound of a lush string melody coming from, of all places, little speakers embedded in the cavernous "natural" walls of the river bed. The "sound track" for the Natural Bridge is meant, I suppose, to enhance the experience for visitors who are apparently considered to be unable to create the maximum experience themselves.

And, for those who want to store the memory of their visit to the Natural Bridge forever, a copy of the album is available at the gift shop on the way out.

Music and moods are conceptually related in lots of other contexts. College students reported that "new wave" rock music was useful to them when they were in the mood to be "rowdy, crazy, radical, energetic, hyped up, when they felt like fooling around, when they wanted to dance or when they were drunk or stoned" (Lull, 1982a). Generally these students found the then unfamiliar music to be useful only under conditions having to do with mood. More generally, the students believed that the fast-paced modern music was not functional for relaxing or romanticizing, two commonly mentioned uses of music made by young people (Gantz, Gartenberg, Pearson, & Schiller, 1978). Larson and Kubey (1983) found music to encourage "higher moods" with friends, but "lower moods" with family members and that music was enjoyed the most when adolescent members of their sample felt "out of control." And for people of all ages, music helps put people to sleep at night and wake them up in the morning.

*Summary*

Music contributes to the construction of meaning given by listeners to the ongoing stream of events that constitutes personal, social, and cultural life. At times these moments involve friends, family members, or thousands of people who are unknown to the user. Music may play a central or peripheral role in human interaction. It may be part of the foreground or background of any communicative situation. Locations for the use of music such as homes, institutions, vehicles, parks, stores, and the street provide contexts for different imaginative applications. The various electronic media that are used to produce musical sound— and the live performance—also contribute to the range of functional resources that popular music supplies its fans.

## Music and Youth Socialization

Popular music is readily available to most young people in the more developed parts of the world via a variety of media, including FM and AM radio, television, cable and video, records, compact discs, and cassette tapes that can be played on home stereo systems or portable units such as ghetto blasters and Walkman-type units. Even very young children begin to develop a special relationship with music reflected in media exposure that differs greatly from their elders (Christenson, DeBenedittis, & Lindlof, 1985). Beyond that, music listeners' personal agendas, vocabularies, language patterns, interaction styles, and what they are motivated to learn about from interpersonal and mediated information sources all begin to take characteristic form long before adolescence.

But adolescence signals a time in the life of young people when dramatic changes take place. Not only does the body reach a stage of sexual maturity, but mental orientations and lifestyle activities begin to change too. Adolescence, for many young people, is a time of turmoil and resistance. Popular music fits nicely into the daily life of adolescents since its lyrical content and the atmosphere that can be created by its sound reflect many of their concerns.

It must be kept in mind that the primary use of all the nonprint media by people of all ages and lifestyles is for "entertainment." But music is a resource that encourages other more complicated and meaningful communicative uses too. Many young people use music in their struggles with unsympathetic power holders such as parents, teachers, bosses, and other authority figures (Frith, 1981). A fundamental adolescent use of music is the "need" to declare independence from parents (Hebdige, 1979). This is often done by the adolescent in his or her own private way, but sometimes adolescents construct social bonds in the form of subcultures that increase the intensity of the conflict. Under these circumstances youth display "subcultural style" through dance, music, fashion, language, and other avenues of expression that help demarcate their cultural space (Hebdige, 1979), a theme that will be taken up in later paragraphs of this chapter, and in several of the chapters that follow.

In contemporary American society, rock, soul, and pop play central roles in the cultivation of many of the personal and social goals of youth. The heavy beat, sexual lyrics, and aggressive tone of much popular music resonates with the emotional character of many adolescents, giving them abundant popular culture material with which to identify and a resource to exploit for personal and interpersonal objectives. Generally, young people use music to resist authority at all levels, assert their personalities, develop peer relationships and romantic entanglements, and learn about things that their parents and the schools aren't telling them.

Music influences socialization in two basic ways. These are not completely separate phenomena, but each reflects a unique focus. The first has to do with the role of music in the emerging *self-concept* of youthful listeners. Here we are less concerned with what children and adolescents learn specifically from the music, but rather how music in general fits into their active lives as they monitor their own entry to the adult world. Second, we will consider the impact of *content themes* to which youth are exposed through popular music. Young people participate ambitiously in their uses of music, a fact that contributes to the power of this medium in their socialization.

### Music and the Self-Concept

Children are born into a world that is saturated with media, including music and the various delivery systems that reproduce it. The easy availability of popular music makes this symbolic form useful to children at an early age. Rock and roll and soul music, early vivid departures from the bland pop music of the Tin Pan Alley era, have become resources that clearly separate certain matters of taste from parents, most teachers, and other aged encumbrances that young people find in the way of fun and self-determined growth. Learning how to use music is a joyful preoccupation of youth.

Very young children can be observed in all cultures to have a special relationship with music. They often sing, dance wildly, even fall down painlessly when they listen to music in private and public locations, apparently greatly moved by the sound. Many of them are unaware or unconcerned about what other people might think of their spontaneous and often creative physical expressions. Although this kind of uninhibited response to music tends to diminish for most children when they enter school, they continue to enjoy music, especially the emotional meanings that can be understood sensually and the power of the beat. This multiple sensory involvement with music gives it special meaning as an agent of communication and socialization. As I have claimed elsewhere (Lull, 1985a), *active involvement with a medium increases its potential as an agent of socialization* and there may be no more dramatic example of this than the actions of youth as they enjoy and employ popular music.

Adolescence is a stressful period for many teenagers. Not only are their bodies changing, but they are casting about looking for excitement and avenues for creative expression and growth that are not available to them within the confines of home and school. The family and television, two entities seemingly inseparable in the Western world at least, no longer provide the kind of stimulation that many adolescents seek. Adolescents typically lessen the amount of contact they have with their families, increase the rate of interaction they have with peer groups, develop greater mobility in their daily routines, and alter their media habits. The amount of time spent watching television decreases during this time (Comstock, Chaffee, Katzman, & Roberts, 1978; Lyle & Hoffman, 1972; McLeod & Brown, 1976), while exposure to audio media increases (Avery, 1979). The time that is spent watching television becomes more of a peer coviewing, sibling coviewing, or solitary viewing experience (Chaffee, McLeod, & Atkin, 1971), especially since the arrival of music video (Miller & Baran, 1984). As a result, the role of parents in the socialization of children of this age diminishes (McLeod & Brown, 1976). There is a general reorientation of youth with respect to sources of information about how to live. The new interpersonal liaisons and media activities interact with each other. Just as television is part of family life, film, radio, and especially popular music are parts of peer group life.

Relationships that exist between and among the peer group, media, and educational institutions must be taken into consideration. Young people are required to spend much of their turbulent adolescent years in school, an institution that introduces students to ways of thinking that generally support mainstream culture and requires of them nondisruptive, conventional behavior. But, the school also becomes a place where friendships are consummated and peer groups formed, developments that are more important to some students than formal learning in the classroom. The roles of music and peers in relation to educational attainment is an issue that has been explored in recent research, and Keith Roe provides a thorough summary of this work and an original contribution to this literature in his chapter in this volume.

Music is rightfully given an important place in the socialization of American black youth in a setting that a black scholar calls the "dance party" (Clark, 1974). The dance party is a learning context for children as young as 11 years old. Here black youth are free to interact in a setting that is not noticeably influenced by white society. In this "cultural ceremony," young blacks are socialized into culturally appropriate patterns of interaction between males and females, black unity and the spirit of community, the realities of alcohol consumption and drug use, and the use of dance as a "celebration" of the culture. As one of Clark's young subjects observed,

When (black recording artist) James Brown says "Everybody over there, get on up. Everybody over here, get on up," you *know* he means you and then when his heavy music starts it's almost like somebody sayin' "It's celebration time" [Clark, 1974, p. 150].

The dance party is a kind of music-based cultural ritual that provides a context for learning social roles from the event itself, *not* so much from actual thematic content of the lyrics. The young consumer of music begins to understand certain vital aspects of social behavior in the cultural context he or she occupies. One can view the dance party as a kind of microcosm of life itself where some of the rules for interaction are learned and imitated. The patterns that develop may or may not be appropriate in other cultural settings. For instance, the sexist and chauvinistic language and interaction style that typifies gender relations at the dance party (Clark, 1974, p. 153) may be completely unacceptable in family or work settings.

Of course, the dance party is only one environment where music is used in black culture. Not only is music heard in the homes and work places of blacks, but it is a lively component of street life in black neighborhoods. Music was singled out from all other cultural materials and media as the most important influence on black youth in a television documentary presented by CBS in 1986 that lamented teenage pregnancy and the soaring number of unwed mothers.

At times preference for a type of music can signal a personal statement in a strong way. Membership in the punk subculture, for instance, announces a lifestyle orientation of a particular type that asserts some vivid features of the self-concept. In the punk subculture there are "rules" for interaction that help its members identify with a peer group, though the forms of punk expressionism are typically paradoxical. These patterns will be discussed more fully in subsequent sections of this chapter.

Apparently the socialization of adolescents to particular behavioral patterns is not distributed evenly among males and females. Gantz et al. (1978) found that girls were more likely than boys to think that music is "gratifying." In the Swedish studies (Roe, 1983; Rosengren, Roe, & Sonesson, 1983), low grades stimulated girls more than boys to become peer oriented and to adopt music listening preferences that favored rock, pop, and punk styles. The punk lifestyle, however, is a blatantly masculine scene. Girls who embrace the music and subculture must make some major adjustments from any behavior that reflects the preponderance of sex-role information they previously received and used (Lull, 1987). In England, Frith (1981) found boys more likely than girls to be opinion leaders in the use of music. Abt (this volume) found that females were more "involved" in music and music video and girls also watch MTV more than boys, at least on weekends (Sun & Lull, 1986).

### Content Themes of Music

Like the content of all mass media, music contains themes that represent particular symbolic versions of reality. Youth and adults are exposed to values represented in music and, to some degree, integrate those themes into the substance of their everyday lives. But popular music is not the first or most pervasive socializing influence on children. Parents and the extended family, television, nursery and primary schools, religious institutions, and youth groups all have an initial, largely uncontested opportunity to inscribe their hegemonic visions and values on the experiences of young children.

Even prior to adolescence, however, children begin to find alternative information about the issues that face them. Music is a primary source of this knowledge that often arrives uncensored in their homes, partly because their parents don't like the sound of it and therefore avoid it. Ideas contained in music are often perceived and interpreted privately or with friends in locations that are not supervised by adults. Of course there is no homogeneous, alternative ideology expressed in music. But much popular and subcultural music does contain themes that conflict with the common ideological orientations of mainstream culture as a whole, and with particular philosophies of life that characterize the social environments occupied by children.

Much criticism has been directed at the record industry and radio stations throughout the years about the lyrics of popular songs because of their suspected "harmful" influence in the socialization of youth. The federal government in the United States through the Federal Communications Commission has issued warnings to radio stations about the airing of songs that contain explicit references to drugs and sex. Religious organizations, particularly those of the "moral majority," have spoken of rock music as the work of the devil and in some cases have alleged that demonic messages could be heard by playing certain records backward, including not only songs by bands such as Led Zeppelin, but even the theme song to the old American television series, "Mr. Ed" (an innocuous program about a talking horse). The music of Prince, who became extremely popular in the mid-1980s in the United States, alarmed many parents when they listened to the lyrics and heard direct and provocative messages about sex. A group of religious leaders in Minneapolis, Minnesota, the hometown of Prince, held a public burning of his records as his popularity climbed. The number one pop record in West Germany in early 1986, "Jeanny" (by Austrian pop singer Falco), was banned because some critics thought the lyrics of the song described the murder of a young girl. Other instances of the power of lyrics to provoke censorship have been noted in previous sections of this chapter. The point should be clear. Lyrics matter.

Especially during stressful periods of world conflict, lyrics sometimes reflect critical political positions. But even during relatively tranquil times there are strong "oppositional" messages in the lyrics of some popular songs, thereby creating opportunities for listeners to hear points of view that contradict the opinions they more commonly receive from institutional sources of information and entertainment. Englishman Paul Hardcastle's single, "19," for instance, became the top hit in Great Britain in 1985, and a popular dance song throughout the world. The song is a powerful critique of the Vietnam war and calls attention to the many problems that veterans from that era have encountered.

Points of view about controversial issues are expressed in the lyrics written and performed by even the most apparently banal artists. Michael Jackson hit the very top worldwide with his album, *Thriller*, which contained a song titled "Wanna Be Startin' Somethin'." The lyrics convey the message that girls who cannot afford to have children should not yet have a baby. The song clearly asserts that the mother and child will suffer greatly and Jackson recommends that this kind of pregnancy be avoided. There is no way to document empirically the effect of this song on young girls. But millions of them bought the record or tape, played it over and over, sang the lyrics perfectly, danced to the song, talked about it with their friends, and interacted symbolically with the artist as they did so. Michael Jackson may have been able at least to bring the issue of birth control to the awareness of literally millions of young girls with simple, practical verses that reflect especially the problems of childbirth among the poor.

Other Michael Jackson songs reflect a different ideology. He sings a duet with Paul McCartney on the *Thriller* album titled "The Girl is Mine," that is not likely to please feminist listeners. The song "Thriller" itself contains references that some people have considered supportive of violence, and other romantic songs on the album surely have stimulated sexual fantasies. Frith (1981), in his cultural studies of English youth, found that music is a commonly used medium of access by girls to new feelings of sexual interest and romantic fantasies of which their parents are not aware. Similarly, young males related to the sexual power of the music, terming it "cock rock," where the guitar becomes a symbol of the penis.

The San Francisco punk study (Lull, 1987) is another illustration of the ideological power of the lyrics as an agent of socialization. Most punks are very young but, contrary to popular belief, a substantial number of them are sincerely interested in social, political, and economic issues and have a desire to change things. The angry sound of much punk music relfects the active and critical orientation of the subculture.

Punk subcultural ideologies are often transmitted powerfully in the context of the live show. At one San Francisco concert put on by the Dead Kennedys, a local band (no longer together) that had an international following, lead singer Jello Biafra said between songs, "Thirty to forty thousand dead in Central America so the bananas keep coming real cheap to Safeway"; about the multinational corporations: "They say, we just want you to go home, turn on TV, shut up, and go to sleep." The singer from another local punk band, the Dicks, introduced a song from the stage shortly after the 1984 presidential election by saying, "I hope all the motherfuckers that voted for Reagan will burn up. And all the motherfuckers that voted for Mondale will burn up. It's too bad that we have to burn up with'em." These are messages that most young people certainly do not get at home, school, or other traditional agencies of socialization. Further, while the "feeling" or texture of punk music may be its aesthetic signature, the lyrics of songs, and interjections made during public performance, are part of the content themes that this form of music represents.

### The Taste Culture Perspective on Music

What kinds of people like what kinds of music and why? Do fans of one genre or another come from similar backgrounds? What do audiences or consumers of particular artists or genres have in common? Social class? Race? Age? Are people with similar personalities attracted to certain types of music regardless of the demographic indicators listed above? Why do some people prefer but one kind of music while others appreciate a variety of song styles? Why do some people maintain their preferences for particular types of music while others change? These are some of the most nagging yet intriguing questions that can be asked about the enormous audience for popular music. We are concerned here with the segmentation of the large audience into groups that prefer particular types of music. These individual groups of fans are sometimes called "taste cultures."

In his chapter in this volume and in his previous writing, George H. Lewis has advanced an argument for the taste culture perspective (Lewis, 1980, 1981, 1982). According to taste culture theory, traditional sociological analyses based solely on demographic considerations (for instance, social class, race, gender, education, and so on) are inadequate. Taste culture theorists believe that audiences are attracted to particular sounds more by "choice" than by opportunities for "access." Taste cultures are said to exist in the United States especially after World War II, since the generally robust economy has permitted the spread of entertainment forms such as recorded music to nearly everyone.

Some theorists in communications and sociology have given "culture" the primary position in their reasoning (Gans, 1974; Carey & Kreiling, 1974; Kreiling, 1978), suggesting that social structure does not sufficiently explain the different preferences that subaudiences have for media content. Some examples from music audiences illustrate the taste culture debate. Dixon, Ingram, Levinson, and Putnam (1979), for instance, found that the early American audience for punk rock was bound together more by their extreme interest in contemporary music than by any social class clustering. Indeed, their research indicated that fans of the Sex Pistols were high in socioeconomic status, a fact that stands in conflict with the socioeconomic origins of this music, especially in England. This research suggests that a taste culture that chooses to participate in the latest rock music developments may exist, and that this informal aggregation is primarily united by the interest its members have in new forms of musical entertainment rather than by any shared demographic considerations. Fans of the Sex Pistols were primarily young, white males. But the point is that the vast majority of young, white males were *not* fans of this band, so purely demographic considerations explain very little.

Peterson and DiMaggio (1975) came to roughly the same conclusion when they studied audiences for country & western music. Though race and age could partly explain the composition of the audience for this music, "more people of the same strata, race and age, do not like country music" (Peterson & DiMaggio, 1975, p. 503). They introduced the term "culture class" as a descriptor of subaudiences, attempting to link preferences in cultural taste with social situational considerations.

While it is true that some taste cultures may have somewhat homogenous demographic characteristics, it is also apparent that some genres, songs, and artists appeal to a wide spectrum of audience members. The music industry has a term for artists who appeal to a wide variety of people. These are "crossover" artists. They are highly coveted stars of the culture industries because they sell to more than one traditional market. While a contemporary artist like Sade, for instance, may appeal greatly to "black music" fans (this is a common distinction made in the music and radio industries and appears under a similar heading in nearly every trade journal), she also "crosses over" into the realm of "new wave/progressive," "adult contemporary," and "contemporary hits." The ultimate crossover artist of the early and mid-1980s, of course, was Michael Jackson, whose music appeals to millions of fans who are black and white, female and male, very old and very young, rich and poor, straight and gay, old fashioned and modern. Artists like Sade or Jackson are comparatively "open texts," cultural resources that permit listeners to read into the performer and the music what *they* want.

Proponents of the taste culture perspective submit that audience members choose cultural materials of their liking and that these choices cannot be explained by traditional theories of social status. Audience members are thought to negotiate the meaning of music and other cultural fare and to "find significance" in these materials (Lewis, this volume). *How* this significance is found—in part, the basis for choice—is an issue that continues to go unanswered by taste culture theorists, though Lewis has recently provided a framwork for examining this issue in a cross-cultural context, and has developed an explanation more fully in his chapter in this book.

## Communication Rules and Music Patterns

In his study of South Africa's Venda tribe, John Blacking found their music-making and music-consuming activities to be highly structured within the cultural context:

The rules of Venda music are not arbitrary. In order to create new Venda music you must be a Venda, sharing Venda social and cultural life from early childhood [Blacking, 1973, p. 8].

Blacking was clear in his analysis that particular understandings underlie cultural behavior, and that these agreements inhere in music activity and all other human undertakings. These patterns of human behavior can be considered *communication rules*. For purposes of this writing, *rules refer not only to explicit or implicit prescriptions for contextually appropriate behavior, but to the deep structural themes that reside in cultural activity as well.* A culture or subculture, therefore, might be identified by its rules. Rules are socially sanctioned patterns of organized cultural behavior that stand in contrast to the possibility of random human energy. The actual content and meaning of communication rules are sometimes unknown except to members of the culture where they exist.

The punk subculture provides evidence of the importance of rules. In order to understand punks, it is necessary to become aware of the codes, modes of expression, and meanings that exist in their social communication. One clear example of the existence of subcultural rules is the concept of paradox—for the punks, this refers to purposive contradictions between appearance and reality (Lull, 1987). Punks routinely create seemingly illogical behavioral sequences where an action is contradicted by a subsequent action. Second, many statements and actions made by punks actually mean the opposite of what they appear to signify. While these communications may be confusing to the outsider—someone who lives according to different rules—they are clearly understood by those within the subculture. Indeed, subcultural membership requires this understanding.

To observe communication rules, one must examine the two domains in which they exist. These contexts are *microsocial* and *macrosocial* (Lull, 1982b). Microsocial settings are the natural interpersonal environments where routine, everyday interactions are conducted (for example, families, peer groups, work groups, neighborhoods, and the like). Microsocial rules reflect interaction patterns that characterize these settings, and are fundamentally determined and controlled within the confines of these locations. A microsocial rule, then, could be any behavior that originates and is controlled in an intimate setting, such as the family home or peer group terrain.

Macrosocial rules, on the other hand, refer to patterns of interaction that exist between media sources and audience members, or between one audience member and another where behavior is influenced by some agent external to their personal situations, especially mass media. For instance, the veejay on a music video channel might strongly recommend the music of a particular band. Stimulated by the media personality and by the music, viewers throughout the nation are influenced to buy a recording made by this artist. The pattern of consumption that results is largely a response to an external authority that has prescribed a cultural behavior in the form of a consumer purchase. Indeed, the mere presence of videos on MTV and the other video channels, and music played on radio stations and in clubs, conditions patterns of consumption, and of culture, a fact that drives the entertainment industries financially and helps define formats for social and cultural interaction.

Interactions between youth and their parents, between youth and their peers, and between youth and media representatives can all be considered from a communication rules perspective. Culture patterns develop in part stimulated and guided by the structural circumstances that surround youth's interaction with music. In the United States, youth typically have a high degree of control over their patterns of music exposure, consumption, and use since they develop private ways to experience these cultural materials. This freedom is not granted to youth in some other parts of the world, the Middle East and the Far East, for example, where the experiences of young people are more closely monitored.

The rules approach to understanding sociocultural activity involves the *choice* of particular behaviors often in relation to the demands of authorities who supervise these activities in some way. In the family, parents and older siblings may control the patterns of behavior. In peer groups, the oldest, strongest, or most clever members may have great influence. In the relations that audience members have with the mass media, the personalities who are featured and their sponsors occupy positions of influence over the audience. So habits develop, choices are restricted to a range permitted or recommended by authority, and the extended interpersonal strategies that emerge from differential motivations do so according to power relations (Lull, 1982b).

The result is patterned human activity that can be peculiar to a small group of people or characteristic of a larger subculture or culture. In the United States, for instance, one might observe the consumer orientation of the larger society, yet also see subgroups who are defined principally by their opposition to consumerism. Communication rules are not only prescriptions of human activity that congeal into patterns, but are evolutionary patterns themselves that become implicitly prescriptive. These are sometimes referred to as "norms" that promote "preferred" behavior (Shimanoff, 1980, p. 65). They may begin as indications of negotiated meaning within contexts where structural relations intercede, then advance in popularity to become normative for the larger society.

Rules are sometimes in conflict with each other, particularly for young people whose behavioral patterns inside and outside the home may reflect immersion in two very different interpersonal contexts, requiring a fair amount of rule switching in order to maintain stability in each environment. There is also a discrepancy often apparent between the rules for living advocated by the family and ideas transmitted to young people from the various mass media. The mediated messages may encourage some family members to participate in behavior that is forbidden at home. In this way adolescents, for example, are socialized to "deviant" perspectives on matters ranging from personal habits to more abstract ideological concerns. Patterns that reflect "normal" or "deviant" behavior are communication rules of competing substance.

Of course, "rules are made to be broken," and departure from the norm is itself a normal characteristic of a dynamic society. Young music listeners are especially good at breaking rules, sometimes because they genuinely feel restricted and need to expand their experiences outside the permitted boundaries, and other times just for the shock value that can be transmitted to authorities who attempt to uphold the status quo. Hippies and punks have been successful rule breakers. The hippie movement was in part a slap in the face of the "establishment" generally and of their parents particularly, since the older generation was typically supportive of discipline, toil, and obedience to the policies of the American government, which was involved in a war that seemed wrong and personally threatening to many young people then. Punks, with a different style, have also outraged mainstream society. And punks slap their own faces too. Some of them, including members of various bands, have started to grow their hair long in order to disturb their own peers, suggesting a symbolic unwillingness to conform even within the deviant subculture (Lull, 1987).

### Subculture and Music

Stuart Hall has pointed out that culture-producing practices are only "tendencies" of a society to "reproduce . . . its structure of domination" (Hall, 1979). There are many pockets of resistance to this loose structure. In some cases, men and women reject much of the dominant culture that faces them each day and invent alternative ways of thinking and acting. Sometimes these paths are forged in fairly individualistic ways. At other times social members cohere in their shared preference for alternative lifestyles. It may be useful to refer to these nontraditional groups as subcultures.

If a culture is a "particular way of life" (Williams, 1965), then a subculture is an alternative particular way of life that contrasts with the mainstream culture. Deviant subcultural style is expressed in ordinary behavior as well as in art (Williams, 1965). This can involve music, of course, but also verbal and nonverbal communication, fashion, gender relationships, religion, food, family, and peer interaction (Hebdige, 1979). Members of subcultures carry out certain behaviors that are codified or implicit in the rule-governed patterns that help define and characterize particular groups.

Subcultures can encompass all aspects of human existence or be specific to a particular part of life. Some people participate in typical patterns of vocational life, for instance, but assume deviant patterns in their political activity, sexual preferences, or artistic tastes. On the other hand, one's commitment to a subculture can reflect total immersion in an alternative lifestyle. Personal commitment to favorite types of music can reflect either of these orientations and it is often difficult from the outside to judge the degree of commitment that a member of a subculture has. The many British subcultures discussed by Iain Chambers and E. Ellis Cashmore in this volume, for instance, possess very different degrees and types of commitment to subcultural ideology. When the commitment to a music-based subculture is strong, it signals perhaps the ultimate "use" of music.

Realizing that their differences fall along a continuum rather than into exclusive categories, music subcultures can be considered to be of two primary types (Denisoff & Peterson, 1972). The most common is the "aesthetic subculture" or taste culture. These groups are composed of musicians and their audiences who create and appreciate music that differs from popular genres in style only. Jazz, classical, and much ethnic music (for instance, salsa, polka, flamenco) are in this category. Aesthetic subcultural music typically has no overt political objectives. It celebrates alternative forms or tempos that are largely excluded from radio airplay because of its limited commercial appeal. Much of this music exists on the periphery of mainstream culture, but is deeply loved by its subcultural adherents. There very well may be socioeconomic associations among audience members in these subcultures, but the groupings do not result from common political interests.

The second category of subcultures discussed here is "oppositional." Their music has a purpose that greatly transcends the pleasure of hearing alternative sounds. It is the music of subgroups that resist particular social institutions or practices. There is an ideological convergence between the artists and listeners of these various musics. Oppositional subcultural music *confirms* political positions held by its creators and listeners. It legitimizes social and political ideologies and movements by reinforcing alternative values and actions. Within a particular subcultural system, information is distributed through recorded music and live performances. As one punk said about the information potential of subcultural music: "We know that Reagan sucks, but we need to know more about *why*. Our music does that." When oppositional sentiments are distributed through record and tape sales and radio airplay, the ideological confirmation process is further enhanced. Members of subcultures find that their alternative lifestyles are noticed and given public exposure, creating the possibility for *diffusion* of an alternative ideology.

In Chapter 1, I discussed at some length the role of protest music in the development of subcultural opposition to the Vietnam war and other related issues. One must be careful not to romanticize the 1960s to the point of blurring the conditions that actually existed. No doubt there was youth culture, more precisely substreams of a large and temporary subculture, that stood in opposition to war and began to question the unbridled development of technology in relation to human problems and goals. At the same time, however, American citizens who were less directly affected by the war, or who stood firmly for "our country, right or wrong" still had an enormous and enduring amount of economic, political, and cultural power in the United States. Further, what appeared to be a transformation of national consciousness toward a more liberal position on many social issues has since been redirected by the rise of conservatism under Ronald Reagan and fundamentalist religious leaders, particularly television evangelists such as Jerry Falwell, during the late 1970s and the 1980s.

### Contemporary Oppositional Subcultures

Presumably there will be deviant subcultures in all historical periods, and for younger groups in particular, music is likely to play important roles in their communication activities. Two vivid examples of this in contemporary Western society are punks and Rastafarians.

*Punks*

Growing from a national background of music-based subcultures, punks created a scene in London and other urban centers in England in the middle 1970s with the basic message that rock had become too esoteric and no longer represented the economic and emotional character of working class youth—rock and roll's basic audience. Punk rock played down musicianship while playing up some of the same "antiestablishment" anger that had characterized the American and British rock scene in the 1960s. Early punk rockers believed that anyone could make music and they should. It was "punk" to grab a microphone and start shouting hostile lyrics over simple guitar droning and drum bashing. This was done basically in the pubs, not in concert halls. For some, at least, punk music was an outlet for expression by people who were seriously disaffected by the social, economic, and political circumstances of life. Punk, therefore, has become not only an art form, but a lifestyle where traditional distinctions made between art and everyday life are blurred (Henry, 1984) and where the relationship between economic conditions and cultural style is made evident. To the degree that record companies can market this type of music, it is also a commodity.

The most famous of the original British punk bands are the Sex Pistols, who broke up shortly after their first album and tour of the United States, and the Clash, still together, but not in the original configuration. Formed in 1976 as an early part of the punk movement, the Clash has always been fiercely political, especially concerning the foreign policy of the United States. While the band's subcultural status and influence have dwindled greatly now, their impact during the early days of punk was powerful, and their messages were clear:

Yankee dollar talks to the dictators of the world
In fact, it's giving orders.
And they can't afford to miss a word.

I'm so bored with the U.S.A.
I'm so bored with the U.S.A.

The early music of the Clash praised active revolution:

Black people got a lot of problems
But they don't mind throwing a brick

White people go to school
Where they teach you how to be thick.
Are you taking over or are you taking orders?
Are you going backwards, or are you going forward?

The Clash became a popular band (thereby self-admittedly losing "punk status") whose work outlived the intense early period of punk music. The textures of the band's music softened, making it more accessible to the public and, at the same time, less "subcultural." The popular *Sandanista* album contained several danceable hits, but also numerous songs about the involvement of the United States and other world powers in international politics and trade. One song, "The Call Up," encouraged young American men to refuse the military draft:

All the young people down the ages
They gladly marched off to die.
Proud city fathers used to watch them
Tears in their eyes . . .

It's up to you not to heed the call up
You must not act the way you were brought up.

Shortly after the album was released the United States became more visibly entangled in the internal political struggles of various Central American countries, particularly Nicaragua. When that happened, the Clash's music became more meaningful for draft-aged men in the United States. In this case, context influenced the salience of a new generation of protest musicians.

Few American punk bands have had such an international impact. One extraordinary exception is the Dead Kennedys, a now defunct band from San Francisco that is well known not only at home but in England too, where white American bands generally are not well received. This band focused critical attention on the role of the United States in its development of foreign markets and labor pools:

In the name of world peace
In the name of world profits
America pumps up our secret police
America wants fuel,
To get it, it need puppets
So what's ten million dead
If it's keeping out the Russians?

When cowboy Ronnie comes to town
Forks out his tongue at human rights . . .
Smile at the mirror as cameras click
And make big business happy.

C'mon bleed.
Bleed for me.

Even the stage presence of the Dead Kennedys and many other punk rock bands has ideological implications. The singers typically throw themselves from the stage into the audience and are routinely thrown back by the crowd in an activity called "stage diving." Audience members similarly jump onto the stage and move to the frantic tempo of the music, then dive back into the crowd, where many of their peers are participating in a churning movement called "slamming" or "thrashing" (see Figure 7.1 and 7.2). This constant breaking down of the physical and psychological distance between performer and consumer of music symbolizes a conscious unwillingness on the part of everyone to draw "class" distinctions between interactants in this unique form of communication (Lull, 1987).

## Rastafarians

Contemporary subcultural protest also finds expression in reggae music. This slow, rhythmic music originated in Jamaica and became a national folk music that speaks of the struggles of ghetto life on the island. While some reggae music is nonpolitical, much of it concerns issues that confront the poor. The hypnotic sound of reggae (the accent is on the back beat with heavy instrumental emphasis on the "bottom"— bass and drums) is unmistakable and universally signals class-based protest. Some reggae music is influenced by the Rastafarian religious movement in Jamaica, a fundamentalist set of beliefs that calls for the symbolic repatriation of black people to Ethiopia, where the black king, Haile Sellasie (a.k.a. "Ras Tafari") ruled. Reggae is appreciated by young people in most countries, particularly those of the Third World. Still, it is seldom played on radio stations in the United States in its authentic style, though pop records sometimes feature a mild reggae beat.

Authentic reggae is subcultural music. When reggae concerts are held in the United States and elsewhere, there is much ceremonial smoking of cannabis in a ritual thought by the Rastafarians to be a divine

Figures 7.1 and 7.2  Exuberant "Stage Divers" at a Punk Concert in San Francisco
(photos by Eric Predoehl)

sacrament. The atmosphere is typically festive and peace loving. Reggae has produced some international recording stars, especially the late Bob Marley (White, 1983), but also Peter Tosh and Jimmy Cliff, among others.

Elements of reggae music, including its politics and lifestyle, have been absorbed into the creative work of other musicians who have recorded in Jamaica, including especially the Clash. Reggae is significant in England where the Rastafarian movement has taken hold in the black immigrant neighborhoods of South London and elsewhere (Hebdige, 1977, 1979; Cashmore, 1984, and this volume).

Even though Rastafarian or "roots" reggae has promised deliverance for blacks from their prison in white Babylon, there is a fascination among some working-class whites in England for this subculture. Distinctive English subgroups such as youthful Skinheads have adopted lifestyle features of the Rastas (and black culture generally) including language patterns, dance styles, and musical preferences. Sharing the same social class and neighborhoods has stimulated appreciation for this music and the formation of some integrated reggae bands, like UB40. The music is usually considered to originate from outside the confines of mainstream culture, a perception that increases its attractiveness to some young urban inhabitants.

In Jamaica, reggae has its strongest appeal to youth of low socioeconomic status (Cuthbert, 1985). Upper- and middle-class youth there prefer disco, soul, and rock music, most of it imported from the United States, England, or elsewhere. In a sense, then, reggae represents the ideological orientations and musical interests of Jamaica's underclass, where it is experienced especially by means of dance hall "sound systems." Reggae records and tapes are sold in mobile record stores (Wallis & Malm, 1984; see also the picture of one of these vans in their article in this volume) mainly to poor youth in the Trenchtown area of Jamaica, the area from which many of the roots artists come. This music, and its outlets for public exposure, are alternative communication channels for some young Jamaicans (Cuthbert, 1985).

## Some Final Thoughts

In 1986, the governor of the State of California appointed a task force to investigate the "problem" of youth gangs. According to the report,

Figure 7.3 Jello Biafra, Lead Singer from the Dead Kennedys, in action at a San Francisco Concert (photo by Eric Predoehl)

the two dominant groups named were "punk rockers" and "heavy metal fans." The subgroups were considered to be "predominantly white and of a middle-class socioeconomic background . . . they listen to . . . rock music. Nothing traditionally held sacred is recognized; their behavior is violent—they enjoy shock value, they have little parental authority and believe in anarchy; and their goal is to destroy, not protect" (San Francisco Chronicle, 1986, p. 3). One might speculate that a policy recommendation potentially forthcoming from official "analyses" such as these would be the banning of particular types of music, at least the prohibition of certain kinds of live popular music shows, a censoring activity that has already begun in many communities. The "fear of music" is more than just an album title.

But we must not lose a realistic perspective on the actual place of popular music in society. The most common uses of music are for entertainment purposes, and the vast majority of these exposures and utilizations have little or no bearing on subcultural life. Even so, popular music is a form of communication and a symbolic sphere of culture that routinely diffuses and amplifies its influence deeply and sensuously into the lives of those who create it and those who listen to it. Popular music is a communicational and cultural resource of distinct character from which many people draw much inspiration, ranging from momentary relief from the drudgery of mundane tasks in perfectly conventional settings to the focus for development of personal and group identities in exotic subcultural locations. Several of the key considerations in the analysis of popular music-as-communication have been raised in this and the other chapters of this book. Researchers and theorists from many academic disciplines may wish to explore this unique and important variety of human communication even more closely in the future, according it the same serious and sensitive attention that youth, and nearly everyone else, already eagerly give it.

## REFERENCES

Avery, R. (1979). Adolescents' use of the mass media. *American Behavioral Scientist, 23,* 53-70.

Blacking, J. (1973).*How musical is man?* Seattle: University of Washington Press.

Brake, M. (1985). *Comparative youth culture.* London: Routledge & Kegan Paul.

Carey, J. (1969). The ideology of autonomy in popular lyrics: A content analysis. *Psychiatry, 32,* 150-164.

Carey, J., & Kreiling, A. (1974). Popular culture and uses and gratifications: Notes toward an accommodation. In J. G. Blumler and E. Katz (Eds.), *The uses of mass communications: Current perspectives on gratifications research.* Beverly Hills, CA: Sage.

Cashmore, E. E. (1984). *No future.* London: Heinemann.

Chaffee, S., McLeod, J. M., & Atkin, C. (1971). Parental influence on adolescent media use. *American Behavioral Scientist, 14,* 232-240.

Chambers, I. (1985). *Urban rhythms: Pop music and popular culture.* New York: St. Martin's.

Chesebro, J. W., Nachman, J. E., Yannelli, A., & Foulger, D. A. (1985). Popular music as a mode of communication: 1955-1982. *Critical Studies in Mass Communication, 2,* 115-135.

Christenson, P. G., & Peterson, J. B. (1986). *The musical tastes of rock's second generation.* Paper presented to the International Communication Association, Chicago.

Christenson, P. G., DeBenedittis, P., & Lindlof, T. R. (1985). Children's use of audio media. *Communication Research, 12,* 327-343.

Clark, R.M. (1974). The dance party as a socialization mechanism for black urban pre-adolescents and adolescents. *Sociology and Social Research, 58,* 145-154.

Clarke, P. (1973). Teenagers' coorientation and information seeking about pop music. *American Behavioral Scientist, 16,* 551-556.

Cole, R. (1971). Top songs in the sixties: A content analysis of popular lyrics. *American Behavioral Scientist, 14,* 389-400.

Comstock, G., Chaffee, S., Katzman, N., & Roberts, D. (1978). *Television and human behavior.* New York: Columbia University Press.

Cuthbert, M. (1985). Cultural autonomy and popular music: A survey of Jamaican youth. *Communication Research, 12,* 381-393.

Denisoff, R. S., & Peterson, R. A. (1972). *Sounds of social change.* Chicago: Rand McNally.

Dixon, R. D., Ingram, F. R., Levinson, R. M., & Putnam, C. L. (1979). The cultural diffusion of punk rock in the United States. *Popular Music and Society, 6,* 210-218.

Frith, S. (1981). *Sound effects: Youth, leisure, and the politics of rock and roll.* New York: Pantheon.

Gans, H. (1974). *Popular culture and high culture.* New York: Basic Books.

Gantz, W., Gartenberg, H. M., Pearson, M. L., & Schiller, S. O. (1978). Gratifications and expectations associated with music among adolescents. *Popular Music and Society, 6,* 81-89.

Hall, S. (1979). Culture, the media and the "ideological effect." In J. Curran et al. (Eds.), *Mass communication and society.* Beverly Hills, CA: Sage.

Harmon, J. (1972). The new music and counter-culture values. *Youth and Society, 4,* 61-83.

Hebdige, D. (1977). Reggae, rastas and rudies. In J. Curran et al. (Eds.), *Mass communication and society.* London: Edward Arnold.

Hebdige, D. (1979). *Subculture: The meaning of style.* London: Methuen.

Henry, T. (1984). Punk and avant-garde art. *Journal of Popular Culture, 17,* 30-36.

Horton, D. (1957). The dialogue of courtship in popular songs. *American Journal of Sociology, 62,* 569-578.

Katz, E., Blumler, S. G., & Gurevitch, M. (1974). Utilization of mass communication by the individual. In J.G. Blumler and E. Katz (Eds.), *The uses of mass communications: Current perspectives on gratifications research.* Beverly Hills, CA: Sage.

Kreiling, A. (1978). Toward a cultural studies approach for the sociology of popular culture. *Communication Research, 5,* 240-263.

Larson, R., & Kubey, R. (1983). Television and music as contrasting experiential media in adolescent life. *Youth and Society, 5,* 13-32.

Lewis, G. H. (1980). Commitment and involvement in popular music: An argument for a mass behavioral approach. *International Review of the Aesthetics and Sociology of Music, 8,* 229-237.

Lewis, G. H. (1981). *Taste cultures and their composition: Towards a new theoretical perspective.* In E. Katz and T. Szeesko (Eds.), *Mass media and social change.* Beverly Hills, CA: Sage.

Lewis, G. H. (1982). Popular music: Symbolic resource and transformer of meaning in society. *International Review of the Aesthetics and Sociology of Music, 13,* 183-189.

Lull, J. (1982a). Popular music: Resistance to new wave. *Journal of Communication, 32,* 121-131.

Lull, J. (1982b). A rules approach to the study of television and society. *Human Communication Research, 9,* 3-16.

Lull, J. (1985a). On the communicative properties of music. *Communication Research, 12,* 363-372.

Lull, J. (1985b). The naturalistic study of media use and youth culture. In K.E. Rosengren, L. A. Wenner, & P. Palmgreen (Eds.), *Media gratifications research.* Beverly Hills, CA: Sage.

Lull, J. (1987). Thrashing in the pit: An ethnography of San Francisco punk subculture. In T. Lindlof (Ed.), *Natural audiences: Qualitative research of media uses and effects.* Norwood, NJ: Ablex.

Lyle, J., & Hoffman, H.R. (1972). Children's use of television and other media. In E.A. Rubinstein et al. (Eds.), *Television and social behavior (Vol. 4)*. Rockville, MD: National Institute of Mental Health.

McLeod, J.M., & Brown, J.D. (1976). The family environment and adolescent television use. In R. Brown (Ed.), *Children and television*. Beverly Hills, CA: Sage.

Mendelsohn, H. (1964). Listening to the radio. In L.A. Dexter & D.M. White (Eds.), *People, society and mass communications*. New York: Free Press.

Miller, D., & Baran, S. (1984). *Music television: An assessment of aesthetic and functional attributes*. Presented at the meeting of the International Communication Association, San Francisco.

Panzarella, R. (1980). The phenomenology of peak experiences. *Journal of Humanistic Psychology, 20,* 69-85.

Peterson, R. A., & DiMaggio, P. (1975). From region to class: The changing locus of country music. *Social Forces, 53,* 497-506.

Pichaske, D. (1979). *A generation in motion: Popular music and culture in the sixties*. New York: Macmillan.

Riesman, D. (1950). Listening to popular music. *American Quarterly, 2,* 359-371.

Roe, K. (1983). *Mass media and adolescent schooling: Conflict or co-existence?* Stockholm: Almqvist and Wiksell International.

Rosengren, K. E., Roe, K., & Sonesson, I. (1983). *Finality and causality in adolescents' media use*. Presented to the International Communication Association, Dallas.

Rosengren, K. E., & Windahl, S. (1972). Mass media consumption as a functional alternative. In D. McQuail (Ed.), *Sociology of mass communications*. Harmondsworth, England: Penguin.

San Francisco Chronicle (1986). State task force blasts punk rockers. (January 6), 3.

Shimanoff, S.B. (1980). *Communication rules: Theory and research*. Beverly Hills, CA: Sage.

Sun, S-w., & Lull, J. (1986) The adolescent audience for music television and why they watch. *Journal of Communication, 36,* 115-125.

Wallis, R., & Malm, K. (1984). *Big sounds from small peoples: The music industry in small countries*. London: Constable.

Warren, R.L. (1943). German parteileider and christian hymns as instruments of social control. *Journal of Abnormal and Social Psychology, 28,* 96-100.

White, T. (1983). *Catch a fire*. New York: Holt, Rinehart & Winston.

Williams, R. (1965). *The long revolution*. London: Penguin.

# 8

# Rock and Roll in Search of an Audience

## LAWRENCE GROSSBERG

The history of rock and roll—if not rock and roll itself—is largely a set of images: musical and visual, live and recorded, personal and public, of performers and fans, of youths and adults, of fun and rebellion. The concreteness of these images belies their transitory nature, and what seems powerful and unforgettable at one moment is quickly displaced in our memories by other images. If their effects and the sources of their impact are not easily recovered, it is not merely because they are no longer present to be interpreted. For we understand the present of rock and roll no better than we do its past.

Consider the enormous popularity of Bruce Springsteen. He has always had a loyal—some would even say fanatical—following. From club performer to folk-rocker to "rock and roll future" to rock poet to pop megastar, his success remains controversial and obscure. Clearly, the music and images have changed, and the audience has grown by leaps and bounds. The appeal of *Born in the U.S.A.* is still hotly debated. Imagine attending a concert with 100,000 other fans. The band opens with the song that some have described as a patriotic anthem and others as an impassioned attack on national politics. The entire crowd passionately sings along, emphasizing their investment in the chorus' repetition of the title. Their participation would seem to express some sort of national pride; except the same response happens in London and Tokyo. How do we explain this? Why have so many different groups—

AUTHOR'S NOTE: I would like to thank Jon Crane and James Lull for their invaluable comments and suggestions.

adolescents and yuppies, working class and middle class, male and female—remained or become such ardent fans? What is their relation to the music? And what is the relationship between the music and their identity as "youth"?

Rock and roll, in fact, is inseparable from its audiences. Consequently, every interpretation of the musical texts also interprets their audiences, as well as the relationship among them. While communication theory increasingly recognizes this in interpreting any cultural event, the specificity of rock and roll forces this equation upon us in particularly urgent and unique ways. Rock and roll works in many ways, at many levels, and in many directions. And there are many different ways of entering into its spaces, of mapping out its relations to and effects upon other aspects of our social lives. The obvious complexity of rock and roll and its relations to its fans' lives, however, is too often dismissed in the attempt to treat it as just another form of mass communication.

## Rock and Roll as Mass Communication

Yet, it is undeniable that rock and roll is a form—perhaps the purest form—of mass communication, and is therefore involved in all the commodity and corporate/state relations with which critics of mass culture often begin. It does—in its socialization of young children into the world of rock culture—also socialize them into the gendered role of consumer; it does—in its celebration of the evanescent qualities of taste and fashion—also undermine traditional notions of quality and historical transcendence. And it does—in its creation of a culture dedicated to the pleasures of fun and raw energy—provide an escape, a temporary distraction from many of the harsh and oppressive realities of the world around us.

Having said all of this, we know little more about rock and roll than any form of culture in the modern world—from the highest arts to the simplest forms of entertainment. In fact, the mass media did not make culture into a commodity: its incorporation into capitalist relations of exchange and production was accomplished long before the twentieth century. But the new technologies of the twentieth century, technologies of mass reproduction and distribution, did alter the terrain of culture, for they gave the great mass of the population some access to heretofore privileged cultural texts; the revolution of mass communications is largely one involving changing relations of cultural consumption. (I do not mean to ignore or underestimate the increasing corporate, even multinational, control of the media—and hence, of both information and images. But control of production, and even more important, of distribution, does not guarantee what the complex effects of any image or message will be.)

But this is hardly an adequate description of any cultural form, including rock and roll. Culture works, not only in an economy of commodities but in an economy of meanings as well. Of course, how we interpret the music, what meanings we give to it, and the relations between those meanings and our world, is never totally isolated from social and political struggles. Thus rock and roll is implicated in a struggle, not only for the money of its fans, but for their minds as well. By communicating certain meanings, or structures of meanings, it offers its audiences ways of seeing the world, of interpreting experiences; it offers them values that have a profound impact on the ways they respond to particular situations and challenges. We can refer to this relationship of music, meaning, and reality as the domain of ideological struggle. But how does rock and roll accomplish this? After all, as both fans and critics have constantly pointed out, it is not the explicit messages of rock music that define its appeal.

Of course, this doesn't prevent many of us, both fans and critics, from speaking as if the lyrics and images (for instance, of performers) were the real locus of its power. This apparently makes the rest of the message (the music, the energy, the fun) just the sugar coating that helps the "ideological pill" go down smoothly. In this view, rock and roll is merely the natural and inevitable expression of its source of production. In such views of the ideological role of mass communication messages, both the audience and the music are entirely powerless. The audience is seen as the passive recipient of already interpreted signs, nothing more than a collection of isolated "cultural dopes," while the message is merely the expression of an intention determined somewhere else. To the extent that its creation is controlled by corporate or capitalist interests, it will likely reinforce the dominant ideologies (for example, it will be sexist, racist, celebrate the life of the wealthy, and the like); on the other hand, when it originates from "the people" as an expression of their lives, their experiences, their oppressions and frustrations, it can become a real—if not very potent—statement of rebellion and resistance. This assumes that corporations produce inherently coopted music (sometimes referred to by rock fans as mere "pop") while the "people" (usually working-class or black youths, but occasionally alienated middle-class kids) produce authentic rock and roll. In either case, the audience is merely the passive victim of an act perpetrated against them, absorbing a message produced for them, even if it is produced in their own name.

## Rock and Roll in Communication Theory

Recent work in communication theory has attempted to give both the *message* and the *audience* a more active role in the processes of meaning construction and ideology. While such efforts are exceedingly important, they are still unable to describe either the relationship between the two terms, or the place of rock and roll in the everyday lives of its fans. There have been two strategies in the effort to move beyond passive views of the communicative process. The first sees the text as constructing the very reality it describes. Rejecting the assumption of a natural, already existing reality outside the text (such as sexuality or youth), which is "expressed or controlled by cultural practice," it argues that messages, through their sense-making practices, produce the very experiences that appear to be interpreted. It seeks to understand how such realities are "constructed by the (communicative) conventions themselves, by the responses they compel listeners to make" (Frith, 1985, p. 22). For example, by giving "private desires a public language," rock and roll not only constructs the parameters of our sexuality (and our experiences) but also constitutes its audiences within its own possible spaces. That is, the audience of rock and roll does not exist independently of the music itself. To be a fan is precisely to stand in the positions that the music makes available to you (for example, as a passive, feminized spectator or an active, masculinized musician). In this view, our individual identities are the products of the social relationships into which we are inserted by particular communicative messages; and so the audience remains passive.

But how does one know that a particular text (that is, the material collection of signs without interpretation) or a particular message within the text is, in fact, effective? How does one know that the "meaning" one finds is what the audience finds, or, if it is, convincing in this rather unconscious way (there is, after all, a difference between representations and fantasies), or even that "meanings" can describe how the rock audience is affected by the text? Perhaps the most obvious example of this is the furor raised in recent years over rock songs that apparently celebrate suicide. After all, millions of us have listened to Ozzy

Osbourne's "Suicide Solution," Van Halen's "Jump," and Blue Oyster Cult's "Don't Fear the Reaper" without following the rather demented example of a small number of already suicidal fans.

The second strategy in recent communication theory seeks to rectify these weaknesses by seeing the audience as the active principle; it is the audience that interprets the text, defines its message, "decodes" it by bringing it into its own already constituted realities, or "uses" it to satisfy already present needs. In either case, the audience makes the text fit into its experiences. Of course, these "experiences" are nothing more than already defined structures of meaning, interpretive practices, or social-psychological functions, which are themselves only the product of previous cultural and communicative relationships. This view potentially leads us back into a kind of passivity—for the audience's interpretation is always determined by something outside of its actual encounter with the text. The audience is not accountable for its interpretations. Furthermore, such views cannot explain why one pays attention to particular texts, in ways that demand particular sorts of decodings, or why some texts are granted an importance and perhaps even a power denied to others. Whether the audience is reduced to the summation of sociological variables or privileged as the creative authors of meaning, the relationship between the text and the audience remains mystified.

Fans may in fact find ways, whether challenging or reassuring, to make sense of their feelings and experiences. Whether this takes place within the musical text itself, or within the ideological structures of already existing social experiences, cannot be decided. We have yet to understand the pleasure or intensity of the relationship to particular messages, nor the choices made in relation to particular texts. Why do some audiences respond differently to different media forms, using them in radically different ways? Why do particular individuals like or dislike particular forms of rock music? Fans' appeals to "taste" (for instance, they like the sound, the singer's voice, the lyrics, the innovative guitar work, the rhythms, and so on) do little to help us understand what has become a socially sustained mass media event. Taste itself is not an answer but a set of questions. If we are to understand the importance of rock and roll to its audiences, and the significance of the audience's youth, we must begin to ask how rock speaks to its fans, in what tongue, or whether it speaks at all. Somehow, we must come to terms with both the activity and the determinateness of both the text and the audience.

## Who Are the Masses
## and Why Are They Dancing?

In fact, rock and roll is apparently different, in its relation to both media and audiences, from other mass communicative forms. Unlike other cultural genres, it is presented in many different mediated forms (such as records, radio, television, films); nor can it be identified with a particular context of consumption (for instance, home, parties, bars, clubs, stadiums). Rather, its functioning depends upon the complexity and the flexibility of, and the differences among, the various possible media and contexts within which it is consumed and enjoyed in different ways. We can also note the ambiguous, even uncomfortable and often contradictory relationship that rock has, at different moments, to the dominant media, even as it depends upon them. The same sense of friction exists between rock and roll and the ways it is written about in the media, even though such writing teaches fans not only how to talk about and judge rock but, often, how to experience it. Thus on the other side of the media which both present and construct rock and roll for its audiences, one must locate the actual functioning of rock music within the lives of its fans—the ways in which it is inserted into their already organized lives, to produce new possibilities for locating pleasure and fun. These possibilities serve, not merely as strategies of resistance and evasion, but rather, as countercontrols that reorganize their lives. Rock and roll is not revolutionary but it is a form of struggle against a certain debilitating organization of pessimism.

There is a second way in which rock and roll works differently from other forms of mass communication: Not only does the rock audience have a particular identity, that of youth, but that identity "bleeds" into the very definition of the music itself. (In what other cultural setting would it make sense to tell someone that they are "too old" to understand or enjoy it?) But we should not assume too quickly that we understand the category of youth, for it is a changing historical structure, inextricably bound up with rock and roll on the one hand and a particular sociohistorical context on the other. But this is not the only way in which rock's relation to its audience is unique: The rock and roll audience is extremely heterogeneous, at least as heterogeneous as the music itself. While this can be said of many mass cultural forms, rock fans often have complex and contradictory relations both to the music and to other fractions of the rock and roll audience. And unlike other media forms, this difference is not merely sociological or interpretive; rather, it lies at the heart of the different relations that audiences have to the music itself, differences that do not correlate to sociological determinations.

Moreover, the differences constituting the rock audience necessarily lead us beyond the category of the "fan." We must also acknowledge the large part of the population which, at least within the past decade, is constantly exposed to it and thus has become a "secondary" audience. Yet this division, however real, is difficult to define at the outset; it is sometimes marked by an opposition between the fan and those who merely seek entertainment; but, as we shall see, it is more accurately a question of the intensity of one's investment in—and hence the politics of—entertainment. The audience of rock also includes those who, by their conscious self-exclusion from either of these two audiences, appoint themselves as aesthetic or moral critics of rock and roll. Yet, by virtue of their opposition, whether because of "taste" or "moral outrage," they also define themselves as a part of rock's audience, often becoming, ironically, promulgators of rock and roll. From the early efforts to eliminate rock by attacking radio practices (such as the payola hearings) to the latest efforts (by the Parents Music Resource Center) to "control" the contents of rock and roll, its rejection by some significant portion of the public has been an important part of its relationship to its audience.

Finally, we must note the peculiar but constant relationship that rock fans define to the music: In an informal survey by the student newspaper at the University of Illinois, students admitted to being exposed to rock music more than any other form of media message, and yet, maintained that it had the least influence on them. There is something paradoxical about this, especially when you consider how commonly the same fans celebrate the power of the music: "My father always blamed it on the rock 'n' roll. The drugs, the sex, the faithless wild boys and girls obeying no authority and bearing no responsibility, playing havoc with America in a mindless quest for the good times they believed was owed them by the world. My father's not stupid" (Duncan, 1984, p. 1). This refusal to take rock and roll seriously does more than deny the right to others. It points to the heart of rock and roll's power, for its "seriousness" in its fans' lives depends upon its negation of the serious.

This unique relation between the texts of rock music and its audience, emblematized in its links to youth, means that it cannot be studied as a set of messages built upon common, specifiable generic conventions, for the limits of rock and roll vary, not only over time but across different audiences. Thus not only is it the case that what "sounds like" rock and roll today (for instance, Einsturzende Neubauten, Joy Division, or Laurie Anderson) would not have sounded like rock and roll 20 years ago, but for some contemporary audiences, these do not sound like rock and roll today either. Consequently, we must find a different way into the space of rock music and its cultures, different questions than those dictated by communication theory: Why is rock and roll so popular for some, and so threatening for others? Why has it been able to sustain a continuous self-identity despite the changing economic, sociological, and even musical parameters that define its place in contemporary society? How are we to understand its place in the lives of its fans—and its enemies? (I will leave aside the question of those casually exposed to its omnipresence in our media culture.) And how do we understand its special—and unique—connection to youth? In fact, what is this "youth" that is somehow so closely connected with the emergence and continued power of rock and roll, given that it is neither external to, nor a mere internal product of, rock culture?

In other words, how do rock fans "empower" the music and how does the music "empower" them? What is it that the music gives to or does for the fan such that it is allowed to hold a special, even privileged place in their everyday lives? And what is the nature of this privileged place? To say that rock music is "about" having fun and celebrating good times is not to dismiss it. For contemporary youth, fun is an extremely important part of life; yet it is also problematic if we begin to think about what constitutes a good time, its relative importance, and its relations with other parts of our lives. Thus rather than beginning with questions of meaning or use—as if we could assume either that the fan is conscious of how rock and roll works, or that the critic has some privileged access to the meaning of the text—I propose to examine how rock and roll works to redistribute our concerns, how it enables the construction of particular maps detailing what matters in our everyday lives. In order to understand the relationship between rock, youth, and fun, I propose to look at the ways in which rock and roll organizes, not the meanings we give to the world, but the ways we are able to invest and locate energy, importance, even ourselves, in those meanings. It is not a matter of interpretation, but rather of identifying the ways in which rock and roll remaps the places and ways in which one can have fun.

## It's All Rock and Roll to Me?

As soon as one begins to look at how rock and roll fits into the actual lives of its fans, one cannot help but be struck by the range of differences that exist, not only in fans' interpretations and uses of particular songs, but in their definitions of the genres of their taste, and in their assumptions about the essential nature or limits of the category of rock and roll itself. The diverse ways in which fans draw boundaries around rock and roll already determine the kinds of sense it can make of their world. In fact, *whether or not a particular song is rock and roll cannot be taken for granted.* This heterogeneity extends beyond the fact that rock and roll (like other cultural forms) allows for a diversity of interpretations, for if it is not the music, it is also not the individual fan who determines whether something is rock and roll. The individual's judgments only make sense within a particular context which has already defined the ways in which rock is constituted and used. Given a small number of judgments from any fan, one can usually construct a cartography of their taste. If you like the early Clash but not the later Clash, if you like Joy Division but not New Order, it is fairly easy to predict that you would probably not like the Pet Shop Boys or Culture Club. If you like the Rolling Stones but not the Beatles, you are more likely to like The Gun Club than Squeeze. The fan is already a fan, and moreover, a particular kind of fan (such as a heavy metal fan, a new waver, a pop fan, and so on) precisely because he or she already makes predictable judgments about the various musics that might be enjoyed as rock and roll.

There is, additionally, an even more striking feature of the way rock and roll fans deals with it in their everyday lives: They consistently make very different, but related, judgments. On the one hand, like any cultural audience, they distinguish between good and bad rock and roll. You may or may not have liked the latest Sting album, or the new Cult single, or the Mekons concert, or the new Motley Crue video. You can argue about such judgments or simply decide that they are a matter of taste; you can replay the text for one another, pointing to its good or bad/interesting or boring qualities, or just appeal to its general texture. Your friend may or may not agree with your descriptions.

On the other hand, fans make a distinction between what counts as rock and roll—whether good or bad—and what is simply not included within the category. Thus one may argue that the Sting record, whether good or bad, just isn't rock and roll—perhaps it's jazz or perhaps Sting has "sold out." You think the new Scritti Politti album, or any synthesizer music, is "pop" or disco, or even worse, "bubble gum" music, or that the new Motley Crue song is just adolescent noise. For someone else, there are unproblematic examples of rock and roll, although they may be examples of bad rock and roll. The same arguments exist at the level of genres within rock and roll; most commonly, is black music (such as rhythm and blues, funk, or rap) a part of rock and roll? In either case, it is not a matter of defining specific criteria, or of adjudicating their application. It is not merely that one doesn't like it or doesn't like "what it says"; it is, quite simply, that one cannot hear it as rock and roll or that it doesn't feel like rock and roll, both of which are common statements. Such judgments often take a particular form: "If you don't like (...), then you don't like rock and roll," or alternatively, "If you think that (:..) is good rock and roll, you don't understand rock and roll." There is an elitism here, as if every fan assumes the right to define the boundary between what is rock and what is not. Even rock and roll songs and performers constantly draw such distinctions by declaring themselves to be rock and roll and celebrating that identity.[1]

If such boundaries are not individually drawn, they point to the different ways in which fans are organized; the structures of such groupings establish and locate fans within different "nominal" groups or invisible subcultures. The relevant social network for fans is determined, not merely by shared tastes in music, but more important, by shared ways of drawing the line between what is and is not rock. Such groups, however, are only nominal because they do not imply any sociological reality, shared community life, or visible style. The essential function of such nominal groups is precisely to define that line: to continuously renominate those texts that deserve the honorific title of "rock and roll."

The relationship between the fan (and hence, between youth) and rock music, as well as the identity of each, can only be understood within a larger context on which both are actively defined, and defined as active. Such contexts will vary for different audiences and different musical relations; they must be considered and described locally, in their concreteness. They include not only implicit definitions and explicit selections of rock and roll, both live and recorded, but also images, styles, dances, modes of performing, forms of social relationships, languages, relations to other media (and their specific histories), and technologies, as well as social, historical, economic, and experiential events and relations.

These contexts of everyday life and culture are not merely the passive background in which rock and roll works; they actively define and give shape not only to rock and roll as a cultural form, but to the specific ways it works for particular nominal groups. Because these contexts are active for each nominal group, because they are themselves productive, it may be more accurate to describe them as rock and roll "apparatuses." The most obvious examples would be the various youth subcultures (often urban, male, working class, with shared experiences and styles that define both its members' identities and the ways in which rock and roll functions), but any fan is located, however invisibly and unconsciously, in some apparatus(es). Insofar as there is some unity to the rock and roll culture, certain features of these local apparatuses will be shared but, insofar as the rock and roll culture is always fragmented, there will be significant differences as well. Only by mapping out these lines of similarity and differences can we begin to make sense of the complex relationship between rock and roll and youth.

### "It Ain't the Meat, It's the Motion"

What is this work that rock and roll is supposed to accomplish? Why do fans incessantly draw boundaries—albeit always temporary ones (although they are often treated as if they were written in stone)— around rock and roll? I want to offer the following hypothesis: By encapsulating rock and roll and defining it as essentially different from whatever is not included, the apparatus also "encapsulates" the nominal group. Marking itself as different and placing the fan within its spaces, the fan takes up a position of being different from those who don't "understand" the music and who cannot make the appropriate distinctions. We can, metaphorically, contrast the encapsulation provided by rock and roll with that provided by the automobile: The latter is a mobile bubble that extends the protection and privacy of the home into the outside world; the former is a mobile bubble that can penetrate both the privacy of the home and the social relations of the public spheres with a unique sense of difference and energy embodied in a particular relation to fun.

This practice of critical encapsulation divides the cultural world into Us and Them, but that difference does not necessarily constitute an identity. While being a rock and roll fan sometimes does entail having a visible and self-conscious identity (such as punks, or hippies, or mods), it more often does not appear visibly on the surface of the fan's life, or even as a primary way in which most fans would define themselves. But it still functions as one way in which we mark our difference from others, especially from what is considered the straight, adult, or boring world. In fact, as individuals and as members of social groups, there are many axes along which we register our difference from others—some are physical categories, some are sociological, some are ideological. We are women, black, short, middle-class, educated, and so on. Any particular difference, including that marked out by being a rock fan, is always augmented and reshaped by other social differences.

At different points and places in our lives, we reorder the hierarchical relations among these differences, we redefine our own identity out of the relations amongst our differences; we reorder their importance, we invest ourselves more in some than in others. We are supposed to grow out of our identification with rock and roll; but even if one doesn't, it is probably wise not to admit to being a heavy metal fan when you interview for a job with a conservative corporation. For some, then, being a particular sort of rock fan can take on an enormous importance and thus come to constitute a dominant part of the fan's identity. For others, it remains a powerful but submerged difference that colors but does not define their social identities.

But what is the nature of the difference rock and roll produces? If being a rock fan automatically marks one as young, youth is simultaneously a biological, material, sociological, and ideological category. But there is something else, another dimension, that rock and roll brings into the field of youth, what I will describe as *youth as an affective difference.* The notion of *affect* points to the fact that there is more to the organization of our everyday lives than just a distribution or structure of meaning, money, and power. There is a variable distribution of concern and energy: Some things *feel* different from others, some matter more, or in different ways, than others. Affect refers to that dimension or plane of our lives that we experience as moods, feelings, desires, and enervation. It is related to meanings but not reducible to them, for an event, even with a specifiable meaning, will have radically different effects depending upon its relations to our affective life, depending on its place in our "mattering maps" (Goldstein, 1983).

The notion of affect is crucial if we are to make sense of rock fans' responses to music, for its encapsulation clearly depends upon how the music feels and how it makes one feel. Rock and roll works on the affective level of our everyday lives, at the level of the strategies we use to gain some control over that affective life, to find new forms of pleasure and excitement to cope with new forms of pain, frustration, and boredom.

A great deal of this affective power depends upon the fact that music (perhaps like visual images) is more than a language, although its precise force remains elusive. Music has a unique and striking material relation to the human body itself, invading it, enfolding it within its own rhythms and textures:

> Why, when I first saw the Grand Canyon and the Piazza San Marco and the Alps, did I feel that these things had all been more moving in Cinerama? Why? Because both God and Man forgot to put in the music . . .
>
> In one sense, it's no surprise that music grabs us—it's supposed to. But once you look at the process, it seems quite miraculous that people can bowl one another over just by jiggling sound waves. It's a miracle akin to that of language . . . But music is more than a language [Rosenfeld, 1985].

This musical excess has often been described in terms of music's connection to emotions. But emotion seems inadequate to describe the range of music's effects, which include not only emotional distinctions (for instance, pleasant, sad) but also quantities of *activation* (such as excitement versus relaxation). At the very least, music seems capable, by manipulating structures of the predictable and the unpredictable, of producing sudden shifts in emotion. Such "thrills" (Rosenfeld, 1985) are in fact more commonly attributed to music than to, for example, sexual activity.

Yet affect cannot be equated with pleasure and pain, and rock and roll is not about pleasure per se, but about a particular use or organization of pleasure, about the attempt to shape pleasures into fun. It brings other forms of pleasure (such as sex, dance, fashion, drugs) into its economy of fun, relocating them affectively and, consequently, redefining them ideologically. There is, after all, a significant distinction, however hard to describe, between them: Consider how it would change the song if Cyndi Lauper had sung "Girls Just Wanna Have Pleasure." Fun involves the negation of seriousness and boredom, and rock and roll works by transforming particular activities and events and making them available as potential sources or sites of fun. While rock and roll is not the only form of culture that works in this way, nor does it work only in this way, it is the dominance of this affective level which is largely responsible for the enormous power and popularity of rock music and its connection with youth.

Rock and roll defines youth as the site of an affective difference, at the point of the contradiction between fun and boredom. Within rock's terms, you are young if you are bored with the straight world, and celebrate fun as an alternative strategy for navigating your way through everyday life. It constitutes youth as an affective state whose primary (if not only) investment is in fun—especially in relation to contemporary forms of boredom (predictability) and terror (unpredictability), arising from new structures of control and the absence of control within our lives. Such strategies emerge in the context of adolescence, but they have long since exceeded that and become implicated in a more historical struggle over the affective organization of everyday life.

## Live from the Postmodern Warzone

If we are to make sense of this struggle, however, we need to understand the "postmodern" historical context out of which rock culture emerged as a viable and even reasonable response. Rock and roll is *about* growing up in the advanced capitalist world after the World War II, but not in the sense of describing, representing, or even interpreting it; rather it is a set of strategies for reorganizing affective lives to cope with the demands of that context by restructuring its very contours, including the shape and experience of youth. *Growing up* (in other words, becoming boring), after all, signals the demise of a rock and roller and, in fact, no rock fans ever feel themselves to have grown up completely.

What brought rock and roll into existence? What were the conditions that enabled a particular set of musical styles (which had existed well before the beginning of rock and roll) to be linked to specific images of alienation and these, in turn, to be identified with a generational audience? Children born after the war—especially but not only the white working and lower middle classes—found themselves in a context defined by its mobility. The economic boom of the 1950s (sustained in part by the Korean war and the government's high investment in weapons development and production) established an optimistic climate and, to a certain extent, real economic prosperity. At the very least, there was a surplus of disposable capital that Americans (United States) invested in their own personal lives (for example, they bought houses in the suburbs, and cars to take them to work in the city and to play in the country; they filled their houses with new consumer goods, including the newly available technologies of mass communication). Following the wars, the "national project" of returning to what was represented as normalcy was interpreted as demanding a serious reinvestment in the family, and in the necessity of "towing the line" in order to realize the American dream of peace and prosperity, not to mention protecting ourselves from the "godless communists."

Thus on the one hand there was an enormously powerful context of mobility and change, defined by images (for instance, advertising, the movies, and the like) but also by experience and desire. The world was quite literally entering a new age, through the redistribution, not only of power and wealth on an international scale, but also of the possibilities of the individual's everyday life and future. And on the other hand, there was a real "conservativism," or perhaps more accurately, a quietism, which justified sitting back and reaping the rewards that America (United States) and Americans had earned. Quite simply, in the best of all possible worlds, why would anyone want to rock the boat? And if this were not the best of all possible worlds, it would surely be so soon, and the new generation of children would reap the benefits that their parents would bequeath to them.

But if the dream were to come true, if there was to be a meaning behind this new vision (or actually, an old vision of the meaning of America updated), it would have to be invested in future generations. People would have to have children, and have children they did! The baby boom created an enormous population of children by the mid-1950s, a population that was seen, on the one hand, as America's future, as the living embodiment of their parents' dreams—this would be the healthiest, happiest and best treated generation of all times—and, on the other hand, as an economic dilemma. For while they represented a large market (not only as future consumers but as the object of their parents' consumption), they also presented new challenges to a society, the institutions of which—from hospitals to schools, from recreation facilities to potential employers—were simply unable to absorb them without enormous investments of capital. For example, while they were to be the best educated generation ever, schools were unprepared to handle them, not only in terms of facilities and teachers, but also in terms of the new educational demands that life in the postwar context seemed to impose (with new sciences, new technologies, new worldwide political struggles, new forms of cultural production and language, and so on).

But another line of change radically altered the landscape of life in postwar America: the wide scale appearance of a set of images, vocabularies, and ideas that represented the world as having gone through a radical, almost apocalyptic transition. If postwar America was to be the beginning of a new age, it also had to be the end of an old age. While such self-images are common throughout history, their absorption into the newly empowered mass media (making them available to the masses) gave them a unique presence and a powerful claim to truth. That these images connected to real historical changes is undeniable; whether the rupture was as total or radical as its representations claimed, or even whether it was experienced as such, is more questionable. Nevertheless, the fact remains that events such as the war, the holocaust, the A-bomb, and the new forms of economic and technological mobility became signs of a new uncertainty. They seemed to call into question our ability to appeal to stable values and truths that gave meaning to our lives and defined the future as an ideal goal.

Increasingly, the words that had provided the framework within which our emotional lives were made congruent with the world seemed to fail. The bomb threatened the security of any future just as the eventual conquering of space threatened the sanctity of the earth. The holocaust made insanity an inescapable fact of human history, and seemed to undermine the possibility of any faith in some ultimate principle of value. If there are no meanings underlying our actions, providing stable supports to our lives, then life is only what appears on its surfaces. For example, it is only after the war that "image-politics" becomes a real, if not dominant form of power in society (finding its ultimate expression of course in Reagan), in which positions and commitments are less important than their surface representations. Moreover, the new electronic media—as technologies, commodities, and languages—practiced a new egalitarianism in which all images are equal, and hence in which the significance of the distinction between the real and the image collapses. Reality increasingly is called upon to fit the image of the media, rather than the media representing a reality which is, in some way, foreign to them. The increasingly common experience of an identity crisis—who am I apart from the roles I play on the surface— was yet another emblem of this crisis. As everything became both dispensable and disposable, America became a "throwaway" society, in which nothing is at stake except the mundane realities of our lives.

Obviously, the experience I am invoking here contradicts the ideology of the 1950s, its optimistic sense of the present, and its strong investment in the future. Yet, both sides of the description are real. How can they be reconciled and lived? This *postmodern* sense of the impossibility of meaning and value can only be understood as an *affective* experience, most potent for the younger generations who had never experienced the values of their parents' generations as particularly powerful representations of life or emotional commitments. There was an apparent rupture. While adults may have been conscious of a crisis of faith—one which had to be met with the strong reassertion of values and a commitment to the future—the younger generation confronted this as simply a fact, an affective difference that, at the deepest levels, separated them from their parents and from the straight world around them. Moreover, this difference—and its various discomforts—was heightened by its similarities to and interaction with the frustrations and ambiguities of adolescence and puberty. It is not that youth did not live the ideological values of their parents; rather, they found it impossible to represent their mood, their own *affective* relationship to the world, in those terms, and increasingly, to invest themselves seriously in such values.

### Bored in Paradise

How was one to respond to this paradoxical structuring of everyday life, what Elvis Presley described in a song as "a rat race at a snail's pace?" The dilemma posed for the baby-boom generations was only magnified as youth was increasingly valorized, as it became the dominant sign of the reality and intrinsic value of the future. Moreover, a sociopolitical atmosphere that demanded conformity to moral and behavioral norms allowed little space within which youth could attempt to live out their unique contradiction. There was, of course, one domain within which their "uniqueness" was acknowledged and deviation from adult norms tolerated: namely, the irresponsibility implicit in their youth or adolescence with its postmodern affective difference. Of course, this was not a conscious strategy and it developed only over time. By locating youth on the affective level, they were able to reserve and even subvert their dilemma, to celebrate their adolescent frustrations and fantasies as an alternative to the empty effect of their parents' lives. In a sense, unconsciously, youth defined themselves by their investment in their affective life, by the penetration of affective difference into social life as a form of protest, by their celebration of their own fantasies and pleasures as a way, if not of giving meaning to life, at least of rebelling against the artificial attempts to impose meaning and order on them.

Given this strategy, we can begin to understand how rock and roll works, why it would be able to sustain its importance in the lives of its fans, and why it would be perceived as threatening by the straight world. For the power of rock and roll lies in its ability to bring together and celebrate the production of difference and fun. It marks its fans as *others*, as outsiders, even while they continue to live within the dominant cultural structures of meaning. It says nothing to be a mod, a surfer, a hippie, a punk or a new waver; certainly such identities do not function as intelligible constructions of the world. They do not carry with them their own alternative ideologies. But they are measures of an affective difference hiding from the obscene light of social power (a light that burns rather than illuminates) and, in particular, from the inability of that power to comprehend youth's affective life. Various rock and roll cultures' constant search for outlandish styles, and the celebration of exaggeration and excess, are signs not merely of the defensive alienation of adolescence, but rather, of a strategy that takes fun seriously, which makes "taking nothing seriously" a serious commitment.

Rock and roll functions, then, precisely by constructing a connection between this postmodern affective difference and the social positions of youth. While it appears to express its audience's adolescent alienation, it rather appropriates the adolescents' investment in fun as a response to an alienation on another level. While it originally depended upon the generational (age) difference of its adolescent audience, it continued (and still continues), even as they grew older, to inscribe its affective difference upon the other social structures it encountered, appropriating them into its affective dilemmas and celebrations.

Rock and roll does not offer a common language or ideology, it does not create common experiences out of private desires. It is not a folk culture linked to a community of youth. While its various audiences may appear to define identifiable communities, they are in fact only the *simulacrum* of such communities, temporary images, like the human wave at stadium events, momentary celebrations of an impossible community in the midst of an enforced anonymity. Rather, rock and roll makes private desires and public experiences into public signs of an unrepresentable affective situation: that is, the domination of terror and boredom as the twin poles of contemporary affective life. Increasingly, the world is marked by random moments to danger, insanity, and risk. And at the same time, it appears to be more predictable and redundant than ever before.

Rock and roll responds by offering "fun" as a strategy, but not as something capable of transcending that reality. It escapes the boredom of *terror-ism* and negates the terrifying omnipresence of boredom by recontextualizing the world according to an alternative map, a map of fun, which relocates the possibilities of predictability and unpredictability. It energizes its fans by transforming the very elements that oppress them into moments of fun, celebrating the noise, terror, and repetition; it does not redefine them, but the ways in which they matter. It remakes the "controlled" panic of contemporary life in its own image. But in so doing, rock and roll also resists and even attacks the very social structures and institutions that give birth to contemporary youth: the family, the school, and the economy of work. It makes fun into the only sign of difference that matters, at the same time that it refuses to see fun as extraordinary. There is nothing extraordinary about rock and roll, and rock and roll does not attempt to create the extraordinary; rather, it celebrates the ordinary as extraordinary and ultimately, the extraordinary as ordinary. Elvis is the king of rock and roll because he was the self-made king: An ordinary kid who just happens to have become rich and famous, he flaunted both as tiresome toys having no function apart from the differences they marked. The ability to have fun in the midst of the straight world, not despite it but with the very tools of its oppressiveness, is what rock and roll offers as the mark of our difference.

### Celebrating the Differences

Nevertheless, there are real differences among different rock and roll apparatuses, differences that are often "punctuated" or foregrounded— in images and behavior—by the music and its fans. These different affective economies provide an alternative basis, both for constructing the history of rock and roll, and for contrasting the political stances of competing apparatuses. These relations can be described at three levels: (1) *Affective difference* refers to rock and roll's relation to the dominant culture, to the kind of boundary with which it surrounds itself; for example, it may explicitly oppose the straight world (for instance, the politicized counterculture), or it may offer an alternative to it (for example, glitter rock), or it may dismiss the dominant culture as completely irrelevant (as in pop culture). It thereby constructs itself as either an enemy, a competitor, or an independent reality; (2) *affective alliance* refers to the ways in which fun becomes important, the ways in which groups of fans invest their energy into rock and roll itself, the ways in which rock and roll matters: For example, rock and roll may be taken as a vision to be achieved (for instance, the utopian counterculture), as an experience to be celebrated (for example, the mainstream pop/rock culture), or as a rejection of the dominant culture to be reiterated (as in post-punk cynicism); (3) *affective structure* refers to the particular forms and possibilities of fun that are available, the things that demand a significant investment of energy, that matter if we are to *live* rock and roll.

One can identify three major "axes" on which rock and roll locates fun: youth, pleasure, and the postmodern. While each of these three axes is almost always active, they can be weighted differently and have different relations to one another. Youth as the site of fun enables rock and roll apparatuses to celebrate the impotence, frustration, and irresponsibility of adolescence. It converts risk and instability, mobility, and the expenditure of extremely high levels of energy (with the subsequent exhaustion that is implied) into new forms of pleasure. If youth is always a transition, struggling to maintain its difference, then rock and roll celebrates transitions and change (for example, this is clearly the dominant way in which the early Beatles, or early Springsteen music was taken).

The celebration of pleasure as fun emphasizes the body as both sexual and sensual (for instance, disco and most rhythm and blues). While such pleasures are not unique to rock and roll, by equating pleasure and fun (and thus denying the responsibilities that are entailed in notions of pleasure itself), rock and roll sets itself against the increasing disciplining of leisure in the modern world (and the puritanism of both the Left and the Right). Further, such pleasures are celebrated without the necessarily romanticized images of love and self-knowledge that the dominant culture attaches to them. (Sex is never as wonderful as its rock and roll image—even pleasure is incapable of giving meaning to our lives.)

Finally, finding fun in the postmodern enables rock and roll to celebrate the artificial and the ironic. Rock and roll substitutes style for authenticity (making the latter into another style), finds pleasure in the very structures of noise and repetition that are so oppressive in the straight world. Quite literally, somehow, noise feels good rather than painful. Rock and roll takes its content and form from outside of its own boundaries and in the very process of appropriating them (for instance, its musical practices, its fashion statements, and so on), it forces the straight world to organize itself in opposition to the rock and roll culture. Rock and roll opposes the artificiality of its own pleasures to the supposed naturalness of the values of the straight world by taking everything to excess. Rather than seeking to become art or to trash aesthetic pleasures, rock and roll constructs an aesthetics of trash (for example, this is the dominant way in which punk and postpunk were received).

Rock and roll is never as homogeneous as its name suggests, nor as diverse as its fans would like to believe. It exists as a set of strategic responses to a particular historical context; it cannot be treated merely as a set of musical messages, for its power and identity as rock and roll depends upon a complex set of differences that cut across generations, genders, time, and space. It remakes the world in its own image—an image of surfaces, fun, and youth.

## Conclusion: Who Is "The Boss" Anyway?

I opened this article by questioning the current success of Bruce Springsteen. Let me close by returning to it. The answers will not be found in the texts themselves, nor in the diversity of interpretations that fans make. For neither explains why Bruce has finally achieved the popularity that critics have long predicted, and become the latest star. This is not to say that these are irrelevant, but that they can only be interpreted within larger interactive contexts (apparatuses) that are available to us only in the behaviors and responses of his fans, for example, as they participate in a concert.

Springsteen's success has been produced by a series of incremental additions to his audience, rather than by either a steadily progressive growth or a sudden emergence from obscurity. The changes in the relations between his music and audience map out an ever-expanding incorporation of different affective possibilities of rock and roll: from oppositional to independent, from visionary to experiential to hypercritical, from celebrations of our postmodernity. More than perhaps any rock and roll performer, Springsteen's career defines the limits and possibilities of rock and roll, and his peculiar commitment to the genre is captured in his relation to his own history as well as to that of rock and roll. Neither is ever allowed to disappear into the past or to dissolve into an innocent nostalgia. History is always being recontextualized and reinterpreted in the music he is playing at the moment. Moreover, despite the changes in his music (most important in his current success is the fact that he has successfully adapted to the three-minute pop format), its constant features—Bruce's voice, Clarence's sax, the interplay between the powerful rhythm section and the idiosyncratic guitars—have consistently produced some of the best rock and roll of the past decade. The power of the music/lyrics is complemented by the image of the relations among the band members, augmented recently by the addition of a female vocalist.

Critics have often identified three appeals beyond the music itself: his images, his populism, and his presence as a performer. While each of these points to something real, they need to be located within the actual contexts of rock and roll's functioning. First, I want to suggest that the power of his images has always been in their ability to invoke affective commitments rather than to interpret shared experiences. Whether the images are of youth on the streets, or freedom as flight, or orgiastic pleasures, or desperate marginality/criminality, the audience need not "interpret" the message in order to enter into its affective economy. What sense can we make of adolescent surburban girls singing "And I feel like I'm travelling on a downbound train" unless we understand that it evokes an affective situation.

But beginning with *The River*, the referent of such images has changed, increasingly invoking the affective dilemma of postmodernity. While the contradiction between faith and common sense, between dreams and realities, between affect and meaning, has always been an important part of Springsteen's music, it has become explicit and dominant in his current success. The contradiction can constantly be heard, as he both attacks and celebrates the simultaneous necessity and impossibility of meaning in our lives, in images both more concrete and less specific (for instance, "Glory Days" and "Dancing in the Dark" end up, in concert, celebrating the very trap that such meanings prepare for us). This relationship to the music can be heard in the ways the audience "punctuates" its own participation in the concert: For example, although they sing along to almost every song, there are particular lines and songs that seem to evoke a widespread, passionate involvement. When Bruce sings "Cover Me" or "I'm on Fire," when he says, "If you're hungry inside, shout it out," we can literally hear, and feel, the audience's investment in the music.

Second, Bruce's image as a performer, including his use of stories, constantly reinforces his ordinariness. He is, after all, like us. He allows us to celebrate, simultaneously, our own ordinariness and to assert our own difference. In fact, the ordinary becomes extraordinary as Bruce celebrates the fan's identity within the mainstream. In their very lack of difference, in their affective relation to the music, an identity is constructed. Finally, his presence—his commitment to the music and the fans—offers an image of affective relief: "So many videos were full of disasters, with everything flying apart, shifting, in the blink of an eye. The random images on the screen were swirling, beyond anyone's control; everything was falling ... but Bruce was still dancing in all that darkness, and the heart of rock and roll was still beating" (Mason, 1985). Bruce's desire to have it all and his willingness to give whatever it takes to get it, constructs both his own romantic faith and his image of "authenticity." But the audience knows that his act is rehearsed and repeatable, while the authentic is not. Yet Bruce's power may lie precisely in having found a way to redefine authenticity onto the television screen. He offers us images of our own affective existence constantly played off against his own commitment to struggle continuously to escape those debilitating dilemmas. The relationship between musician, music, fan, and history is constructed around an increasingly common celebration and production of energy in the midst of a global "black-out." And isn't that the heart of rock and roll, and the soul of youth?

## NOTE

1. The power of this elitism does not depend on whether or not fans actually use the term "rock and roll." In fact, increasingly, fans are having to find other terms to draw the distinction, partly under pressure from the popular press, which has appropriated "rock and roll" in different ways. For example, there is a return to vocabularies of authenticity and cooptation apart from the nomination of the music. Whether this can work is an open question, since the way in which rock and roll names itself is in marked contrast with other forms of popular music, which either rarely name themselves (for example, Tin Pan Alley), or which name themselves by reference to experiences outside the music (for instance, blues, country), which define criteria of one's right to play or enjoy the music.

## REFERENCES

Duncan, R. (1984). *The noise: Notes from a rock 'n' roll era.* New York: Ticknor and Fields.
Frith, S. (1985). Confessions of a rock critic. *New Statesman* (August 23) 21-23.
Goldstein, R. (1983). *The mind-body problem.* New York: Laurel.
Mason, B. A. (1985). *In country.* New York: Harper and Row.
Rosenfeld, A. H. (1985). Music, the beautiful disturber. *Psychology Today* (December), 48-56.

# 9

# Patterns of Meaning and Choice:

## Taste Cultures in Popular Music

### GEORGE H. LEWIS

Popular music has long concerned members of the culture in which it is played and sung. As far back as Plato's *Republic*, it was held that "the introduction of novel fashions in music is a thing to beware of as endangering the whole fabric of society, whose most important conventions are unsettled by any revolution in that quarter" (Conford, 1941, p. 394). This concern about music as a focal point for the articulation of social protest—and as a seedbed of potential revolutionary activity—has been a recurrent theme in the critique of popular music, especially in the music of political subcultures, such as the American Left of the 1930s and 1940s (Denisoff, 1972; Dunaway, this volume), the international youth culture of the 1960s (Lewis, 1972), the British punk movement of the late 1970s (Hebdige, 1979), or the new wave sounds of the 1980s (Lull, 1982). Such studies emphasize the power of ideology in music—especially in the lyrics—in contributing to the solidarity of social groups and movements (Frith, 1978).

On the other hand, there are theorists and social critics who have looked to popular music as a strong supporter of the status quo, noting that most composers and players have been financially supported by the dominant institutions of their societies (Denisoff, 1982), or that the music, by focusing attention in a nonpolitical sphere, actually detracted from the creation of revolutionary ideology and substituted the symbols of "false pop consciousness" for it (Adorno, 1959; Gramsci, 1971).

Although these two positions on the *effects* of popular music are vastly divergent, they are similar in that they agree that music is meaningful to those who play and listen to it—that it is, in fact, a means of symbolic communication that has an impact extending far beyond the concert hall or the radio (Sheperd, 1977). This view of music as symbolic communication is one I share and will develop in this chapter, merging it with the idea that such communication is a symbolic resource and has power in defining or reaffirming people's views of their social worlds and the social groups to which they aspire or already belong.

## Music as a System of Meaning

Music is symbolic communication. When we hear a "golden oldie" it can easily evoke a whole time and place, our feelings and emotions, who we were, and who we were with when we first listened to it. Music can also be a theme, a rallying cry, a protest around which we gather to do something about social conditions. Or it can be a badge of identity—a means of showing others (and ourselves) to what group, or groups, we belong, or aspire to belong, as members.

Music, viewed this way as symbolic communication, is an ordered system of meaning and symbols in social interaction. In contrast, what I refer to as the "social system" is the *network* of social interactions itself—those interactions that focus on the balancing of biological and psychological needs, on cultural integration, and adaptation to physical and social environments (Lewis, 1979). Thus on the one level in popular music, there is a framework of beliefs, expressive symbols, and values in terms of which individuals define their world, express their feelings, and make their judgments. On the other level, there is the framework of interactive behavior, called social structure, that is composed of social classes, groups organizations, and subcultures. Clearly the relationships between these two levels are of critical import in the study of modern, complex societies.

The study of popular music, then, should be the study of the *meanings* of music to those individuals and groups who create and consume it. As W. I. Thomas, the Chicago social psychologist said, "If people define situations as real, they are real in their consequences" (Thomas & Thomas, 1928, p. 572). Thus definitons of the situations of people are reflected in the creation and assignment of meaning to the musical artifacts of their worlds. It is important for a student of music to discover how, as a world of symbols, music expresses the images, visions, and sentiments of the people who find significance in it, as well as how such music reflects the values and norms of social groups and systems, or even the ideology of a social class or classes. Such an approach is increasingly urgent in the fast-paced and socially heterogeneous world of today, where many music patterns and cultures can slide in and out of favor with the speed of kaleidoscopic images.

### Individual Preference or Group Taste?

We all have our musical preferences and tastes—the records we purchase, the performances we attend, the tunes we hum along with on the radio. In America, with our ideology of democratic choice, we also feel that taste is an individual matter—that since we are free to choose anything (or, at least anything that the music industry puts on the market and that we can afford), our choices reflect our free spirit and individuality. The ecleticism that this freedom permits encourages diversity in personal taste to some extent. We all have our few idiosyncratic choices—the classicial music lover who listens to Bob Dylan, or the country & western fan who chooses Tina Turner's "You Better Be Good to Me," are examples. But, in general, such choices are but window dressing. The central fact is that *we pretty much listen to, and enjoy, the same music listened to by other people we like or identify with.*

Adolescents understand this and are constantly checking out the record and tape collections of influential friends (to see if they themselves are "covered" in their own collections), or of newcomers seeking admission to their group (to see if they "fit"). Bits of musical trivia are hoarded and exchanged (Is that Sting singing on the Dire Straits LP? What was Madonna wearing on her latest video? What did the lyrics to "Louie, Louie" really mean?). Knowledge of this trivia is like money in the bank in the game of who's OK and who is not in youth culture.

Such social uses of music are not new in America. Prior to the explosion of rock and roll in the mid-1950s, sociologist David Riesman oberved the same things to be true of Tin Pan Alley tunes, dating back to the 1930s and 1940s. He noted that young people used popular music to create socially shared meanings and common states of awareness. Then, as now, young people identified with certain singers, used popular music as a conversational resource, and, by predicting which songs would become hits and knowing musical trivia, created and established their positions within the peer group (Riesman, 1950).

Nor are these social uses of music purely an American phenomenon. In Sweden, sociologist Keith Roe collected panel data on Swedish youth in the town of Vaxjo in 1976, 1978, and 1980, and found that involvement in popular music in Sweden is clearly a group phenomenon (Roe, 1985; see also Roe's chapter in this volume). Swedish youth who were most oriented toward their peers (as opposed to their families or school) most often agreed that "music creates a good atmosphere when I'm with others" (Roe, 1985, p. 359). Listening for the sake of the lyrics also correlated highly with peer orientation, leading Roe to suggest that knowledge of lyrics "may be useful as a coin of exchange in peer group discourse" (Roe, 1985, p. 359).

Finally, the statement that "music fits in well with my life" correlated highly with listening to rock, new wave, and punk music, the forms that were, in 1980, the most clearly identifiable as subcultural or group styles. As Roe concluded, "Such subcultures possess their own distinct norms and values in matters of clothing, hair styles, attitudes, and modes of behavior. They demand allegiance and identification as the price of entry. Music becomes a main avenue of expression for group values and identity" (Roe, 1985, p. 361).

Studies have also been carried out in England revealing similar patterns. In 1959, Mark Abrams published a "teenager consumer report," which showed that consumption of popular music was by far the most important pastime of British young people (Abrams, 1959). And, sociologist/music critic Simon Frith conducted an intensive survey of 14- to 18-year olds in Yorkshire, from which he concluded that music is important to British youth for two main reasons—it is a means by which groups define themselves and it is a source of in-group status (Frith, 1978, p. 46).

As an extreme example, Frith points to what was known in the early 1970s in England as the "northern soul" scene, with an estimated 25,000 adherents across the country whose lifestyle revolved around all-night dancing to obscure (in England) American black music. Those who Frith interviewed told him: "I can't stand to be with anyone who doesn't like soul . . . My whole life centers around soul . . . I couldn't imagine going out with a girl who doesn't like soul . . . I like black films and I like the lifestyle they depict . . . Soul has given me so much that me and my girl have contemplated adopting a black baby!" (Frith, 1978, p. 57).

But, even as it seems true that music, by itself, has a lot to do with defining the identity and boundaries of groups and subcultures, Frith warns that music should also always be looked at in its larger social context. Youth from different social class backgrounds, for example, can—and do—interpret similar music differently. Middle-class youth seem more concerned with the lyrics and their meaning, while working-class youth are more into the beat and danceability of the song (Frith, 1978, pp. 37-58). Girls, on the whole, relate to popular music differently and listen to different tunes than do boys. Black youths usually have different listening patterns than do whites (Lewis, 1980).

So, although music helps to define the important groupings and subcultures of British and other youth cultures (for instance, punks, Teddy Boys, hips, new wavers; see Hebdige, 1979; Brake, 1985), one must never lose sight of factors such as social class, age, education, race, religion, and sex as important variables in determining who listens to what and with whom.

### Taste Cultures in Popular Music

The term "taste culture" was coined by American sociologist Herbert Gans to refer to the set of cultural strata in a society that roughly parallels the strata of social class of that society (Gans, 1967). What Gans had in mind was the fact that members of a society—all members, from upper to lower class—have definite ideas about the worth of musical, or, more generally, cultural material. Indeed, if they all could vote—or if some smaller group of them was politically so powerful they could make the decisions for everyone else—these persons would establish a cultural ranking of, in this case, musical materials, from highest to lowest.

This ranking would, according to Gans, roughly correspond to the patterns of consumption representative of the various social classes. For example, classical music would be consumed primarily by the upper classes, while polkas (in the United States today) would be most often associated with working class/folk culture.

In this way, given the perspective provided by Gans, a primary determinant of the music one enjoys is one's position in the class structure of society. Conversely, if a person's musical preferences are known, his or her social class might also be indicated. Gans was too sophisticated to see this as a totally one-to-one relationship between musical or cultural taste and social class. Still, he felt this correlation was quite significant, and certainly too important to ignore.

Gans's idea of taste cultures, as they apply to musical preference, was first tested in Los Angeles (Denisoff & Levine, 1972). They found partial support for Gans's theory, in that the social class level of college students was an important determinant of the type of music they preferred. However, these researchers also found that students' age and, most important, race, was critical in determining musical preference.

When tested on other American and Canadian college-age groups (Fox & Wince, 1975; Skipper, 1975) and on the American adult population (Lewis & McCarthy, 1974; Dixon, 1979), further evidence of a similar sort was found. Social class level was important, but other demographic factors were, in addition, just as important—factors such as age, education, religion, race, and where people live.

At about the same time, Richard Peterson and Paul DiMaggio (1975) published a study of taste culture as it applied to listeners of country & western music. They concluded that social class-based lines of distinction were, interestingly, not much in evidence. There were clear groupings of people who liked the same music but did *not* fit together in terms of social class: "Not only are country fans more clearly distinguished by race and age than by social class . . . more importantly, many people of the same strata, race, and age do *not* like country music" (Peterson & DiMaggio, 1975, p. 503; italics mine). These authors used the term "culture class" to refer to that aggregate of individuals who seek out similar cultural forms, even as this aggregate is nondefinable in the traditional, social class sense of taste cultures.

And yet, even as there is evidence that music preference in America is grouped along lines other than social class, the picture is by no means completely clear. In studying young Californians, communication researcher James Lull and his associates concluded that demographically predictable radio audiences can be identified for various musical types (Lull, Johnson, & Sweeny, 1978). In a study of a midwestern American town, researchers found three main categories of musical taste—what they term "highbrow/traditional, contemporary progressive, and middlebrow/traditional" (Deihl, Schneider, & Petress, 1983), categories that are linked, to some extent, to social class.

### Musical Culture and Social Structure: How Does It Link Up?

What does all this ultimately suggest about taste cultures and the correlation of musical preference and social class? Clearly, the relationship between the two is not the clean and neat one that some, perhaps naively, have assumed it to be—especially in our modern, mass-mediated technological society. In such a society, under conditions of relatively high social mobility, greater discretionary income, easy credit, efficient distribution of goods, high diffusion rate of cultural products, conspicuous consumption, and a greater amount of leisure time, the linkage between social and cultural structures, such as popular music, becomes a question, not a given. Rather than assume it to be simply correlative, it is perhaps better to view it as contingent, problematic, variable, and—to a higher degree than we might imagine—subjectively determined (Lewis, 1983).

Said more simply, there just does not seem to be the one-to-one relationship between social class level and music consumption that the social-structural way of viewing music has assumed. Music does not just reflect social structure. It is dynamic, charged with subjective meaning, and may dramatically cut across the standard social structural variables such as class, age, or education, in creating groupings with common musical expectations and symbolic definitions, yet with members in widely divergent positions in the social system. Princess Caroline of Monaco, for example, shares a love of Stevie Wonder's music with many American ghetto blacks—but she likely shares very little else with them, in a sociological sense. Conversely, *within* the same social area, structurally defined, there may be many varied, and competing, musical taste groupings, a point that can be demonstrated by a visit to any American high school.

And, to make things even more complicated, there may well exist, side by side with these more demographically diverse groupings, other, more traditionally defined taste cultures. For example, country & western music fans may well cut across the standard socioeconomic variables in group definition. This is one of the reasons why the country & western style exploded from the 1950s to the 1980s from a small, regionally and subculturally based music, to a national mass cultural form, drawing an audience from people representing various classes, ages, educational levels, and geographic regions. But, along with something such as country music, one can have a taste culture in the same society and at the same time that is very narrowly defined by the standard demographic variables (such as the new "go-go" music that is defined by region—mid-Atlantic America; race—black; and socioeconomic class level—lower).

As a matter of fact, the more complex a society becomes, the more likely it is that all these patternings and musical connections to the culture will exist simultaneously, whereas in less socially mobile class-based societies, the simpler model of traditional taste cultures matching up with social class is more likely to be the norm, a point Pierre Bourdieu has made impressively in his studies of French society (Bourdieu, 1984).

Such an awareness of the complexity of structure and definition of taste cultures in modern society makes the fact of discrepant tastes and conflicts over these tastes an object of sociological investigation. The "politics of music" takes on new meaning when one can interpret clashes in the political arena or the commercial marketplace to represent conflicts among various culture groups over the legitimacy of their musical tastes, values, and moralities. Musical artifacts symbolize the group that identifies with them and its style of life. Hostility directed toward musical symbols, then, can be interpreted as hostility directed toward those whom these symbols represent. As Kreiling (1978) points out, in modern society there is a more or less continuous struggle—at times quite visible and at other times relatively dormant—among groups that seek public legitimacy for their lifestyles and public sanctions against the visible cultural symbols (like music) of alternative styles of life. Such struggles are at the heart of change in any social system.

Viewing musical taste groups this way, defined largely by alternative styles of life, is close to the way in which social theorist Max Weber distinguished between classes and what he termed "status groups": With some oversimplification, one might thus say that classes are stratified according to their relations to the production and acquisition of goods; whereas status groups are stratified according to principle of their consumption of goods as represented by special styles of life" (Weber, 1968, p. 937).

With the added *caveat* that those sharing a style of life may well not all have social structural variables in common, this model suggests the vitality of an approach to the study of popular music that does not automatically assume correlative linkages between the cultural and social structural levels of a society, but, instead, examines at the cultural level the way groups of human beings produce, sustain, and transform meaning in the creation and consumption of their music. Phil Spector, the famous rock and roll writer and producer, was asked during an interview what the million-selling 1963 song "Da Do Ron Ron" meant. He said, "It's not what I say it means, it's what it makes you feel! Can't you hear the *sound* of that record, can't you hear that?" (Marcus, 1969, pp. 11-12).

## *Inventions and Conventions in Music*

All popular music is composed of two types of elements, labeled by American Studies researcher John Cawelti as "inventions" and "conventions" (Cawelti, 1970). Inventions are the unique insights, discoveries, and aesthetic techniques contributed by the musician's creative power. Conventions are the socially shared stereotypes, formulae, myths, and musical patterns lodged in the "collective consciousness" or the musical heritage of a society or group. In the study of the meaning of music to people and groups, a focus on both of these elements is important. Study of inventions will give some insight into the transformation of musical meaning due to the sociopersonal insight of the artist and the unique social position of the artist and the audience. However, perhaps the more sociologically crucial area of study is that of conventions—their appearance and transformation in musical development.

Historian Russel Nye has expressed this sentiment with respect to popular art:

> Popular art tends to confirm the experience of the majority, in contrast to elite art, which tends to explore the new . . . thus [popular art] can provide an unusually sensitive and accurate image of the attitudes and concerns of the society for which it was created. It provides metaphors for expressing common experience. It gives us information we can obtain in no other way about the basic ideologies and operative ideas that drive society [Nye, 1972, pp. 5-6].

Thus conventions in popular music reflect the meanings understood by those individuals and groups who consume it. For example, the themes of rebellion in both the words and music of heavy metal rock groups such as Motley Crue reflect and reinforce very successfully the values and feelings of preteen and early teen male adolescents, those who make up the greatest part of this music's audience.

Not all aspects of social life can be effectively translated into musical culture. Some aspects are better than others for embodying dramatic tension and possibilities for resolution and thus are more likely to be reflected in the conventions of myth and patterns of the music. Others are included or excluded because of political decisions of the cultural power elite of the group or society in question. For example, the lyrics of heavy metal rock were under attack in America in the mid-1980s by conservative pressure groups such as the Parents' Music Resource Center, who somewhat successfully sought censorship of this form of musical expression within the record industry itself.

In any case, most popular music will be organized around a few accepted basic formulae that are then expanded by means of accumulation of audience expectations and symbolic associations over time. The Tin Pan Alley "June, moon, spoon" romantic love themes of the 1930s and 1940s is one such example of accumulation of meaning over time and songs. The rebellious themes of drugs, sex, and revolution of the 1960s and early 1970s music of the Rolling Stones, Janis Joplin, and others is another. A final example is the case of various political concerts and songs of the mid-1980s that were produced to raise funds (and consciousness) for groups such as the starving people of Ethiopia, the American small farmer, and the victims of South African apartheid. As diverse as these causes are in terms of performers, types of music, and political focus, the shows and recordings have been pretty much the same in terms of format, production, and performance, and have created definite audience expectations and shared symbolic associations.

Through such cultural forms—some rigidly stereotyped (country & western music, middle-of-the-road) and some more loosely organized (jazz, rap, reggae)—a variety of meanings can be expressed. These meanings may be relatively stable until either groups push for new and more relevant (for them) forms of meaning or a musical "prophet" breaks through the censoring cultural establishment with forms that symbolize necessary, but ignored, aspects of people's lives—an Elvis Presley, a Bob Marley, a Bruce Springsteen, a Prince, even a Frank Sinatra.

New music, in terms of meaning, is many times tied to the traditional meanings and consciousness of existing taste cultures. This is one of the most effective ways in which music of social protest arises—yet is, at the same time, familiar sounding to the people. For example, the Nueva Cancion songs of Chile, popular during the socialist Allende regime, were traditionally Chilean in form and instrumentation. They shifted lyrical content just enough to be critical of Western influences and to extol nationalistic solutions to Chilean problems. Yet, when these songs were transported to Mexico, they were never associated with a strong protest movement, as they had been in Chile, but instead were fragmented in various directions—toward rock or jazz or even traditional Mexican music (Finlay, 1982). This has also been the case of reggae music in Jamaica. Transplanted and torn from its traditional context and meaning, reggae loses its specific social effectiveness—though it has continued to diffuse internationally as a popular form, and has been built on by groups as diverse as Britain's The Clash and Nigeria's King Sunny Ade to form protest music of new types.

## Popular Music as a Symbolic Resource

If music is viewed as a symbolic resource shared by a group, then one can ask how in different historical periods, or in the songs of different groups or taste cultures, different elements are drawn from the larger societal "pool of culture" and how different uses are made of them. This would be a most fruitful perspective from which to examine, in America for instance, the fusion of the taste cultures of Anglo-Appalachian country music and Afro-American blues in the 1940s and the 1950s to form rock and roll, its diffusion across the Atlantic in the early 1960s to the British working class (whose youth added their own distinct elements to the mix), and its reintroduction to the American scene in the mid-1960s. Crucial to such a model of musical change would be determining the way in which some musical elements are continually enriched with new meanings while others are allowed to die, as well as a determination of the various taste cultures who hear their values symbolically reflected in the music, perhaps contribute to it, and adopt it as their own.

One can, using this perspective, trace the way symbolic elements move through a culture and are put to different uses by the members of different taste cultures. Disco, for example, originated in Paris in the mid-1970s by the young, urban middle class as a means of dancing to records, rather than live bands, during a time of economic scarcity. The music spread to America selectively. It became popular in gay dance clubs on the East Coast and also with blacks and Latinos, who could develop musical rhythms and more sexually explicit messages via this form than with that of media-controlled popular music (Lewis, 1982).

Disco then catapulted to fame in America primarily on the strength of a multiple-taste culture base, but also because of some strong songs by artists such as Donna Summer and Gloria Gaynor, an economic crunch that made record dancing an attractive way to spend an evening out, and the popularity of John Travolta in the film *Saturday Night Fever*. From there it was marketed throughout the world, enjoying great popularity in Third World countries—especially West Africa—even while it was fading from the forefront of the American music scene. The disco phenomenon raised the research question of how a musical form, transported to a different society entirely, takes on different symbolic meanings. What is the meaning of disco for West Africans? The music of Bob Marley for Europeans? Elvis Presley for the Japanese? (These questions are taken up by Roger Wallis and Krister Malm in their chapter in this volume.)

Shifts in power relations among large social groupings and social classes may well be reflected in changes in the popular music of the society—changes that could perhaps be examined profitably in analyses of English and French-based popular music in Quebec and across Canada, or in the revival of traditional Hawaiian music and its transformation into a vehicle for social protest in that state (Lewis, 1984). As well, shifts in ideology and power negotiations both within and among small nations can be examined, as in the case of the shifting "approved" popular musical content of culture in the People's Republic of China in the 1980s.

Finally, this approach to taste cultures and the meaning of music suggests the crucial role of the production of music in this whole cultural-social equation. Although a detailed examination of the culture industries that produce much of our popular music is beyond the scope of this chapter (see especially Frith, Abt, and Rothenbuhler in this volume), some quick observations are in order. How systems of musical production and distribution unite or fail to unite subcultures, communities, and groups in which musical resources are shared may affect the balance between formal development and substantive change in a society's musical tradition. Will subcultural forms (such as ska, metal, rap) remain within their own small taste cultures and communities? Will they only selectively be introduced as new and isolated symbols into the larger society by the music industry, thereby adding on meaning to established forms, but not symbolically altering them? Or, will taste cultures become connected via communication and distribution systems that powerfully inject their "new" music into the larger society, thus altering its symbolic content, as occurred in the diffusion of British rock and the "San Francisco sound" in the United States in the late 1960s and early 1970s (Lewis, 1972)?

The answers to questions such as these lie in close examination of the parameters of taste cultures in a given society and at a given point in time. How socially and culturally powerful are its members? How closely do its values and attitudes, as reflected in its music, parallel that which is accepted as "correct" within the larger society? How powerful is the music as a resource of definition and self identity? To how many different taste cultures do members of a song group belong, collectively and individually? How stable are taste cultures across time? To what extent do taste cultures correspond to social class levels in the society and how deeply and in what manner do they cut across these levels of social class?

## Conclusion

There is still a long way to go in developing a clear understanding of taste cultures, their boundaries, and linkages to contemporary society. I have attempted to suggest an approach that considers music to be a system of symbolic meaning to individuals and members of social groups. Meaning is created by the members of these groups in their internal interaction and in interaction *among* other groups as they jockey for position within society, or attempt to maintain their cultural or political dominance.

Clifford Geertz, the anthropologist, suggested an analogy concerning culture that is appropriate here when he said that "people are animals suspended in webs of significance they themselves spin" (Geertz, 1973, p. 31). I am not convinced that the musical webs of taste culture that we have examined in this chapter are quite as neat and symmetrical as such an analogy suggests. Rather, I imagine that taste cultures are ragged and incomplete—filled with repetitions of similar symbolic patterns and blank spaces—that are even tied together at times in nonlogical ways. Yet these musical webs of taste culture are extremely resilient. When studied carefully, they can reveal a great deal about the creatures who created them, are influenced by them, and who eagerly live out their lives enjoying the music they contain.

## REFERENCES

Abrams, M. (1959). *The teenage consumer*. London.
Adorno, T. (1959). *Introduction to the sociology of music*. New York: Seabury.
Bourdieu, P. (1984). *Distinction: A social critique of the judgment of taste*. Cambridge: Harvard University Press.
Brake, M. (1985). *Comparative youth culture*. Boston: Routledge & Kegan Paul.
Cawelti, J. (1970). *The six-gun mystique*. Bowling Green, Ohio: Popular Press.
Conford, F. (1941). *Plato's republic*. Clarendon: Oxford.
Deihl, E. R., Schneider, M., & Petress, K. (1983). Dimensions of music preference: A factor analytic study. *Popular Music and Society, 9*, 41-49.
Denisoff, R. S. (1972). *Sing a song of social significance*. Bowling Green, Ohio: Popular Press.
Denisoff, R. S. (1982) Democratisation of popular music. *Media Development, 1*, 29-30.
Denisoff, R. S., & Levine, M. (1972). Youth and popular music: A test of the taste culture hypothesis. *Youth and Society, 4*, 237-255.
Dixon, R. D. (1979). Music in the community: A survey of who is paying attention. *Popular Music and Society, 5*, 12-27.
Finlay, B. (1982). *Nationalism in musical protest*. Unpublished manuscript.
Fox, W., & Wince, M. (1975). Musical taste cultures and taste publics. *Youth and Society, 7*, 198-224.

Frith, S. (1978). *The sociology of rock*. London: Constable.

Gans, H. J. (1967). Popular culture in America. In H. S. Becker (Ed.), *Social problems: A modern approach*. New York: Wiley.

Geertz, C. (1973). *The interpretation of cultures*. New York: Basic Books.

Gramsci, A. (1971). *Selections from the prison notebooks*. New York: International Publishers.

Hebdige, D. (1979). *Subculture: The meaning of style*. London: Methuen.

Kreiling, A. (1978). Toward a cultural studies approach for the study of popular culture. *Communication Research, 5,* 24-63.

Lewis, G. H. (1972). *Side-saddle on the golden calf: Social structure and popular culture in America*. Pacific Palisades, CA: Goodyear.

Lewis, G. H. (1978). The sociology of popular culture. *Current Sociology,* 1-160.

Lewis, G. H. (1979). Mass, popular, folk and elite cultures. *Media Asia, 6,* 34-52.

Lewis, G. H. (1980). An examination of commitment and involvement in popular music. *Popular Music and Society, 7,* 10-18.

Lewis, G. H. (1982). The rise and fall of disco. *Stockton Record* (March 19), 4-5.

Lewis, G. H. (1983). The meaning's in the music. *Theory, Culture and Society, 3,* 133-141.

Lewis, G. H. (1984). Da kine sounds: The function of music as social protest in the new Hawaiian renaissance. *American Music, 2,* 38-52.

Lewis, G. H., & McCarthy, J. D. (1974). *Popular music and the American audience: An examination of the taste culture hypothesis*. Paper presented at the American Sociological Association meeting, Montreal.

Lull, J. (1982). Popular music: Resistance to new wave. *Journal of Communication, 32,* 121-131.

Lull, J., Johnson, L., & Sweeny, C. (1978). Audiences for contemporary radio formats. *Journal of Broadcasting, 22,* 439-453.

Marcus, G. (1969). *Rock and roll will stand*. Boston: Beacon Press.

Nye, R. (1972). *Notes on a rationale for popular culture*. Bowling Green, OH: Popular Press.

Peterson, R. A., & DiMaggio, P. (1975). From region to class: The changing locus of country music. *Social Forces, 53,* 497-506.

Riesman, D. (1950). Listening to popular music. *American Quarterly, 2,* 359-371.

Roe, K. (1985). Swedish youth and music: Listening patterns and motivations. *Communication Research, 12,* 353-362.

Sheperd, J. (1977). *Whose music? A sociology of musical languages*. New Jersey: Transaction.

Skipper, J. K., Jr. (1975). Musical tastes of Canadian and American college students: An examination of the massification and Americanization theses. *Canadian Journal of Sociology, 1,* 49-59.

Thomas, W. L., & D. S. Thomas (1928). *The child in America*. New York: Knopf.

Weber, M. (1968). *Economy and society*. New York: Bedminster.

# 10

# The School and Music
# in Adolescent Socialization

## KEITH ROE

> It is probably cultural inertia which still makes us see education in terms
> of the ideology of the school as a liberating force [Bourdieu, 1974].

After the family, the two major agents of socialization in modern
societies are the school and the mass media. This fact has stimulated a
vast sociological literature that attempts to describe and explain the role
of these agents in the individual's social development. Such work should
be seen as a valuable and necessary, but not sufficient, condition for
understanding the process of socialization. Simple relationships between, say, the individual and the family, or the individual and the
school, tend to conceal the complex interrelationships of social life as a
whole. It is necessary also to examine critically the ways in which the
family, the school, and the mass media, including music, interact in the
socialization of youth.

While there exists a long and respectable tradition of research in the
sociology of education regarding links between the home and the
school, other interconnections have received considerably less attention.
There is now a growing literature that focuses upon the importance of
family relationships for the ways in which children use the media (for
instance, Chaffee, McLeod, & Atkin, 1971; Chaffee and Tims, 1976;
Marschak, 1980; Faber, Brown, & McLeod, 1982). Studies of the
relationships between the school and young people's uses of the media
have been more limited both in number and quality. The purpose of this

chapter is to examine these relationships in light of the existing research and then to discuss the general implications of them for the school/media debate with particular attention paid to a medium of special importance to young people—popular music.

International research on the relationship between the media and school achievement is as old as the media themselves. This research agenda developed in part because educators very quickly came to regard the media as competitors for the minds of the young. This concern was amplified by the rapid spread of television in the period after World War II. By the early 1950s, researchers, mainly American, became concerned with the belief that televiewing could adversely affect children's school work. The results of this research, however, provided little support for such apprehension (Maccoby, 1951; Battin, 1952; Himmelweit, Oppenheim, & Vince, 1958; Greenstein, 1954).

Despite the lack of empirical evidence, this early concern with the effects of television on school work quickly developed into the dominant theoretical perspective of the relationships between the media and the school. This dominant perspective is represented in Figure 10.1.

More recent research has also been unable to provide consistent support for this perspective. While it is true that some studies have reported results indicating that television does negatively affect school work (Slater, 1965; Emery & Emery, 1976; Sharman, 1979), others have reported positive effects (Ridder, 1963; Smith, 1972; Neuman, 1980), while still others have reported highly qualified effects depending on such factors as age, gender, and ability of the child (Bailyn, 1959; La Blonde, 1966; Harrison, 1978; Murray, 1980; Williams, 1982). The simple negative effects perspective has increasingly come to be viewed as unsatisfactory (Morgan & Gross, 1980; Roc, 1983). Yet it remains the dominant theoretical paradigm for explaining the media-school relationship.

Often the arguments put forward on behalf of the negative effects hypothesis are based solely on ideological or rhetorical assertion. A good example of this type is Postman's (1980) polemic on the school as a conservative defense against the supposed evils of the modern media. Postman's work has been influential and has partly been responsible for sharpening the debate surrounding school-media relationships in recent years. Unfortunately, many of the arguments used in such attacks on the media lack the scientific criterion of falsifiability and criticism of the media tends to be tautological because observations are selectively

ASPECTS OF
TELEVISION ---have (detrimental) effects on--> ASPECTS OF
SCHOOL EXPERIENCE

Figure 10.1 Dominant Perspective on School-Media Relationship

interpreted to "prove" basic presuppositions (McQuail, 1969).

We all attend, and are socialized by, some educational institution. The school is one of the few genuine universals of modern social life. More than this, we accept the legitimacy of the schools' pedagogic authority and of its social sorting function, fulfilled by means of the grading of "ability" and "achievement." Inherent in the acceptance of this authority is a tendency to see success and failure in individual terms and, second, to see the origins of failure as largely external to the school and its practice. Stated baldly, teachers and educational researchers usually locate causes of academic failure and behavioral disturbance outside of the school—in intelligence, motivation, family background, language and other cultural "deficiencies," the peer group, the media, and so on. Of course, all of these can and do play a role. That is not the point. The point is that rarely are causes of failure sought within the structure and praxis of the school itself. If failure is caused by deficiencies elsewhere, then why bother to look inside? It is in this context that we find the major reason for the continued predominance of the "media-damage-school-achievement" perspective.


### What About Popular Music?

The preoccupation with the alleged effects of television has diverted research activity away from the possible relations that schooling may have with other media. Apart from occasional studies examining film, radio, or comics, very little more than lip service has been paid to media other than television. In particular, the role and importance of popular music in the teenage environment has been seriously neglected, despite the steady accumulation of powerful evidence for it from other fields, especially within British subcultural studies.

While the neglect of popular music may have been understandable during the early history of rock and roll, it is remarkable that this oversight has persisted until now. More and more studies show that the whole adolescent milieu is penetrated at many levels by an active interest in music; that many adolescents employ it as a social lubricator; that a great deal of adolescent discourse centers around the language and terminology of rock; and that music provides the core values of numerous adolescent subcultures (Willis, 1978; Hebdige, 1979; Brake, 1980; Frith, 1981; Lull, 1985a, 1985b, 1986). Consequently, it is becoming increasingly difficult to escape the conclusion, in terms of both the sheer amount of time devoted to it and the meanings it assumes, that it is music, not television, that is the most important medium for adolescents.

## A Theoretical Reconsideration

A realization of the various inadequacies of the orthodox theoretical perspective leads me to propose a respecification of the school-media relationship, a perspective that can, moreover, be tested empirically. It is argued that it is possible to reverse the traditional causal direction and hypothesize that school experience, in various ways, independently influences aspects of media use (including music) and the gratifications obtained from it; and, furthermore, that such a perspective is more fruitful than the dominant view. In its barest form such a reversal is represented in Figure 10.2.

Very important in this respecification is the need to examine media other than television, especially music and, subsequently, video. In addition, existing research clearly indicates that children and adolescents do not relate to media or to school in a social and cultural vacuum. In particular, the importance of the peer group as a mediating factor between individuals, their lives in school, and the media is identified. It is, therefore, necessary to refine the respecification by incorporating the peer group in general and youth subcultures in particular. The final specification is represented in Figure 10.3.

## Functions of School in Society

The functions of school in advanced industrial societies are particularly complex and the subject of considerable political and ideological conflict. Historically this conflict has largely been responsible for the fact that schools have been assigned three major mutually incompatible, even contradictory, functions. First is the education of the child into what is considered "useful" knowledge, usually incorporating the ideology of individual and social liberation and growth. Second is the cultivation of the discipline, outlooks, and attitudes necessary for the expressive functioning of the industrial system. Third is the instruction of skills and knowledge, along with the sorting and allocation of individuals into vocational categories, necessary to meet the demands of modern technology (Katz, 1968; Bowles & Gintis, 1977).

Much of the work of the schools is concerned with human differentia-

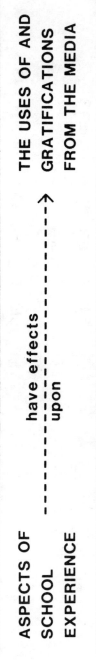

ASPECTS OF SCHOOL EXPERIENCE ----have effects upon----> THE USES OF AND GRATIFICATIONS FROM THE MEDIA

Figure 10.2 Respecified Perspective on School-Media Relationship

217

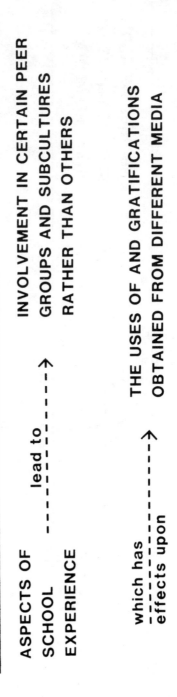

ASPECTS OF
SCHOOL          ------ lead to ------>
EXPERIENCE

INVOLVEMENT IN CERTAIN PEER
GROUPS AND SUBCULTURES
RATHER THAN OTHERS

which has
------ effects upon ------>

THE USES OF AND GRATIFICATIONS
OBTAINED FROM DIFFERENT MEDIA

Figure 10.3  Fully Respecified Perspective on School-Media Relationship

tion and allocation. The primary mechanisms of these processes are the giving of grades, examination certificates, and degrees. Every act of grade giving is also an act of differentiation and as such an act of allocation into socially legitimized and recognized categories. Central to these mechanisms is the giving of the status labels "success" and "failure." In effect, then, schools have received from society the power of conferring success and failure on young people (Bowles & Gintis, 1977; Meyer, 1977).

This argument also implies that schools assign status. Collins (1972) sees the main activity of schools as being the teaching of particular status cultures both inside and outside the classroom. Imparting knowledge is not really important. What schools really teach are "ways of using language, styles of dress, aesthetic tastes, values and manners" (Collins, 1972, p. 187; see also Collins, 1979). This model regards society as made up of associational groups sharing common cultures or subcultures usually composed of persons who share a sense of status equality based on participation in a common culture.

Some of the most sophisticated work in this area has been that of the French social anthropologist Pierre Bourdieu and his associates. Bourdieu argues that educational institutions are involved in structuring society into status and cultural hierarchies. Indeed, the requirement to produce individuals who are selected and arranged in a hierarchy for their whole lifetime is regarded as one of the major functions of the school (Bourdieu & Passeron, 1979).

Bourdieu employs the concept of "cultural capital" in order to enable us to see the ways in which individuals and groups form status hierarchies. An important component of cultural capital is "academic capital," which is given its most explicit form in grades and degree certificates. The use of the term "capital" is a deliberate analogy to economic capital. Just as economic capital may be used to create and reproduce wealth, so may academic capital be used to create and reproduce status distinctions. Cultural capital may be employed to create and reproduce cultural distinctions such as what constitutes "taste" and "good taste," "high culture" and "popular culture," and so on.

Indeed, the economic analogy may be carried further. Academic degrees may be used as a form of currency on the labor market. They are subject to inflation and devaluation. They may even be squandered and wasted. The amount of possession of academic capital is therefore largley dependent upon various socially legitimized judgments of the individuals' worth as defined by criteria currently employed by the school (Bourdieu, 1974, 1980).

That schools help to structure society by allocating students to different roles and statuses is not to say anything particularly new. What has not been made explicit or deep, however, is what consequences this has for cultural taste in general and for media use in particular. The essential point is that schools, by means of these activities, necessarily create socially homogenous status groupings with different values, styles, and general predispositions toward cultural taste, including media habits (Morley, 1980).

It follows from this discussion that the degree of possession of academic capital may be regarded as an important intervening variable between the individual's social background and all cultural forms and tastes. Specifically, we may expect to find an empirical link among indicators of differential possession of academic capital and preference for legitimate or oppositional cultural forms as between classical or punk music.

### The Importance of Social Background

Social background is an important factor in this relationship. Much work in the sociology of education has analyzed the significance of social background as an influence on educational achievement. In terms of academic and cultural capital, it is obvious that children are born into homes possessing different amounts of each. For Bourdieu in particular, the influence of social background is the strongest differentiating factor in the student world and is, moreover, far broader, more subtle, and more pervasive than is normally assumed. In addition to the material, linguistic, and parental factors usually discussed, social background influences are seen as affecting the whole of social life to reach their purest consequences in differences of taste and lifestyle by which different social groups are able to identify one another.

In discussing social background, especially when dealing with matters of taste and cultural activity, therefore, it is necessary to look beyond mere differences in income. Cultural privilege (as opposed to economic privilege)

is only manifest when it is a matter of familiarity with works which only regular visits to theatres, galleries and concerts can give ... in every area of culture which it is measured—be it the theatre, music, painting, jazz or the cinema—students have richer and more extensive knowledge the higher their social origin [Bourdieu and Passeron, 1979, p. 8].

It should be remembered that the transmission of academic and cultural capital is no longer direct from parents to their children but now takes place through the mediation of the school. This implies that some individuals from lower classes may, by means of achievement in school, accumulate extra academic capital and overcome the academic and cultural handicaps of their background. Conversely, students from more privileged backgrounds may squander their advantages and fail to accumulate sufficient academic capital (in other words, degrees or examination certificates, and so on) to maintain their status. Both of these groups will, as a consequence of their experience, suffer from some degree of status incongruity between their social background and their current academic status. Such status incongruity is often important in the formation of subcultures, since compensatory strategies are required to resolve these incongruities.

For academically successful students from low social backgrounds the problem does not usually become acute. They often merely adopt the cultural values and styles of their newly acquired status. Often more visible are those school "failures" or school "rejectors" who come from more privileged social backgrounds. For them, the dislocation of social background and current academic status is in a negative direction and, consequently, compensatory strategies are more necessary. In general, an aesthetic concern with music, art, and other forms of cultural expression are characteristic reactions to disenchantment with, or failure in, school for children from privileged backgrounds.

Before we proceed we should also note that social background is not the only important background variable in the experience of schooling. It must also be remembered that schools are age-based institutions where children are compelled to attend by adults. This means that schools are also arenas of age-based conflicts that can at times assume great significance in the formation of youthful subcultures. Moreover, this age-based conflict is common to all youth, though it may be expressed in different ways. When discussing the importance of popular music in particular, this aspect of the makeup of schools is of major importance.

To recapitulate, the main argument is that one of the major sociocultural effects of the school's allocative function is a structuring of the audience for cultural products. The result of this structuring is a hierarchy of individuals. Inseparable from the whole process is the ascription of the status labels of "success" and "failure." It is argued that the main activity of schools is the teaching of particular status cultures both in and outside the classroom. Knowledge transmission, the "official" business of schools, is seen as less important than the teaching of styles, tastes, values, and so on. The result is a society composed of groups sharing a sense of status equality and possessing common cultures or subcultures. Such groups also tend to have relatively homogenous tastes, styles, and media preferences.

This argument is supported by a substantial number of research results. First, there is evidence that formal differentiation of pupils by the school leads to polarization of students as a result of the accompanying labelling process. The consequences of this polarization are that the failures are predisposed to react negatively to the system that has thus labelled them while the successful tend to be predisposed to accept the school's culture. In the extreme case, this polarization may result in specifically antischool subcultures developing among the failures. One expression of this reaction may be a negative commitment to the school, manifesting itself in truancy, bad behavior, and low motivation. Various studies have found that successful students tend to stay at home more in the evenings, read more, and watch more television. The less successful students go out more, are less cooperative with parents especially concerning friends, clothes, hairstyles, and the like, and are generally a greater problem to parents over a wide range of behavior. In addition, they tend to prefer more socially disapproved popular music (Hargreaves, 1967; Lacey, 1970; Martens, 1981, 1982).

### The School, Teenage Subcultures, and Popular Music

We have traced here a direct causal chain. Differentiation by the school leads to a polarization of students, which can lead to the formation of pro- or antischool attitudes which, in turn, may result in the formation of distinct subcultures. These achievement-related subcultures may then form distinct orientations toward the media in general and preferences for certain kinds of music as well.

One of the first researchers to explore some of these links empirically was Coleman (1960, 1961, 1966) in his classic study of the American high school. He found that adolescents who failed to achieve in school tended to turn toward heavier media use as an escape from confronting the meaning of their failure. This work was subsequently given added impetus by British studies of the role of the school in the formation of subcultures (Sugarman, 1967; Brown & O'Leary, 1971). These studies showed that commitment to the teenage role expressed in dress, adornment, music, dancing, and slang has the function of asserting independence from adult authority.

In particular, frequency of popular music listening and the display of identity symbols of teenage subcultures were found to correlate with unfavorable attitudes held toward school, poor conduct, and low achievement. The main function of involvement with teenage pop culture was therefore seen to lie in symbolically expressing alienation from school. The impetus for involvement in pop music was located within the school and was dependent upon the school as an institutional base. High achievers were found to be less involved with pop music than low achievers and academic work and pop music were, partly at least, alternative centers of interest, even alternative sources of reputation, for these groups. Pop music could become a source of prestige for the less academically successful. One study (Murdock & Phelps, 1973) went so far as to claim that given knowledge of social background, gender, commitment to and achievement in school, the media habits of most older school students could be predicted with some accuracy.

Much of the work of the British subcultural theorists has supported these findings. The interaction of social background with various aspects of schooling as being of great significance in the formation of youth subcultures has been repeatedly confirmed in the studies of specific groups (Cohen, 1972; Clarke, 1976; Willis, 1977, 1978; Brake, 1977; Frith, 1981; Hebdige, 1979). In these studies special attention has been given to the last years of schooling, since the anticipated entrance into work may strongly influence subcultural styles (Willis, 1977, 1980).

What most of the subcultures had in common was a very strong commitment to some form of popular music. Indeed, in many cases music provided one of the most explicit expressions of group identity (Willis, 1978). However, popular music must not be regarded as an undifferentiated whole. It should be borne in mind too that the popular music audience is not homogenous (Denisoff, 1975; Frith, 1981) and varies according to both ethnic origin and social background. As Denisoff complains, there are few definitions of popular music of any substance. He observes,

> Taste publics and genres are affected by a number of factors, predominantly age, accessibility, race, class, and education. As such the designation of popular music is more a sociological than a musical definition [Denisoff, 1975, p. 39].

The importance of separate peer groups for popular music has been indicated by Clarke (1973). He shows how knowledge of popular music can be used to form impressions of peers at school. Music preferences give the adolescent information about others and knowledge of popular music can be used as a coin of exchange in peer interactions. Two distinct groups of users are identified: those who are members of a peer group sharing musical preferences and those who are relatively isolated and listen for reasons other than social ones. He further notes that music may also become important for various subcultures in their resistance to the agencies of adult culture and authority as sources of "collective power."

## The Swedish Panel Study on School, Media, and Music

The link between school achievement and the media has recently been explored in a full-length study conducted on a panel of 509 Swedish adolescents aged from 11 to 15 years (Roe, 1983). These young people were followed through four years and interviewed by means of questionnaires on three different occasions, when aged 11, 13, and 15 years. The results, therefore, represent relationships *over time for the same individuals* thereby enabling us better to assess causal relationships. The end-of-term school grades of the respondents were also collected for the ages of 12, 13, and 15 (the 6th, 7th, and 9th years of school).

A theoretical causal model was subsequently developed for testing based on the respecified relationship between the school and the media described earlier. In addition to school grades, respondents' levels of commitment to school were also measured by means of the scale developed by Murdock and Phelps (1973). Also measured were social background, gender, orientation to parents and peers, interest in popular music and preference for different musical genres, television use, future educational plans, and occupational expectations at the age of 15.

It should be kept in mind that all relationships between factors described are unique, all other factors in the model having been simultaneously controlled. This means, for example, that when discussing relationships between school achievement and various music preferences we are discussing the strength of those relationships *after* the effect of other relevant variables (for instance, social background) have been taken into account.

The results of the study provide substantial support for the hypothesis that both school achievement and attitude toward school may operate as independent causal variables with respect to adolescent music uses and preferences. Effects were both direct and indirect, mediated by the peer group. It should be noted, however, that the causal mechanism revealed by the model operates quite differently for males and females. The effects of school achievement and attitudes held toward school were nevertheless in the same direction for both sexes, the differences lying in the roles played by male and female peer-group involvement.

Specifically, a strong direct relationship was found between higher school achievement at the age of 12 and a greater expressed disliking for classical music three years later (remembering that social background effects have been controlled for). For the females this relationship was particularly strong. As an extra check to remove doubts that the results might be influenced by social background, those adolescents who came from the lowest social background (as measured by both parents' occupation and level of education) were analyzed separately. The results showed that the higher their school achievement, the more likely they were to express a liking for classical music. Thus even students from the lowest background tend to move toward a liking for classical music (a genre normally associated negatively with low status) *if they are high achievers*. Here we see clearly that high achievement itself predisposes students to accept a liking for acceptable cultural forms.

Relationships between achievement and other music-type factors first came into operation a year later when the respondents were aged 13. Higher school achievement at this age was negatively associated with a liking for punk and rock music two years later, indicating that low achievement provokes a preference for this type of music. Mainstream popular music, on the other hand, was positively associated with earlier school achievement.

In addition to these direct relationships, there was an indirect causal path from school achievement to music preferences. At the age of 13, lower school achievement was associated moderately strongly with a greater orientation toward peers. Orientation toward peers was itself related to a greater liking for punk and rock music two years later. Here we see the causal chain identified in the research cited above—namely, that low school achievement leads to a greater involvement with peers, leading to a greater preference for socially disapproved music.

At the age of 15 the "school commitment" variable was introduced into the analysis. For both sexes it became one of the most powerful explanatory factors in the whole model, exerting an influence independent of that stimulated by school achievement. Once again, both direct and indirect effects were in evidence. For both sexes a negative commitment to school was directly related to a greater liking for punk and rock. Conversely, a more positive commitment to school was related to a greater liking for mainstream popular music among boys and to a stronger tendency toward classical music for both sexes. Indirectly, a negative commitment to school led to a greater orientation to peers, and thereafter from peer orientation to a greater liking for punk and rock, the same mechanisms identified for school achievement.

**Music Versus Television**

The results, then, clearly showed the causal role of the specified aspects of school experience with regard to adolescents' music uses and preferences. Much more equivocal were the results concerning the use of television. At each stage of the analysis, the television-use data manifested complex, even contradictory, tendencies. While there was some evidence of a negative relationship between school achievement and television use at the earlier ages, especially among females, television use subsequently became increasingly irrelevant in the causal relations of the model. Even school commitment, which at the age of 15 related to every other variable in the model, witnessed no significant relationship with television use. In addition, there was evidence of curvilinearity in the relationship with students most positive to school *and* students most negative to school viewing least. This obviously argues strongly against the simple negative relationship between school and television. We are led to conclude that at the time of puberty the expression of conflict in the school-media relationship centers on certain oppositional music forms, while the relationship between school and television comes to be characterized by, if not mutual irrelevance, then by more or less peaceful coexistence.

*Summary*

The results of the Swedish study firmly support a number of conclusions. First, the significance of school achievement as a causal variable in relation to media use was established. The findings unequivocally support the argument that music preferences are dependent upon earlier levels of school achievement.

Second, the results clearly indicated the mediating role of the adolescent peer group in these respects. Taken together, the presence of these two causal paths, the direct and the indirect, provide substantial evidence for the empirical link, postulated earlier, between indicators of differential possession of academic capital and preferences for traditional or oppositional cultural forms. The more successful students, even when they come from the lowest social status background, show a greater liking for classical and mainstream music forms. The failing students move instead toward socially disapproved and oppositional music and at the same time orient themselves more fully to school peer groups. Here we see that through its certification and allocation activities, the schooling system does indeed help to structure preferences and behavior of the media audience.

Further evidence of the importance of school was provided by the efficacy of the school commitment variable. By age 15 it was the most powerful single explanatory variable in the whole model. The relationships between school commitment, peer orientation, and music preferences, in particular, clearly support the view that high involvement in certain teenage groups and musical styles helps to provide a symbolic expression of alienation from the school.

Involvement with music was also significant in another sense. This has to do with the question of anticipatory socialization, meaning that adolescents adjust their present values and styles in response to their anticipated future social status. The results showed that social background influences on most music preferences were very weak. On the other hand, some music factors were related to perceived *future* status. For example, 11-year-old girls who were heavy users of popular music anticipated getting lower status jobs after school, even when social background was controlled. Similarly, at the age of 15 boys who preferred socially disapproved music also anticipated getting lower status jobs after high school. Both of these relationships remained after controlling for school achievement. Thus there would appear to be an independent link between certain music uses and tastes and perceived future status for some adolescents. In particular, the results suggest that perceived social mobility (upward, downward, or stationary) may be intimately connected with music tastes.

Implications of these results for the whole school-media debate are compelling. We have seen that the practice of schooling itself provokes attachment to values and subcultures that stand in opposition to those of the school. Teachers themselves, in fulfilling the certification function, may be provoking some pupils to adopt the very values that the same teachers later criticize.

It could be argued that results obtained in Sweden cannot be generalized to the United States. DiMaggio (1984) has nonetheless argued that there are in fact striking similarities between the two countries, especially in the relationships between class and taste and between taste and school achievement. To a very large extent these similarities are grounded in the universality of schooling in modern industrial societies and the broad functions that schools perform in most Western democracies. All schools evaluate and allocate in one way or another and in so doing they create predispositions to cultural taste and subcultural involvement.

We have seen that one-sided criticisms of the media do not provide adequate explanations of the school-media relationship. These two agents of socialization are much more intimately related than the bare "negative effects of the media on school" perspective suggests. Some criticism of the media may certainly be justified. However, it is time that educators begin to look not only at the negative effects of the media, but of the negative effects of what they themselves are doing.

## REFERENCES

Bailyn, L. (1959). Mass media and children: A study of exposure habits. *Psychological Monographs, 73*, 1-48.

Battin, T.C. (1952). The impact of television on school children in regard to viewing habits and formal and informal education. *Dissertation Abstracts, 12*, 343.

Bourdieu, P. (1974). Cultural reproduction and social reproduction. In R. Brown (Ed.), *Knowledge, education and cultural change*. London: Tavistock.

Bourdieu, P. (1980). The aristocracy of culture. *Media, Culture and Society, 2*, 225-254.

Bourdieu, P. & Passeron, J.C. (1979). *The inheritors: French students and their relation to culture*. Chicago: University of Chicago Press.

Bowles, S., & Gintis, H. (1977). *Schooling in capitalist America*. London: Routledge and Kegan Paul.

Brake, M. (1977). *Hippies and skinheads—sociological aspects of subcultures*. Unpublished doctoral dissertation, London School of Economics.

Brake, M. (1980). *The sociology of youth culture and youth subcultures*. London: Routledge and Kegan Paul.

Brown, L. R., & O'Leary, M. (1971). Pop music in an English secondary school. In F. G. Kline & P. Clarke (Eds.), *Mass communication and youth: Some current perspectives*. London: Sage.

Chaffee, S. H., McLeod, J. M., & Atkin, C. K. (1971). Parental influences on adolescent media use. *American Behavioral Scientist, 14*, 232-240.

Chaffee, S.H., & Tims, A.R. (1976). Interpersonal factors in adolescent television use. *Journal of Social Issues, 32*, 98-115.

Clarke, J. (1976). Style. In S. Hall & T. Jefferson (Eds.), *Resistance through rituals.* London: Hutchinson.

Clarke, P. (1973). Teenagers' co-orientation and information-seeking about pop music. *American Behavioral Scientist, 16*, 551-566.

Cohen, A. (1972). Social control and subcultural change. *Youth and Society, 3*, 259-276.

Coleman, J.S. (1960). The adolescent subculture and academic achievement. *American Journal of Sociology, 65*, 337-347.

Coleman, J.S. (1961). *The adolescent society.* Glencoe: Free Press.

Coleman, J.S. (1966). *Equality of educational opportunity.* Washington, DC: Government Printing Office.

Collins, R. (1972). Functional and conflict theories of educational stratification. In B. R. Cosin (Ed.), *Education, structure and society.* Harmondsworth, England: Penguin.

Collins, R. (1979). *The credential society.* New York: Academic.

Denisoff, R.S. (1975). *Solid gold: The popular record industry.* New Brunswick, NJ: Transaction.

DiMaggio, P. (1984). A review of "Mass Media and Adolescent Schooling: Conflict or Co-existence?" by Keith Roe. *Theory and Society, 13*, 874-877.

Emery, F., & Emery, M. (1976). *A choice of futures.* Leiden: Martinus Nyhoff.

Faber, R.J., Brown, J.D., & McLeod, J.M. (1982). Coming of age in the global village. In G. Gumpert & R. Cathcart (Eds.), *Inter/media.* New York: Oxford University Press.

Frith, S. (1981). *Sound effects: Youth, leisure and the politics of rock 'n' roll.* London: Constable.

Greenstein, J. (1954). Effects of television upon elementary school grades. *Journal of Educational Research, 48*, 161-177.

Hargreaves, D.H. (1967). *Social relations in a secondary school.* London: Routledge and Kegan Paul.

Harrison, L.F. (1978). The relationship between television viewing and school children's performance on measures of ideational fluency and intelligence. *Dissertation Abstracts International, 39*, 412.

Hebdige, D. (1979). *Subculture: The meaning of style.* London: Methuen.

Himmelweit, H., Oppenheim, A.N., & Vince, P. (1958). *Television and the child.* London: Oxford University Press.

Katz, M.B. (1968). *The irony of early school reform.* Cambridge, MA: Harvard University Press.

LaBlonde, J.A. (1966). A study of the relationship between the television viewing habits and scholastic achievement of 5th grade children. *Dissertation Abstracts, 27*, 2284-A.

Lacey, C. (1970). *Hightown grammar.* Manchester: Manchester University Press.

Lull, J. (1985a). On the communicative properties of music. *Communication Research, 12*, 363-372.

Lull, J. (1985b). The naturalistic study of media use and youth culture. In K.E. Rosengren, L.A. Wenner, & P. Palmgreen (Eds.), *Media gratification research.* Beverly Hills, CA: Sage.

Lull, J. (1986). Thrashing in the pit: An ethnography of San Francisco punk subculture. In T. Lindlof (Ed.), *Natural audiences: Qualitative research of media uses and effects.* Norwood, NJ: Ablex.

McQuail, D. (1969). *Towards a sociology of mass communication*. London: Collier Macmillan.

Maccoby, E.E. (1951). Television: Its impact on school children. *Public Opinion Quarterly, 15*, 421-443.

Marschak, M. (1980). *Parent-child interaction and youth rebellion*. New York: Gardiner.

Martens, P. I. (1981). *Socio-economic status, family structure and socialization of early adolescent children*. Stockholm: Stockholm University Project Metropolitan.

Martens, P.L. (1982). *Achievement-related behavior of early adolescents*. Stockholm: Stockholm University Project Metropolitan.

Meyer, J.W. (1977). The effects of education as an institution. *American Journal of Sociology, 83*, 55-77.

Morgan, M., & Gross, L. (1980). Television viewing, IQ and academic achievement. *Journal of Broadcasting, 24*, 117-133.

Morley, D. (1980). *Reconceptualizing the media audience: Towards an ethnography of audiences*. Birmingham: Birmingham University Centre for Contemporary Cultural Studies.

Murdock, G., & Phelps, G. (1973). *Mass media and the secondary school*. London: Macmillan.

Murray, J.P. (1980). *Television and youth*. Nebraska: Boys Town.

Neuman, S.B. (1980). Television: Its effects on reading and school achievement. *Reading Teacher, 33*, 801-805.

Postman, N. (1980). *Teaching as a conserving activity*. New York: Delta.

Ridder, J.M. (1963). Pupil opinions and the relationship of television viewing to academic achievement. *Journal of Educational Research, 57*, 205-206.

Roe, K. (1983). *Mass media and adolescent schooling: Conflict or co-existence?* Stockholm: Almqvist & Wiksell International.

Sharman, K. (1979). *Children's television behaviour*. Melbourne: Australian Council for Educational Research.

Slater, B.R. (1965). An analysis and appraisal of the amount of televiewing, general school achievement and SES of 3rd grade students. *Dissertation Abstracts, 25*, 5651-5652.

Smith, D.M. (1972). Some uses of the mass media by 14 year olds. *Journal of Broadcasting, 16*, 37-50.

Sugarman, B. (1967). Involvement in youth culture, academic achievement and conformity in school. *British Journal of Sociology, 18*, 151-164.

Williams, P.A. (1982). The impact of leisure-time television on school learning: A research synthesis. *American Educational Research Journal, 19*, 19-50.

Willis, P. (1977). *Learning to labour*. London: Sage.

Willis, P. (1978). *Profane culture*. London: Routledge and Kegan Paul.

Willis, P. (1980). *Symbols and practice: A theory for the social meaning of pop music*. Birmingham: Birmingham University Centre for Contemporary Cultural Studies.

# 11

# British Pop:

## Some Tracks from the Other Side of the Record

### IAIN CHAMBERS

Looking back from deep inside the 1980s over the last 30 years of British pop music is not dissimilar to browsing through a photographic album. As Roland Barthes noted of photography, we are struck by an "ontological desire" wanting to know what it "was like" (Barthes, 1981). Yet sounds in the ear, tastes on the tongue, the feel of certain clothes on the skin, have fallen away. Without the contexts we are left with only some of the texts—records and a series of images, signs of a presence.[1] I want to look at some of these traces, and, in particular, to look at the other side of the official record of British pop where it becomes possible to connect these sounds and signs to a wider set of social and cultural rhythms. This involves moving away slightly from the names and major musical waves usually associated with the British scene—The Beatles, Rolling Stones, the beat and rhythm and blues boom of the early 1960s, psychedelia, glam rock, punk and new wave, even reggae.

### Some Signs, Some Sounds, Some Beginnings

Rock and roll is a visual culture [Stewart, 1981, p. 5].

Style is essentially a dynamic phenomenon. It develops from more or less identifiable antecedents, articulates the feelings and attitudes of its adherents of a period before atrophying or metamorphosing. The discarding of a style by its original catchment may signal its adoption in a modified form by another social group with fresh symbolic requirements. Thus the dynamics of style supply a fascinating index of social *change* and the continuing struggles to negotiate identities of those occupying different positions in the power structures of society (Chibnall, 1985).

In the early 1950s, before Hollywood film and rock and roll music had broadcast the image of youth rebellion to the world at large, there emerged out of working-class districts in south London narcissistically dressed youths known as "Edwardians" or Teddy Boys. Their clothing crossed the Edwardian wardrobe of *fin de siecle* English dandyism with the long, wide-shouldered, North American zoot suit handed on from a more recent, but equally dubious, London style—the Spivs. Laboring under these extreme precedents—aristocratic extravagancy and shady, low life fashion—the teds' fancy waistcoats, shoestring ties, drape jackets, thick soled shoes, hair piled up into a sculptured quiff held in place with lashings of grease, were destined to produce shock waves in Britain. Wartime clothing coupons and utility clothes were still of recent memory, and the flagrant finery of these working-class youths suggested the brazen posturing of subversive fashions and criminal conduct—a world of black marketeering, violence and gangs, of those who bucked authority and betrayed the civic duty of austerity and restraint (Cosgrove, 1984). "Edwardian Suits, Dance Music and a Dagger" is what the *Daily Mirror* announced in September 1953.

Behind the headlines, and the real and presumed violence, the teds' style was an amalgam that temporarily overthrew the relations of power in the male fashion world. Instead of foppery and fashion being passed down from a select coterie in London's west end to a wider public, here were working-class males publicly taking the initiative on the streets of south London. The select snobbery of Saville Row was upstaged by a wild sartorial style produced on a mass scale by the "lower orders." Hollywood, rather than *haute-couture*, set the tone:

> We made our way along the market, walking in the fashion of the time. Jacket undone, hands in pocket, feet pointing slightly to the side as they shot out. This gave a walker a slightly swaying motion, creating an impression of toughness. It also make you walk with a . . . bounce, indicating a couldn't-care-less attitude. Why the boys felt they had to walk like this, I can't say. I think the gangster films had a lot to do with it [Barnes, 1976, p. 173].

In one sense, the whole Teddy Boy thing was an isolated phenomenon. Unlike later youth cultures it had no music of its own to provide a less precise, and therefore more accessible, symbolic allegiance to its public (and increasingly publicized) style. To be a ted meant wholeheartedly adopting and defending the immediate signs of an uncompromising dress and attitude. It was invariably a choice for those who held few other options—a sort of lumpen existentialism. But as the first of recognizable postwar British youth cultures, the Teddy Boys' self-gestated street style and dramatic announcement of YOUTH laid down many of the public coordinates for a subsequent series of juvenile identities in which clothes, music, and what the art critic John Russell once called an "imaginative involvement with America," was to become central (Russell & Gablik, 1969).

In Britain, in fact, clothes have been inextricably bound up with changes in popular music. Clothes form part of the cultural context, connecting music to styles and situations, and in turn become mythological icons for some of the sounds of the time: the greasy collared drape jacket of the later post-rock and roll Teddy Boy, out on the dance floor with his crinolined-skirted jiving partner; the sloppy pullover, jeans, and sandals of the beatnik in the bowels of a jazz club; the neat, neat, mod, moving in his shades, two tone shoes and Italian-styled suit to the cool, cool, sounds of black soul music; the disintegrating wardrobe and sounds of punk, held together by sellotape, safety pins, and noise; the back-to-front baseball cap, Ellese track suit, and Nike "kicks" of the Battersea B-boy. All these particular connections orbit around what, at least in Britain, are familiar landmarks—public male youth cultures mixing up the imagery of class society and street life in stylistic and imaginary response to their lot in the narrow prospects of everyday Britain.

But if subcultural analysis offers a by now well-trodden path through the semantic universe of British pop, suggesting some sociological, cultural, historical, and aesthetic sense for what was once considered nonsense, it is by no means the unique guide.[2] Thirty years of music, from the crooning complacency of the hit parade in the early 1950s to the cosmopolitan college sounds of the 1980s, cross, and in turn are crossed by, multiple histories—histories of the record industry, of radio and television, of youth, fashion, gender, class, race, sexuality, consumerism, marketing, entertainment, leisure, and politics. Music has consistently assisted in signifying a passing sense inside all of them.

## A Native Beat

Most accounts of British pop begin with the breach made in popular music by American rock and roll in the mid-1950s. Initially, however, both British youth and the native record industry found some difficulty in assimilating rock and roll. Attempts at producing a British variety— Tommy Steele, Terry Dene, Wee Willie Harris—failed to reproduce convincingly what was then a totally alien form. Memphis was just a place on the map and blues, gospel, and country music were the names of almost unheard-of American musical styles. Physically and culturally separated from those sounds and places, British rock and roll was largely a pantomime of borrowed accents and stolen gestures.

If direct contact was initially too difficult, there did exist the possibility of more oblique approaches to the body of American music that rock and roll represented. Although fundamentally conservative in scope, the revivalist fervor of the British "Trad Jazz" movement had been providing an exposure to a largely obscured part of American popular music, to early New Orleans and interwar jazz, and the blues, since the late 1940s (Melly, 1970). It offered sounds and pleasures that were quite different from those being broadcast by the radio and hit parade of the day. In the darkness, dance, and drink of the jazz club new cultural connections were made—you gave yourself over to the fresh mystery of sounds and sensations that escaped an obvious daytime logic. It was in the night, in the after hours of official culture, that other possibilities could be met:

> We used to think it was real going down to Chinny's, to the dance. Getting black drainpipes on, and a long duffle coat, and you looked exactly like a bopper. I couldn't bop, but I used to think it was real, and we felt it was smashing going out with greasy faces. We just used to put HiFi on, smear it all over our faces, no powder or anything and lots of black mascara. Then we'd go down in the dark and we'd feel exactly like boppers [Jackson, 1968, pp. 1-2].

Clearly, these "boppers" are hardly being true to the image of their 1940s New York jazz namesakes, but in borrowing the label they are seeking a space in which to produce some local sense, a statement about how to experience everyday possibilities and endow them with meanings.

The whole jazz scene was itself highly heterogeneous and included several factions. There were the "traditionalists" who followed pre-1914

New Orleans jazz, and the "revivalists" who championed the 1920s "hot" Chicago style. Quite apart from these two camps were the "modernists" who went for be-bop and contemporary jazz. Here's the male teenage observer of Colin MacInnes's *Absolute Beginners* describing a coffee bar encounter with two friends: one—the Misery Kid—is an admirer of Trad Jazz; the other—the Dean—is a "sharp modern jazz creation":

> If you know the contemporary scene, you could tell them apart at once, just like you could a soldier or a sailor, with their separate uniforms. Take first the Misery Kid and his trad drag. Long, brushless hair, white stiff-starched (rather grubby), striped shirt, tie of all one color (red today, but it could have been royal-blue or navy), short jacket but an old one (somebody's riding tweed, most likely), very, very, tight, tight, trousers with wide stripe, no sox, short boots. Now observe the Dean in the modernist number's version. College-boy smooth crop hair with burned-in parting, neat white Italian rounded-collared shirt, short Roman jacket *very* tailored (two little vents, three buttons), no turn-up narrow trousers with 17-inch bottoms absolute maximum, pointed-toe shoes, and a white mac lying folded by his side, compared with Misery's sausage-rolled umbrella.

> Compare them and take your pick! I would add that their chicks, if present, would match them up with [trad boy's girl]: long hair, untidy with long fringes, maybe jeans and a big floppy sweater, maybe bright colored, never-floralled, never-pretty dressed . . . smudged-looking's the objective. [Modern jazz boy's girl]: short hem-lines, seamless stockings, pointed-toed high-heeled stiletto shoes, crepe nylon rattling petticoat, short blazer jacket, hair done up into the elfin style. Face pale-corpse color with a dash of mauve, plenty of mascara (MacInnes, 1961: 50-51).

In these sharply separate tastes and styles we can recognize many of the later distinctions between the scruffy rhythm and blues fan identifying with the earthy "authenticity" of the blues, and the up-to-the-minute tastes (contemporary soul, Continental scooters, and fashion) of the mod subculture intent on "clean living under difficult circumstances" (Weller, 1981, p. 35).

Rock and roll was despised by the jazz followers. It was considered a commercial din, something dreamed up by the American record industry to extract cash from the pockets of the latest commercial discovery—the teenager. Yet it was a jazz club offshoot, skiffle, that in the mid-1950s offered a further possibility of being directly involved in some of the musics that had gone into the making of rock and roll.

Drawing upon American folk musics (both white and black), and the simple instrumentation of guitar, a single string bass (often home-made from a tea chest) and elementary percussion (washboard, kazoo, paper and comb), thousands of teenagers took to skiffle as an opportunity to make music, the rhythms and lyrics of which were quite distinct from native folk sounds, yet not so distant as to be inaccessible.

Produced almost by accident in the British jazz world, largely due to the unsuspected success of ex-Trad banjo player Lonnie Donegan, skiffle widened the horizons of popular music. Young Britons wrapped their tongues around "Rock Island Line" and "Freight Train" and placed their fingers on "blue notes" guitar picks and syncopated rhythms. Skiffle opened up various directions—folk music, the blues, and contemporary Afro-American music. Against the Tin Pan Alley model of the singer accompanied by an orchestra, it suggested the small group responsible for its own sound. It involved an important demo-cratization of popular music making and provided the first steps in the formation of many of the British groups of the next decade from the Shadows to the Beatles.

Then in the late 1950s, also coming out of the jazz clubs, and from the bohemia and art school ambience that hung around its sounds, there was a further development—rhythm and blues. Just like Trad Jazz had been, R&B was considered anticommercial and antipop, although its raw vocals and electric instrumentation caused some consternation among the older English purists used to an acoustic delivery of the blues and the polished performances of Big Bill Broonzy and Josh White. The music was about being "authentic," about identifying with the sound and carrying on a crusade on its behalf. The obvious discrepancies between the black American lifestyles that had produced the blues and white, suburban English boys trying to play them produced a compensa-tory "outsider" style destined to encounter social disapproval. Long hair, dirty sneakers, jeans, and a dishevelled appearance were all signs of "having paid your dues."

In the early 1960s, R&B began to develop with an increasing autonomy from the Trad Jazz movement. By now the latter had become a rather predictable institution and was increasingly discredited among the purists after a brief season of commercial success in 1961-1962. It was in this climate that R&B took over from Trad Jazz as the white bohemian sound of the early 1960s. Out of one-time jazz clubs and blues revivalism came the Rolling Stones, the Animals, the Pretty Things, the Kinks, Manfred Mann, Them, and a wave of lesser names.

Also from the same jazz background, but adopting the more sophisticated contemporary Afro-American sounds of soul and Tamla Motown, came the hip, cool style (sartorial descendants of the Dean) of a cosmopolitan mod sound best represented by Georgie Fame and the Blue Flames. Initially introduced by these white male groups and a rare female voice (Dusty Springfield), these black sounds—Marvin Gaye's "Can I Get a Witness," the Isley Brothers' "Twist and Shout," Arthur Alexander's "Every Day I Have to Cry," the Marvelettes' "Please, Mr. Postman," Sam Cooke's "Bring It on Home to Me"—found a home among the hip huggers, polo necks, drip-dry shirts, Cuban-heels, mini-skirts, and loafers, and became a crucial part of British pop. Soon afterward, at a teenage-crowded Studio 9, in London's Kingsway, Rufus Thomas, Marvin Gaye, the Isley Brothers, James Brown, Martha and the Vandellas, would be performing among the dancers for the cameras of *Ready Steady Go!*—the hippest TV pop program of the time (and since).

But whether it was R&B, contemporary black girl groups, or soul music, it was in weekly and nightly dancing patterns that black American music was increasingly inscribed into British popular culture and tastes. Whatever were the actual records dominating the charts, it was invariably black music and its white derivatives from the rare soul record collections being spun in clubs in northern England and the disco frenzy of every holiday resort and Saturday night dance to the patois-drenched rhythms of reggae and the electro-beat modernism of contemporary funksters, casuals, and B-Boys that has provided the rhythms for Britain's danceland since the early 1960s.

### Inside the Sounds

"Passion . . . danger . . . desire" [Nona Hendryx, "A Girl Like That," 1985]; "Flesh comes to us out of history" [Carter, 1979, p 11].

At this point we have arrived at a complex cultural mix. The limited sense of particular male subcultures with which I began has been supplemented by the altogether wider sweep of youth styles in which less precise sartorial and musical tastes were being cross-indexed in far less obvious fashions. Meanwhile, American-derived sounds, frequently of black origin, were being translated, via local enthusiasms, into more immediate concerns, naturalized and reworked inside the details of everyday British popular culture and tastes.

These are among the more explicit signs of the development of pop music in Britain since the 1950s. But while pop culture is invariably perceived as being a public event—the stars of radio, television, video, and cinema; or the spectacle of punks on the streets as the ragged jesters of crisis; or crowded clubs, dance halls, and discotheques filled with fashionably dressed bodies moving to an insistent beat—that is only a small part of the social space it actually occupies.

Pop music provides the possibility of living "in exile"—for the mods a fashionable "cool" removed from the dull prospects of everyday routines, for the motorbike boys ("Rockers") the mythological highway of masculine fulfillment. But exile also provides the opportunity to experiment with new cultural possibilities: social, sexual, and stylistic. Jon Savage has recently provided a fitting metaphor and example of the consequences of such a possibility:

> In a then notorious homosexual novel of 1953, *The Heart in Exile*—whose pink spine was a crucial signifier in those treasonable times—Rodney Garland's hero visits the Lord Barrymore and falls, as one will, into reverie: "The young were living mostly in exile, but exile gave them possibilities of which they had seldom dreamed before. Everything around them became slightly abnormal, the new occupation, the environment, the dress they wore, the physical and emotional climate. The concrete things of the past, like postal addresses, time-tables, road-signs, became less probable and friendships became all-important because it was unlikely that they would last. Nearly all of them, willingly or unwillingly, became creatures of the moment, living in an everlasting present; the past had vanished, the future was uncertain [Savage, 1985, pp. 22-25].

The removal of the past and an uncertainty about the future leads to a concentration of attention—social, sexual, psychological—in the present. It creates a situation in which a self-conscious style becomes increasingly imperative. Style provides a socialized network to bind the heterogeneity of the possible into an affective shape and sense.

The postwar Britain of newly built housing estates and rebuilt city centers, where the local ecology of the street community, the corner shop, and nearby pub were often replaced by slicker, more impersonal services and solutions, provided, at least for many working-class youth, the context for such a stylistic exile. But male street styles coupled to American-inspired sounds involved more than simply a response to the remaking of postwar class culture. In a world formed by the popular press, radio, cinema, and popular television, the adoption of particular musics and forms of dress were also part of a subconscious strategy for traversing and inhabiting it, providing a certain shape and direction among its multiple senses and signs.

The temporary arrest achieved by a particular record collection or wardrobe, a choice of make-up, skirt, or group—all involving objects plucked from the mobile spectacle of the present—permits a personal and tactile sense (for the collector is "speaking only about himself" or herself—Benjamin, 1973, p. 59) to be etched across the flux. This grasping of the present, this seizure of time, permits the exercise of local power:

> One of my clearest memories from nine years ago is of a bus ride from my housing estate in Birmingham into the city center. An atmosphere like a cup final coach, but with all of us on the same side and with one even more radical difference—there were no boys. At every stop, more and more girls got on, laughing, shouting, singing the songs we all knew of by heart. We compared the outfits and banners we had spent hours making, swapped jokes and stories, and talked happily to complete strangers because we all had one interest in common: we were about to see the Bay City Rollers [Garratt, 1985, p. 140].[3]

But it is finally around and across the body—the ultimate signifier in the chains of power and meaning—that the social, cultural, and sexual referents of pop come to be most intensely organized. Here in pop, as elsewhere, there is the most obvious (and therefore largely overlooked) history of representing the subordinate female body—object of the dominant male gaze—that nevertheless grows increasingly complex as the look itself is exploited by women, becomes autonomous, separate from male desires, finds its own powers:

> "Get into the groove" goes her most recent single smash, "you gotta move if you want my love." Quite what she had in mind is open to several interpretations, at least one of them threatening: currently posters are being amended to "Madogga-slag-cunt-tart" by boys who run away laughing nervously [Simmonds, 1985, p. 60].

There is also a history of British pop music that can be written across the changing body of masculinity, across the diverse presentations of the male body—as pop icon (a "star"), in the artistic camp and "confusion" (sexual, ideological) of David Bowie, in male fashions, in subcultures, and on the dance floor.

In both these histories, dancing occupies a central space. Although public, it permits important transgressions, frequently offering the connective occasion between social bodies and sexual (both hetero- and homo-) desire. Forms of corporeal expression that would not be considered acceptable elsewhere find a temporary realization on the dance floor, a space where there are "rhythms saying more about sexuality and the body than the lyrics will admit to" (Fleming & Muirden, 1985, p. 53). Not by chance, it was the corporeal pulse of disco music that became one of the more privileged expressions for the "coming out" of male gay culture in the early 1970s.

And unlike most other public aspects of pop culture, dance also directly involves girls and women. With the gradual break-up in heterosexual dancing patterns since the late 1960s, and a subsequently more indiscriminate mixing on the dance floor, girls no longer need to depend on the male invite. "Do you wanna dance?" is a phrase increasingly consigned to the rock and roll archive and dance hall memories of the 1950s.

There are different bodies moving to diverse beats, and shifts in sexual and cultural power are inscribed across their surfaces in various manners. Young black Britons, who through the 1970s had increasingly looked to the rebel music of reggae and the religious credo of Rastafarianism as a response to living in the cold currents of Britain's racial discrimination and chronic unemployment, are today beginning to exchange that imaginary solution for more concrete confrontations. Religion has not simply been replaced by riot, the limits of one's own history—inevitably brought to the surface living in a multicultural reality—are also increasingly confronted through everyday experiences. British Lovers Rock singer Carroll Thompson:

> In Jamaica, it's always been roots and the men singing about their culture and Rasta. . . . And because of that women always had a low profile. At first it was the same in England, because you only had Louisa Mark, Janet Kay, 15, 16 & 17 and Brown Sugar who had any real success, and I don't think the producers really took women seriously.

Sheryl Garratt takes up the story:

> In 1981, Carroll Thompson gave up waiting for attitudes to change and formed her own company, C&B, starting to write, sing, and produce her own records. . . . Her first album, *Hopelessly In Love*, was distributed by

Carib Gems and packaged with a photo of Carroll sitting on a car bonnet outside their office in Harlesden. The picture was slightly fuzzy, the title Letraset over her legs—everything about it said cheap, but it is a Lovers Rock classic which with very little airplay has sold well over 35,000 copies [Steward & Garratt, 1984, p. 140].

The signs are there. Some black male youth instead of adopting Ethiopian colors and Rastafarian stigmata (dreadlocks, woolly "tams," I-tal diet, Jamaican patois) are opting for Italian tracksuits and, imitating the cosmopolitan style of the New York B-Boys, are beginning to mix sounds with black British roots rather than a mythologized Jamaica. Out of Clapham Junction, south London, comes Smiley Culture's local toast complete with translation—"Cockney Translation."

## Into the Critical Groove

The indeterminacy of musical texts has been noted, but writers attempt to eliminate it rather than explore it [Hustwitt, 1984, p. 96].

So, what do the last 30 years of British pop suggest? Certainly it has involved a widening circle of sounds accompanying the spreading presence of youth, where "youth" has invariably been seen as the frequently unwelcomed spearhead of cultural change. A simple visual example: the shift from those adult-supervised beach movies of the 1950s (the British equivalent were the Cliff Richard films of the early 1960s, *The Young Ones, Summer Holiday, Wonderful Life*) to the knowing sophistication and autonomy of *The Face* busily recycling every trend and taste, both past and present, across its glossy pages. In the late 1940s, youth was not even considered a significant category. In the 1980s it had become the symbol of (post-) modernity, of the present, of the NOW, presided over by the "brats" of the fashion, music, video-clip, and cinema world. It is a crucial division, both in historical and cultural terms—a symbol of an altered landscape that reveals the profound remaking of popular culture under the impact of new sights, sounds, and sensations. It represents a new "structure of feeling" (Williams, 1965) of tastes and aesthetics.

Meanwhile, the heterogeneous sense of pop music continues to run beyond the more obvious manifestations of concerts, television, video clips, clubs, and even dance. It is in this "beyond" and its extended sense of popular culture and tastes, that sounds, not necessarily tied to the hit parade, radio airplay, or television exposure, become our own and connect to the felt sense of our lives. Such public occasions as the appearance of Bowie clones in the early 1970s, Madonna-styled female iconography, and independence in the very material world of the mid-1980s, male subcultures, school cultures, letters to the musical press, pirate radio programming, dance floor mannerisms, club spins and requests provide an important index. But it is through their place in the everyday (whether through involvement or apparent distance and separation) that they ultimately connect to a more private dimension where individual fantasy and fact, romance and realism, sounds and sentiments, are stitched into the fabric of different daily lives.

The music is not restricted to single objects or "texts"—the song, the record—but exists in an intertextual or transtextual reality in which producing, dancing, or listening to it, we all, in a certain sense, become its authors. It is through these varied points of contact that sounds are translated into sense. And across our bodies, the music joins and becomes entangled with other histories—clothing and class, fashion and fantasy, style and sex, race, gender, desire, and so on. The diverse elements that make up these histories—black music, Hollywood, Continental fashion, Jamaica—have been adopted and reworked into more local accents and sense, acquiring a "British" shape in the translation. The mutability of such objects, whether it is a record or a scooter, suggests that they form part of a complexly determined, but finally endless, sign play:

> We think our dress expresses ourselves but in fact it expresses our environment and, like advertising, pop music, pulp fiction and second-feature films, it does so at a subliminal, emotionally charged, instinctual, non-intellectual level. The businessmen, the fashion writers, the designers and models, the shopkeepers, the buyers, the window dressers live in the same cloud of unknowing as us all; they think they mold the public taste but really they're blind puppets of a capricious goddess, goddess of mirrors, weathercocks and barometers, whom the Elizabethans called Mutability. She is inscrutable but logical [Carter, 1982, pp. 85-86].

To understand the cultural "play" involved at this point—the heterogeneity of determinancy, the transitory quality of the meanings—forces criticism out of the shelter of neat abstractions and away from the art of critique into the more profane art of collecting.[4] In other words, critical "distance" is undermined and supplemented by critical involvement. This also leads to abandoning the romanticism traditionally invoked in most discussions of contemporary popular culture and its music. "Romantic" misleads because the criticisms implicitly appeal to abstract "alternatives"—the apparently lost equilibrium of an earlier "folk" culture or the ascetic sublimation of a textbook utopia. Both fail to connect to the complex movement of the present, except by negation.

Central to such romanticism is the formalist argument that the instruments and ownership of production are unilaterally capable of determining the cultural content of its products. On this basis a critique of the "culture industry" is mounted and a negative, ahistorical verdict returned.

But there is history, and an important one, of the changing composition of the record and entertainment industry in Britain over the last three decades: from the four major gramophone companies (Decca, EMI, Philips, and Pye) that dominated the British record market in the 1950s to today's mixture of small independent, national, and transnational holdings, as much involved in visual (video, cinema, computer software) as audio entertainment. That particular history not only involves the increasing complexity of the music industry, but also the increasing complexity of the culture in which it operates.

For what we are talking about at this point is not simply cash and hits. We are also talking about sounds that serve to signify something in the daily and not always predictable textures of popular culture. It is that extra, that "something more," that betrays the lie of obvious control and direction. And it is surely from the edges of that potential "more" that the critical eye and ear moves. The overall situation is by no means obvious, it is subject to unplanned pressures: The "anarchy of the market" is finally also a symptom of cultural unrest.

## NOTES

1. I have attempted elsewhere to evoke some of the "presence" and textures of British pop music within a series of historical contexts (see Chambers, 1985).

2. For subcultural analyses, see Hall and Jefferson (1976); Willis, (1979).

3. The Bay City Rollers were the Duran Duran of the mid-1970s.

4. Without venturing into the contemporary debate on postmodernism, the different implications of a choice between a rigorous "critique" and a more open-ended critical "collecting" can be found in the correspondence that took place in the 1930s between Theodor Adorno and Walter Benjamin over Benjamin's proposed study of nineteenth century Paris (see Adorno, 1973).

## REFERENCES

Adorno, T. W. (1973). Letters to Walter Benjamin. *New Left Review, 81.*

Barnes, R. (1976). *Coronation cups and jam jars.* London: Centerprise.

Barthes, R. (1981). *Camera-lucida: Reflections on photography.* London: Cape.

Benjamin, W. (1973). *Illuminations.* London: Fontana.

Carter, A. (1979). *The Sadeian woman.* London: Virago.

Carter, A. (1982). *Nothing sacred.* London: Virago.

Chambers, I. (1985). *Urban rhythms: Pop music and popular cutlure.* New York: St. Martin's.

Chibnall, S. (1985). Whistle and zoot: The changing meaning of a suit of clothes. *History Workshop, 20,* 56-81.

Cosgrove, S. (1984). The zoot suit and style warfare. *History Workshop, 18,* 78-91.

Fleming, D., & Muirden, A. (1985). Notes from practice. *The Media Education Journal, 4,* 50-61.

Garratt, S. (1985). Lover's rock. *The Face, 59,* 66-71.

Hall, S., & Jefferson, T. (Eds.). (1976). *Resistance through rituals.* London: Hutchinson.

Hustwitt, M. (1984). Rocker boy blues. *Screen, 25,* 89-98.

Jackson, B. (1968). *Working class community.* London: Routledge & Kegan Paul.

MacInnes, C. (1961). *Absolute beginners.* London: Ace Books.

Melly, G. (1970). *Owning-up.* Harmondsworth: Penguin.

Russell, J., & Gablik, S. (1969) *Pop art redefined.* London: Thames and Hudson.

Savage, J. (1985). Gender and pop. *Monitor, 4,* 22-25.

Simmonds, D. (1985). Madonna. *Marxism Today* (October).

Steward, S., & Garratt, S. (1984). *Signed, sealed, and delivered: True life stories of women in pop.* Boston: South End.

Stewart, T. (Ed.). (1981). *Cool cats.* London: Eel Pie.

Weller, P. (1981). The sixties: The total look. In T. Stewart (Ed.), *Cool cats.* London: Eel Pie.

Williams, R. (1965). *The long revolution.* Harmondsworth: Penguin.

Willis, P. (1979). *Profane culture.* London: Methuen.

## *12*

# *Shades of Black, Shades of White*

### E. ELLIS CASHMORE

Interestingly, during the 1970s punks had struck up quite a liaison with blacks because of their music. That was, of course, reggae and punks seized upon it enthusiastically. Reggae in the later 1970s was heavily suffused with a rastafarian inspiration and was, in effect, a protest music. There grew an intriguing correspondence between punks and members of the developing rastafarian movement: Punks wanted to change the system totally, although they lacked a firm vision of what they wanted to replace it with; rastas also wanted total change, what's more, they had a name for the system—Babylon.

The rastafarian movement manifested in the United Kingdom in the mid-1970s, drawing adherents from young blacks in the inner cities. Originally a Jamaican phenomenon, the movement grew rapidly during the 1970s in such places as the United States, Australia, New Zealand, and Holland (Cashmore, 1981). But it was in England that the movement established its most vigorous presence.

Basically, rastas drew their inspiration from the black leader, Marcus Garvey, who, in the 1920s, preached the philosophy of "Africa for the Africans," imploring black people in West Indies and United States to organize themselves for an exodus to their ancestral homeland. At some stage in his career, Garvey is reputed to have prophesied, "Look to Africa when a black king shall be crowned, for the day of deliverance is near." When, in 1930, Ras Tafari was crowned the Emperor of Ethiopia

AUTHOR'S NOTE: This article is reprinted from E. Ellis Cashmore's book, *No Future*, Heinemann Educational Books, London. Reprinted by permission of Gower Publishing Company Limited.

and renamed Haile Selassie, many made the fairly logical connection between the new emperor and Garvey's black king, believing the coronation presaged the "day of deliverance," and the mass return to Africa. Their conviction was based on the view that, contrary to Garvey's view, Haile Selassie was God and it was he—not them—who would organize and execute the exodus, at the same time breaking the whites' world domination. In other words, the movement to Africa would coincide with the dissolution of the system called Babylon—to emphasize its inherently evil nature.

The movement's growth in England was unarguably the most socially important development in British postwar race relations; it became a vital source of identity and purpose for young blacks. Coiling their hair into dreadlocks and adorning themselves in the red, green, and black of Ethiopia, they began to see themselves as a misplaced presence, sitting oddly astride the West Indies of their parents and England where they were domiciled when, in fact, they should really have been in Africa. This thought spurred them to new postures and they sought to detach themselves culturally from society, cultivating their own distinct way of life.

In many ways, the rastas fit into the same mold as many of the other youth subcultures: They were mostly quite young, drew inspiration from music, identified positively with each other, dressed similarly and, most important, emphasized their sheer difference. But there is another dimension to the rastafarian movement that is not found amongst similar subcultures: That is, it was a response to racism. Black youths felt themselves to be locked into a system that worked persistently against the interests of black people. Babylon had been formed in the early days of slavery and had remained intact, with minor modifications, ever since; blacks were not slaves in a physical sense, but they had to endure what rastas called "mental slavery." The movement's growth was inextricably linked to the perception of a world racked with racism: It wasn't so much white people who were the culprits, but the system of which they were part. The point was captured in the movie *Pressure*, where the black youth, having grasped this point, remark about whites: "They're colonized too, just like we are. The only difference is we see the bars and the chains."

Well, certainly punks saw the bars and chains, and, over the last years of the 1970s, formed an affinity with rastas. The link, as I've pointed out, had its source in the music of reggae and punk—reggae clubs and discos appeared on the scene. But, there was a deeper level to the relationship:

Punks and rastas were both highly critical of and antagonistic toward the existing social order, Babylon. Rastas opposed it because its power structure maintained blacks in a position of subordination and whites in domination. Punks accepted the fundamental wrongness of this power arrangement, but thought they, as young people, were also oppressed, or to be precise, restricted.

Punks believed the system was weighted against both the young and blacks. "Rock against racism" concerts were regular in the late 1970s; they signalled the willingness of punk and reggae musicians to use their music in the campaign against the rising forces of skinheads and organizations such as the National Front and the British movement. No one ever determined what the punk doctrine was all about; it was a vague package of criticisms, very few constructive, aimed at everything. The enterprise had negative views on politics, the monarchy, morals, religion—it found virtually nothing to approve of in the social order. And in its place? Anarchy.

Hebdige (1979, p. 65) calls punk "white ethnicity." He wrote, "It is issued out of nameless housing estates, anonymous dole queues, slums-in-the-abstract. It was blank, expressionless, rootless. In this the punk subculture can be contrasted to the West Indian styles which had provided the basic models." The idea here is that punks sprang from the same well-daubed tower bocks and were educated on the irrelevant curricula as young blacks and wanted to articulate the same kind of protest. But, armed with rastafarian ideas, black youth had a theory of history and a vision of the future; punks had neither. Hence their creation of important symbols out of mundane items such as safety pins, paper clips, and chains. These were the elements of the "modern world" and punks attached to them new significance: They represented a culturally barren world in which they were locked and condemned. Unlike rastas, they had no alternative of a culture based on a black Zion; so they took what was available and remixed the elements to create a new product. And that product was based totally on urban youth: Punks decried anyone or anything connected with the established social order as boring old farts (BOFs). They regurgitated the impulse behind the mod slogan of the 1960s, "I hope I die before I get old" (from the Who's *My Generation*), refusing to acknowledge the validity of the views of anyone over 20. It was at once a celebration of youth and a recognition of the hopelessness of it; it pleaded for an end to racism while conceding the inevitability of its growth.

Rastas for their part were equally as vitriolic in their condemnation of society, but guided by the vision, albeit a utopian one, of a future in which black-white relations would be transformed. "Must come," was the typical rastafarian endorsement of the imminent crash of Babylon.

The longevity of both movements attests to their lasting significance: a span that is momentous for youth subcultures, many of which are fragile and ephemeral affairs (usually the artificial manufactured kind, such as the new psychedelics, who were totally products of consumer capitalism). Punks and rasta weren't short-lived episodes, because they articulated genuine and deeply held sentiments. They gave air to the bitterness, resentment, sometimes fury, of urban youth in the 1970s and 1980s. They, more than any other youth movement, reflected the transformation of youth from young people prospering in partially real but largely illusory affluence, proclaiming their collective identity and revelling in their lack of responsibilities and abundance of time and resources. The continuing theme is that, like the subcultures preceding them, punks and rastas maintained their collective identities as youths and were, for the most part, impermeable to people who weren't young. But if the teds, mods, and others were loud choruses of difference, but general approval with the way things were, punks and rastas were shrill, unmelodious screeches of defiance and bitterness. So what happened at the turn of the decade?

A general sense of a worsening economy, poorer living standards, deteriorating race relations, and a collapse of the optimistic consensus of the 1950s and 1960s are obvious causes behind the changing posture of youth, though it would be unwise to try to specify a dividing point between the age of affluence and the period of decline. If decline is in any way measurable by using unemployment as an index, we can plot a gentle course from 1970 to 1974 with the percentage of the total number of employees out of work rising from 2.6 to 3.6 then back to 2.6; then, in 1975, it shot up to 4.1% and in 1976 it rose to 5.7%. After a slight drop in 1978, it went up to 6.1% in 1979 and from then on into the 1980s and the days of double figure percentages. The groups usually most affected are: the young, ethnic minorities, and women. From the first two were drawn punks and rastas. Marsh described punk rock as "the music of the unemployed teenager" (1977, p. 114); it captured perfectly the emergent mood of frustration among the young. Reggae functioned similarly for black youths.

At one level, unemployment meant a reduced spending capacity for youths, black and white, particularly when coupled with price inflation.

The days of affluence were over by about 1976; no more spending vast amounts on smart clothes and motor vehicles; torn T-shirts and Shanks's pony became the order of the day. But, at another level, unemployment was to have a more profound effect. Unemployment meant depriving young people of the activity through which they are supposed to derive satisfaction, their identity; it's that activity that's supposed to occupy the largest chunk of anyone's time between birth and death. Obviously, we hear time and time again of the boring monotonous, drill-like alienating nature of much work; but, at least, as one youth put it, "It's something to do; the alternative is do fuck all, all day."

The conditions of job security and intensifying competition for positions were exactly the ones precipitating the conflicts between whites and blacks in the later 1950s. The contraction in the labor market after the immediate postwar expansion brought new faces to the dole queues. Blacks, prior to this time, were seen as auxiliaries in the sense that they were welcomed to the United Kingdom to fill in the gaps in the labor force: The economic "boom" of the late 1940s and early 1950s had ensured virtual full employment and migration from, principally, the British West Indies, and, second, South Asia (India and Pakistan), supplied basic labor. The white working-class prospered from the situation, enjoying freedom of mobility and a range of options.

Imagine a department store with a promotion system based on its floors, so that if you're the tea maker, you work in the basement. Around Christmas time, the store gets busy, so all the employees get a chance to move up. Those on the third floor move up to the fourth, those on the second to the third, and so on, with the basement workers rising to the ground or the first floors. But there's no one to work the basement. The solution: Bring in outside workers, who are prepared to put up with not-too-pleasant working conditions, without terrific wages, and with long and often awkward hours. Everyone upstairs is happy, as are the new workers brought in and the store profits nicely from the system. After Christmas, however, sales drop and the store's management begin to cut jobs; but the basement workers have got used to their jobs and it would be impossible to fire them and funnel everyone downstairs. So jobs are chopped on all floors, some third-floor workers lose out, as do those on all floors, including the basement. Now, those who've lost their jobs look at the basement workers in a different light; they think, "If they hadn't been brought in here in the first place, there'd still be jobs around, even if they were only those in the basement." In effect, they will blame the basement workers who've managed to hang on to their jobs. An equation seems plausible; it goes: If there are 100 jobs lost and 100 outsiders working in the basement, then those jobs would still be around if the outsiders weren't here. The logic of the argument may be flawed, but the equation gains credibility for the worker who feels he's pushed out of work by outsiders.

In the 1950s that equation applied to immigrants. If there's a half-million blacks here, and a half-million on the dole, then those blacks are the cause of the unemployment; if they weren't here, the jobs would still be open. This kind of logic propelled the teds and their accomplices in the 1950s, as it did the skinheads in the 1970s, but it's by no means confined to these and their sons and daughters. Scapegoating outsiders is a convenient way of blaming one group for all the ills of society, when in actual fact that group is in no way to blame and, in many circumstances, is more badly affected by the social ills.

The persistence of this specious reasoning will become much more evident when I recount the views of youth in the 1980s, but, for the moment, let me simply document the fundamental logic behind a lot of racist thinking: The outcome is to identify one or more visible and obviously different groups and attribute them with causes of deteriorating social conditions. Unemployment and general economic decline may be the primary cause behind losses in spending power, poorer housing, education cutbacks, worsening social services, and so on, but it's much simpler to look for a tangible target to blame and hit. After all, you can't beat up social processes but you can beat up Pakistanis. And this is exactly what some groups thought and did in the later 1970s and early 1980s.

Unemployment is certainly not the explain-all concept it has been made out to be. Those mounting the moral barricades and making pronouncements about youth violence, delinquency, and drug abuse, among other things, are quick to cite unemployment as the sole cause. It isn't. It may well be the single most important factor behind the excesses and problems of the young, but a full understanding can't be grasped without paying attention to the other elements involved, and this is what I intend to do.

This stated, we can certainly point to the lack of work from the late 1970s as a most powerful influence in the postures of youth, white and black. Punk and rastas believed themselves to be trapped in a bizarre bureaucratic maze with no apparent way out; many youths perceived every avenue of advancement blocked.

The critique of society is articulated in particular by young blacks was a very pertinent and trenchant one. At a general level, for example, a rasta told me how: "I now understand how the Imperial Machine of the West and the religions that served it were designed to oppress all black peoples in the world." More specifically, another rasta reckoned: "I experience certain things: that a black youth cannot walk the streets without a chance of being picked up by the police, a chance of being beaten up by the National Front . . . we can't get a job because of our religion, the color of our skin" (Cashmore, 1983, pp. 130-131). In 1978, a punk told me: "We're on the same side as the rastas. People think they're their own people, projecting their own image" (Cashmore, 1983, p. 179).

### Punk-Tafari

The affinity felt between punks and rastas was based on a recognition of a common plight ("We're on the same side"), a resentment of the system that perpetuated that plight, and a longing to change it, albeit through different means, though neither group did anything obviously constructive to further that change. The perception, however, was clear enough and the affiliation between black and white youth, though not strong, had been forged out of a common recognition. The link was captured in a piece of graffiti I noticed in a Birmingham subway: "Punk-Tafari."

It was not a lasting link, however, and it became progressively weaker as the end of the decade loomed. As with most other exploitable phenomena, punk became amenable to commercialization and the music and products were quite quickly integrated into what we might call mainstream pop culture: Movies such as *Jubilee* and *The Great Rock 'n' Roll Swindle* used punk themes; clothes shops all over the country specialized in punk fashion; punk or punk-derivative records shot into the popular music charts and the critical impulse was all but lost. The rastafarian package also underwent a kind of commercialization: Parallel processes ensured that a distinct rasta commodity industry was built upon records, films, and so on. Again the critical impulse was dampened but not entirely extinguished. A residual number of punks retained integrity of sorts and were assisted by new, unexploited bands and less commercial clubs and discos. In the 1980s, there was more or less a "second generation" of punks: Youths of around 16-17 (who would have been about 11 when the subculture first emerged) asserted the vitality of punk and its relevance at a time of severe depression for youths. Rastas continued to attract younger and younger affiliates, many subscribing to the general ideas such as the conspiracy of Babylon and the importance of Africa, without plumbing the theological depths of the movement in its religious aspect.

## 400 Years

The rastafarian movement continued to exert an important influence on vast portions of black youth in the 1980s. Even a small minority of inner-city whites locked their hair and proclaimed allegiance to Ras Tafari as if to demonstrate their affinity with the black youths with whom they grew up with in the inner cities. It became possible for a white band such as the Ruts to release a rasta record like *Babylon's Burnin'*.

For a moment, let me determine that being a rasta involves the individual accepting two linked beliefs: (i) the divinity of Haile Selassie; (ii) that all black people should ultimately go back to Africa. Beyond these, there are no meaningful doctrinal points of unity. Some rastas won't eat pork; others will. Some smoke herb (ganja) as a ritual; other's don't. Some insist that the whites' domination of blacks through imperialism is in a process of dissolution; others feel that the whites are as much in command as ever. The list is almost endless. In fact, one of the main reasons why the movement caught on in the United Kingdom was that there was no clear, unambiguous doctrine that the would-be member had to accept in order to call himself or herself a rasta. The rastafarian beliefs were open to interpretation—so long as the member believed in Haile Selassie and the return to Africa.

But, as the movement developed, many blacks dipped into the rasta beliefs and pulled out whatever they felt appropriate without whole-heartedly becoming a rasta. For example, a youth might fashion his hair into dreadlocks, but identify with the movement without actually being a rasta. One youth who did so justified his actions to me: "It's I's way of showing my naturalness; of rejecting the western world's materialism and showing that I am a roots man. This is not rasta: it is natural to blackness. . . . I can't accept Haile Selassie as my god. Christianity is my way, Haile Selassie was a mere king."

The look of dread was immensely popular, but so too was the acceptance of one of the central rastafarian beliefs. In the 1980s, it was no longer necessary to be a rasta to believe in the existence of Babylon. This may, in the 1970s, have been an obscure way of comprehending the world, but, in the 1980s, Babylon was the reality experienced by black youths. Babylon was felt to exist everywhere: on the streets, in the churches, in the dole queues. Babylon became the single most important concept in the rastafarian repertoire. It provided thousands of black youth with a tool for analyzing the nature of society and their position in that society. In a *New Community* article called "After the Rastas," I speculated on the increasing relevance of Babylon to young blacks and its role in promoting the kinds of awareness that resulted in the Brixton riots in 1981 (Cashmore, 1981). The basic problems of bad housing, lack of job opportunities, perceived harassment by the police were explicable in terms of the existence of Babylon: Whites had kept blacks down and were doing everything possible to keep it that way. Racism was a main tool to this end: By separating out black people and subjecting them to unequal treatment in many spheres of society, such as education, employment, and the law, whites, it was thought, could maintain their grip—and so keep Babylon intact.

This was precisely the kind of awareness that spread among black youth; in the eyes of a young black person who found difficulty getting a job at all, let alone an apprenticeship or some sort of training scheme, everything fell into place in terms of the Babylon conspiracy. What's more, belief was contagious and even schoolchildren, armed with ideas from the elder brothers and sisters, began to think in terms of Babylon. This was first brought home to me when I witnessed a scene in Handsworth: A group of two black youths and some younger children are walking along the street when a panda car draws up; two police officers spring from the car to apprehend the youths, corralling them into the car and driving off to the continual shouts of "Babylon, Babylon!" from the children.

The disaffection of black youths wasn't all caused by the growth of rastafarian beliefs. Rather, those beliefs gained purchase because social conditions permitted it. In particular, the concept of Babylon drew great credibility from the worsening situations blacks found themselves in at the start of the 1980s. If they wanted some kind of comprehension or explanation of why they were in that position, they needed to look no further than rastafarian theory.

To understand the phenomenal rise not so much of the rastafarian movement, but of the general rastafarian ethos, the spirit and beliefs of the movement, we have to recognize two features. One is obviously the widespread availability of rasta ideas. Originally these came to England via Jamaica, mostly through reggae records—though there most certainly were groups of rastas in the United Kingdom since the 1950s, as I have noted in *Rastaman* (Cashmore, 1983, pp. 50-53). Although in my study, few rastas would consciously acknowledge that reggae was the major inspiration, on occasion they would concede: "I suppose music was my first contact with Ras Tafari; and it was this that made me look inside myself to find the true rastaman within I," or "I used to listen to music and sometimes a certain record might stick in my memory and I would meditate on that record. The words of it got stronger, began to make meaning for I" (Cashmore, 1983, p. 106).

The first wave of rastas, say from 1976 to 1980, were stimulated to probe in reggae and use it as a kind of revelatory experience, taking themes and "reasoning" them through in long, intense conversations with other rastas. The second wave of youths inspired by rasta had all the ideas available to them: The movement had, by the end of the decade, attracted a formidable following and had been reasonably well attended to by the media—becoming the source of at least one moral panic in Handsworth (Cashmore, 1983). But this doesn't tell us why more and more non-rasta black youths swallowed up rastafarian ideas. The basic answer is that they were rendered suggestible by the social conditions through which they grew up. This is the second feature we need to recognize. Disenchanted with educations they found irrelevant and unmotivated by families that failed to play adequate supporting roles in their general educations, black children tended to do badly at school and so finished up "underachieving" (Taylor, 1981; Rampton, 1981; Tomlinson, 1980). Having no qualifications of note, they began from a disadvantage and so lacked the kinds of commitment needed to progress in a career. The situation was compounded by the outright racism they encountered when trying to get on such things as apprenticeships and training programs, and there is good evidence to suggest that this type of racism operates fairly systematically (see Lee and Wrench, 1981). Then, the massive youth unemployment affected blacks more than any other single group. All the factors combined to depress the morale, drain away energies, and generally demotivate the black youth from taking an active part in society.

The rastafarian posture was one of detachment and, in the 1980s, more black youths are striking up this posture. Intrigued by the rasta analysis of society and its conclusion that it will simply not allow black people an active role, many blacks nowadays take the view that the basic rasta idea of Babylon is correct and that the system is working to the detriment of blacks. Faced with the future as they see it, who can blame them? The plausibility of rasta ideas is enhanced by every fresh round of school-leavers who will take their places in the dole queue, attempt to find a job for a few months, then sense the pointlessness of their search. As one youth told me: "I'm not a rasta personally but I know many and they are all good roots brothers. . . . I don't think it's necessary to believe totally their whole philosophy: one is an individual and one must worship as you believe. But much of rasta is truth, it is a philosophy of black people and I say it is a philosophy for all black brethren!"

The rasta explosion was like someone throwing a stone into the center of a still pond: For long afterward the ripples extended outward toward the periphery. The movement's impact in the late 1970s was momentous and its influence continued, prompting many to favor the popular view that there were "genuine rastas" and "masqueraders." To pose such a division is to mistake the nature and quality of the movement: There were never any hard and fast distinctions between rastas and non-rastas; no oaths, rituals, or ceremonies to go through. Being rasta was always a process of becoming. "The learning never stops," one rasta told me, referring to the way in which acquiring rasta knowledge involved comprehending the world in a different perspective and always seeking to add to the comprehension through study and reasoning. In my study of the movement, I identified the critical point in the whole process as the acceptance phase, when the youth accorded Haile Selassie with divine status. But perhaps my analysis was even then too linear: Being drawn to the movement is not an inexorable drift toward acceptance; rather it can involve all manner of deviation. There is a kind of selective perception in which the youth sees in the movement exactly what he wants to see. So vague and amorphous is the rastafarian philosophy that virtually every individual can extract whatever meaning he or she likes from it. But the central meaning was captivity and repression. The whole rastafarian ethos was structured around these themes and they took on significance for the whole black youth. "Four hundred years" of slavery was how rastas described their condition: It was a description recognizable to thousands of other black youths, who in their own, perhaps idiosyncratic, ways identified with rasta in the 1980s.

The effect growing up in a world of material abundance had on youth prior to the mid-1970s was for youths to form, quite self-consciously, cultures based on their age. Those almost grandiose cultures of affluence and expansion were supplanted by grimmer, more sullen movements based on poverty and constriction. Maturing black youths found their lives double-bound by the ropes of unemployment and racism. The withdrawal of many into predominantly black cultures of resistance was both a response to this condition and a creative attempt to construct an alternative existence based on blackness. That many others were to follow their examples without perhaps the totality of commitment of rastas attests not so much to the inherent plausibility of rastafarian ideas, but to the willingness of black youths generally to seek out alternative beliefs and lifestyles to the ones offered. They had little or no investment in a world with no jobs in which blackness was to be disparaged and used as a basis for exclusion.

Very few black youths in the 1980s escaped the resonance of what the late rasta musician and, to many, prophet Bob Marley called "rastaman vibration" (from *Positive Vibration,* 1976). Rasta was a main influence on the consciousness of young blacks in the period and continually asserted itself in the way they dressed, the way they spoke (in patois), the way they walked even (a loose-limbed bouncy stride); but, most important, in the way they postured themselves in relation to the wider society. They grew weary of the futile search for acceptance as equals and so effected a sort of detachment, severing their links with society and opting out of the race for jobs, careers, security, and the rest of the trappings young people are meant to aim for. Those goals and the values underpinning them were seen as unattainable and so blacks jettisoned them.

As one black youth, two years out of work since leaving school, said: "You get told about careers and things when you leave school and then you go for a few jobs and maybe there's a white kid there and he gets the job and he's got no more qualifications than you; and so it starts you thinking. . . . Is it harder for a black man? Then when it keeps happening and your mates tell you the same thing, you know it's true . . . so you get to the realization that there's no point."

"And the rasta influence?" I asked him (he was wearing the colors). He replied with a question that captured the mood of the times: "How can you deny what rasta is saying is untrue? Where is the truth in what the white man has been telling blacks for years? Where indeed?"

Before concluding this section, let me add that it's misleading to view all black youth as in some way involved in rasta. A less popular, though still relevant, subculture was that revolving around the music called jazz-funk. This was a predominantly black form with the adherents eschewing any political influence: Music, dancing and dressing were the important items. A great many blacks, uninterested in the rasta posture, opted for this pleasanter, altogether milder, subculture, creating for themselves a nonpolitical world of sound and movement, music and light, where Babylon never intruded.

### Two-Tone

"The ghost town" is what some call Coventry, a Midlands city 20 miles southeast of Birmingham, once a symbol of postwar affluence with a thriving motor industry, now a degenerating indicator of the 1980s recession. It's so-called because of its desolation: The city center precinct was the focus for so much violence that an 11 p.m. curfew was imposed, resulting in the center's desertion after that time. Hence ghost town.

Coventry was overrun with clashes between youths in the late 1970s: Intergang rivalries spiralled into a continuous series of violent outbursts. New policy measures were introduced, but the violence was virtually uncontrollable and the curfew was an extreme measure. It was from this conflict-riven context that there emerged a youth culture brimming with a vitality and enthusiasm for an end to violence and a greater harmony in relations between whites and blacks. "Why must the youths fight each other?" asked the band called The Specials in their number, "Ghost Town." This band was the vanguard of the movement called two-tone, perhaps the most impressive ethnically integrated youth subculture in the postwar period.

The punk-rasta relationship had become unhinged by the turn of the decade. Both movements continued to attract adherents, though there were no meaningful links between them as there were in the 1970s, when rastas and punks joined at clubs such as the Roxy, the Vortex (in London), and Rebecca's (in Birmingham). But cultural connections between white and black youths were enlivened by the coming of two-tone. Here was a potent unifying force that brought youths together in a social stand against racism and indeed many other reactionary elements of the 1980s.

Two-tone had unlikely origins. In 1978-1979, there was a mod revival. Kids of 16 and 17 began dressing up in the garb of the mods: parkas, striped blazers, tab-collar shirts, and so on. Motor scooters, decorated with multiple lamps and chromed side panels, began appearing on urban streets; "mod sounds" discos opened. A feature movie based on the Who's album, *Quadrophenia,* which plotted the experience of a mod youth of the 1960s, was released with some success. There was even a reissue of Cohen's sociological study, *Folk Devil and Moral Panics!*

The revivalists looked very much like the original mods, though the music they listened to was substantially different: The sounds of the revival were basically white, mainly bands such as the Small Faces and the Who, who were mod bands all right, but not the real stuff of which mod sounds were made. In fact, the whole revival had a somewhat hollow ring about it. Maybe it was a little more than a coincidence that *Quadrophenia* came out at precisely the same time as the revival because the second coming of the mods seemed to be more a product of commercial "hype" (for hyperbole, an exaggeration) than street creativity.

Still, the importance of the mod revival for our purposes was that it prompted renewed interest in the ska and bluebeat music so popular— and, in some cases, emblematic—among the first mods. In particular, the "Rudie" songs made a strong comeback. Rudie was a sort of a folk hero character who cropped up in song after song: Rudie's in Love, A Message for Rudie, and so on. He was the prototype rude boy: an impoverished black youth, barely scraping a living through hustling and scuffling (as Jamaicans call it), getting his kicks through stealing, fighting, and opposing authority at every turn. Michael Thomas described the original Jamaican rude boys as "the hustlers and ratchet men and small-time superflies of West Kingston. They haven't been to school and they can't get a job and a lot of the time the reason they can't is because they don't want to work" (1973).

The rebellious violent image of the rude boy struck chords with the skinheads of the 1970s and rudie music was enormously popular. Many black youths were accepted by the otherwise xenophobic skins because of their connections with what was then called rock steady music (an outgrowth of bluebeat and ska and a predecessor of reggae). In a way, the rude boy lyrics captured the growing spirit of the day: dissident, angry and, sometimes, just plain aggressive.

The rude boy became a sort of generic concept, symbolizing those factions of youth alienated by the media's commercialization of punk but still retaining the vital critical impulse of the 1960s. The mod revivalists were attempting to recreate the heady, antiauthoritarian spirit of the 1960s, but were awkwardly anachronistic and more than fractionally influenced by the media hypes. Yet their importance lay in their exhumation of the rude boy figure.

At the very start of the 1980s, it was difficult if not self-defeating to try to disentangle the intermeshing complex of mod, rude boy, and two-tone. Ostensibly, "two-tone" was the name of an independent record label; it was a company started in Coventry by young people with little resources but an abundance of musical ideas. Local bands like the Specials, the Selector and, from London, Madness, were the first to record on the label. The music was straight from the 1960s mod era. Madness, in fact, drew its name from a hymnal bluebeat track by the West Indian figure, Prince Buster, who attracted what some call "cult status" among early mods. This band, in particular, captured the rude boy ethos. Songs were a blend of old revamped bluebeat and ska sounds with new originals incorporating rude boy lyrics; the overall effect was an almost perfectly authentic recreation of the sounds of the 1960s. The influence of punk was evident in the pronunciation of lyrics; no mimicking of American accents, but a very sharp accentuation of London or Midland dialects as if to emphasize that this was the music of the streets.

Bands, old and new, began to identify with (or, more accurately, be identified with) two-tone; as Timothy White put it, it "combined a ska revival with the frantic energy of punk" (1983, p. 21). From Birmingham came the English Beat, a combination of aging West Indian musicians and white school-leavers. Already established as a force in the early punk days was Paul Weller's brainchild, the Jam, from London; the trio dressed in mod-inspired clothes, like mohair suits and French shoes, and mixed straight love songs with clever invectives against the social order. The Jam, in general, and Weller, in particular, became the most successful products of the period, attracting mod, punk, and two-tone adherents—though, of course, there was no clear demarcation between these groups—before they broke up in late 1982.

To varying degrees, all the groups identified with two-tone were critical of aspects of society, whether it be general phenomena such as inequality, violence, and unemployment or specific institutions such as marriage or mental asylums. Their followers, again to varying degrees, associated with the critiques. The single unifying bond of the whole movement was the abhorrence of racism. Two-tone was meant to convey the feeling that whites and blacks were simply two different tones of one skin color; there was no natural break between youths, but a continuum of tones—and, at the two extremes, were white and black.

Hence two-tone. Virtually all the bands had black and white members. Some, like the influential UB40, whose name was derived from the code number of the form received when registering as unemployed, had dreadlocked rasta members playing alongside neatly groomed mod look-alikes. This band, based in the west Midlands, treated racism among youths as one of its central issues and used its popularity in the early 1980s as a platform for youth, often offering concert concessions for those producing evidence of their unemployment.

Two-tone was perhaps the most invigorating movement of the early 1980s; its performers and followers were dedicated to a steadfast opposition to racism in its every manifestation and committed to encouraging more mixing and understanding between blacks and whites. Two-tone concerts were quite often more than purely musical events and were geared to political campaigns, as were the Rock Against Racism gigs of the late 1970s. In this respect, two-tone was the countervailing force to the other great motive power among youth of the 1980s—fascism.

Two-tone concerts were events of celebration and criticism. They celebrated the unification of youth, white and black, yet criticized the growing presence of forces that threatened that unity. Its followers were a mixture of whites and blacks and, to a much more limited extent, young Asians—all dressed in a manner reminiscent of the original mods: sharply cut jackets, slim lapels, pork pie hats, narrow trousers, and tennis shirts came back into vogue. Two-tone became a truly dialectical movement because its music was both vox populi, a reflection of the voice of the people, and a stimulus to those people. It conveyed the feelings, sentiments, and emotions of kids on the streets, yet, at the same time, translated these into coherent messages that were, in turn, picked up by those kids, thus prompting clarity of thought and maturity of perspective. The process was reciprocal and dynamic.

I might be accused of exaggerating the importance of two-tone, for, at the end of the day, like other youth subcultures, it achieved nothing tangible. But so what? It did lend form and coherence to a vague set of apprehensions about the world as it confronted many inner-city youths. Not all youths were disposed to look for easy scapegoats and identify Asians or blacks as the causes of their problems; some at least were prepared to probe more deeply and locate the source of the problems at a deeper level, at the same time recognizing that hostility between whites and blacks/Asians was ultimately destructive and of no relevance to their general interests.

Some said that the end of two-tone as a distinct movement came in 1981, symbolized perhaps by the splinter of the Specials to Fun Boy Three. This three-man (two black, one white) outfit became a total commercial success and, indeed, outstripped the residual band they left behind as Specials. Madness had an interesting history; in the wake of their early success they left behind an embarrassing legacy of a substantial skinhead following, which obviously jarred with their two-tone devotees. The band left the "two-tone" label and became a major commercial success with a chain of hit singles and albums. During the successful period, the band abandoned the two-tone identity and became integrated into the mainstream of popular music.

I prefer to view two-tone less as a recognizable youth movement, more as an impulse felt by certain sections of youth. If viewed in this way, two-tone's life wasn't necessarily linked to the developments of the bands. If it were, then two-tone was dead by 1981; alternatively, we can see the spirit of two-tone as living on, unattached to any particular bands, but continually being enlivened by the necessary opposition to racism. As nazism and racism spread among some factions of youth, then two-tone grew and remained as a countervailing tendency.

### Romantic Indifference

Sandwiched in between the two extremes of two-tone and the mark two skins were groups of youth who exhibited no identifiable stance on racism or other socially significant issues. Two-tone was a genuinely collective enterprise like other youth cultures based on music, but constructed around common efforts, shared aims, and perceived enemies. Of course, all youth subcultures are collective in the sense that they just can't exist without the cooperation, recognition, and identification of others. You can't create a youth culture by yourself; unless others identify you as either one of "us" or perhaps one of "them," then you are condemned to being an eccentric—particularly if you choose to adorn yourself with somewhat bizarre clothing. So, it would be impossible to envisage the rise of new romanticism in the 1980s without a gigantic collective effort.

The irony of it all is that the new romantics were totally and utterly committed to being unique; they went to the most extreme lengths in their strenuous efforts to be completely different. Hair was dyed in not just different, but often fluorescent, colors, sometimes in intricate patterns; it was then fashioned into petrified manes—spikes, like long icicles, jutting from the scalp. Clothes were made from outlandish fabrics and designed to project the image of exotica: hugely wide trousers, elongated jester-pointed shoes, flamboyant, frilly blouses. There was no gender differentiation for clothes; nor for the stark make-up worn to great dramatic effect by males and females.

New romanticism was the most utterly narcissistic youth subculture: Its adherents were preoccupied with one thing—themselves. More accurately, the new romantics were interested in displaying themselves for others. It was carte blanche for these young peacocks. If it looked different and could attract others' attention, then it was worn. So, men wore dresses and dropper earrings; women wore soldiers' uniforms, boots, and the like. Literally, anything went.

The Blitz wine bar in London's Covent Garden is popularly taken as the first authentic haunt of new romantics. A discotheque over the bar acquired a reputation for attracting the more exotically dressed. The clientele became known as "blitzkids." This was about late 1979 and, during 1980, the influence spread north. In Birmingham, for example the Rum Runner club, previously a middle-aged club-cum-gambling-casino, underwent a transformation. Subtle dress restrictions were introduced, like "nothing too straight!" Every patron of the new romantic clubs and discos was an example of studied desire to be different—and be recognized as such. As David Bowie, himself idolized by new romantics, characterized the movement: "There is a grim determination to be fashionable at all cost."

The bands enthused over by new romantics reflected the effort to be extravagantly dressed. Spandau Ballet believed their appearance to be equally as important as their music to the stage act. Japan, a sort of hybrid of Bowie and Roxy Music, showed a similar concern. Other bands to capture the new romantics' imagination were Simple Minds, Kraftwerk, and the precommercial Human League. The common factor in the "futurist" music was the use of electronics: Synthesized sound replaced the more conventional instruments to the point where some bands would simply tape record their whole set and operate consoles on stage, virtually eliminating any need actually to play instruments "live." The aforementioned German band Kraftwerk took this to extremes, on occasions, substituting themselves with plastic dummies and leaving the stage completely while the taped music played.

New romanticism was totally self-indulgent, a predominantly white culture with no focus beyond the individual: The youths make a most dramatic bid to divorce themselves from the drab monotony of the working day by escaping into an artificial fantasy world in which people dressed up as swashbuckling pirates or Rob Roy characters. Emphasis was always on appearance, form as opposed to content. There was no political edge to the movement unless you allow for the fact that dressing up as a response to everyday life may in itself be a political statement. Overtly, there were not even broad programs. Important social matters affected the lives of young people, such as the lack of work, racism, inadequate schooling. New romantics felt these, but withdrew from them, sealing themselves into a make-believe world populated by beautiful people who were similarly unconcerned by material affairs and who structured their lives around looking good and listening to music.

The other great force of political indifference of the time was, almost predictably, heavy metal, by then a dinosaur of youth culture, surviving its contemporaries and lasting seemingly without change into the 1980s. The dress remained the same, as did the political apathy and, of course, the music. HM was, by this time, a complete industry; its items ranged from full-length feature movies (about 15, at the time of writing) through lapel buttons and T-shirts—these mundane items providing turnovers in the millions of pounds brackets. One of the features of heavy metal was the penchant of its devotees to collect memorabilia, particularly souvenirs of concerts, so a T-shirt bearing the legend "Black Sabbath, 1983 Tour" would signify the follower's presence at that event.

New romanticism was not nearly as resilient as heavy metal and had exhausted itself by the end of 1981. Clothes and make-up became less bizarre, music grew less avant-garde. The new romantics, unlike heavy metal kids, had no sense of belonging to a succession of generations originating in the past and extending into the future. Like a millenarian episode, new romanticism grew out of the new spiritual crisis of youth in the early 1980s, exhibited itself in an orgiastic, ecstatic near-religiosity, then died quickly and quietly. It was a sort of celebration of contemporary decadence with males and females dressing alike, yet at the same time an expression of the anxiety of youth. The social upheavals were taking their effect on youth in the early 1980s and the future depression was unstoppable and imminent. Since society seemed to have little future, it made sense to live only for the moment, to concentrate solely on oneself, become a connoisseur of the art of self-attention.

It's facile to discard new romantics and the everlasting heavy metal kids as unimportant in the general span of postwar youth cultures. True, they were less political, less vocal, and more private than many of the others. But, at another level, they were saying something significant about the passion of youths to live for themselves without worrying about the situations of others, about the development of purely personal preoccupations, and about the erosion of political awareness. We can't suggest that just because these two cultures weren't as obvious and as strident in their demands as, say, two-tone kids or punks, that they weren't conscious of the deteriorating situation in which they found themselves. I would suggest that these people too sensed the intensifying futility of trying to improve their material lives and so convinced themselves that what really mattered was that portion of their lives over which they could at least exert some control.

In this chapter, I have dealt with two basic strategies of youth reflecting a growing despair of changing society and a broadening understanding of it. In the late 1970s and early 1980s, the sense of loss and a concern with the future were commonplace. Some groups seemed to understand it with a sociological brilliance: Punks, rastas, and two-toners, for example, posed trenchant critiques and, in their own sometimes eccentric ways, alternatives. New romantics and heavy metal kids continued more disguised critiques but opted for strategies of measures designed to enhance their own lives, to ensure their own health of mind as opposed to upgrading others'. It was as if they could all foresee a nuclear holocaust; but while some outraged groups began marching in protest, others busied themselves building their own fragile and ultimately wasteful fall-out shelter. All were fated similarly; all their strategies suggested a widespread loss of confidence in the future.

Each youth subculture showed celebratory elements, but these belied the desperate concern for survival, which gave each subculture its point. In punk, the concern was disguised as anarchy, in the new romanticism as hedonism. But for every youth touched by these movements, there was another reality—the reality of the streets. In the 1980s, racial violence in the ghettos and in the school generated an atmosphere of chronic tension that occasionally erupted into full-scale riots. Unemployment hit the poor, the young, and blacks most severely, then spread to the middle class, whose standard of living was systematically eroded. (The decreasing number of white-collar jobs, for example, required less skill and so conferred less security.) To this reality could be added events from far-flung corners, all of which contributed to the sense of no future: distant wars in the Middle East, uprisings in South and Central America, occupations in Afghanistan and Poland, escalations of the arms race, the economic decrepitation of the West. These were small but complementary elements in the atmosphere of domestic crisis.

The modes adopted by youths to express their discontent and an .iety had the effect of actually attenuating the sense of crisis. Gone were the days when youths went through a phase of panic before settling down to mere fashion or style; gone were the simpler forms of the teds, mods, and rockers. Now, there was a bewildering complex of cultures, each harboring vague, sometimes contradictory, frequently impossible, and usually bizarre aspirations. But each of the modes dealt with so far were responses to things youths felt to be wrong, such as racism, unemployment, insecurity; these were novel and growing features of the social world young people were growing up in and they were features felt to be undesirable. In a very different way, other sets of young people were reacting to elements they thought were undesirable, but for different reasons. The groups in this chapter were young and fresh enough to want to encourage change, if it was positive change. For others, the new was an abhorrence; they wanted to revert to an older, more traditional, altogether more solid way of life. And, in their way, the mark two skinheads made perhaps the single most significant impact of any postwar youth culture and most certainly captured the mood of the 1980s with an electrifying horror.

## REFERENCES

Cashmore, E. (1981). After the rastas. *New Community, 10.*

Cashmore, E. (1983). *Rastaman.* London: Unwin Paperbacks.

Hebdige, D. (1979). *Subculture: The meaning of style.* London: Methuen.

Lee, G., & Wrench, J. (1981). *In search of a skill.* London: Commission for Racial Equality.

Marsh, P. (1977). Dole-queue rock. *New Society, 39,* 112-114.

Rampton, A. (1981). *Committee of Inquiry into the Education of Children of Minority Groups, West Indian Children in our Schools: Interim report.* London: HMSO.

Taylor, M. (1981). *Caught between: A review of researching into the education of pupils of West Indian origin.* Berkshire: NFER-Nelson.

Tomlinson, S. (1980). The educational performance of ethnic minority children. *New Community, 8,* 213-234.

White, T. (1983). *Catch a fire.* London: Elm Tree.

# About the Contributors

**Dean Abt** is Research Associate in the San Francisco office of the Opinion Research Corporation. In addition to practical applications of research methodologies, his interests include the study of popular culture, especially popular music. He earned his master's degree from San Jose State University.

**E. Ellis Cashmore** is Senior Research Fellow in Sociology at the University of Aston, Birmingham, England. His books include *No Future, Rastaman, Black Youth in Crisis* (coeditor), *Approaching Social Theory, Introduction to Race Relations* (coauthor), and *Dictionary of Race and Ethnic Relations*.

**Iain Chambers** is Associate Professor of English at the University of Naples, Italy. He is author of *Urban Rhythms: Pop Music and Popular Culture* (St. Martin's Press/Macmillan, 1985) and *Popular Culture: The Metropolitan Experience* (Methuen, 1986).

**David King Dunaway** is a professional writer who teaches biography, communications, and oral history at the University of New Mexico. He is author of an award-winning life of Pete Seeger, *How Can I Keep From Singing?* and is principal editor of *Oral History: An Interdisciplinary Anthology*. He received the first doctorate in American studies offered at the University of California, Berkeley and has served as Fulbright Professor at the University of Nairobi, Kenya.

**Simon Frith** is a Senior Lecturer in Sociology at the University of Warwick, Coventry, England, and author of *Sound Effects: Youth, Leisure and the Politics of Rock 'n' Roll*. He has written about music for numerous magazines on both sides of the Atlantic. He is a columnist for the New York *Village Voice* and is the rock record reviewer for the London *Observer*. He is currently at work on a study of the aesthetics of popular music, to be published by Pantheon in 1988.

**Lawrence Grossberg** is Associate Professor at the University of Illinois, Urbana-Champaign, with appointments in speech communication, communications research, and criticism and interpretive theory. He has written extensively on rock and roll and contemporary cultural theory. He is coeditor of *Marxism and the Interpretation of Culture* (with Cary Nelson), and is currently completing work on two books: *Cultural Studies* (with Stuart Hall and Jennifer Daryl Slack) and *Another Boring Day in Paradise: Popular Music, Culture and Postmodern Politics*.

**George H. Lewis** is Professor of Sociology at the University of the Pacific, Stockton, California. Long interested in the sociology of popular music and culture, he is the author of numerous research and theoretical articles in the field, appearing in journals ranging from *American Music* and the *Journal of Popular Culture* to *Theory and Society* and the *British Journal of Sociology*. He is author of *Side Saddle on the Golden Calf: Popular Culture and Social Structure in America* (1972), *The Sociology of Popular Culture* (1978), and *Symbols of Significance* (1983).

**James Lull** is a communication researcher, writer, and broadcaster who lives in San Francisco, California. He is also Professor of Radio-Television-Film at San Jose State University, San Jose, California. He has been program director and announcer for several radio stations in the United States and abroad. In addition to his professional and scholarly work on music, he has conducted numerous naturalistic studies of television audiences, including recent research in the People's Republic of China. He is editor of *World Families Watch Television*, forthcoming with Sage Publications.

**Krister Malm** is Director of the Music Museum in Stockholm, Sweden. He is Assistant Professor of Musicology at the University of Gothenburg, Sweden. He is also a member of the board of the International Society for the Study of Traditional Music. He has conducted music research in numerous countries, notably Tanzania, Tunisia, and Trinidad. He is coauthor (with Roger Wallis) of *Big Sounds From Small Peoples*. He was Secretary to the Swedish Government Committee on the phonogram industry.

**Keith Roe** is a British researcher currently working in Sweden as Research Fellow at the Unit of Mass Communication, University of Gothenburg. He served as a member of the Media Panel Program at the Department of Sociology, University of Lund, Sweden, where he received a doctorate in 1983. His doctoral thesis, "Mass Media and Adolescent Schooling: Conflict or Co-existence?" was given the top dissertation award by the Mass Communication Division of the International Communications Association. He is now jointly responsible for a major research project entitled, "Teenagers in the New Media World," and has other interests in the impact of cable television, the relationship between school and media, and the sociology of music.

**Eric W. Rothenbuhler** is Assistant Professor of Communication Studies at the University of Iowa. He received a doctorate in communication theory and research at the Annenberg School of Communications, University of Southern California, in 1985. His research interests cover the range of the sociology of communication and culture.

**Roger Wallis** studied at Cambridge University in England before moving to Sweden to do research in economics. He is coauthor (with Krister Malm) of *Big Sounds From Small Peoples* (Pendragon, 1984), a highly acclaimed analysis of the impact of the international music industry on 12 countries. He is affiliated with the Swedish Broadcasting Corporation and the Department of Mass Communications, Gothenburg University, Sweden. He reports news for the British Broadcasting Corporation, and is now at work on a research project that examines the relationship between media policy and music activity.

# NOTES

# NOTES

# NOTES

**NOTES**